VENET

Previous titles from Severn House by Virginia Coffman

The Orchid Tree
The Lombard Cavalcade
The Lombard Heiress
Tana Maguire
One Man Too Many
Hyde Place
The Jewelled Darkness
A Few Fiends To Tea
The Candidate's Wife
The Venetian Masque

THE VENETIAN MASQUE

by

VIRGINIA COFFMAN

·PARRAGON·

This title first published in Great Britain 1991 by
SEVERN HOUSE PUBLISHERS LTD.

This edition licensed by Severn House Publishers Ltd., produced by Magpie Books Ltd., and published by Parragon Book Services Ltd. in 1994

A copy of the British Library CIP data is available from the British Library.

ISBN 0-75250-062-7

Printed and bound in Great Britain

One

Just before dawn, the old nightmare returned.

Once more, she lived through the magical days and nights which led always to the horror of those dark waters, the howling sorrow of her loss. It must be a sign. It wasn't the first time Rick had tried to reach her, to let her know he was alive somewhere. But the quiet whispers of her dreams were growing louder, the nightmare visions more vivid.

The authorities and the private investigators had looked into and discounted all the possibilities in the three years which had passed since the tragedy. But the question wouldn't go away: what if Rick wasn't dead? If he hadn't drowned, but been stricken by amnesia? The doctors and police had dismissed this one with shaking heads and private glances.

O.K. He might be hiding from some problem too terrible to face in his past, that past of which only she knew Rick was afraid.

He was still alive. She sensed it. He had to be.

In her dream it was all there, in little fragments.

Her encounter with the devastating stranger who called himself Rick Kimberly. His tantalizing hot-and-cold behavior of those early days, when she hadn't known what he thought of her. The raw passion of the first time they made love, in that funny old Venetian hotel. The memories rolled past in her dream, some flickering past on fast forward, others exquisitely slow and lingering. Her sleeping body relived them all.

Then, as always, with a sickening jolt came the oily black waters, the agony twisting Rick's face, barely visible in the churning darkness.

Her screams. Other sounds coming over the lagoon.

A ship's bell.

Harsh voices.

Rick gone.

If I relive the dream just once more, she told herself, maybe I will find a clue. He can't be gone forever. I won't let him be. They never found his body. He is living somewhere at this very minute, living some other life, for whatever reason.

There were secrets in his past – she had always known that. But he loved her, and he still lived, no matter what the doctors and the investigators and all the other soothing voices told her about the unlikeliness of his survival. What did they know? They hadn't been there.

A score of false leads had led her to nothing, but always she preserved in her memory the day and hour when the relationship had begun.

In Venice.

For twenty-three-year-old Jacqueline Godart, the Venice trip was meant to be strictly business, and her first chance to prove that Godart Bakeries International had not jumped the gun in voting her onto the Board of Directors. For the family business, she knew she was only a figurehead. For the moment. With Nigel Chilton-Brown's help, she could learn on the job, and she intended to do so. It wasn't as if she was an outsider.

No-one had been closer than Jacqueline to Grandmother Berthe Godart, the deceptively sweet and rosy-cheeked old lady who had founded the company. Still, she knew that it was the Nigel, the General Manager, who now sat firmly at the helm of Godart Bakeries International. His adoring Executive Secretary, Miss Heffernan, made that quite plain.

Jacqueline had made up her mind that her solo Italian trip would be her best shot at bringing off the purchase of a company that manufactured liqueur-centred chocolates. But that was before Angela Godart, her newly-divorced mother, swept in on her the hour she arrived in Venice.

"Just for a day or two, Darling," Angela assured her. "Before I go off to inspect Sigurd's estate. Some Godforsaken heap in Bavaria, but it might be fun to own a castle. For a change."

Angela had recently replaced goodnatured, womanizing Marcel Godart with Prince Sigurd von Ulsbach, the latest in a long line of youthful gigolos.

It was generally hoped at Godart International that Angela would not marry any of her male acquisitions. Angela was an exceedingly expensive piece of bric-a-brac. She constantly overspent her generous settlement, and her male companions had tastes that were every bit as expensive.

Jacqueline was fond of her mother, but a little of her company went a long way, and it was with some relief that she watched the elaborate preparations for Angela's departure to meet her gigolo-prince.

Angela Godart lived for the amusement of Angela Godart, and she had the handy ability to make others do the same. Her ex-husband and her daughter had discovered this long ago.

At the very last minute, with her bags packed and her maid standing there in the Hotel Danieli suite ready to leave, Angela had a sudden, unexpected attack of Mother Love. She protested,

"My poor baby, I shouldn't be doing this. Even His Highness wouldn't expect it. Especially after that awful accident near O'Hare last month. Baby, how could you be so careless as to drive without brake fluid, or whatever?"

Jacqueline brushed this aside. "Accidents will happen, Mother. I'm only human."

This was all she needed. To give the company, and especially the ever-competent Nigel, the chance to keep gossiping about her carelessness with cars. Damn! Why had the darned thing happened anyway? She had been lucky to swerve into the hard shoulder without hitting anything.

Her mother was still talking. "And now, my poor baby, to leave you alone, handling this boring old business for the family. I know – Prince Sigurd could be of invaluable help to you. Why don't we send for him? I can go back to Germany with him after he has finished whatever little thing you are supposed to be handling here. We could put him up at the Gritti – no, the Cipriani. It would be a perfect business proposition for him, and such fun. Sigurd is so charming, darling. You are going to love him."

I can just picture him, Jacqueline thought. Angela's puppet-string control of her lovers, which she brought to bear partly with her barely-fading charm, but much more with her money, had made Jacqueline resolve at an early age never to fritter away her time with, let alone marry, any man who assumed that Godart International would support him for life. It was a well-known decision which limited her love-affairs considerably, but at least she knew that Nigel Chilton-Brown, to name one of her admirers, was attracted to her for herself, whatever that was.

Jacqueline was acutely conscious of the fact that, no matter how hard she might try to do a good job, she was still far too inexperienced to succeed without Nigel's help. He had covered for all the bumbling mistakes her father and mother had made. It must seem ridiculously unfair to him that she, at twenty-three, should be considered the prospective heiress and head of Godart International.

She laughed off her mother's suggestion. "No thanks, Mother, this is your fairy-tale. You run along to your handsome prince, and I'll stay here and get Ruggiero Chocolate Liqueurs signed on the dotted line. No prompting from the gallery. Besides, I'm sure what the prince wants is your delightful company, not some tiresome business deal. Nobody here is pretty enough to hold him."

Angela preened a little. Petite, blonde, and still lovely, she had some reason to believe that something more than her Godart stock held these lovers for as long as she chose. Jacqueline had long ago learned to take her mother as she found her. She looked fragile, but her clinging strength could outlast all the stronger people around her.

Like a charming vampire, she drained the strength from those who loved her.

"Well, dear, it may be just as well. I'm sure Sigurd would prefer a beautiful, tall girl like you to – but you understand."

"Perfectly, Mother. Run along, now. You'll miss your plane."

"Very true, Madame," Matilde, the frigidly correct maid warned Angela. Matilde looked exactly like what she was. She wore her white-collared black dress and its matching, close-fitting coat as if they had been starched and glued to her sparse form, and her manner was chillingly correct. In her view, the young and beautiful Jacqueline posed a threat to the social position and publicity enjoyed by Angela Godart, whom Matilde had tyrannized over and mothered for years.

The well-trained bellman had just arrived and stood like a statue with two Vuitton bags in hand, the third, fourth and fifth within reach.

Angela gazed around vaguely. "I don't see my jewel case. Ah! Matilde. Good . . . Yes, yes. I must be on my way. *Allez. Allez*, Matilde."

She squeezed Jacqueline lightly and brushed her daughter's cheek with her own. By the time Jacqueline had leaned down to kiss her forehead, Angela was already standing back, patting her arms. "Be good, darling. The Leland Appersons will be calling you, and the Reverend McAllister should arrive with his dreadful wife any day. And the Del Sartos are likely to follow you around. They have a thing about kidnappers. You have my phone numbers, if anything goes wrong. But I do wish you would get in touch with Nigel, darling. He likes you so much. I often think – if only he were a marrying man, we'd all be better off. I'm sure he's back of all that ridiculous interest in whether or not I marry Prince von Ulsbach. If you could only see your way clear to marrying Nigel, darling – it isn't as if he weren't fond of you, you know."

"He called me from Paris last week. Wanted to give me some advice, as usual. This time on dealing with the Ruggieros." Jacqueline added mischievously, "He threw in another proposal."

"Jacqui!"

"So romantic. He suggested if we got married it would save on telephone bills. What's worse, he broke off in mid-stream for another phone call and left me hanging on while he dictated a note to Miss Heffernan. Then he came back on the line for my answer."

"He was only teasing, dear. You know Nigel."

"That's just the trouble, Mother," Jacqueline confessed, "We know each other too well. He's the best friend I've got, and God knows, friends are thinner on the ground than husbands."

Angela sighed, shrugged her elegant little shoulders, and gave up. With a glance at the diamond figures on her watch, she hurried to the venerable old double doors, followed at a respectful distance by Matilde. She waggled her fingers at Jacqueline from the doorway, then blew her a kiss.

After she had gone, Jacqueline found herself feeling momentarily but surprisingly lost. It was as if a petted but favorite poodle had gone its merry way, leaving her bereft. This was an absurd feeling, and she shook it off. She didn't see her mother often enough to let such emotions bother her for long.

Inspired by her grandmother's example, Jacqueline had always had an ambition to succeed in the family business. Refusing to continue with college after her sophomore year, she had started on the bottom rung in the huge, antiseptically hygienic family bakeries in Northern California, as a "gofer" for one of the baking inspectors. Her appetite for the cut-and-thrust of business whetted, she had gone back to her native Chicago for two semesters of Business Administration.

And now the Venice trip – a chance to clinch a deal with one of Northern Italy's most successful corporations, and to show Nigel Chilton-Brown that all Grandma Berthe Godart's training hadn't gone to waste. Berthe's death, ten years before, had left a hole in the company so large it had taken her protégé, Nigel Chilton-Brown, Jacqueline's easy-going father, Marcel Godart, and an entire board of directors to replace her.

Jacqueline had a keen sense of family responsibility, which now reminded her that she had only a few hours in which to enjoy herself before getting down to some serious business. Tomorrow she would have to be at her brightest and best, to tackle the Italian chocolate magnate.

For now, she would begin with a slow meander across bridges, through narrow, shadowed byways, past intriguing old palazzos, the water-eaten remnants of past glories. She would get her exercise and maybe some ideas to stun Nigel Chilton-Brown and the board when they met in the fall to discuss the spring campaign.

Though she would never have admitted it to anyone else (perish the thought that Nigel or the board should suspect her of sentimentality), Venice reminded her of a film her mother had played in her projection room at home, when Jacqueline was a child. It was an old film even then; Katharine Hepburn was the star, and Venice her co-star. But Jacqueline and, she suspected, her mother, had had eyes only for Hepburn's leading man, Rossano Brazzi. Of course, there were no Brazzis in real life, except the fakes like Prince Sigurd, and they were unlikely to be attracted to her for herself alone.

She gave a quick brush to her thick mane of smoky-black hair, slung her well-worn Gucci shoulderbag into place, then rushed out into the corridor of the elegant old hotel. She was fully aware that no-one would ever take this leggy American in the tightly-belted swinging skirt and casual cotton shirt for an heiress. She was simply a young tourist, breathing the free, if somewhat tangy, air of Venice.

Jacqueline didn't bother with the elevator. She had too much energy to get rid of. She ran down the heavy staircase to the lobby, where a gaggle of tourists was signing in at the desk. No-one gave her a second glance.

Out on the pavement, with the busy lagoon glittering before her in hazy sunlight, she abandoned her plan to explore the unknown. Instinctively, she turned right and headed for St. Mark's Square with its army of tourists.

This was familiar territory, like the Piazzetta opposite the Doge's filigree palace, where Katharine Hepburn had met the love of her life in the movie.

The chairs were all occupied, not one of them by a Brazzi, Jacqueline noted ruefully. Hardly anyone raised his eyes to watch her pass, but that was how she preferred it, she told herself firmly.

Jacqueline strolled into the great rectangle of the square itself. The noise was deafening, a cacophony of human voices, pigeons skirling, orchestras tearing at full blast into Rossini. All this was punctuated at that minute, by the sudden metallic "bong-bong" of the hour being beaten out, setting the pigeons in a wild panic.

Jacqueline stood there for a minute with her back to the ornate facade of the cathedral. She had seen this sight many times. Still, it never failed to fascinate her as it had millions of others in the past thousand years.

She decided not to walk around the square under the arcades – she knew all the shops by heart. She adored the historic Florian's Café, but it was too late for lunch and a little too early for an aperitif. The little side streets forming the Merceria, Venice's shopping center, called to her, and she responded, crossing the Square and walking from sunlight into shadow as she passed under the arcade.

Wherever she went, Jacqueline's business nose drew her irresistibly to the windows of bakers' shops. The magic of Paris, Copenhagen and Vienna for her lay partly in their breathtaking pastries. It still amazed her how a simple "Danish" eaten in Copenhagen's Walking Street could taste so much better than those at home – apart from Godart's, of course.

Striding across her first bridge, she noted the green canal water glowing in the blocks of sunlight between the shadows of the ancient buildings that bordered the canal. Entrance steps, beneath the water now, were covered with slime, but the mooring poles, each striped in a different pattern for the colors of an aristocratic house, reminded her of the city's unique, water-borne quality. She wondered what mysterious and sinister events had occurred here. A lean cat, huddled against a long-unopened door near the water, bared its teeth at her.

Beyond the bridge, and continuing through the narrow alleys that made up the Merceria, her eye was caught by a shop selling blouses and lingerie. As she looked in at the display, she could see her mother's eyes raised heavenward in disapproval. She had never heard of the designer; the cut wouldn't be right, or the colors subtly wrong.

Jacqueline went into the shop anyway. A bar of afternoon sunlight cut between the shops across the way and illuminated the dark interior. The shopkeeper, a short, stocky, exuberant man, reminder her of her father. If Marcel Godart had not thought to provide himself with a brilliant and energetic mother, he might have ended up very like this little man, who danced around her, showing her a dozen blouses of exquisite, old-fashioned silk, which he laid out on the counter.

There were only a few, classic designs. The colors were like an array of luscious sherbets.

A shadow blotted out the sunlight for an instant. The owner made a gesture shooing away a mischievous-looking youth who peered in at the window. The youth put his tongue to good use, along with a finger and thumb, defying the man, but then he loped off along the twisting, turning little street. Jacqueline thought no more about him, and turned to more immediate matters.

The baby-pink blouse wouldn't do at all, in spite of the shopkeeper's ecstatic praise, but she liked the simple apricot shirt. When she paid, she poured out what looked like a king's ransom in Italian notes. A quick calculation in her head told her, however, that the purchase was reasonable, in dollars. She crammed the remaining wad of lire into a pouch, dropped it into her bag and went out highly satisfied with herself.

In one of the offshoots of the busy little alley she smelled frying food and looked in at a miniature delicatessen serving counter food. Nothing of interest to Godart Bakeries, but it sold the tiny, soft-shelled crabs that she hadn't seen since her last visit to her aunt's house in Tidewater, Virginia. The shell-fish were deep-fried and probably indigestible, but the sight made her homesick and she entered the narrow shop feeling like a true Venetian.

There were several customers at the counter, a stout tourist and his wife speaking in German, and another pair, Americans, the wife complaining in muttered tones to her husband. Nearest to Jacqueline was a tall Anglo-Saxon male in tight blue jeans, lingering over a ruby-colored drink that was probably a Campari. He had slung a black sweater over his shoulder. Jacqueline found him so unexpectedly attractive that she blinked and surreptitiously gave him another look.

This time he grinned at her, though something about his raised dark eyebrows told her he was used to women staring at him, and the smile was probably automatic. She wished she hadn't made her interest so obvious.

The man at the counter repeated a question in Italian.

The tall man translated. "I think he's asking what you're going to have."

"Yes. I know." She turned to the counter man, ordering in Italian, 'A bag of soft-shell crabs, please."

She felt through her handbag and into the smaller pouch for the bundle of lire. In doing so she dropped the package containing her blouse. The tall man had already set his drink aside and leaned over, reaching the blouse first. He presented the package to her with a bow. She was grateful, but she found his gesture a bit overdone and wondered if he was being sarcastic.

She thanked him. He said nothing. Convincing herself that he probably thought he was irresistible, she was careful to appear indifferent to him. He went back to his Campari and she paid for the greasy little packet that was given to her.

She saw his reflection in the window as she left. He had paused with his glass to his lips and was definitely watching her. Feeling surprised and a little better, she crossed another bridge and was able to glimpse the Grand Canal in the distance.

Nice timing. She would find a canal-side cafe and have a drink with her soft-shell crabs.

She reached the wide, bustling area around the canal and the Rialto Bridge. This sight always thrilled her, with the storybook impression the bridge left as it straddled the canal. But she decided to leave it for another time. She strolled along against the violent pedestrian traffic, looking for a cafe that was not sufficiently important or glamorous to attract Angela Godart's friends.

A crowd of passengers poured off one of the big ferryboats, a *vaporetto*, with one destination in mind, the narrow confines of the Merceria. People rushed by her on both sides, pushing and jostling. For a minute she saw the youth who had peered into the silk shop. Then he was lost in the crowd.

She hadn't expected quite this great torrent of humanity and she was thrust from side to side, knocked away from the rough protection of other bodies. A hard elbow dug into her rib-cage and she went hurtling into space. Another second or two and she would plunge into the dingy green depths of the Grand Canal.

Furious and badly shaken, she caught at a low fence that separated the crowd from a little outdoor cafe on the cobble-stones overlooking the canal.

She had found what she was looking for, a little table just being vacated by a male and female with back-packs. Aware that all her muscles had been painfully strained, Jacqueline slipped into a chair beside the canal.

By this time she was able to think more clearly about the jostling she had just endured. Accidental, but it might have been dangerous. Like the near-miss with her car. Her fault, undoubtedly. Unless her garage attendant was awfully careless.

And today's jostling was a commonplace. It happened all the time, just an elbow painfully stuck into her ribs.

"God! I hope I'm not becoming accident-prone. Still, two risky moments in areas as far apart as Venice and Chicago could hardly be a lifelong pattern!"

The waiter, tired, bustling and abrupt, stopped at her table. She ordered a Cinzano, but she forgot and pronounced it in the French fashion with a hissing "s" sound at the beginning, which made him look blank. She was sure he understood. Plenty of French tourists showed up in Venice, but she realized this was his way of telling her that she was stupid and he'd had a hard day.

She corrected herself and apologized. He softened, gave her a longer look. She smiled and that reminded him that he was on duty. He bustled away.

Opening her bag of miniature shell-fish, she began to nibble. She was fascinated by the sounds around her, the hum of voices, the musical rise and fall of the Italian language, the curious traffic noises on the canal. Cutting across those ageless sounds came the roar of a motorboat that almost swamped a venturesome gondola trying to cross the canal. A clumsy, utilitarian *vaporetto* moved ponderously along past celebrated Fifteenth and Sixteenth Century palazzos toward the wider lagoon. It would eventually pass the Piazza San Marco and her own hotel.

She received her Cinzano, pale amber with a lemon rind and one small ice cube. The waiter discreetly left her bill in the saucer. She sipped the vermouth and stared out thoughtfully at the noisy canal, wondering about her mother's future.

Angela had no interest whatever in Godart's except to increase her own profits. Angela's stock dividends paid handsomely, but when she made her monotonously regular complaints about the meanness of her divorce settlement, she never counted the stock dividends. They were her reward for producing an heir to Godart's, even a female heir.

"At least she produced something," Jacqueline thought ruefully. "I'd better get moving. A few more of these clumsy accidents and I'll be in no shape to hustle anything, even a lover."

Passers-by moved in other directions, managing not to collide with each other. They glanced at her, a few smirking at the sight of a woman alone, but most of them resenting the fact that a single woman had taken up a table for two. She stirred, examined the small statement of her debt and reached into her shoulder-bag.

The trouble with such bags was that most heavy objects dropped to the bottom. She rummaged through the bag, her fingers tossing aside a comb, Kleenex, book of Italian city maps, endless souvenirs and gadgets, her passport, and a diamond-studded cigarette case belonging to her mother, which Angela had asked her to hold yesterday at lunch.

But the money pouch proved elusive.

Jacqueline felt panic wash over her. This had never happened to her before, in a strange place where she couldn't easily reach someone she knew. Like her Grandmother Berthe, she had never thrown money away as her mother and father did. From the time Jacqueline was old enough to be taken under her the shrewd Frenchwoman's wing, she had known the value in human sweat, labor and individual abilities that went into a single dollar.

She pushed aside the glass, the greasy half-eaten bag of crabs, and looked down into the shoulder-bag. The smaller pouch was gone, and she had left her credit cards in the hotel.

She fished all over the bottom of the bag, hoping to dredge up either some coins or a couple of those paper notes representing more than a thousand lire. No luck

What do I do now?

Her mother had many friends in Venice but she couldn't see herself calling the Leland Appersons or the Del Sartos in order to borrow a dollar or two.

She looked at her hand. If she turned over her plain but heavy gold wristwatch to the waiter as a hostage she would never see it again. It was worth too much.

She wore a small garnet ring given to her in token of a passionate fling with a boy in her Business Management class, as a pledge of eternal fidelity. She had thought for a short time that they would be married "when they got somewhere in the world." It had been one of her few affairs to date, which made her something of an anomaly among her knowing friends, and it had petered out when they became separated by a continent. Bobby Averbach's engagement to the receptionist in his father's legal offices was another complicating factor.

So it looked like Bobby's garnet had to go. She could hardly sacrifice the three-carat diamond solitaire that had once been worn by Grandma Berthe. She twisted the garnet ring, trying to force it off the ring finger of her left hand, but nervousness and the warm day had made her knuckles swell. She stuck her finger in her mouth and tried to force the ring off with her excellent teeth. She saw the waiter standing before her, looking suspicious.

Red with embarrassment, she took her finger out of her mouth.

"I'm afraid my purse is gone. I must have left it on the counter when I –"

The waiter looked her body up and down, saw nothing that indicated money until his gaze travelled to the watch and Berthe Godart's ring. His suspicion faded. She didn't like the twist of his lips.

"Maybe the signorina leave the watch. For security? She come again with lire. The watch return."

Before she could say anything a welcome male voice entered the one-sided conversation, speaking Yankee-English.

"How much does the lady owe, Compadre?"

She was sure she knew that voice, though she had only heard it once. She looked over her shoulder and up into the face of the good-looking young American who had been drinking vermouth half an hour ago. For an instant she wondered if he had also stolen her money when he picked up her package for her.

Two

The waiter resented the "compadre", or perhaps the likelihood that her bill would be paid. He offered the little paper to the American who looked it over, shrugged and reached into his hip-hugging jeans and dug out some coins. The waiter scowled.

It was an awkward moment. Jacqueline translated the scowl. "I think he wants a tip." She added in a hurry, "I'll make it right with you. I can promise you that."

"You'd better." His grin took the curse off the remark and he fished around, found another coin and threw it into the saucer. The waiter scooped it up without enthusiasm.

Jacqueline got up. "I can cash a check at my hotel. Do you mind coming with me?"

He looked surprised. "You've really got it? This wasn't a put-on?"

"Certainly not. I'm good for it." She thought fast. No harm in playing a game of her own. "I'm staying in a place beyond St. Mark's Square. Past the Doge's Palace."

"Okay. Don't forget the crab-legs. Or whatever that stuff is."

She glanced back. "I'm through. I wanted to recapture the times when we visited my aunt in Virginia. But it didn't taste the same and I remembered something Thomas Wolfe said. 'You can't go home again'. He was right."

"Tom Wolfe?"

"No. The other one. He's been dead quite a while."

He didn't look as if he understood the literary distinction. "Sure. Well, here goes." He plunged into the Merceria crowd. Jacqueline kept up, scarcely aware that her earlier fall had pulled her muscles painfully. Her long strides almost equalled his. He looked around to see if he had left her behind. Her close presence surprised him. "Nice going," he congratulated her, then deliberately slowed down and took her arm, his hand warm, the lean fingers hard as they closed around her flesh just above the elbow. She stared at his hand, aware that his possessiveness brought a prickle of excitement to her body. Her first impulse was to pull away. After all, she knew nothing whatever about him. But she let his hand remain in charge.

He was asking, "Is this on the level? You really lost your purse?"

She was enjoying herself more than she had in ages. "We – ll, not exactly. You know how it is when you find yourself stoney broke."

"Believe me, I've been there."

"– Because you lost your money. Or maybe had it lifted."

"Sounds likely. If you had it in the beginning, of

course." He saw her dark eyes widen.

Someone had once said to her, after too much Irish Whiskey, "Those wonderful depths really take their toll." She had wondered if he was putting her on and had hurt his feelings by laughing. Her present companion added quickly, "Not that I doubt you. Or anything like that."

"If you don't doubt me, why are you acting like my jailer?"

His free hand roughed up his thick, windblown hair. "Maybe I just like your company. Whatever your ethics about money. Incidentally, where is this hotel of yours?"

She gave him a smile that she could only think of as smug in the circumstances. "Around the Danieli."

"Nothing around the Danieli. Except –" He considered. "There's the old Doge's Prison. For malefactors and debtors. Hey! We're passing the place where you got your crabs' legs."

"Little dollar-sized crabs. Soft ones."

"Sounds kind of nasty to me. Cruelty to dumb animals, and all that."

"Don't be funny. Let's go in and see if they found my pouch."

They hadn't. The cook who had sold her the crabs made a pretense of looking around the counter. He came up triumphantly.

"Not here. There was a boy who followed you. Many teeth. I think he is the one. He snatch the purse out of that so-large bag you carry. It would not be difficult."

"He's probably right, you know," the American said.

It might have happened when someone, very likely the boy, had almost knocked her into the canal. She agreed and directed him, "We go beyond the next bridge and then through the arcades."

"You don't want to go back and find this toothy character?"

"Don't be ridiculous. We'd never find him at this hour. So if you want to be paid, it's onward and upward. To the left after the Piazzetta."

He shrugged. "You shouldn't be wandering around Italy on your own. No wonder you're broke. Boyfriend run out on you?"

While she was considering an answer (put him in his place with the truth? Or keep him in his present state of abysmal ignorance?) he shifted his arm to her waist and boosted her onto the hump-backed little pedestrian bridge. This time, having enjoyed the contact but finding no excuse to prolong it, she decided enough was enough, considering their short acquaintance. Since he had no idea of her identity, however, and appeared to find her reasonably attractive, she gave him one of her best smiles as she released herself.

They had just stepped in under the San Marco arcades and were about to cross the huge square itself when the young American glanced in the direction of the campanile – or maybe beyond it to Florian's crowded outdoor cafe. He frowned.

"See someone you know?" she teased. "Someone you want to avoid, that's obvious. An old girlfriend?" It was her revenge for the crack about the deserting boyfriend.

"Nothing like that. But I left the States to get away from pests. I don't need 'em here."

Whoever he thought he saw was no friend. She pursued the mystery with interest.

"I hope no ex-girlfriend brought on that frown." She pretended to examine his face carefully. "You could be quite – personable, when you aren't looking as if the Mafia's after you."

He gave her his attention. "Not the Mafia." He added with his infectious grin, "Just the Feds." He went on, "You see, I'm one of the Rockefellers and they just won't let us poor devils alone. Awful responsibility – being rich."

"Poor you. Tell me something. Honestly. Why are you so anxious to get back two or three dollars? That's all I owe you."

"Just a thing with me. We all pay our debts." He considered, adding with a curious little grimace, "Well, some of us. I'm doing you a favor, keeping you honest."

"You're so good to me."

His mood which had briefly darkened, was mischievous again, his eyes lively as they looked into hers.

The most rewarding aspect of this impromptu relationship was that he had no idea who she was.

They crossed the Piazzetta, passed the Doge's Palace, and carried on over the next hump-backed bridge, which gave them an excellent view of the Bridge of Sighs.

"There it is. Where you'll wind up if you don't make good your debts," the American reminded her, pointing to the prison.

She looked at her arm which he had taken again. He said, "Sorry," and released her. She regretted the loss of that warm, sensuous touch. There had been a good deal of touching, feeling, mauling and other familiarities with would-be lovers in her past, but they hadn't affected her like this man who was a total stranger.

They reached the doors of the Danieli Hotel. They could see the lobby inside. It was still crowded, this time by other arriving tourists. The young man seemed upset.

"Don't tell me you live in this classy dump."

She had been planning her explanation for the last few minutes. "I work for a woman who is staying here. Mrs. Godart. I'm a kind of secretary, companion and gofer. She's in Munich right now."

"So that's it." He shrugged, sounding so uninterested she thought she had lost him. Then he added casually, "You free tonight?"

Pride and caution demanded that she play this game just as casually, "What did you have in mind?"

"Nothing much. A drink at Florian's or Quadri's and maybe a walk around the Square. They play a lot of schmaltzy music in the Square."

She wondered if his walk had a definite direction. He was no Brazzi, but then, she was no Hepburn. Still, it was close. She was wondering how she would get some money at the desk to pay him without revealing her name, but to her surprise he said,

"Meet me at Florian's at ten. You can bring the money then."

Curious that he didn't want to meet her here at the hotel. Probably he didn't like what he thought of as "snobbery."

His sudden smile took the curse off the abrupt invitation. But he seemed to feel that both required an explanation. "That debt of yours is one way I can count on your showing up." He reached for her hand. She wondered if he was going to do anything as quaint as kiss her hand. But for a fleeting time she felt the hardness of his thumb and forefinger upon her flesh, as though sending messages to her pulses. Instinctively she closed her fingers over his.

Recalled to her customary cool behavior with strangers, she withdrew her hand rapidly, a gesture that amused him.

"I don't bite, you know."

While she stared at him with her mouth open, he flipped his hand in an easy salute, turned and strolled away toward St. Mark's Square. He looked back once as he crossed the bridge which gave such a good view of the Bridge of Sighs further up the narrow canal. He pointed to it, then to her. She saw his teeth and knew he was grinning. She laughed, nodded that she understood, and went into the hotel, feeling more pleased with the world than she had in ages.

Only then did it occur to her that it was all very well for him to be at sea as to her identity, but she herself had no idea who he was. He could be anything unsavory. Still, the mystery of the affair gave it a special excitement.

When she got her key the concierge asked solicitously, "You have injured yourself, Signorina Godart? You limp a trifle."

It was the first time she had noticed it and she dismissed it lightly.

"The crowd near the Rialto Bridge tried to drown me in the Grand Canal. They failed though. I'm quick on my feet. Besides, nobody in Venice knows me well enough to kill me."

They both laughed. She swung the key between her fingers and headed for the elevator.

Three

During her solitary dinner at the hotel, Jacqueline asked herself just what she expected out of tonight's meeting between two strangers who didn't even know each other's names. He might – probably would – make a play for her because it was expected these days. But he wasn't the type to give her any trouble if she put him down. He was too self-assured. There would always be another female for such a man.

He was sexy in an offhand, tantalizing way. He amused her by his total indifference to her as Jacqueline Godart. But that was pure luck. It couldn't last.

Obviously, he figured he would get more from her for the price of a drink at Florian's, but that was his problem, Florian's was not some cheap pick-up joint. Meanwhile, she could at least have a bit of fun posing as Mrs. Godart's underpaid secretary.

To keep up the illusion, Jacqueline had to find something suitable to wear in her expensive wardrobe. The immaculate cut of the simple black and white raw silk dress she chose gave away its exclusive origins instantly, so she took the edge off it with a large scarf.

Setting out on her adventure, she couldn't help wondering if it would bear any resemblance to the Katharine Hepburn movie. She scolded herself for her romantic fantasizing; after all, he might be into drugs like too many other men she had met. She would be on the lookout for any signs of this; the drugs scene was not one which captivated her.

As usual at this time of year, St. Mark's Square was full of noise, music, voices and lights, with flashing colors like a Chinese lantern. The lights formed romantic little pools with thick darkness in between, making Jacqueline conscious of the great blanket of blackness overhead.

Two lonely American sailors looking for a pick-up called to her as she reached the campanile. She smiled, shook her head, and saw them follow two stunning young Italian girls whose parents probably didn't know they were out.

In spite of the crowds crossing the Square or lingering around the orchestras, Jacqueline was aware of the echo of steps close to the shops under the arcades. Not many people spent this hour around the shops and it was easy to note the rhythm of the footsteps behind her. Almost exactly even with her own. Her encounter with the sailors had meant nothing. She was lucky they hadn't pinched her in the age-old Italian tradition. But these steps, timed to match hers, were annoying.

She stopped, looked around and was almost run over by a tourist foursome who had to walk around her and go on, raising their voices to drown the music a few yards away. She reached Florian's. The tables and chairs in the Square near the orchestra were all occupied and she saw no sign of her unknown date. She checked again but he wasn't there.

Had she been stood up?

It was past ten. She had deliberately seen to it that she wouldn't arrive early. Too eager. So this meant that he had pulled that trick on her. The idea amused her, reluctantly.

"Serves me right. I was too eager, after all, damn him!"

She strolled on, very casually until the music faded a bit and once more she heard the annoying single pair of footsteps that seemed to match hers. Not funny! She slowed to a stop, pretended to re-arrange her scarf, and glanced over her shoulder.

She had stopped in one of the pools of darkness and saw only faceless, chattering strollers some yards away in the Square itself. Eventually, they passed her without a glance.

Then she remembered her mother's mention of the Del Sartos who might "look after her". They had affiliate connections with Godart and would always try to oblige either the family or Nigel Chilton-Brown, whom they recognized as the true head of Godart International.

The far end of the Square was shrouded in darkness and Jacqueline turned back, this time cutting across the busy Square itself. Like a kind of crazy patchwork quilt that defied any design, others also crossed at intervals in every direction. No longer concerned over some troublemaker following her, Jacqueline could concentrate on the unpleasant, not to say disappointing, knowledge that the attractive American hadn't thought her worth a date, even to get his precious few dollars back.

Probably, he would have overwhelmed her with his attentions if he knew her real identity.

Two hands clasped her shoulders from behind her and she cried out in shock. But there was no mistaking that voice, teasing, easy tantalizing.

"Thought you'd jumped bail. You're about half an hour late."

She swung around in his arms so fast her breasts were crushed against him for a minute before she freed herself, reminding him, "You're the late one. I passed Florian's ages ago. You were nowhere to be found."

"Florian's? I said Quadri's."

He sounded so indignant that she had to remind herself that this was no doubt a favorite tactic of his: "Get 'em on the defensive."

Because she was so glad he hadn't actually ditched her, she was cool about it.

"A likely tale. Anyway, Florian's or Quadri's, does it matter?"

"Not in the least. It's nice to see you honor your debts. Come along. If we get the right table we can look across at Florian's. Two glorious antiques for the price of one. I'm referring to the cafés, not to you and me."

The night had begun to cool and this, with the lateness of the hour, gave them a choice table. When Jacqueline paid him the coins she owed, she warned him,

"This will just about cover the tip."

He took the money from her and pocketed it. He was still wearing the skin-tight denims but his windbreaker looked expensive. She realized that though she was enjoying this little masquerade, she wanted very much to know who he was. It would be too much to hope for if he was playing her own game. Did he actually think she might only be attracted to his financial background? Life wasn't that neat.

When they had given their orders, she brought up the subject. "I'm Jacqui. What do I call you?"

"Richard Kimberly. Call me Rick."

"Backpacking around Europe?"

He was watching her over his Vermouth Cassis. The colored lights, and his frown, made his wide, frank eyes look unexpectedly sinister.

"You're awfully full of questions, Jackie."

"J-A-C-Q-U-I. My grandmother was French and she had the –" She had almost said "money." She added, "influence . . . I'm sorry. I just find you intriguing. All you backpackers wandering over the world. As a matter of curiosity, where do backpackers sleep in Venice? Those canal steps look slippery. And cold."

He relaxed, grinning. "That wouldn't be an invitation?"

"Funny Fellow." She buried her embarrassment by taking a long swallow of her drink.

"O.K. I know when I've been rejected. Do they work you hard?"

Had he guessed about Godart International and her real job?

"Who?" she asked sharply, so sharply he set his glass down and stared at her.

"Well, that woman and her husband. The ones you work for."

What a suspicious idiot I am!

"Not too hard, no. Just tedious. Boring."

He reached across the little table. His forefinger traced her profile, lingering over her lips, which trembled slightly at his touch.

"You're wasting your talents, Jackie. You're pretty enough to be on TV. Doing some of those ads. I've seen plenty of them that didn't have your looks. And that goes for your legs, too. Say! You'd be great demonstrating panti-hose, or something."

"Thanks, Richard. That's a beautiful compliment. I think."

She must remember to tell Nigel that he need look no further for a new promo star. She could dance on a box of Streusel, or something. Even Nigel's neat British mustache would fly up that.

Rick Kimberly looked around at the thinning crowd in the Square. He appeared thoughtful, more serious than she might have expected from his previous flippant conduct. In fact, was Richard Kimberly his real name? (Judging everyone by myself, she thought.)

He said, "We could learn a lot about using beauty to attract crowds."

"Are you in a business that –?" Questions again. If she had secrets, she would do well not to inquire into his.

"Me?" She had startled him out of an unexpected reverie. "Not any more. No. Just looking at that foursome there."

She turned in her chair and was surprised to see that his attention had been caught by a man and woman, each carrying a child. One child, about four and all legs, was yawning as he straddled his father's neck. The other, smaller child, perhaps a girl, was in her mother's arms.

Kimberly remarked, "They'd make a nice little group to paint. Corny, but – well, popular."

A painful idea made her ask, "Do you have children?"

"God, no! Do I look like a family man?"

His contemptuous denial was almost worse than her first suspicion. He was a free and easy artist, of course. That remark about painting was the giveaway of the rest, too. A charmer, and she liked him more than was wise.

She glanced at her watch. "I'm afraid I'll have to be getting back to the hotel. My employer may have called while I was here enjoying myself."

His eyes had been following the Family Foursome but he heard her and surprised her by his sudden plea, "Don't go yet. Stay a few minutes. One more drink."

She was pleased but puzzled. "No, really. I shouldn't have been gone this long." She pushed her chair back. He got up too. She wondered if her imagination made too much of that curious expression on his face. Unhappy? (Surely not over the end of one date with a stranger!) Troubled, anyway, and not about her.

They crossed the Square and headed for the Doge's Palace and her hotel facing the lagoon beyond. Rick Kimberly had reverted to the easy charmer by this time and was teasing her about playing Cinderella on the stroke of midnight.

He made no reference to seeing her again.

Before they reached the doors of the Danieli he maneuvered her back against the aged wall of the hotel. With one of his arms extended against the wall on both sides of her she found herself a willing prisoner. She was sure he intended to make another date, and she hoped he was going to kiss her.

His head was close to hers. She looked up, found her flesh brushing his lips. One of his hands shifted to her throat and left jaw.

In that instant terrorists, Red Brigades and kidnappers ran through her chaotic thoughts, but her scream was smothered by the hard pressure of his lips that crushed both her scream and any thought of protest. The heat of his lips and his body against hers fired her to a passionate response that dazed her by its force. She realized that she had never known the strength of real passion until this minute. His hands moved over her throat, tracing flesh and muscle far more subtly than his kiss.

When he released her she managed to laugh, seeing that he himself was a trifle breathless. She moistened her lips, found herself hoarse and had to start her goodbye all over again.

"Thanks for the drink. And your company."

He grinned, jammed his hands into his pockets.

"Same here. All the way. Tell your boss not to overwork you or she'll have me to answer to."

He swung around and strolled off toward the ferryboat landing.

So much for her expectation of another date. Or maybe he was just playing some cagey game.

Pulling herself together, Jacqueline walked to the Danieli, puzzled by one thing among many: Why hadn't he taken these last few steps with her? Did he have something against luxury hotels?

She was still puzzling over the peculiar Rick Kimberly when she reached her rooms and found a telephone message from Paris awaiting her. Nigel Chilton-Brown or his secretary, Miss Heffernan, of course.

"Dear Old Girl,
Forget business this week and enjoy yourself.

"By coincidence, Ruggiero is in Paris. Business has been settled. He is giving out the story here on the Continent. I have instructed Esther Heffernan to give U.S. the news of the merger, from our point of view.

"Best always.

"N.C.-B."

Jacqueline was not nearly as pleased as Nigel might have expected. She was furious. The first time Godart International had entrusted her with something big, it had been snatched out of her hands. Evidently, Nigel was afraid he couldn't trust her to handle Ruggiero herself. It was one of those annoying qualities that kept Jacqueline from falling in love with Nigel Chilton-Brown. She might admire him, as Heffernan, his worshipping secretary did, but at times like this she wondered how she could ever have thought of him in any warm light.

While running water for her bath, she wrote to Nigel, congratulating him on his coup, and adding snappishly that he could call off his Del Sarto watchdogs. She didn't need any body-guards just to walk through St. Mark's Square.

She took care not to mention Rick Kimberly. She was absolutely sure of one thing. Nigel would never approve of her new acquaintance. Even though it was none of his business, the less said about Rick, the better.

Would he try and contact her again? Tomorrow, she decided, she must notify the desk that any messages to "Mrs. Godart's secretary" should be delivered to her. She was playing a little joke on a new friend.

Which was true enough, she hoped.

Four

Angela Godart's svelte figure provided the Italian press with a good many column inches. Jacqueline normally found it amusing to start the day with a wildly inaccurate account of her mother's social activities. Her breakfast tray came complete with a number of glossy magazines, as well as the influential dailies of Milan and Rome. This morning, she saw at once that Signore Ruggiero had been busy. The news of his merger with Godart's had a prominent spot in both papers, along with a blurry photo of Ruggiero shaking hands with the tireless Nigel.

So much Jacqueline had expected. Unfortunately, as the two men were not especially photogenic, the story was embellished with an inset picture of Angela Godart, and beside her an unmistakable likeness of "her glamorous daughter, Jacqueline, soon to become an active partner in Godart International."

"Damn!"

Would Richard Kimberly see the Italian newspapers? Did he read Italian? Probably not. Luckily, the picture hadn't appeared in the *International Herald Tribune*.

That would certainly have given away her identity to him.

Her curiosity, not to mention her anxiety, had a longer run than she had hoped for. Her mother's friends, the Leland Appersons, called to exchange dinner invitations with her, and Jacqueline put them off with a guilty conscience. They were friendly, entertaining people in their own way. The clever Tita Apperson's knowing gossip about Rome's middle-to-upper crust was just as intelligent as Jacqueline's own dazzling chit-chat with Richard Kimberly. It was also hard to outwit Lee Apperson who tried so subtly to find out just what Godart's International was up to.

But she heard nothing from Richard Kimberly.

Three days later, leaving the hotel on her way to a cocktail party at the Gritti Palace, Jacqueline saw a familiar figure lounging against the wall of the Danieli. Richard Kimberly had perched himself in almost exactly the spot where they had shared that memorable kiss – how many nights ago? Maybe he rationed his valuable talent.

She walked toward him, her smile practiced, casual, more easy than she felt. He reached out for her, took her wrist and stopped her. He didn't return her smile and seemed to be angry about something. His anger faded as he looked her over. He started with her hair, faintly ruffled by the wind off the Lagoon. Then his attention was caught, rather obviously, by the wide, boat-neck of her dress that just tantalizingly covered her breasts, and travelled down over her neat hips and thighs, coming at last to the silver pumps with their high, spiky heels.

The rest of this close study was highly satisfying to her. She was glad she hadn't put a jacket on. She was already somewhat heated by his conduct.

It was Rick who broke their highly pregnant silence.

"You really can be a knockout when you want to be."

"Thank you. All considered, you're pretty adequate yourself. Why the handcuffs, figuratively speaking?"

He kept his firm grasp on her wrist but this time he grinned. "Just want to be sure you don't slip away . . . Keep going."

"Is this a kidnapping?"

"You could call it that."

They had reached the Piazzetta. She would have turned toward St. Mark's and the cafés beyond the Piazza but Kimberly maneuvered her toward the canal and the Lido Ferry moorings.

No man ever ordered her around – except Nigel Chilton-Brown in his polished way. She knew it was a big mistake to be attracted by this stranger's bossiness. But she put up no resistance. She found his touch as sexy as his eyes and certainly his lips, whose bruising passion she hadn't forgotten.

"Are we going to the Lido?"

"This time. Why not?"

It didn't matter where they went. She had gotten those promising words: *This time*. There would be other times.

While they waited for the big ferryboat to dock and the mob of passengers to scatter, she asked directly,

"Why didn't you come to the hotel and call my – my employer's suite?"

His hand, sliding past her cheek, pointed out a huge male and female leaving the ferry. They were adorned with dangling cameras, viewfinders, a movie camera, and assorted souvenirs. Kimberly chuckled.

"One guess what they are doing."

"Tourists. Like us. Why didn't you go into the hotel lobby?" When he didn't answer she made her own excuse. "I guess you saw me out here before you went into the hotel."

He was casual. "That's about it. Here we go. Watch your step . . . Speaking of steps, you have very fetching insteps. And ankles too, when it comes to that."

She was careful not to tell him he repeated himself.

She expressed her thanks with a warm smile. On innumerable occasions she had been to the long spit of land called the Lido, but never with anyone who excited her. Until this evening.

"Here. By the rail," Kimberly directed and then elbowed their way through the crowd to positions at the after-rail. One of his arms reached around her again, pointing out various campaniles, some tilted like the Leaning Tower of Pisa.

"Do you come to Venice often?" she asked, very much aware of his body practically encasing her.

"Who? Me?" He seemed to find this a joke. "In the first place, I don't swim. Not a lot, anyway. So Venice was never my idea of paradise. I just got here because it was kind of the end of the line, after the rest of Europe. I wouldn't be in Europe at all if – Now, that over there, that's the Island called Torcello."

It wasn't. It was the island where Venetians buried their dead, but she thought it wiser not to correct him.

On the other hand, things might be going too easily for him, considering the long wait he had given her. When he leaned forward, pointing to a smudge on the horizon as "The glass island, Murano," she disengaged herself from his arm and his body. Catching his eye, she murmured,

"Fascinating." She added quickly, "What are we going to find on the Lido?"

Her conduct struck him as funny. "Are you afraid of me? If you don't want me hanging around, just tune me out. I'm not really your Average Freewheeling Rapist."

She refused to apologize. "Frankly, I don't think you're an average anything."

He rather liked that, but he didn't put an arm around her again. When they got off at the earlier stop, around what Jacqueline thought of as the back of the Lido, he walked along just a step ahead of her and she felt like an Indian squaw dutifully following a brave. She had no idea where they were going and in some respects didn't care. She felt that he had laid the ground rules and wouldn't try out any of his undoubted sexual talents until she gave him the signal.

It would have been more exciting if he made love to her of his own volition. However . . . She was philosophical about it. You can't have everything.

On this grassy back alley of the crowded and fashionable Lido she was about to walk past an outdoor pizza parlor called "Casa da Napoli" when Kimberly stopped her.

"Whoa! We're here."

She should have known. Highly charmed by all this democratic exposure, she was amiable and pretended she hadn't been in the least surprised.

"Marvelous. Just like a little place I remember on Capri."

They were about to seat themselves when he leaned on the fragile back of his chair and asked, "Who were you with? On Capri."

She remembered crossing the Atlantic on the Queen Elizabeth 2 that year to meet her father and celebrate her sixteenth birthday, but she said casually, "Heavens! That was ages ago. Probably a relative."

"Probably." He looked suspicious but he didn't pursue the point until he had placed their orders "Pizza and trimmings," he announced in English, "and some of your chocolate ice cream."

Jacqueline accepted all this more readily than her stomach would, she was sure. But it was worth it. She was captivated by his sheer nerve and insolence. She looked around at the few other diners. None of them seemed to be enjoying the evening as much as she was. Two Italian males talked with furious animation. A boy and girl lingered over the Casa's celebrated chocolate ice cream. Both played with their spoons. A few of the more audible words in Italian reached Jacqueline.

"What's their problem?" Kimberly asked, watching them, then shifting his attention to Jacqueline's face. She tried to give no indication that their problem saddened her.

"The usual summer romance breaking up. In this case, make that spring. He's returning to the States. She goes home to Verona."

He grinned. "Now, that I do know about. Verona is Romeo and Juliet country, isn't it? Not for me. All that heavy business."

I might have known, she thought, slightly let down.

Still, the evening air warmed up again when she and Kimberly had finished the so-so pizza and dipped into the delicious ice cream under the golden glow of lanterns strung along the green lattice fence. She knew things were better because he made the observation, leaning on one elbow and studying her while the spoon in his left hand turned the ice cream to mush.

"You know, Jacky, you warm me up. Not even this stuff cools me off when I'm looking at you."

She reached across the table, touched his fingers and then brought her hand back to her lap, slowly.

"Thank you. I never had a nicer compliment."

"Wasn't just flattery. I never knew a girl quite like you." He kept leaning on his elbow with his chin propped on his knuckles, his lively eyes suddenly dreamy. "Tell me, how does a girl like you get to be – well, like you?"

"Practice. Practice."

"Where do you live?"

"Chicago."

He let his chin slide off his knuckles with a jolt. "You aren't married, or anything?"

"Well, I'm not married."

He pursued the matter of her birthplace. Chicago struck him as terribly prosaic ". . . for a girl like you.

Hog butcher of the world. All that Sandburg jazz I read in school."

"I like it. Hogs and all. What about you? Are you married?"

"Me? Princess, do I look that gone? So you were born in good old Chi. How come you're here in Venice working for some old bag who leaves you high and dry?"

"Where were you born?" She was about to ask what he did for a living but just possibly he did nothing; so she hurried on. "I'll bet you're from the Coast. You've got a Californian look. Southern, probably Los Angeles? San Diego?"

"Do you really like it in Chi? Tell me the truth?" He reached for her hand, played with her slender wrist and shook his head over Grandma Berthe's ring which had been on her finger so long she put it on almost unconsciously every morning. "Somebody's going to think that's real and murder you for it." He changed the subject suddenly. "What's she like? Hard to work for? Does she pay well?"

It was hard to think of Angela paying anyone. That job usually fell to Nigel or Jacqueline's father.

"I get by. She's very agreeable. Nice disposition."

"Funny. You don't look alike."

"Why should we look alike?" She looked up, glanced at her ring again and understood. The knowledge was a blow. He had seen the papers. He knew her real identity.

It explained a good deal. Most of all, it explained why he had suddenly appeared near her hotel, hoping to meet her, after that hiatus. She had meant nothing to him at their first meeting except a free hour or so, including the kiss. But Jacqueline Godart might be worth pursuing; so he had come back. To make it worse, he harped on about the value of her ring.

"That stone is the real thing; isn't it? Don't you think it's kind of dumb to be wearing it all over the place, where you can get mugged?"

"Yes," she agreed with an icy smile. "You never know what kind of pickup you can run into."

"Ah, that's too true."

"How long have you known who I really am?"

He was too casual. "Couple of days. Saw it in one of those skin mags from Rome. Why keep it a secret?"

She went on eating her ice cream. "I prefer to be Miss Nobody. It's a hangup."

"Sure is. I'd let everybody know if it was me."

"Well, that's the difference between us."

The conversation definitely lagged. He tried again, bringing up Chicago and when that got an indifferent response, he praised the chocolate ice cream for which the little Pizza Parlor was famous. Suddenly, he looked around and as if the idea had just occurred to him, began to study his wristwatch.

"If we make a run for it, we'll get the ferry without too long a wait."

She got up so fast she knocked her chair over.

"Great. Let's be on our way."

Since their conversation on the returning ferryboat was casual and reasonably friendly, she half-expected to continue their relationship. She thought she could handle a love affair with Richard Kimberly, while keeping in mind the basic truth. Her attraction for him was not 100% passion. The Godart money would make any female look good.

As the passengers pushed forward to land at St. Mark's, they edged Kimberly and Jacqueline against the stern-rail. Neither of them moved for a few minutes. The moon was clouded, and there was nothing romantic about the night except the position in which they found themselves.

They found themselves staring into each other's face, as if trying to read something that was deeply hidden. She moistened her lips, preparing to make some trivial remark about joining the Thundering Herd as they left the boat. His mouth, sensuous and humorous and mocking, suddenly crushed hers so hard her head hit the man behind her. She was in no position to apologize. Kimberly semed to want to invade her body through her lips, giving her no chance to breathe before the assault.

Strangling or not, she had responded with a draining kiss, twining her arms around his neck and caressing the flesh beneath the unruly dark hair that seemed to have been cut with a hacksaw. She touched a tiny mole below his left ear.

He broke away even while her insides still fluttered, leaving her to crave his body as she had never craved anything in her life. He said "Whew!" and gave her his careless, boyish grin.

He took her arm and they walked off the ferryboat. On the Piazza he stopped and still breathing a little rapidly, he let her go.

"See you, Princess."

Then he was off on a loping run toward the *vaporetto* wharf. He did not look back.

Five

The affair with Richard Kimberly appeared to be over before it began. He didn't like deception any more than she did, and he obviously understood her suspicions. Jacqueline assured herself many times during the next few days that this was all for the best.

She kept herself busy with company entertaining, once flying to Rome and back. No messages from Richard Kimberly had been left in her absence, but there had been calls from Nigel in Paris and several from her mother. Angela's letter of explanation arrived shortly after.

Poor Prince Sigurd's Schloss von Ulsbach, an estate which had given Angela the notion of marrying him, had turned out to be in the boondocks of Germany, with very little plumbing.

"No point in marrying the poor darling and losing my perfectly good Godart name for a penniless princeling," wrote Angela. She added, "But Sigurd has agreed to accompany me to London, where one desperately needs an escort."

So Angela, unlike her daughter, was happy with her gigolo.

An amusing card from her father, saying, "Miss you, Chérie," persuaded her that it was time to return home to Chicago, even though Marcel Godart, as western head of Godart's, was currently enjoying his beach estate at Malibu, handy to the Los Angeles headquarters of the family corporation.

Two days before flying home, and quite by accident, Jacqueline saw Richard Kimberly. He was enjoying a Campari at an outdoor cafe near the Santa Lucia Railway Station across the canal. He was not alone.

The blonde with him was French or Northern Italian, and appeared to be in the badly dated Brigitte Bardot style, all piquant, sexy curves and the pouty look of a girl with one thing on her mind. To Jacqueline's critical, and not unprejudiced eye, her wet mouth didn't seem to be getting her very far.

Richard Kimberly was reading the International Herald Tribune. He nodded at the girl's babble without looking up. Seeing the two together was not the most pleasant experience of Jacqueline's life, but it did take her mind off this persistent, creepy feeling that someone was following her again. She could never identify anyone when she looked around, and when she stopped suddenly, trying to trick her shadow into revealing himself, either a male or a female close behind passed her without looking back. Still, the sound of footsteps echoing through the lean, shadowed passages of Venice, persisted. Maybe there was more than one. Did they spell each other?

And if so, the bigger question remained – why?

When Jacqueline saw Rick Kimberly and the girl she was returning from the railway station, where she had seen two family friends off to Vienna over the Italian Alps. In spite of the last passionate kiss with which Kimberly had startled Jacqueline the night he took her home from the Lido it seemed he had actually had a – wife? Girlfriend? Mistress? – all the time, damn him!

Jacqueline remembered that kiss vividly and now she saw him with this Brigette Bardot nymphette and decided the girl was the reason why he hadn't troubled to look her up again. He was better occupied elsewhere.

Jacqueline observed one thing with pleasure. He certainly seemed bored by the girl's attentions. Very likely she pleased him only in bed. Jacqueline thought she herself could do better than that. Mentally, she flipped a coin: heads she would blunder on and play the indifferent amused witness. Tails, she would sneak away and say goodbye.

Her imaginary coin came up heads. She strolled down towards them from the bridge. She crossed the square. It was not busy at this later morning hour and the girl saw her first. She looked Jacqueline – or rather her clothing – over in a speculative way. Jacqueline was sure price tags had something to do with it.

She whispered something to Kimberly who turned a page, folding the paper in half lengthwise, making it easier to handle. He went on reading. The girl added something derogatory about Jacqueline's hair, gesturing to her own wild golden mop and wrinkling her nose in distaste. The mention of Jacqueline's hair was the

"Open, Sesame!" to Kimberly's mind. Still holding the paper, he turned abruptly and saw her.

No matter how negative her thoughts might be at having found him with the blonde, Jacqueline could not miss the pleasure that shone in his eyes and his whole manner as he dropped the *Herald Tribune* and got up, signalling her to join them.

"Over here, Jackie." He raised his voice and repeated her name, although she had heard him the first time. She walked across the paved cobblestones toward their table, smiling, friendly but aloof too, as if Kimberly and the blonde were acquaintances of whose identity she wasn't entirely sure.

"It is you, Mr Kimberly. How very nice! A beautiful day, isn't it? I've been seeing a friend off to Vienna. So this is your part of Venice. Charming." She looked around. "A little like Trastevere in Rome."

Kimberly had pulled out a chair between him and the girl. "Here. Make yourself comfortable."

"I'm afraid I've only a minute."

She was amused by his order to make herself comfortable; since the webbing of the chair was torn and badly faded. However, she accepted the chair, showing the blonde a friendly face and the innocent question,

"And this is Mrs Kimberly? A pleasure to know you!" She offered her hand to the blonde who looked big-eyed and confused but took her hand. The girl obviously liked the title bestowed on her by this elegant and perceptive foreign lady.

It was Kimberly who looked shocked. "Who? Babette? This is Babette Cuneo, my landlady's daughter. Babette, Miss Jacqueline Godart has some business to discuss with me. You run along now, honey, and tell Mama I won't be in for lunch."

The girl looked sullen, and with reason. Her bee-stung lips pouted and she hesitated, glanced from Jacqueline to Kimberly. Then she pushed her chair back slowly.

Jacqueline said, "Please don't go on my account. I can only stay a minute."

Kimberly had no problem with her indifference. "That's all right. Babette has to go. Her mother needs her. She was on her way to the fish market. Weren't you, honey?" As Babette grumbled something under her breath he added, "Babette's mother insists on fresh fish at all times. Great cook. Goes for a lot of polenta, too."

Jacqueline didn't want to make an enemy of the girl. As a matter of fact, she thought Babette Cuneo had been treated rather cavalierly. It didn't reflect well on Richard Kimberly. She started to rise.

"I really do have to be going." But his hand held her forearm and Babette saw it. The girl flounced away. She had a remarkably sexy walk. Jacqueline said coolly, "May I ask a favor of you?"

"You know it."

He paid no attention to the girl. He was watching Jacqueline in a way that made her skin prickle. She said sharply, "Don't ever call me honey. Not in that voice."

She had been sure that by her unexpected appearance she held the upper hand with him in this encounter. She hadn't allowed for his physical effect on her and she resented her own weakness.

Without taking his eyes off her, he said, "When I came to the Pensione Cuneo, Babette was madly in love with two French sailors. When they sailed off into the sunset I guess I inherited all that passion. Sorry. Not my type."

He had been staring directly into her eyes. Suddenly, he scowled and slapped the table with his paper, making her jump.

"You think I'm a heel, don't you? Two-timing poor, innocent Babette, and chasing after you for your damned inheritance."

"I didn't say that."

"It was all over your face. Well, for your information, I don't need your stinking money."

She recognized sincerity in his anger. She felt guilty and didn't know what to say. They were both silent. He pretended to study the folded paper but his mind wasn't on it. He grinned reluctantly.

"Sorry. I seem to have overreacted. To be honest, I didn't expect to see you again and there you were. I got carried away."

She tried to joke about it. "So here I am. All your attempts to avoid me were in vain."

She was feeling better than she had in days. If he had actually been attracted by her financial background, he would have kept up his pursuit of her. But he hadn't. Quite the contrary.

"Thank you. That's good to know." The softness of her tone told him more than the words.

He took a deep breath and then, looking a little sheepish, burst out, "Jackie – I can call you Jackie, I hope – I'll bet there isn't an hour since we said goodnight at the Danieli that I haven't thought of you."

"Any daylight hour?" She tried to make this light, joking.

"Wrong. I dreamed about you last night." He considered this. "No. Sorry about that. It was the night before last." She couldn't help laughing.

"I believe you. And you stayed away because I might think you were after my money."

"Wouldn't you?"

"I also think you don't want to be seen at the Danieli."

He hesitated, reached for his glass, but it was empty. He took a deep breath. "I haven't killed anybody. I haven't robbed anybody. That's not why I avoid the glamor hotels. Tourists stay there, and I have what you might call an enemy, who must be looking for me about now."

"Somebody is really after you? About a woman, of course."

"No, this is strictly between me and somebody I – I was about to have a small dispute with the IRS."

She stared at him, this somewhat disreputable fellow with his faded jeans and shirt, and that sweater hanging from one shoulder – this time a white sweater. At least, his clothing was clean. That was something. Then she burst into laughter that attracted others passing back and forth in the little square.

With some reluctance he began to smile. "O.K. I don't look like a guy who'd have trouble with the Infernal Revenue. We've got that out of the way. Have you been in a gondola lately with anybody under sixty-five? Let's go for broke as my Hawaiian friends say. Take a gondola and just get acquainted.

He leaned over, kissed her suddenly, lightly, on the nose and then further surprised her by pulling back her chair and practically lifting her to her feet. "Come on. We're off."

Like an eager boy, he hurried her back through alleys and canals by which she had come and reached the motorboats and gondolas lined up at the Railway Station, waiting for the arrival of the Milan Express.

He stopped on the steps, looked at her questioningly.

She said only, "You're on," and they headed for the nearest gondola whose black hull bobbed up and down in the wake of the *vaporetto* that had moved out into mid-canal a minute before.

Against the sun-warmed back of the seat Kimberly pulled Jacqueline close and the lanky gondolier in his Buster Brown hat, threw his weight forward on the sweep.

Richard began by pointing out various lacework palazzos, several times mixing them up, telling her the inspiring tale of George Sand's tryst with Chopin in the Ca d'Oro, which was interrupted (according to Kimberly) by Henry James in search of the poet Shelley's letters. Jacqueline listened with awe, more impressed by his imagination than by his lies. He delighted her. She had never known anyone quite like him. He might have been a boy of ten, and probably was, mentally!

Gradually, he stopped talking. He stared at the narrow canal, whose waters lapped gently at ancient steps on either side, between the mooring poles. She doubted if he even concentrated on what he saw. He appeared to be deep in troubled thoughts.

"I ought to go home," he said finally.

To Jacqueline it was like a splash of cold water in the face. She shrugged out of his clasp. Her smile was glittering.

"A very sensible idea. Think of all those people on the Coast who miss you."

"Sorry. Boise, Idaho had no coast." But he was amused by her transparent jealousy.

He carefully drew her head against his shoulder. She tried to keep her wits about her, but it wasn't easy. She was relieved to be distracted by the "traffic calls" of the gondolier as he made turns or adapted his weight to the pressure exerted by a passing motorboat.

Kimberly went on in that curious way, as if a shadow had fallen over his light, romantic thoughts. She wondered if it was her influence on him that made him go serious. She didn't know whether to be glad or sorry.

"I've no business getting involved until – Well, let's face it. I'm not a serious guy. That's been my trouble."

"Your trouble back home. Is it something I could help out on?" That sounded awkward, in view of their recent conversation about his true interest in her. She tried to patch it up. "I hope you don't think I'm trying to offer money to solve everything."

This struck him as funny. He said frankly, "Honey – I mean Jacky, if I thought a little money would solve it, I'd take you up on that loan. It was a loan; wasn't it? But it's too late." She raised her head. He waved away the idea of her interference. "I'm not a criminal. At least, I don't feel that way about it. Just a point of honor, you might say."

Only half joking she suggested, "You've left an abandoned wife? A pregnant girlfriend?"

"God! I hope not. It's nothing like that." He laughed; an abrupt, almost nervous sound. "Is it just vaguely possible that this thing between us might get serious?"

"Who knows? Why don't we wait and see?"

All the same, they knew without saying any more that their relationship had reached another stage.

By the time the gondola shoved in to the tiny mooring basin of a hotel behind St. Mark's Square, she was calling Kimberly "Richard," and he was calling her "Sweetheart." He only forgot once and called her "Honey."

They stood alone in the afternoon shadows in front of an old hotel, neither wanting to leave the other. They kissed, pressed hard against each other, clinging there on the edge of the gently moving waters. Jacqueline shivered with pleasure as he bowed his head and his lips lingered over the side of her throat, tickling and exciting her senses.

He muttered hoarsely in her ear: "It's not a bad place, from the looks of it. The hotel, I mean. I want you. I need you, Sweetheart. You'll never know how much."

She said nothing but her eyes gave him his answer.

Holding hands and with their bodies close they walked into the depressing lobby of the two-story hotel. The combined desk clerk and concierge, a stout, bored man, his forehead glistening with sweat, made Richard sign in and show his passport but paid little attention to Jacqueline. He watched them until they disappeared from his view up the winding staircase to the floor above.

Jacqueline saw very little of the dingy interior where, now and then, the stench from the stagnant canal reached the upper floor.

Richard sniffed as he unlocked the door of room 331. "We seem to be at the front, overlooking that damn gondola basin."

"What can you be talking about? Smells like Chanel Number 5 to me."

"Canal Number 5, you mean. Here we are." He pushed the door open and stood there looking at her. From outside the window the dusk gave her eyes shadows of promise. Suddenly, he reached for her, whirled her up off the floor and into his arms. He cradled her there, ignoring her amused protests, and carried her over the threshold, such as it was. He dropped her on the big brass bed whose mattress sank deep, not so much from her moderate weight as from long use.

The back of her neck struck the hard bolster and she winced, but her pulse-pounding desire for him was great enough to overcome such small impediments. At least, the faded coverlet was clean.

She wanted to hold out her arms to welcome him but curiously enough, Richard seemed to feel the same way her first lover had felt. He liked to be the only aggressor in love. He wanted to conquer. he came down upon her with an enthusiasm that made the springs creak and almost made Jacqueline laugh.

"What? No preliminaries?"

"We've had our prelims. Every minute we've been together. Come on now. Open up. I'm taking you right-this-second."

He had unzipped his fly with one hand and was pushing her quilted skirt up with the other. She thought she should make a token protest, but he managed to silence that by the first pulsating touch of his flesh against hers. She blamed his flattering enthusiasm for the rough pain of his entry into her body. Her few early experiences had prepared her for amateurish fumbling, even after several episodes. But she knew at once that Richard was skilled and highly experienced. The implications of that didn't trouble her. She had convinced herself that he felt genuine love for her. It might be temporary but it was the real thing, as nearly as she could tell by her own reactions.

Her body had never known such pleasure. The excitement rose in her until each nerve shuddered with his grinding assault. She locked her arms around his shoulders, holding him tight against her body, wanting to prolong the moments of delight. She heard his sexual whispers, his urgent commands:

"Come, Sweetheart! You're with me. I knew you would be . . . Now!"

They came together as he had commanded and he seemed to find this miraculous. When the tremors passed and he withdrew, lying beside her, he muttered,

"You're wonderful. And this is new to you; isn't it?"

She frowned at his description of love as "This" but she was proud of have pleased him. She was convinced that no one in all her life would ever mean as much to her. But she hesitated.

He turned his head. An uncombed lock of his longish hair fell over his forehead and he pursed his lips and blew the lock of hair back. He looked impatient. No. Nervous. Was he about to let her down easy?

"Sweetheart –" He broke off. His left forefinger traced the bridge of her nose. "Anybody ever tell you you're pretty?"

Uneasily, she recognized that he had been about to say something else and lost his nerve. But she laughed. Perhaps she could get him to trust her, eventually. In his own sweet time he could confide in her and they might work out his problem together, whatever it was.

"Pretty is as pretty does, my grandmother used to say. Of course, it sounded a little wiser in French."

He leaned over her. His lips touched the bridge of her nose again. "You know what?"

"I can't imagine." Her voice teased but her thoughts were incoherent. Something good? Or something bad, to separate them?

He confessed, "I love you. Honest, I do. And it's all a mess, you and me, Gorgeous."

"I figured it was."

He raised up, propping himself on one elbow while he looked down into her face. He burst out suddenly, "I'll bet you never slept in a fleabag like this in your whole life."

She was so surprised at this non-sequitur that she opened her mouth and found nothing to say. What was he getting at?

He bent lower, staring into her face. "God! You have gorgeous eyes, now that I think of it. Almost as nice as your legs . . . I'm a leg man, you know."

She grinned. "I'd never have guessed."

His free hand roamed over her body, along her flanks where it lingered, examining every crease, all of the ivory flesh down to her knees. She craved that delicious touch.

Whether he approved of her aggression or not, she reached out to him. They wrestled playfully on the aged mattress, laughing and teasing, but she couldn't persuade him by example to indulge in any foreplay, tender or otherwise. No matter. He loved her. She was sure of that. She was at an age when sexual compatibility was everything, and their abrupt joining again produced the excitement and the thrill of union with another human being that she had never known in her twenty-three years.

He was playing tic-tac-toe on her bare breast, a sensation that went far towards making up for his previous lack of finesse and foreplay. She shivered with pleasure.

An officious knocking on the door ruined this moment. Richard groaned. Jacqueline scrambled into her clothes while he opened the door. She heard the oily voice of the concierge-clerk.

"Time is two-hour. You like pay four?"

Jacqueline began to laugh. Could anything be more sordid and less romantic?

No matter. Nothing was perfect. And there was always tomorrow.

Six

Jacqueline reminded herself not to rush into this relationship, but the next afternoon she postponed her flight home for a week.

During these days and nights they spent less time making love than they did getting acquainted. They wandered together, talking, sometimes arguing over absurdly small matters – she preferred saffron in her risotto and he despised it. She was a morning person. He was a night owl.

He saw her looking around uneasily at night as they walked, and got all excited, insisting he would get to the bottom of this Del Sarto shadowing business.

"Suppose it isn't this Sarto gang trying to protect you. Maybe it's terrorists or something. Or here's an idea. It might be someone in your company. You've got a pretty cushy job. You must have jarred a few jealous characters along the way."

That was ridiculous. She couldn't see anyone at Godart's spying on her. She hadn't taken anyone's job. Only Nigel might have the right to complain that she had been put in over his head, and he was her mainstay, her teacher and greatest help.

But she let Rick play his little detective game. Maybe he would come up with something.

They agreed the next evening that she would walk out alone and he would trail her, find out what was going on.

Nothing mysterious happened, so far as Kimberly could discover. He caught up with her after half an hour of this, complaining that they were wasting a lot of precious time they might otherwise spend together.

So that was one matter solved.

Two more flights home were pushed back. The hours went by, days and nights during which Jacqueline laughed and loved and exchanged confidences with the only true lover she had ever known. Another flight home loomed up within twenty-four hours.

They hadn't discussed this last flight date of hers. She wondered if he would let her go without a word to stop her.

The afternoon before their last evening together she was deeply touched by his possessive attitude, his frequent kisses, and the way he insisted on their walking arm in arm, like two young Italian lovers. All this when she would soon be gone from him forever. She could hardly see him flying to Chicago just to contact her.

"I want you to see my hangout, Sweetheart," he told her. "Got to show you proof that I'm a respectable man."

This was promising, and she made no objections.

They took a speedboat across the Grand Canal and up a side canal to a footbridge. The steps beside it were slapped by the murky green waters.

Jacqueline walked with Richard to a narrow three-story house painted pink and looking slightly the worse for wear. A thin, severe-looking woman in black was sweeping the alley. She was directly under the words printed in white over the door PENSIONE CUNEO. She looked at Richard, her stern features about to crack into a smile. Then she saw Jacqueline and scowled. Richard explained apologetically, "I'm going to show Miss Godart the view from my room."

"Eh? You take my daughter's time. She is cleaning there." Then she shrugged. "Go up, but do not take her time."

"No, Signora."

Feeling the intruder she was, Jacqueline climbed the creaking stairs to the top floor where the door to the room on the right stood open and they could see blonde Babette dusting under the legs of a heavily carved table. Her hips flounced in a silent rhythm and Jacqueline erased her smile when she saw Richard frown.

"You work too hard, Babette. You're usually done with my room before noon."

Babette stood up, perky as a maid in a French farce, with her hair half-covered by a cotton scarf.

"I give this room extra care. For you, *Caro mio*." She glanced sulkily at Jacqueline who pretended to be deaf and went to the window. Everywhere she saw tiled rooftops. A view of sorts.

Babette meanwhile accepted her dismissal and went out, leaving the door open but waving her duster around madly as she crossed the landing to the other room on this floor.

Jacqueline felt Richard's arms around her middle.

"Sweetheart," he began, looking at the view over her head, "You won't have to live like this as my wife."

She started. "What's wrong with it? If there's love to keep you warm. All the old tunes promise that."

"We don't have to live your way, either," he added, guessing her private thoughts. "I'm not a poor, poverty-stricken slob. I must have a few talents I haven't tried yet." He laughed. There was an edge to the sound. "I can handle a mean deck of cards, for instance." He felt the tension in her body. "No. That's not how I'm going to make our living."

"Can I regard this as a proposal?"

He looked around her head into her face. "Why not? We'll draw up one of those legal things where I can't touch your money and you can't touch mine." She smiled. He added reasonably, "You never know. Anyway, I've got one job to do first. I want to settle that debt of honor I told you about. A letter will do it. I'll tell them where they can find the money I owe them. And the slate's clean."

She suggested, "If you tell me about it, I could help. If you need good legal –"

"Nope." He kissed her hair over her left ear. "I can handle it. I'll have to go back and testify –"

"Testify?"

"Make a deposition. But before we go back into the jungle, we ought to be entitled to a short honeymoon. Then, just before we fly home, I'll send my letter, deposition, that stuff." He added, after a moment's silence, "And I'll give you the straight dope. I swear to God I'm not a criminal. But I ran away when I was needed. Now, I'm going back. Whether you marry me or not."

"Thank you, my darling."

"Will you? I mean – marry me?"

Her lips gave him his answer, rubbing softly against his.

She felt painfully, fearfully happy.

As they walked down the long, aged staircase, Jacqueline settled another matter.

"Darling, two friends of my mother's were on the plane when I came back from Rome. Dr. McAllister is a Methodist Minister. He's been here on church business. His wife, Myrtle, was awfully proud that he'd performed eleven Protestant marriages in Catholic Rome. They're at the Gritti Palace. They leave for the States sometime this week. They'll know the red tape. Are they O.K for us?"

"Anything to get this show on the road, Mrs. Kimberly."

She put her hand over his mouth. "Bad luck until it's my name legally."

He was also anxious to find a place for himself in the workforce, as he put it. He said this with a grin but his eyes were serious. Jacqueline was proud of his independence but suggested that he put aside the problem of a job until he settled his other problem with the I.R.S. at home.

Besides, he didn't seem too sure where his talents lay. He kept talking about bookkeeping ". . . which I hate with an unholy passion, but I do know a little about it."

Jacqueline, however, saw him as a Godart plant manager or maybe an inspector of the company chain.

She explained this with some passion to Dr. McAllister when he hinted that Kimberly might have a few motives other than his overwhelming love for a girl he had known less than five weeks.

It was Myrtle McAllister, bustling and authoritative, who ruled her genial husband, and she had taken a fancy to the prospective bridegroom.

"George, of course you will perform the ceremony." Her strident voice rose still higher. "I'll bet you could point out one partner in every other marriage whose eye is on the money. Oblige Jackie, like a good fellow." She confided to Jacqueline, "I can't wait to see Angela's face when she hears you have beaten her to the altar. She always did have abominable taste in men."

Jacqueline stared in shock and Myrtle McAllister backtracked hurriedly.

"I meant – in her extra-marital affairs, naturally. No one is more fond of your dear father than I am. Delightful man. Be sure and give him my best when you phone him about this business. Now, dear, you rush right back to your beloved and tell him it's all settled. I adore his grin. So boyish. He positively oozes sex-appeal. And he's so shy."

"Shy? Richard Kimberly?" This was a new side to her lover.

"Oh, yes. I think he has an inferiority complex, bless the boy!" Myrtle went on. "He was positively afraid to walk through the lobby to meet George. Kept his head hanging like a little boy. Wouldn't look to left or right. I don't think he's used to the high life. Do run along, child. We'll handle everything. Just leave your passports."

"Really, Myrtle," her husband protested in a futile way as Jacqueline hurried out of their Gritti Palace suite.

When she came through the intriguing little alleys between the Gritti and St. Mark's Square where she was to meet Richard, it wasn't until he hugged and kissed her with great gusto, almost spilling her freshly ordered Cinzano, that she was able to tell him the good news.

"I figured the guy wasn't tickled all over at the prospect," he admitted. "But his old lady seemed friendly enough. She probably swung it for us."

He set his own glass down and reached for her hand again, closing his fingers around it. "Happy?"

His eyes watched her a bit anxiously and she asked, "Can't you tell?"

He began on a new tack, "Honey, have you any ideas for our honeymoon? We've got to do something special. But here we are in a honeymooners' paradise; so the question is, where do we stay? I sure as hell don't want to spend our wedding night in one of those Beautiful People Palaces."

She had been thinking about that very thing, but she didn't want to make all the decisions. He might be reminded too vividly of Mrs. McAllister. She hesitated, then ventured, "It's just a thought. But have you visited any place in the Lagoon besides the Lido? Like the islands? Murano. Burano. And –"

"Torcello!" They said it together.

His eyes lighted. "There's an old inn with great food. A perfect place if we can escape Hemingway's ghost. He hung around the island a bit." He confessed, "I'm not much of a swimmer. Pretty dry country where I come from. Not many pools until I was half-grown. But I sure as hell can zoom over the bounding main in those demon speedboats. So long as I'm on top of the waves. And Torcello is like being off at the ends of the earth. Nobody can touch us."

For some reason the idea of escape seemed vitally important to both of them. Jacqueline was anxious to avoid her parents and Nigel Chilton-Brown, at least until there was no turning back from the marriage.

The Reverend and Mrs. McAllister staged the wedding in their suite. It was not precisely what the prospective bride and groom would have chosen, but they found themselves tugged along in the wake of the all-conquering Myrtle. The renaissance splendor of the salon had been disguised with enough flowers, hothouse and otherwise, to bring on the Reverend's hay fever. A bower of irises, daffodils and greenery stood in for the altar. Roses lined what Mrs. McAllister called "The Aisle." She herself would stand in as a witness, though she referred to herself with a goodnatured chuckle as "Your Matron of Honor". In the circumstances it seemed ungrateful to refuse her offer.

"Besides, Darling," Jacqueline reminded Richard who was less than enthusiastic, "The sooner we get this thing out of the way, the better."

That made him laugh. "I like the respect you show for our great moment, the sacred event that hooks us up for life." He was stroking her hair and wrapping the long dark locks around his neck. The gesture brought them together and they lingered over their last pre-nuptial kiss. They were in the maid's bedroom of the McAllister suite where Jacqueline was putting the finishing touches to her bridal finery.

Richard had sneaked in from the hall and been slightly dazzled by his first sight of her. She had chosen an oyster-white, silk crepe tunic over silk trousers. The tunic was just below knee-length, with a high Nehru collar whose severity was relieved by her best three-strand pink pearl necklace. Matching earrings dangled among the strands of her hair, which she wore unconfined.

Richard was not the only one a little shocked by her long slide from the traditional. Myrtle McAllister had shuddered.

"Jackie, isn't that a teeny bit dated? Right out of the Sixties. Are you sure you don't want to wear something just a mite more feminine?"

Surprisingly enough, her husband had disagreed with the redoubtable Myrtle.

"On the contrary, my dear. I'v never seen anyone more feminine. It takes a special kind of – er – form, I always say, to wear trousers and Jacqueline certainly has it. She looks like a Manchu princess."

"Whatever that means," his wife grumbled, but she was mollified when Jacqueline agreed to carry a lace handkerchief of hers as "something borrowed."

Only minutes before the ceremony Mrs. McAllister came to the maid's bedroom, rustling in pale pink *peau de soie*. She ordered Richard out to the living room.

"Bad luck. Bad luck. Don't peek. There's a good boy." She returned to more important matters than the bridegroom. "Jackie, you do like gardenias, I hope. They seem so appropriate with that dress, or should I say those trousers?"

The gardenias were small, enchanting flowers, unlike those great, lush blooms once used in corsages. They were threaded to fall in a graceful ribbon from Jacqueline's fingers.

Jacqueline adored them. They made her think of trips to Hawaii in her childhood.

A good omen. She had been happy then.

It never occurred to Jacqueline to ask about wedding music. She merely wanted to marry Richard Kimberly in the simplest legal way. But no detail was too trivial for Mrs. McAllister. She had ordered her maid, Ethel, to press the "play" button of her Sony tape recorder at a signal, and the Lohengrin "Wedding March" would begin its inexorable lock-step.

Mrs. McAllister's carefully set blonde head popped around the hall door into the big living room. She nodded. The maid pressed the button and, as Jacqueline thought wryly, "The show is on the road." Myrtle took the bride's arm, pressing it and assuring her,

"This is it, Dear. Head up. One of your nice smiles . . . Lock! Step! Lock! Step!"

Damn, Jacqueline thought . . . I wish she would shut up!

They lock-stepped into the living room. A half-dozen of the McAllister acquaintances watched the little procession of Myrtle and Jacqueline. There were audible murmurs at their first sight of the bride. Thank heaven, they were flattering!

But most important was Richard. He seemed a long way off, at the end of the room. He wore a "respectable" business suit – his only one, he had confessed to Jacqueline. But his hair was tumbled, slightly windblown, and he looked the way she loved him best. Casual. A free spirit.

Just as Jacqueline entered he passed a handkerchief to the Reverend McAllister who was trying desperately to stifle a sneeze. Then Richard saw Jacqueline. Though he had already seen her in her wedding finery, his face lit up and his eyes widened. Then he winked.

Overwhelmingly relieved that he had broken the mood of this ridiculous ceremony, she was dying to wink back but restrained herself, content to stifle a smile that he must have seen.

There was no Best Man. Mrs. McAllister had goofed there. But otherwise, the ceremony went like clockwork. The whole thing was over in less than ten minutes. Richard made his responses loud and clear. Her own were low-pitched, a bit husky. Once she was drowned out by the minister's strangled sneeze. She found herself far more nervous than she had expected to be.

There was no engagement ring either, but Richard had insisted on spending most of his ready cash on her wedding band, a simple twist of yellow gold. She wanted it that way. It was simply engraved, at his suggestion: "Ever and ever." Her stiff, chilled body didn't warm up until he pushed the ring over her knuckle, forcing it a little.

"You may kiss the bride, my boy," the Reverend McAllister managed to get out before accepting a cocktail napkin to muffle a paroxysm of sneezes.

"All over but the shouting," Richard announced and pulled her to him, threatening to crush her ribs as he kissed her exuberantly. He made her wince and everyone laughed but she returned his kiss, pretending to strangle him.

The babble of congratulations, spiced with champagne, followed, only partially interrupted by Reverend McAllister's whispered plea to his wife: "In heaven's name, get these flowers out!"

The bride and groom exchanged glances, trying hard to keep a respectful demeanor when they both felt all the symptoms of a laughing jag coming on.

Freedom at long last. They had only to change into comfortable clothes, and grab their luggage, her Hermes overnight case priced at $4,000, and his back-pack worth about a hundred times less. They rushed off to hire a speedboat for the half-hour ride to Torcello.

In spite of Richard's efforts several men with cameras and a female reporter caught at them as they passed, but the afternoon was foggy and they got nothing except what appeared to be a pair of poorly dressed tourists on the run. That was lucky. Jacqueline wanted no publicity to reach anyone she knew until she could announce it. Richard was even more relieved.

Seven

In other circumstances the unexpected gloomy weather would have dampened their plans. But the feel of the thick, misty fog on their flesh as they climbed down into the speedboat only made the bride and groom burst out laughing again.

"It figures," Richard remarked finally, surprising the boatman who was busy making excuses in Italian for the unseasonable weather.

"Goes with the territory." Caught between the boatman and Richard, and still laughing, Jacqueline let herself be boosted down into the boat. "He does know where we are going, I hope."

"Sure thing. We go Torcello. No?"

Before they could say "yes" he started up with a snap and a roar and they headed out from San Marco Piazzetta into the choppy gray lagoon, spanking the water smartly.

In spite of the jolting that made their teeth rattle, bride and groom settled back, bodies pressed close. They sighed in unison.

"Mine at last," Richard murmured melodramatically, his lips tickling her ear.

She played up. "My own, my very own." She let him place her head against his shoulder, her hair lashing across both their faces as the Adriatic wind played around their heads. He sneezed and that set them off again. "Poor Dr. McAllister!" she said when she could speak. "He really is a dear. Incidentally, I saved the flowers. I suppose I should have thrown them at someone."

"If I know the redoubtable Myrtle, she'd be sure to catch them."

"Still, it's because of her that we're man and wife. We owe her that."

'You may have something there." he turned his head and kissed her cheek. "You taste of salt. Is that the spray? Don't tell me it's going to rain."

"Wouldn't surprise me. Who cares?"

He squeezed her and kissed her again. She cooperated passionately. They clung together, ignoring the spray of lagoon water and the bump and slap of the speedboat over the waves.

The boatman grinned. "Lovers?"

"Better. Married," Richard told him proudly.

The boatman wrinkled his powerful nose. "Bah!"

Everything struck them as special this evening, the Lido lights fading romantically in the mist on the horizon, even the boatman's cynicism about marriage. It seemed just another joke.

"Is that going to be you ten years from now?" she teased.

"I said 'ever and ever' and I meant it. Are you cold,

Honey? Your face is wet. You look like a water nymph, whatever that is."

"Who cares? As long as you like it."

"I like it." he followed the trail of her hair with his finger. In spite of the fog and mist, she felt his gentleness and touched his wrist with her lips.

He studied her face in a curiously somber way. She wondered what he was thinking.

They had changed their course somewhat and could now see the first evening lights of St. Mark's Square on their left, shimmering and beckoning across the lagoon. It seemed especially beautiful to Jacqueline as the setting for her great love. Even the mist and the chill Adriatic wind added to the glamor of this moment.

"Like an old movie," Richard said, following her thoughtful stare.

She sat up suddenly, shocked by the gigantic gray apparition that cut across their bow on a course toward the San Marco moorings. It appeared to be floating on the misty night. She cried out, but the boatman deftly turned the little speedboat, avoiding the Lido Ferry by a safe margin as it chugged by. He chuckled at Jacqueline's terror, took a hand off the wheel and made a circle with thumb and forefinger.

"Nothing, Signora. No problem."

Jacqueline tried to relax but the feeling that had formerly wrapped her in a cocoon of safety was now torn away.

They might be lovers, and legitimate at that, she and Richard, but they were not free of the dangerous world around them.

By the time the quiet, dimly lighted island came

into view on the horizon both Jacqueline and Richard were half-frozen. The boatman headed for the mooring pole at the end of a marshy canal. He waved them ashore.

"You walk with canal. Not far."

"I devoutly hope not," Richard said as he fished in his pack for an extra jacket. He did the noble thing, wrapping the faded blue denim around the shoulders of his shivering bride. She was laughing, so things could have been worse.

The boatman, anxious to drum up trade, suggested, "I got business and come here, I see you tomorrow."

"What?" Richard demanded. "Only one night?"

Jacqueline put in lightly, "Give us at least a couple of days. And nights."

"Okay. Day after? Two day after, maybe? Right here. Same place. Maybe same time?"

"Maybe."

Jacqueline waved to him as she and Richard started toward the distant lights, following along the dark path made even more indistinct by the foggy mist. They walked arm in arm, saying nothing, merely savoring their togetherness and the far-away atmosphere around them, as though everyone they saw was a phantom. He said finally,

"Makes you feel like you're on a desert island. You know. Romantic and otherworldish."

She agreed. "Maybe. But those lights ahead look mighty good. I'm so – hungry."

"Well, that's sure as hell a romantic statement!" He considered for a few more steps. Then he hugged her shoulders and confessed, "Me, too."

They began to run, challenging each other, laughing again.

A few daring spirits, probably locals, were out but nothing slowed the newlyweds until they reached the inn and signed in. The inn was unimpressive and rustic on the outside but single story accommodations framed an enchanting little garden on three sides and only the latticework separated the terrace restaurant from the garden on the fourth side.

Jacqueline had eaten there many times and was greeted with warm enthusiasm and some veiled inquiries about her esteemed mother. Registration produced a problem, since her passport was issued in the name of Jacqueline Martha Godart. After much fluttering and many regrets from the clerk it was decided that she should sign her passport name and write her married name beneath in parentheses. Meanwhile, congratulations were in order and Giulio, the clerk, promised to send a bottle of Orvieto and the sommelier's best Chianti to their little rooms, since they preferred this to the usual champagne which the clerk insisted would follow later.

Jacqueline guessed that the news of their marriage would travel fast now; so she scrawled brief notes to her father and Nigel Chilton-Brown, announcing the event and her ecstatic happiness, and Giulio offered to see personally that these went off from Venice early in the morning "when the chef visits the fish market near the Rialto."

Richard sent no messages. He informed Jacqueline with some pride, "My letter – you know the one – goes out the day after tomorrow. I wrote it yesterday, the whole business, and gave strict instructions. That gives us a few days, anyway."

"Thank you, darling. And I'll do my share. I won't write to Mother yet. She and her prince are much too close here in Europe."

He laughed but agreed.

The Terrace Restaurant was deserted, due to the weather, but for Jacqueline and Richard as they followed the bellman to the last vacant room facing the garden, this murky world look perfect.

Unpacking presented few problems, so few Jacqueline had another laughing jag when three Agatha Christie paperbacks fell out of her husband's backpack.

"What's so funny? They're my worry beads," he explained.

On his part, he found it hilarious that with only one change of clothing she should take up room in her case for an Instant Camera and a set of electric curlers.

"And here was I, thinking that mop was natural."

Before going to dinner they uncorked the Orvieto for Jacqueline, the Chianti for Richard, and drank out of the festive glasses provided along with a tray of inviting antipasto which they didn't eat until they had made love.

It was not like their recent frenzied, hurried love-making, chiefly in the dingy hotel off San Marco. They spent this time exploring each other's bodies with lascivious delight. They lay together in the big, comfortable country bed, wondering at their luck in finding each other.

It was well into the evening when Jacqueline exclaimed suddenly, "I'm still hungry."

"Well, there goes the marriage."

He assumed a hurt expression but there was a humorous quirk about his mouth. He rolled over, bounded out of bed, and stood up. "I believe, on second thoughts, I could eat something too." He leaned over her, threatened to take a bite out of her elbow.

They dressed and stepped outside into the Italian night, marvelling that the garden and the lonely terrace (so enchanting in good weather) could seem romantic and mysterious on a night like this. Voices came to them from somewhere inside, but stubbornly, they insisted on eating by the garden, where they could stare at the arbor and the door of their honeymoon home. Looming in the gray mist beyond the garden was the narrow, square tower of the church whose foundations had seen the beginnings of Venice fifteen centuries before.

"Kind of like us," Richard murmured, unexpectedly impressed.

"What? Fifteen hundred years old?"

"No. Because it wants to be eternal."

"You want to be eternal?"

"If it's always going to be like it is here, tonight."

"Amen to that." She took his hand. "Whatever happens, let's never be less happy together than we are this minute."

"I'll drink to that," he joked, to break the strange tension that seemed to have come over them.

Jacqueline could never afterward remember what she ordered for dinner. Richard ordered Scampi Risotto and tried to feed it to her because he didn't like the saffron flavor. She did recall taking the bites off his fork, because she loved his touch and wanted to please him.

But the evening was magical. The world they had left was far away on another planet.

Afterward, they walked around the garden, stopped under the flower-scented arbor and kissed each other, and resumed their walk. They didn't even mind when they discovered that the guests were peering out at them from the dry haven of the other garden rooms and from the main quarters of the inn itself. They heard the penetrating giggle of a young female quickly hushed by her companion. Richard waved at the unseen giggler.

"Just jealous, poor devils!"

Jacqueline wouldn't have been surprised if the entire world was jealous of them that night. There was a good deal of romping and fun in their lovemaking, but the youthful passion remained to be satisfied. Neither of them had much practice in finesse and foreplay.

Richard was nothing if not direct, and Jacqueline, in the throes of her first genuine love, welcomed him and his boyish enthusiasm.

Anything else was beyond her experience, if not her knowledge.

Only one disturbance occurred when they were awakened in the early hours of the morning by newly arrived guests, a male and female, who quarrelled about "her," some mysterious being whom they had failed to find on Torcello.

For a breathless moment or two Jacqueline lay there wondering if the voice she heard outside their door could be her mother. The idea alarmed her as much as if Angela had meant nothing but evil. She got up, careful not to disturb Richard, though this was not easy. He lay on his face with his arm stretched out across her body as if he was afraid she might get away.

She drew the light, silken skirt of her Pucci nightgown through his fingers and freed herself, then moved quietly to the window.

The woman was not Angela Godart, though she was small and curvacious, like Angela, with her deceptive fragility. This one lacked Angela's radiant golden look and she seemed a bit tight, something Angela never permitted in herself. The mysterious "her" that the woman seemed to be looking for was her husband's mistress, according to their argument, which was conducted in English.

Jacqueline grinned and returned to bed. Richard murmured sleepily, "Time to get up already?"

"No, darling. Just some people looking for someone."

He grunted, turned over, then sat up abruptly. "Who are they looking for?"

"One of your ex-mistresses," she said and curled up in bed again.

Gradually, he sank down beside her, chuckling. "Jealous, Sweetheart?"

"Frantically. Good night."

He was disappointed. Obviously, he would have preferred her to show a little concern about his former girlfriends.

When they awoke and luxuriously ordered their breakfast in bed Richard complained that no one in Europe could give him his ham and eggs the way he wanted them, the eggs hard-boiled, the ham underdone. These ideas produced such a shocked reaction on

Jacqueline's part that they discussed eggs and other curious eating habits for the next half-hour.

The day slipped into evening, the hazy sun had come out and dutifully sunk somewhere around dirty, smoggy Mestre on the Mainland and the two lovers agreed over Cinzano with Lemon Peel that this had been the most perfect day in their lives.

Shortly afterward Richard was captivated by the children of an Italian pair they met over cocktails when a ball, sticky with chocolate ice cream, rolled up to his feet and the three children hurtled into him as they chased it. Their stout, substantial parents insisted in Italian that they apologize and, somewhat to Jacqueline's surprise, they did so. The boys mumbled and dashed away but their little sister blinked her big black eyes at Richard, shyly tried to speak and hid her head.

How tender he was with children, Jacqueline thought.

The child gave her parents a side look, but apparently had no fear of her father's stern features. She put her hand in Richard's, then pulled it away quickly and pelted after her brothers.

Richard swallowed his Cinzano, still watching the three children chasing each other around the garden.

Jacqueline said, "You like children, don't you?"

He looked at her and shrugged. "Not particularly. Just reminded me of the fun kids have."

She didn't know what to think. She decided he simply didn't like to admit his sentimental side. He began to talk about tomorrow and where they might go.

"We've almost used up Torcello."

She wondered at his sudden boredom after telling her that today had been the happiest day of his life.

Maybe he could only handle one Happiest Day at a time.

The evening was fun, more strolls about the island, more of the same Italian family with the lively children, and yet, there was a subtle difference. She felt that he wasn't really with her. His thoughts were far away in some room that she was afraid to enter.

Did he have a family somewhere, with children . . . A wife? No. That was ridiculous. But children? She tried to make a joke out of it.

"You don't by any chance have a ready-made family waiting for you back in the States; do you?"

He looked offended. "Christ, no! You do get the damndest ideas, Honey."

"O.K.," she said casually. "But hadn't we better send cards at least, to your folks."

"I told you, I don't have any folks."

"Not even in Idaho?"

"Oh, them. They don't pay any attention to cards and stuff: X marks my room . . . The casino's over yonder . . . Wish you were here! I'd feel like a hypocrite."

She paid great attention to a fingernail she had broken. "Are there any children in your family?"

"Lord, no. What made you think of that?"

She changed the subject.

When they went to bed, they made love as passionately as if for the first time – she would always remember that with gratitude – and eventually she went to sleep. The last thing she remembered that night was a glimpse of Richard lying there staring at the ceiling, while one arm lay close and warm against her hip. She was reassured.

The next day they took a roll of instant snapshots of each other and got the gruff but obliging Italian father to take some of them together. Without discussing it they tacitly accepted the fact that they would leave Torcello that evening when their boatman came for them – if his business warranted.

It wasn't until they were packing their few honeymoon belongings late in the afternoon that she realized they were getting closer to whatever it was that bothered him.

"Sweetheart?"

Her throat was tight. She managed a sound or two. "Hm?"

He zipped up the canvas roll that he would balance between his shoulder blades. The screech of the zipper set her teeth on edge.

"Sorry." He grinned boyishly and leaned across the bed, touching her arm and stopping her as she folded a half-slip. Badly shaken by her premonitions, she stood there watching him, waiting.

"Honey – I mean Sweetheart," he began again and then poured out the question without taking a breath. "What would you say to us grabbing a plane for home without any time over in Venice. I mean – tomorrow morning."

She was only half relieved. "Tired of married life. I see it all now."

He ignored her wry, humorous tone. "I mean it. I could settle that IRS thing. And I could sure use your moral support, as the guy says."

Jacqueline found this a double relief. Once and for all, they would settle the matter. And even better, he still loved and needed her. She thought about her mother. How could she possibly explain her desertion of Angela who would undoubtedly come hurrying back to Venice when things didn't work out with the dashing prince?

The devil of logic came to her rescue. Strictly speaking, she had no doubt that Richard needed her more than her mother did. Besides, he was her husband now. Closer to her than her mother had ever been. She would leave a note for Angela, hope her mother understood, and suggested that if things didn't go well for Angela, she should follow Jacqueline's flight and come straight home to Chicago. Not that Angela had ever felt that Chicago was her home, but that was Angela's problem.

"Let's do it," Jacqueline said and he closed his two hands over hers, drawing her across the rumpled bed toward him. She added, "I'll call Mother just before we leave. It will be too late to stop us."

"Honey, I love you like – I don't know what. I'm going to turn over a new leaf." He kissed her cheek boisterously. "Get a job." His lips pressed hard on her mouth. "And get rich. All for you." He kissed her throat, lingering deliciously in the low v-neck hollow of her blouse until she begged him laughingly, "Please. I'm ticklish."

They clung together while the seconds slipped by and the last rays of the sun were blotted out by a thick roll of fog. It didn't matter. They had arrived in fog. They would leave the same way. What difference did it make?

The fog had thickened when they left the inn after carefully splitting their expenses. It made them shiver when they had paid their bill in the cozy, timbered interior and abruptly met the foggy drizzle outside. They walked arm in arm, silently remembering the moments they had shared in the little haven they were leaving behind them. At least, Jacqueline hoped they were both thinking the same things.

She did have other matters not too far back in her thoughts. She broached them as casually as possible while she and Richard made their way to the canal.

"Maybe if we discussed your trouble now, before we arrive there, you would be better prepared. I certainly would be. By the way, Darling, where is it we are going in the States?"

"Don't worry. I'll give you the full lowdown the minute we get settled on the plane." He grinned at her. "Then it'll be too late for you to back out."

"Never." She got carried away and hugged him until he grunted. She assured him, "Never, never, never! Where you go, I go. That's how it's going to be."

His lips brushed the crown of her head and her body felt the heat of his touch in spite of the clammy fog creeping around her jacket and her bare toes in their expensive but worn sandals. She was just about to ask: "What will happen to our beautiful plans if the boatman isn't there?" when they heard a motor cut off with a sputter at the public ferry dock. There, illuminated by the mooring light, was the boatman, waving to them in great glee.

"You come like you say. I come with the promise. We are of our word. No?"

They climbed into the speedboat. The boatman insisted on helping her. She caught a whiff of his breath and wished she hadn't. His dinner had been heavily lubricated by wine. It made him very jolly. He related in Italian the story of a group of tourists who had behaved ridiculously this afternoon. He received a rewarding laugh, though Richard hadn't understood much and Jacqueline failed to get the point.

They didn't care. They looked at each other and huddled together for warmth, with the feeling that they shared an unforgettable experience.

"Cold, Sweetheart?"

"Don't be silly. Me, cold?"

"Funny thing. We'll laugh about this ten years from now."

Her imagination worked on the problem. "We'll make it a starry night, with the crescent-moon rising out of the Adriatic, and lucky me in the arms of a bodice-ripping pirate."

"That'll take a bit of doing, but I could oblige with the bodice-ripping." He hugged her more closely, then frowned. "Our buddy here can't see a foot in front of us, it's so foggy. And I doubt if he could see much better if it happened to be clear. The vino has him fogged up. But what the hell? By tomorrow night this time, if we get the connections, we might be high in the clouds over the Rockies. Or the Sierras. I got everything else in Europe. I only missed one thing. The Banbury Cakes."

"What?" She sat up. "You can think of a thing like Danish Pastry on a romantic night like this?"

"Not Danish, Sweetheart. English. They call them Eccles, too, I think. Anyway, they are terrific. Funny. I hung around England at first, but I completely forgot about them. I've got an idea. Why don't you tell your bakery to do them? I'll bet they'd go like – well, like Banbury Cakes!"

She laughed at Richard's businesslike suggestion and Richard raised his voice to the boatman. "Buddy, we've got an early plane to catch. This weather won't hold us up; will it?"

"What? Me? Hold up? No way. We get you there."

The spray rose up around them like a brisk, icy shower.

"Please," Jacqueline put in. "You're only responsible for the first lap. To San Marco. After that, we're on our own."

That might be, but the boatman had other ideas. He was obsessed by the passion to get them home as rapidly as possible. They skimmed past a sun-bleached skiff that was moored to a buoy marking one of the passages through this stretch of the lagoon. They seemed to be headed for Murano or Burano, a land mass that hovered on the near horizon with faint lights already shrouded in the gloom of a foggy night.

Unable to think of "Slower!" or even "Stop!" in Italian, Richard nudged the boatman with an elbow, shouting, "Whoa, damn it!"

"Si, si!" was the enthusiastic response as the boatman cut away sharply toward open water.

His passengers were soaked. Jacqueline screamed and Richard poked the boatman harder.

"Slow down, damn you!"

They caught a flash of the boatman's teeth. "Si. Like you say. Catch the plane."

Night had fallen over the lagoon so gradually they were not quite aware of it until Jacqueline shouted in

Richard's ear, "We can't see a thing. Make him slow down, for heaven's sake! We're liable to find ourselves adrift in the Adriatic."

Their little bow-lamp, too small to be dignified as running lights, could scarcely be seen more than a few yards across the water. Jacqueline found herself straining forward, hoping against hope that she would see anything the boatman missed. Nor was it reassuring to note that Richard had done the same thing.

She knew the area well enough to guess they were crossing the main shipping lane used by the international cargo liners that anchored in the lagoon.

"Never saw it so black," she yelled, but her voice was swallowed up among the muffled noises of the sea, the distant clang of a bell, the horns announcing the snail's progress of shipping leviathans, the moan of the rising wind, and above all, the sound of their own little boat slapping the churned up waters.

Somewhere nearby, cutting across the surface of the lagoon, they heard the first clang of a ship's bell announcing the time and the changing of the watch. In seconds the clanging, brassy sound seemed much louder.

"There's a ship anchored out here somewhere," she warned Richard. "We've got to go easy."

Trying to make himself heard, Richard yelled a warning to the boatman who waved a free hand and nodded.

"Si. A Slavic tanker. Hold fast. We make the turn." He thrust his body at the wheel and they spun around, barely saved from capsizing either by the boatman's skill or by his incredible luck.

Suddenly, the thing was before them, an anchored mountain, the ship's bell deafening at these close quarters. A harsh voice shouted a warning down to them in Croatian. The little speedboat spun again on a turn. The abrupt change of course had been too much.

The boat heeled over. Jacqueline heard her screams, Richard's shouts and then she was in the water, drawn under as if by some terrible hand from the depths. She swallowed oily water, choked, made an effort, using every ounce of strength, and bobbed back to the surface. The boatman had seized the overturned boat and clung there, his eyes wild and glazed in the blinding light flashed down on the water from the tanker.

Jacqueline made out Richard's head as he swam toward her, the water boiling and foaming around him. She cried out. Trying to conserve strength she floated for an endless few seconds, watching, bobbing to the surface again when the current would suck her down. She realized in a ghastly, heartsick way that Richard had been right. He was not a good swimmer. He struggled too much.

"Easy," she screamed, getting another mouthful of oily water. "Easy, Darling."

She swam toward him, long, experienced strokes born of many years at Cannes and Deauville and Sardinia, and especially in swimming pools. There had not been many swimming pools in Richard Kimberly's life.

She caught glimpses of his head. Once his hand almost touched hers. She called his name but she doubted if he heard her.

Something hurtled down to the water, making a great splash. It was a life-preserver, weatherworn but still adequate. She shortened her strokes, bringing her body to the preserver, floating it toward Richard. She caught a glimpse of his agonized face.

She screamed, "Darling! Don't give up. Hold on. Hold on."

His head disappeared beneath the waters. He pushed up again in his struggle, but his last, desperate energies were spent. His fingers groped toward her before he went under.

She kept screaming, "Hold on . . . please . . . please . . . Hold on . . ."

By the time the tanker's boat was lowered only the Italian boatman clinging to the hull of his boat, and Jacqueline, clutching the preserver, remained on the surface of the water.

Strong, callused hands pulled her over the side into a ship's tender. She made it harder for them by her struggles, her flailing arms: "Find him! He's out here . . . close by! Please . . . Oh, please . . . I know he's here . . . Please . . ."

A gloved hand, smelling of tar and oil, pressed firmly against her mouth, silencing her cries. They must think she was hysterical.

She hated her rescuers; yet she knew even then that they couldn't do anything else in this deep, murky dark.

Eight

Afterwards, she remembered those first days after the accident as an unbroken series of nightmarish hours. Jacqueline recovered her physical strength almost at once, and was able to lead the endless stream of authorities, even the Venice Fire Department, to the place where the collision occurred.

The Yugoslavian tanker had already sailed out into the Adriatic after turning over the rescued Jacqueline to the Venetian police. According to the Yugoslavian report, no one else had been picked up, although Jacqueline had seen the drunken speedboat pilot floating in his life-preserver.

When every effort by the harbor authorities, including police and fireboats, had been exhausted, she hired a string of private investigators: a company from Rome, a private agency from Milan, and finally a French agency recently responsible for uncovering Shiite terrorists in Paris.

They all agreed that the testimony of the vanished speedboat operator would be invaluable, but when a life-preserver from the Yugoslavian tanker washed ashore on a tiny islet off Burano, it was generally agreed that the missing operator had drowned and only the hope of discovering Richard Kimberly's body remained.

It was never found.

Much against her will, but yielding to her parents' pleas, Jacqueline returned home on the understanding that her agents would continue the investigation.

The hours became months and at last the search failed off into intermittent reports, all of them false.

It was in late October, three years after the accident, that Jacqueline awoke in her high-rise apartment in Chicago with the icy sensation that Richard had sent her a message through the horror of a nightmare.

Only hours later Jacqueline saw the photograph which seemed to her the proof that her premonition had been true. That she saw the photograph at all was an accident. She was due to attend a TV ad campaign meeting downtown in Nigel Chilton-Brown's office. At the last minute the call came through from her father, asking if she would meet him at O'Hare airport. He was flying in from the Coast "with a surprise you will love, *Cherie*."

She was always happy to see her father and immediately notified Nigel's adoring Miss Heffernan that she would be late for the ad campaign meeting.

Marcel Godart's good nature was proverbial, in spite of an occasional Gallic outburst which disappeared in seconds. Physically, he took after his mother, the celebrated "Berthe." He was stocky and a little on the plump side. This was not entirely due to heredity. He loved few things better than a good Bordeaux, unless it was a pretty woman. He was always urging his only child to "Eat up, *Chérie*. You are so thin, you look like a giraffe. All legs. My father was like that, and you remember, he died young. It is bad, this skinny-thin business."

Although he had been born in Chicago, his mother's accent and six years of study under the chefs of Paris and Lyon had left him with a "Frenchness" that fooled most people into believing he was a foreigner.

The traffic to O'Hare was horrendous as usual, but at least since that stupid carelessness about the brakes three years ago, Jacqueline was more careful.

She had barely gotten out of the car at the airport when she saw Marcel Godart trotting toward her, accompanied by a tall blonde with European chic who was, like Jacqueline, a head taller than Marcel, even allowing for his heavy, graying mane.

He seemed very pleased with himself, which was not surprising. Even at first glance he looked like a prosperous impresario, or perhaps an operatic tenor, except that his brown eyes were too gentle, too sentimental.

A skycap followed in his wake, with a set of expensive foreign luggage plus Marcel's old, familiar brown valise and folded garment bag. The European luggage certainly did not belong to him.

Sighting his daughter, he forgot the chic blonde and threw himself into Jacqueline's arms, yelling at the top of his lungs, "Happy Birthday, *Chérie*!"

Her birthday had been two days ago, but she took the will for the deed and returning his embrace as he complained, "There is nothing to squeeze. You are so skinny. And your complexion, so pale. You should come out to the Coast. Soak in some of our L.A. sun."

Laughing but firm, she reminded him, "Nature made me pale. Blame Grandfather."

"Look at the contessa here;" boasted Marcel. "She has a fair complexion. She soaks every day beside my pool, and her skin is like gold."

While the Skycap stored the surprisingly large collection of luggage in the trunk, Jacqueline reached around her father to shake hands with the elegant blonde who was such a great commercial for sunlight. The contessa had an easy continental charm and Jacqueline could see why her father had shared his pool and probably his heavily furnished Santa Monica beach house with her. After all, his ex-wife was still parading around Europe, with her headquarters in London, accompanied by her perennial escort, Prince von Ulsbach.

This contessa was whole planets away from Marcel Godart's last "travel-mate", a conceited little *ingenue* fresh from a triumphant four-year TV series.

"Now then," Marcel insisted, "You climb in the back seat with the contessa and get acquainted. I drive."

"Papa, you are a born chauvinist." Jacqueline watched goodnaturedly while her father assisted the contessa into the somewhat worn interior of her four-year-old Chrysler LeBaron. Nigel Chilton-Brown had picked it out for Jacqueline. She often said she was lucky he hadn't patriotically picked up a Rolls or a Bentley.

When Jacqueline got in on the opposite side of the car the contessa held out her hand again.

"I am Irina Fabrini. Your dear Papa is so delighted to see you he has forgotten his manners."

"Jacqueline here."

The contessa accepted this gracefully.

There must be more to Marcel's relationship with the contessa than met the eye. Few of his Hollywood pool-mates felt confident enough to scold him in this easy, proprietary manner. Jacqueline seated herself, stretching her legs, and immediately became aware of a nasty comparison. Her legs were as good as Irina Fabrini's, but that was as far as it went. The contessa's gloriously-fitting suit, the color of golden sand (it looked like a Feraud) with its hot pink blouse, was matched by high-heeled Italian pumps as supple and creamy as butter.

Quite a contrast to Jacqueline's long, draggy, full skirt and her suede flats. She had worn them to ease the ache of a twisted ankle caused by a pushy pedestrian on State Street. But today the limp and her wardrobe made her feel like Hans Christian Andersen's Little Match Girl.

She hadn't long to worry, however. Marcel Godart started up with a zoom and a thrust that made her rock in her seat, though she was familiar with his driving. The contessa was even more familiar. Her gloved hand firmly pinched the back of the driver's seat for security and to Jacqueline's further surprise she said with gentle authority, "Marcel, *attenzione*!"

Marcel was out in traffic now, with the afternoon wind whistling through the open windows and the sky a vivid, clean-washed autumn blue. To Jacqueline's private satisfaction the contessa was forced to anchor her chic, floppy-brimmed felt hat with her other hand. Still, her blonde hair in its low twist stayed beautifully in place on the nape of her neck.

"The contessa comes from Italy," Marcel explained, watching them a trifle anxiously in the rear-view mirror.

"She's been doing costumes for one of those nighttime soap operas. They want her for the new Newman-Streep next spring."

"I can see why." Jacqueline felt better. The woman's job was an acceptable excuse for her superb look. "Then your home is in Italy. Florence? Or Rome?"

The contessa slung her big Hermès handbag off her shoulder and onto her lap. "Neither. I am what you Americans call the maverick in Italy."

Marcel cut into the left lane, ignoring the fury of a young Honda driver. He was trying to watch his daughter at the same time. "The contessa has a palazzo in Venice. It has been in the Fabrini family for centuries."

Jacqueline said, "How nice!" She saw that her fingers were curling up in her palm. The knuckles had lost color, she was so stiff. She added with more calm than she felt, "I spent my honeymoon there."

Irina Fabrini sensed the tension behind the simple answer. "I beg your pardon. I do not understand, quite."

Marcel blurted out, "I forgot to tell you. My daughter's husband was drowned in Venice."

Jacqueline cut in brightly, not wanting to talk about it with this stranger, "A long time ago. Actually, I've been a widow for over three years. Don't let it bother you."

The poor contessa still seemed to be embarrassed and Jacqueline tried to relieve the atmosphere by praising the Venice that she had tried for so long to blot out. It was less painful than it might have been a year or two ago, but the whole ghastly thing swam suddenly before her eyes. By the time they roared their way through the Loop traffic and reached the Imperial Towers off Michigan Avenue the two women were at least acquaintances, but one thing still troubled the contessa.

"Please forgive my mentioning your tragic loss, Miss – Mrs. Jacqueline, but you see, I was in London last spring on business for the Preservation of Venetian Antiquities, and I met your mother."

Jacqueline was a little jarred. "I knew she was in London, but she didn't mention Venice."

The contessa said, "What is more strange, if you will forgive me, we had several intimate conversations, especially when I mentioned that I was bound for Hollywood. But your connection with Venice – she made no mention of it. She did speak very highly of you and Marcel. It was your mother who gave me dear Marcel's private number in Los Angeles. It was very gracious of her. So broadminded."

"That's Mama, all right."

The contessa looked as if she didn't quite know how to take all this broadmindedness. She said hurriedly, stroking her Hermès bag,

"I have photographs here of the Venetian Antiquities affair, the one that took place in London. I thought they might serve as my introduction to Mr. Marcel Godart, and so they did. One of them is an excellent shot of your mother, Jacqueline."

"She's awfully photogenic."

The contessa glanced at Marcel who nodded as they turned the car over to the young attendant in the well-lighted lower-level garage. Although the Imperial Towers were serviced by three elevators, only one went up beyond the twelfth floor to the fifteenth and the penthouses above.

The young attendant rang for his Number Two man, a lean, scholarly Lebanese, to take over the garage and he himself took the luggage under his wings.

Once the four were in the elevator and Jacqueline was debating tomorrow's weather with Raul, the young attendant, the contessa reached into her bag and took out an eight-by-ten glossy that had been taken by the photographer of a British weekly. Under the tulip globes inside the period elevator, Jacqueline studied the photo.

She was only casually interested. Her feelings for her mother hadn't yet recovered from the fact that Angela had forgotten her birthday entirely.

In the picture her mother was chatting away as usual, small, beautiful and volatile, her little hand possessively clutching the upper arm of the sleek, blond Prince Sigurd von Ulsbach. She always photographed well. But if Jacqueline knew her mother well, His Highness would soon be ready for the discard. Angela seldom supported her protegés and escorts longer than two years.

The photo included half a dozen other international jetsetters, along with waiters carrying trays of champagne and hors d'oeuvres.

Another man was distinguishable at the rim of the photo. Jacqueline's hands shook as she stared at him. The man was a dead ringer for Richard Kimberly. The resemblance was great enough to bring back all the old anguish.

Was it Richard?

She had insisted all along that he wasn't dead, but through the horror she remembered. She had seen him drown.

Nine

She closed her mind to that other traitorous memory. Her dream this morning really had been a sign, a message to her that Richard was alive. Absurd as it might sound to her family and the Italian police and the private investigators, she had been right all along. The proof was here.

It took a minute or two for her to pull herself together and return the glossy without betraying her turmoil by the tremor of her hand. She thought the contessa was watching her with a peculiar intensity. She wondered if the woman knew the identity of everyone in the picture. But Marcel supplied her with a simpler explanation for the stare.

"Young Man! Why are these lights so bright? They make the flesh look most unflattering."

"Sorry, Sir," young Raul explained, "With all the crime in the inner cities these days the ladies, especially ladies in the tower, requested more light."

"I do not consider this the inner city." Marcel was still worried about Jacqueline, who turned to study her reflection in the mirrored back wall of the elevator. He was right. Her face looked the color of skimmed milk. The shadowed hollows under her dark eyes and beneath her high cheekbones didn't help either. She hoped this was due to the lights and not to the photo she had seen. She managed a fleeting smile.

"Oh, Papa, it isn't Raul's fault. Let him alone . . . Contessa, are you acquainted with all the people in that picture?"

"I do not know. I do not think so. Still –" The contessa studied the photo, a tiny frown barely disturbing the smoothness of her brow.

"Either she has no problems, or she gets some terrific facials," Jacqueline thought enviously.

The elevator whizzed by Jacqueline's floor to the one two stories above, where Godart had what he called his "*pied à terre*," an apartment considerably larger than Jacqueline's. She had one bedroom and liked it that way. Her parents were too much in the habit of dumping their friends on her, reminding them that if they happened to be in Chicago overnight (or longer) they must not dream of camping out in some dreary, impersonal hotel when they could stay with Jacqueline.

As they put it: "It will be a favor to our little girl. She spends far too much time alone."

Jacqueline had ended this by selling her larger apartment after she returned from a business trip last year, buying one with a single bedroom. Except for a few special pieces, she had decorated her apartment comfortably, the way she thought Richard might have liked it. As for guests, at a pinch there was always one of the couches in her spacious, living-dining room. This lack of beds discouraged casual hangers-on.

On the sixteenth floor Raul unlocked the big, impressive bronze-studded door, fussed around, turning on half a dozen lamps, looking into closets, checking every corner and promising to send them Glover, Marcel's part-time man of many parts, who would see to his wants. He avoided mentioning the contessa but when he was gone and Jacqueline was about to broach the subject of the London photo, Marcel produced his little explosion.

"Irina will be staying with me."

"Of course." Last year's little *ingenue* had been something of a disaster as his house guest, but Jacqueline knew her father, an incurable romantic. And then too, the contessa looked like a woman who knew how to get along with a somewhat spoiled older man who could be "adorable" when he got his way.

Marcel coughed. "No. This is different. Irina has done me the honor of accepting my proposition."

"Proposal, dear Marcel," the contessa corrected him with her controlled little smile.

Jacqueline's thoughts were several thousand miles away in Venice, and this new shock further confused her. She stammered, "But – how wonderful! Now, we have something really worh celebrating."

One more complication.

Marcel squeezed her elbow in his gratitude. "That's my girl. Nothing surprises my Jacqueline."

Jacqueline and the contessa exchanged forced pleasantries. They didn't know each other well enough, Jacqueline thought, to have much enthusiasm for the enforced relationship. Also, this news was completely alien to Jacqueline's real interest in that glossy photo.

All her thoughts were devoted to knowing more about that man. Besides, it wasn't as if this was the first time Marcel Godart had gotten himself involved since the divorce from Mama, for which he had gallantly accepted the blame.

Jacqueline, who always did her own packing and unpacking, looked around at the beautiful pile of luggage discreetly stacked in a corner just off the foyer.

"May I help you?"

The contessa quickly covered her surprise. "Thank you, no. My maid will be arriving in the morning. In the meanwhile, I shall live out of my carry-on case, as we say."

Somewhat mortified, Jacqueline bristled. "Naturally. I'll leave you to get settled. I am afraid I must be off. I've got to change for a meeting. I'm already late."

She hugged her father, congratulated him again on his engagement, and tried to shake hands with her future stepmother, but the contessa embraced her, cheek to cheek, in the European style. Nevertheless, Jacqueline could feel the chill indifference of a stranger. It was reciprocated. Maybe things would warm up between them after they got to know each other.

Just as Jacqueline was leaving she asked in a casual way, "Do you have any more photos of that London party?"

The contessa was fingering the crimson portieres that Marcel had insisted upon in his living room. Clearly, her ideas did not run with her fiancé's heavy, Bourgeois-French tastes. At Jacqueline's question she blinked.

"More photos? But yes. Several. Would you care to see them?" She drew out a thin, beige European envelope of eight-by-tens and offered them to Jacqueline. "Take them. I have others."

Trying to hide her nervousness and avoid discussing the still painful details of her old tragedy aloud, Jacqueline thumbed through the glossies. The man who looked like Richard Kimberly was not in any other picture. She couldn't make up her mind about him.

He was taller than the closest men in the shot. That fitted Richard. He had a profile whose features seemed a trifle more regular than those of the delightful drifter who was Richard Kimberly. The way he held his head was different. There was pride in it. Richard had an impudent, devilish way about him. But he might be quite different after his near escape from death.

Those vivid, blue eyes, unexpected in a man with dark hair, might have told her more, but she couldn't make out the eyes. They were shadowed.

The mouth of the man in the picture, what she could see of it, had the sensuous curve whose power she remembered so well upon her own body. Richard slouched a bit. The man in the glossy was slightly hunched over, possibly because he was looking down at something in his hands. A program? A notebook? The nose appeared to be the same, perhaps a trifle thinner than she remembered. The shape of it had always seemed perfect to her.

She had thought Richard was exceptionally good-looking. There weren't many men whose general description fitted his. Still, she could be wrong. She probably was wrong.

But if she was right?

"This man, the one in three-quarter view. Do you know him?"

Controlling her curiosity with an effort, the contessa studied the picture.

"A photographer, perhaps."

Marcel looked at the picture over her shoulder. "Who is he, *Chérie*? A friend of Angela's? That prince-fellow she has been seeing so much of?"

"Not the prince. No."

"Most unlikely," his fiancée agreed. "The man is not in white tie. Perhaps from the press? I believe there was a sketch artist present. Some of the committee thought dollars could be earned from a book with sketches and portraits of each palazzo. The book was to include some of the sponsors, the Beautiful People, as we called them."

"Correctly." Marcel assured his fiancée, squeezing her shoulder.

"I'll leave you two ladies to get acquainted. I see Glover looking distressed. As usual, he objects to the way I packed . . . Coming, Glover."

"And I must go," Jacqueline said. "I have a company meeting in town, and I suspect I'm late already."

The contessa walked with her to the foyer and the elevator. "Meetings in town? With the Englishman, I suppose. But one would think they would be held at Marcel's convenience."

Jacqueline was surprised that the woman did not understand Nigel Chilton-Brown's position.

"Well, Nigel does run the company."

"Yes, but – a pity he is not a Godart. My poor Marcel feels that such a position belongs within the family, as one says."

Jacqueline managed to keep her polite smile.

"And Father feels left out? Even though he controls the Western Outlets?"

The contessa made a graceful little gesture, inviting understanding. "Several of the Western Board at Godart's feel that Marcel, as the only son of the founder, should be the controlling head of the company." The contessa tapped Jacqueline's hand with a tender movement. "You, of all people, will appreciate that."

"Of all people," Jacqueline agreed and watched the contessa, summoned by Marcel, drift away to meet him. On her way she reached out, touched Marcel's glassed-in collection of Napoleonic lead soldiers, shook her head and hurriedly withdrew her hand as if it had been contaminated.

Jacqueline was relieved when she left them. She suspected that her father had better say goodbye to his clutter of knick-knacks, bric-a-brac, and the other remnants of his somewhat cumbersome Old World tastes. Irina Fabrini would soon have it all shipshape and "pip-pip", if indeed, she let him keep the apartment at all.

An hour later Jacqueline arrived at Nigel Chilton-Brown's suite in the aging office building on State Street.

She was still nervous and had been uneasy since meeting the contessa and her father, but that was more or less routine.

Marcel's delightful insouciance, his extreme excitement and optimism, qualities so evident in her own Richard Kimberly, were lovable but tiring in a father. They also had a habit of suggesting to Jacqueline all the ways Marcel's optimism could go wrong. With two feckless parents Jacqueline would not have been true to her genes if she hadn't inherited some of that optimism. Luckily, it was tempered by her grandmother's sound realism.

Recent happenings had not calmed her nerves, but she still managed to dazzle the pretty new receptionist in the outer office as well as Miss Heffernan, Nigel's adoring, highly organized Executive Secretary. In fact, Jacqueline's appearance brought Miss Heffernan right out of her chair.

"Good heavens, Mrs. Kimberly! How very stylish you look! Isn't that a St. Laurent? Or do I mean a Givenchy, or –"

"Closer to home. Oscar de la Renta. But thank you. I needed a pick-me-up." She wondered if she was conspicuous in her sleek, black suit with its multi-colored scarf and button detail and changed the subject quickly. "I'm not late, am I? I got stuck. Papa introduced me to his new fiancée and I have a hunch this one will stay the course. A Contessa Fabrini, no less."

Miss Heffernan rolled her eyes. "Like that, is she? I hope she won't try to put a hand in the works here."

"She's a fashion designer, not a baker, thank God! May I go in?"

"Please do. He is always delighted to see you, even aside from business. But you know that. Anyway, he wouldn't start the meeting without you. Meanwhile, I'll check on this Fabrini."

Jacqueline thanked Miss Heffernan with her best smile but took care to knock before pushing the door open.

After providing such an unwelcome contrast with her prospective stepmother, Jacqueline felt that her reception by Nigel, plus an advertising man and a female TV executive, made her self-esteem really climb. Her black pumps, with their multi-colored insert barely visible, had the highest heels she could find and she was a graceful walker, knowing just how far her stride would carry her before she stretched her slit skirt.

Nigel got up at once and crossed the room to greet her. In the background the painfully neat advertising man made a bluff of rising a few inches, then settled back. The TV woman turned away from the window where she had been studying the busy State Street traffic below. She examined Jacqueline from head to toe, missing nothing. She was a goodlooking woman, probably about Jacqueline's age, but her kinky, shoulder-length hair in the popular blow-dried frizz dragged down her long face.

As it turned out, the woman was here to sell her product, not herself. Jacqueline, who was basically a feminist, gave her full marks. The woman knew her business. Still, it was a waste of good material, not to do something about her assets.

Nigel took Jacqueline's forearms, leaned over them and kissed her cheek, his neat, 1930s mustache tickling her as always. A lean man of forty with few outstanding features except his pleasant, polished British manner, he did not excite Jacqueline, but he had been by far the most comfortable person for her to be with until she met Richard Kimberly. And that was no mean quality.

"Here you are, looking quite like a million – my dear." The familiar "Old Girl" almost slipped out. They had been friends so long that the "Old Girl" was a form of endearment.

He introduced the advertising man and the TV woman. The man was impressed by her identity and became positively ingratiating. But the woman, Theba West, caught Jacqueline's attention at once, in a way that had nothing to do with the business at hand.

"Mrs. Kimberly, sorry to move off the pad at this early stage but you may have a puzzler out there." She waved her business-like folio toward the windows. "Did you come here alone?"

Everyone was startled. Nigel had pulled the armchair over to the enormous mahogany desk as usual, giving the illusion that Jacqueline presided at the meeting. He straightened up, glanced at her, and then at the windows, frowning.

"Good Lord, why? Have they ticketed her car?"

"I came by taxi."

"Coincidence, I guess." The TV woman shrugged. "Shall we get on with matters?"

Jacqueline crossed to the nearest window.

"What is it? What happened?"

Theba West joined her at the window.

"Sorry. Just a man. He's nothing. Unless you have a bodyguard. He was following you. I saw him as you walked up the street. From the cab, I guess. I couldn't miss that outfit of yours. Marvelously photogenic, the way you wear it. This character was pretty close behind you. You stopped for a few seconds and did something to your ankle."

"I was rubbing it. Yesterday, I twisted it. Still hurts a bit."

"Well, the thing is, this character stopped too."

Nigel asked sharply, "What? Somebody following Jacqueline?"

"That's what got me," the woman went on. "Then you turned in here, Mrs. Kimberley. And he started in too. A crowd came pouring out. Probably the girls from the big real estate offices on the third floor. Anyway, he's disappeared now . . . Shall we get on. Now, then, Mr. Chilton-Brown, we've signed that fat little actor you wanted for the reverse twist on the Baker-and-the-Girl Bit."

But Miss West's casual snooping had distracted Nigel. "Might it have been a coincidence? Or even a purse-snatcher?" His reaction did nothing to calm Jacqueline. She watched the woman shrug again and didn't believe her when Miss West brushed the matter aside, hoping to get back to more important matters.

"Very likely. I didn't see his face. His hands were in his pockets . . . Now, here is the layout that Bernstein and Kent have come up with. I think you'll find it plays well on the soaps."

Nigel looked at Miss West's folio without seeing it. His calm demeanor didn't fool Jacqueline. He was tense. He began to feel across the desk for the pipe he had given up two years ago. Then he went over to the windows, tilting the Venetian blinds to study the sidewalk far below. His actions disconcerted the others.

Miss West squirmed in her chair. "We just need a little more input on the Joby Marks tape." She gave her partner a side-glance, but in spite of their discomfort, Nigel gave no definite approval to the plans for the "Croissants With Sex Appeal" commercial and eventually Miss West, with her cohort, gathered up the evidence of their campaign and left.

Jacqueline threw her arms around Nigel, thanking him for a basket of birthday roses. He, at least, had remembered. He looked gratified and returned her enthusiastic hug in his moderate way.

"Happy Belated Birthday, Old Girl. And many more."

Then he broached the subject that bothered him. "Have you any idea who could have been following you? Or is it all that toothy female's free-flowing imagination?"

"It can't be the Del Sartos. I was followed long ago in Venice by somebody from that family. Your instructions, I believe."

"The Del Sartos are on a visit to the USSR. I doubt if they would have sneaked over to follow you here."

She leaned over, pulled up her narrow skirt and gave him a view of her left leg in its sheer black nylon stocking.

He was duly impressed, but not with what she intended.

"Gorgeous. Can this be an offer?"

"Get your mind out of the gutter and look at that ankle. Still swollen. Yesterday, some idiot pushed me in front of a bus. Almost, anyway. I was out there, crossing State Street."

"Well, I'm damned! Then it was serious."

"The pain was. You'd better believe it."

He called to Miss Heffernan. "We're leaving, Esther," but when his Executive Secretary came in to lock up he was still at the window with Jacqueline. On the street below there were a dozen prospects for the man Miss West had seen following Jacqueline, but every single one of them managed to cross State Street or head Uptown without looking back.

Miss Heffernan called, "I hope you had a nice birthday, Mrs. Kimberly," and locked up the inlaid mahogany cabinet where Nigel Chilton kept his now-forsaken pipe rack, his liquor, and his pewter soldiers representing Wellington's Army at Waterloo. It was the latter collection that almost cost him Marcel Godart's friendship. Marcel had more than once threatened to send his own land army of Napoleon's "Old Guard" downtown to thrash Chilton-Brown's "Old Contemptibles."

Jacqueline thanked Miss Heffernan and Nigel wished the woman good night, adding as always, "And have a splendid evening," to which she answered almost by rote,

"Oh, I shall, Mr. Chilton-Brown."

What those splendid evenings consisted of, no one had any idea. Miss Heffernan lived alone and her work was her real life. She had once told Jacqueline who sympathized over her complicated job,

"I adore every minute of working for a man like Mr. Chilton-Brown. I wouldn't trade my position to be – to be the wife of the president."

Going down in the elevator they found themselves alone. Jacqueline suggested, "How about my going ahead, pretending to be by myself. You tag along and see if Mister Zero, or whoever, follows me."

He shook his head, taking her upper arm firmly in his grasp. "Sorry. We've no notion what his object is. We can't afford to let him get too close. I'm having a little talk with your father about the matter. It's my suggestion that we hire some sort of protection for you until we discover whether there is anything to this business."

That would be almost as bad as the original follower, assuming there was one. "This isn't a game, Old Dear. All that private eye stuff."

"You must remember, one day you are going to be an exceedingly rich woman."

"I'm not complaining right now. If they leave it all to me, it's only going to go for causes that irk you so much. Hunger and Elderly Indigent, and Anti-Nukes and Environment, and –"

He threw up his hands. "Spare me. I am thoroughly acquainted with your charities. Luckily, a good percentage remains in the corporation."

"Suppose Mama marries Prince Sigurd von Ulsbach and makes him her heir? And when Papa remarries he may have a curly-headed little male heir to take over the name. And I'll be out on my – reputation, such as it is."

"Both prospects you envision are highly unlikely."

She grinned but said nothing for the moment.

Out on the sidewalk Nigel signalled to the chauffeur of his hired limousine. He looked around carefully as they got in, then settled beside Jacqueline. Once they were on their way through the roaring afternoon traffic, he remarked,

"Marcel arrived, I take it."

"Papa and my future stepmother, that Unlikely Prospect you were talking about."

He opened his gray eyes at that. "I hope you are being funny."

"Not a giggle. She is the Contessa Irina Fabrini of Venice and she designs for Hollywood and the Beautiful People."

She could see that he didn't like that at all. It hurt his sense of propriety, considering Marcel Godart's age and track record. "Young and beautiful, of course."

"Of course. About my age, or possibly more. Maybe thirty or so."

"Good God!"

He sat there digesting this and a minute later, remembering the other Godart problem, he leaned forward.

"Albert, we are on our way to the Towers. Keep a weather-eye out for anyone following us. It's just possible –"

The chauffeur, a discreet little man with a pinched face and small, sharp eyes, kept his curiosity in check, nodded and glanced up at his mirror.

"Too much traffic to tell right now, Sir."

Nigel nodded and settled back again.

Jacqueline played nervously with her black snakeskin handbag and attache-case. She didn't approve of using snakeskin – she liked most snakes – but she couldn't bear to part with the bag. It so exactly fitted her needs. Finally, she drew out the thin beige envelope.

"Would you do me a big favor and look at these? My prospective stepmother gave them to me because Mama is in them. They were taken in London about ten weeks ago. Some affair for the preservation of Venetian palazzos."

He took them, looking politely interested because she had asked him, but she knew he was wondering what could be so special about them. He flipped through the glossies.

"She holds up very well. Doing her hair lighter, I see."

"No, no. Not Mama. Do you recognize anyone else you've seen in other pictures? Color prints?"

The throb of excitement in her voice caught him, but he couldn't figure out what it was she wanted from him. He studied each picture and had to admit defeat. Her impatience and tension puzzled him.

"Are you blind? Look at that man on the side there. Haven't you seen pictures of him before? In a dozen color shots, at least. Instant prints."

He frowned, then suggested hopefully, "Angela's latest? The successor to that Prince what's-His-Name?"

"You are impossible. It's Richard Kimberly. My own Richard."

He dropped the entire set of glossies, scattering them over the floor of the car. He reached for them but she beat him to it. Carefully placing the Richard picture on top she took another set of pictures, this time stiff Instant prints, from a zippered compartment of her bag.

"Just look at that profile and then at these prints."

"But these are full face," he complained.

"Can't you see the resemblance? His dark hair, for instance. It's true, this man's hair seems neater. It's brown, you know. Richard's hair was a bit windblown. But that was eighteen months ago. Well – he might have cut it recently. It's still not what you'd call short." She was studying the pictures with great intensity. Quite possibly, she didn't hear her own words.

"Jacqueline . . ."

She colored, coming back to the present. Trying to conceal the absurdity of her conversation, she laughed.

"That's if it were Richard, I mean. And who knows how he would change after such an experience?" Very cheerful, as if her claim had been a joke, she added brightly, "Would you believe it? I dreamed of Richard last night."

"Yes. I would believe it."

It was not what he said but the way he said it that disturbed her. She hated compassion directed at her.

"Just because you thought I needed a psychiatrist after the accident doesn't mean I really am crazy, you know."

"I know that." He returned the color shots to her.

She understood. "You don't see any resemblance at all, do you?"

"Not a shred. I'm sorry . . . So you are about to acquire a stepmother. is she in those pictures?"

She had forgotten all about Irina Fabrini. She looked over the glossies more carefully. In the shot showing Richard Kimberly's double, the contessa, a bit blurred by movement, was at his elbow, looking down at something. The pad in his hand. Although she apparently did not know him, she certainly seemed close to him in this picture.

Embarrassed by the deep, suppressed emotion he sensed in her, Nigel leaned forward again.

"Notice anything yet, Albert?"

"Hard to tell, Sir. Got a Hyundai and a Cad on our tail, and a whole bunch of Compacts behind the Cad. You can take your pick."

"Unlikely."

Nigel gave Jacqueline a side-glance, reached for her hand, and felt the thin, cold fingers curl up resentfully in his. She cleared her throat.

"They never did find his body. They say that's unusual in Venice."

Ten

She was angry and depressed all the way home, so much so that she felt she owed Nigel something when he was about to leave her apartment. He looked puzzled, hurt too, and she said abruptly,

"Father is holding Open House to introduce his Lady Love. You're invited, of course. But we're not due for a couple of hours yet. Why don't you come in and have a drink first. We'll see if we can rustle up some of that crumbly old Cheddar you're so crazy about."

"Sounds like an offer I can't refuse."

He seemed to be relieved. He was certainly pleased.

At her invitation he went to the bamboo bar in the big living room and dropped ice cubes into highball glasses, then reached for the Scotch decanter. She was in the kitchen getting out the cheese board, the cheese and crackers, when he reminded her,

"Everything humanly possible was done to find your husband, assuming he was alive. No one in Europe, including that Venetian landlady, knew anything about him, or his past. He seemed to come out of nowhere. It isn't natural for a man to have no ties to the past."

"Never mind that. Richard undoubtedly had his reasons."

'I'm sure that he did. May I use your phone? I must call Esther Heffernan."

"Help yourself."

She resented his remark about Richard but didn't pursue it. She was well aware that even Richard's "Boise" story hadn't worked out. No relatives or anyone else had responded to ads in the *Idaho Statesman*. Jacqueline's investigators failed to locate any sign of "Richard Kimberly." He had covered his tracks too well.

She didn't tell Nigel, or anyone else, for that matter. She could be sure of only one thing. The Richard Kimberly she knew had genuinely loved her, and with that knowledge a lot could be forgiven.

When she returned to the living room Nigel had gone to the long windows with his glass. He sipped the Scotch while he stared at the ragged line of skyscraper lights against the black sky. Lake Michigan was within sight several blocks to the left, but a good view of it required opening the long windows and craning your neck.

Anxious to let him know she was not depressed, she suggested brightly, "The lake is mysterious at this hour. The witching hour."

With one hand encumbered by the highball glass he handed her she leaned against the left window to point out the lake view. The window gave way, swinging outward. The rush of night air off Lake Michigan whirled around her. By what seemed a miracle, she caught hold of the window with her free hand. A second later Nigel, muttering "Good God!" reached over her head and closed the window.

"You nearly took a spinner there, Old Girl."

"Fourteen floors down." She shuddered but played it lightly. "No harm down. Well," She raised her glass, clinked it against his. "Here's to us."

He refused to be mollified. "See here, Jacqueline, do you make a habit of leaving these windows unfastened?"

"Don't be ridiculous."

He was taking an immoderate interest in the window-latch. "Not broken. But it seems to have been left unlocked. You could have been killed."

Annoyed that he should dwell on it, she contradicted him. "Don't be melodramatic. There is a wrought-iron railing out there."

"About a foot high. That would be poor comfort if you tumbled out."

She finished her drink in one long gulp. "If you're going to bring up pursuing gangsters and enemies pushing me off the sidewalk again, Old Dear, you can take your Sherlock Holmes cap and go home. Richard and I checked out that sort of thing in Venice. Nothing!"

"I still think –"

"Did you ever hear of someone forgetting to latch a window? Either Milly Yee or I forgot. That's all. Really, there's no need to make a federal case out of it."

He swished the ice around in his glass, but he kept staring at the window-latch. His concentration made her nervous.

"Not to change the subject," she began hopefully, "But what do you really think about this woman who calls herself 'The Contessa Fabrini'?"

"Well, to begin, the title is authentic."

"Damn! How on earth do you know so soon?"

"Surprisingly easy. I just called Esther Heffernan. She started in on the woman the minute you mentioned her an hour or two ago. There isn't any fact she can't get for me. The secret, Old Girl, is not necessarily to cram one's head with information, but to know exactly how to acquire that information at a moment's notice."

"Efficiency is your middle name. And Esther's too. So the beauteous contessa has you on her side before you even meet her." But she still had one more card to play. "Anyway, I have a feeling she has already taken over Father's life. And you know what that means."

"Oh?"

"Oh, yes. I saw the way she eyed Papa's apartment and his driving in the car, and his manners. She's going to want to be back here at the heart of things, so to speak. Next step will be running Godart's. She's already mentioned giving you the heave-ho."

He set his glass on the cocktail table behind him. "My dear girl, when you are dealing with a susceptible man's passion for a clever young female the matter requires finesse and time. I strongly advise you not to interfere. You will only antagonize Marcel."

"But what are we going to do?"

"*You* are going to do nothing, I devoutly hope. There are big interests behind her. Corporate interests. Esther has already taken soundings. So, I suggest you leave the matter to the experts."

"Meaning you?"

"Meaning me."

"It must be nice to be so sure of everything."

He merely nodded. "Very pleasant."

"All right. You take on the redoubtable contessa, with my blessing. Where do you begin?"

"Possibly where the lady herself began. In Europe."

"What?"

"Certainly. I've been giving some thought to the packaging of Eccles Cakes as a frozen item. You mentioned them some time ago."

Richard Kimberly's beloved Banbury Cakes. She cried, "Why, you rat! You paid no attention to my idea when I mentioned it at some of those interminable meetings."

"Ah, but I'm paying attention now. A very handy suggestion, for our present purpose. The lady is not unknown in corporate circles."

She had pursued the Eccles Cakes in England on several visits and she sighed now at the memory. "Banbury Cakes, with that cinnamon and almond filling. I adore them."

"What better excuse to get me overseas to look into our charming contessa's background?"

"If you mean it – about the Banbury Cakes, I have some other ideas I am dying to try out on the company."

"Perhaps next spring. Meanwhile –" He got to his feet. "If that marriage is imminent, and the woman proves to be a Trojan mare, so to speak, Godart's may be ripe for a very hostile takeover. Marcel will surrender to the contessa, and to the Europeans behind her!"

"They'd have to get Mother's shares." She considered. "But that wouldn't be difficult. To Mother, money buys everything. Her example has been one reason I've never married again."

He laid a hand on her shoulder. “Don’t worry. If the woman is using Marcel to get control of Godart’s for some rival, we’ll stop her. And whoever is behind her. You have my word.”

“Where will we start?”

“England first, to make the whole thing plausible, using that Banbury Cakes thing. But it must be done as soon as possible. Especially Switzerland. And Northern Italy because Venice is her home ground. Or maybe Turin and Milan. Make my excuses to Marcel; won’t you?”

“You are going to start the wheels moving tonight?”

“I have the reports to study, and I want to get things under way.”

“Dear Nigel, what would we do without you?”

“I wish you meant that.”

In the foyer they kissed goodbye, this time with genuine feeling. Still in a warm embrace they looked at each other, trying to read each other’s thoughts.

She ordered him softly, “Take care of yourself.”

“What concerns me is you. Esther will contact an agency about your protection. You may be the key to this entire business.”

“Me? Don’t be silly.“

“Quite serious, I assure you. Consider. you are the only heir to Godart’s, barring the few of us with subordinate holdings. Unless, of course, either Marcel or Angela should remarry and produce children. In Angela’s case, I imagine we can rule out that likelihood, but she is quite capable of being coerced into leaving her husband her shares, whoever he may be. As for Marcel, a young woman like the contessa – it seems to me that you could be a threat to either the contessa or any child she might claim Marcel sired. You understand your position?"

It seemed preposterous. And the idea of having spies following her around was revolting.

"No way. Have nasty little Sam Spades in hot pursuit of me? I'd have no privacy at all."

She had dealt with private investigators for too long after Richard's accident and gotten nowhere, except that they charged more than their TV counterparts and were a great deal uglier.

The elevator was already waiting as she protested. Nigel waved to her and was gone.

A minute or two afterward her phone started jangling. She knew it must be her father or the contessa calling her up to the Meet the Contessa bash. She almost ignored it but finally crossed the foyer, opened the door and picked up the phone without enthusiasm.

It was London calling.

That would be her mother. She was more touched than she had expected to be that Angela should remember even if, like her father's good wishes, they came a little late.

"Mother?"

She heard voices, one of them male, then Angela came on the line.

"Jacqui, darling! Happy Birthday . . . Sigurd, where is that cigarette? Ah, thank you . . . Darling – No, Sigurd. I am speaking to Jacqui now. What man? Do not be funny. You know quite well Jacqui is my little Jacqueline." There were sounds suspiciously lke a kiss. "Now, stand over there. That's a dear boy. My little girl is a very grownup lady today . . . Jacqui dear, I was interrupted by that naughty Sigurd von Ulsbach. His Highness sends you his greetings. Well, well, Jacqui, it seems like only yesterday that you were crawling about the house in your rompers."

That puts me in my place, Jacqueline thought wryly, guessing that her mother was anxious to plant in her lover's mind a baby and not a grown woman.

"Thank you for calling, Mother. It's awfully nice to hear from you."

"Oh, Jacqui, one more thing. We hear the most ghastly rumors here. Is it true that Marcel is thinking of marrying that dreadfully pushy Italian woman?"

Jacqueline looked into the phone's mouthpiece in her surprise. "You ought to know, Mother. You gave her Papa's unlisted number. It was at a charity to save Venetian Palaces or something." She held her breath, wondering if Angela had forgotten the entire Venetian Antiquities affair.

Thank heaven, she hadn't. "Yes, dear. But that was out of sheer desperation. She had her claws in the prince and – Well, never mind. I wanted to get her mind off every man she saw. Besides, I thought you or Nigel would stop her."

"Give him time." Jacqueline rushed on nervously. "You do remember that Venetian Benefit you attended in London?"

"Heavens, yes! Cost us a pretty penny, believe me. But it gave us an *entrée* to the most delicious masquerade balls and parties in Venice this winter. I can hardly wait. I have to run over to Paris to have a few little things whipped up before Venice, of course. I'll attend to that in a week or so."

On such "little things" kingdoms have fallen, Jacqueline thought.

"Yes, Mother. But some pictures were taken. The contessa showed them to me. Eight-by-ten glossies. Do you remember a man of around thirty, standing back of you on your right, drawing sketches or taking notes on a pad?"

Angela stopped to consider. She covered the phone, doubtless checking with Sigurd von Ulsbach. Jacqueline's hands began to sweat.

"Vaguely, dear. Nobody important. I do remember a tall, darkish young man. Very serious-looking. Some of the girls remarked on his looks. Personally, dear, I prefer blonds."

That would be for her companion's benefit.

"Mother, could you possibly remember his name? Or find out? And call me back as soon as –"

"What in the world? Darling, I mean really! Who is he?"

"Don't you understand? He may be someone I once knew. Someone terribly important." She didn't dare suggested Richard's name. There had been too many false alarms that first year after the accident.

Angela was obviously intrigued. "Of course, I'll do it, dear. If it means that much to you. Sigurd will help me. He's very clever with such things . . . Darling – I'm talking to Sigurd now, dear. My Jacqui wants to talk to you. Here you go."

A moment's international static provided difficulty. Then there was no mistaking Prince Sigurd von Ulsbach's practiced, sexy voice.

"And how may I help my Angel's little girl?"

She explained about the photos taken at the Venetian Antiquities affair.

Thank God, he made it his business to know details. Like Nigel Chilton-Brown, he didn't miss a trick.

"But of course. We have a dozen or so of the photographs. I would not dream of destroying a photograph of my Angel."

Jacqueline could hear her mother's flattered giggle in the background. "And the man I described?"

"A moment. I have them in the escritoire." He gave the phone to Angela, who said anxiously,

"Jacqui dear, we can count on Nigel getting rid of that dreadful woman, can't we? There must be something about her that will shake Marcel."

"We'll do our best, Mother."

To her intense relief Prince Sigurd came back on the line. "Yes," he said. "I recall him. A Yankee, about thirty, from the West somewhere. California. Perhaps he is a sketch artist. Photographer, too, as I recall. Has an Irish name. Conor-something." He snapped his fingers. "Kimball Conor. Yes. Devlin Kimball Conor."

Kimball. Kimberly. Coincidence? Jacqueline took a long, deep breath again.

"Could you tell me one thing? Did anyone make any remarks about this person? Describe him more clearly."

She could almost see his shrug. "Nothing beyond the usual Old Biddy gossip. I remember Viola Sears, the general's widow, twittered a lot about his being handsome. Sexy. Reserved. Any male under sixty is handsome and sexy to some of those women. They haven't my Angela's careful eye."

Flattery was his stock in trade.

"Mother said he was dark."

"Dark, yes. But Mrs. Sears remarked on his blue eyes. I recall that. What do you think, Angela? About six feet tall?"

"Just a trifle taller than you, Darling," Angela put in. It wasn't the most diplomatic thing to say but Jacqueline suspected Angela put in these little darts occasionally to keep her men on their toes.

All this byplay mattered very little to Jacqueline. Her hands were trembling, but she managed to speak coherently.

"Thank you, dear Sigurd. Hold onto those photos. I'll see you at the Savoy if I can make the first Concorde available. Tell Mother. And give her my love."

It couldn't be true. Not possibly.

But the "Kimball" and "Kimberly" clues, and the appearance of the man, even his background, gave her hope, after three long, terrible years.

If he didn't want her, that would be something to worry about when it happened. She would gamble that if he turned out to be her Richard Kimberly, the love would still be there.

Eleven

Angela had a hair appointment in London at the time of her daughter's expected arrival, which suited Jacqueline very well. She wanted to devote her first hours to getting the facts on the unknown Devlin Kimball Conor.

Prince Sigurd von Ulsbach volunteered to pick Jacqueline up at the airport and escort her to the Savoy Hotel. On their drive into London the prince provided Jacqueline with the all-important photographs of the Venetian Antiquities affair. She was so busy examining them that she hardly heard von Ulsbach remind her that "My little Angela prefers Claridges. She complains that too many Americans are found in the Savoy."

"Americans like Mother?" she asked absently.

The prince shrugged. "It is her little joke. She likes to be European. What the French call 'Le Snob' appeal."

But Jacqueline had stayed in one particular little corner mini-suite since she was old enough to remember her travels, and having been left alone a good deal of the time, in the care of hired Nannies, she had learned to regard the elegant and stately hotel as her home away from home.

She began to examine the pictures again.

Conor appeared in five shots, mostly in profile, or quarter view. One was almost full-face. He seemed a trifle older, more serious, but three years and an almost fatal accident might explain that. The hair was worn a little differently, not quite so wild, but the back of the neck where the dark hair had curled and her fingers had played with it so sensuously looked the same in one photo.

Von Ulsbach took his eyes off the road ahead to remark, "I am jealous, Jacqui. You look only at the pictures. You do not even see your good friend Sigurd."

They had met on only a few occasions, but she smiled and studied him, admitting to herself that the prince would have been impressive even without his title. London's rare sunlight gleamed on the crown of his golden head and glanced off a haughty Aryan profile that Hitler might have adored. This was softened by the prince's easily-turned-on smile which cushioned life for him.

The prince had drifted into his natural milieu, obliging rich women, partly because he and his family couldn't keep up the old homestead, a craggy castle somewhere beyond Munich in Bavaria. As he had often explained with fetchingly modest frankness, "We are not among the rich Ulsbachs."

The liaison with Angela had lasted over three years. Jacqueline wondered if the prince hadn't found the perfect niche at last.

He had greeted her with the slightly barbed, "Ah, Jacqueline, how long as it been? After all this time, still looking lovely."

There had been no "it" between them, and he seemed to infer that a decade had passed instead of a few months. She eyed the tiny golden hairs of his mustache and said, "So are you."

He refused to be ruffled. "I'll take that as a compliment."

"I like your car," she told him, not too surprised that the Porsche was painted fire-engine red. "It must be so easy to find in a parking lot."

He was more complacent than she remembered. "Angela thought I should have a Mercedes. She even suggested a Rolls. For the long haul, you know. But I remained firm and here I am in my little Porsche. Let the others have second-hand Rolls. Not Sigurd Ulsbach."

"How nice for you!" She was careful not to give the sentence a special inflection.

"Yes. It makes things easier for my darling girl. She detests driving, you know. But –" He reached across to her lap and squeezed her hand. She remembered his own hand as surprisingly soft and it hadn't improved. "– enough about Angela and me. My Angel, as I call her. Our little private joke. You must tell me about this photographer, or sketch artist, whatever he really is. An old lover? Must I be jealous? Tell me it is only Godart business."

She said quickly, "Only business. We need him to do some shots. TV promotion, you know. A new line. Have you ever eaten Banbury Cakes?"

He leaned closer. "Would it please you if I ate these Banbury Cakes?"

Alarmed by a lorry headed directly for them, she raised her hands wildly. "It would please me if you watched the road. My God! That truck almost hit us."

"Left-hand driving. This is London, you know. Anyway, Angela always says she feels as safe as churches, to borrow her expression, with me at the wheel."

"I wouldn't set too much store by that. Churches aren't her natural habitat."

He seemed to find this highly amusing, but at least he let go of her and took his hand away.

Surreptitiously, she glanced at the photos in her left hand, then, unable to resist, she studied the top one again.

Prince Sigurd was nothing if not observant. He kept on looking ahead but suggested, "I imagine the address of this artist would be worth something to you, and Godart advertising, of course, if I could locate it for you."

She was much too interested to treat this casually.

"You know it! It would save me, and the company, a lot of valuable time. Do you think you can do it?"

He pursed his full lips. "Quite possibly."

She took this as her cue, reached into her handbag and brought out a folded check. He removed one hand from the wheel, unfolded the check, read the amount, and nodded.

"There is something reassuring about round numbers. Reach into the pocket of my topcoat. The right side."

She followed directions and took out a page torn from a Pocket Agenda, with an address in Richmond, Surrey, written in his sprawling, spendthrift hand. She looked up. He said,

"The fellow has modest digs in a little hotel on Richmond Hill. General Sears' widow, Viola, provided it. She's one of Angela's coterie. I think she had her eye on your artist. She says he's a bit of a loner, so she must have struck out."

"Sigurd, you are a darling!" and she meant it.

Her enthusiasm didn't exactly bowl him over.

"Somehow, I suspect that was a tribute to your artist and not to me."

She laughed. She felt as lighthearted as if she were sure of Devlin Kimball Conor. But she felt she owed the prince something and as they headed along the Strand toward the Savoy, she suggested, "Just let me out and drive away fast. And remember, I'm not at all sure I can see you and Mother tonight. Jet lag, you know."

He smiled. "But if you meet this Conor, the jet lag goes, eh?"

A minute later they turned off the Strand and headed for the familiar, elegant hotel which loomed up at the end of the tiny street with its perverse right-hand traffic. They said their brief goodbyes. The bellman took her bags, and the prince drove off to wait for Angela at her beauty shop.

The assistant manager on duty knew Jacqueline well and the formalities of registering and being escorted to her small corner suite were handled with a minimum of fuss.

As the assistant was leaving he stopped in the doorway to ask, "Are you expecting to meet anyone here in the next hour, Mrs. Kimberly?"

"Not that I know of. Possibly Mr. Chilton-Brown if he is in the city, but I will be out this afternoon."

"Not Mr. Chilton-Brown. We know him at sight, of course. This was a rather –" He hesitated. "Quite a different sort. Not the type of our usual guests. The bellman said he acted a trifle furtive. A small man. Wouldn't leave his name, and lingered until you were at the desk. I'm told he was solely interested in your movements."

"Good heavens! Where is he now?"

"We haven't seen him since you left the desk. If we do, we will certainly have a word with him."

She thanked the young assistant and he closed the door. She was relieved to hear the lock click behind him.

While she changed to a last year's Geoffrey Beene pine-green sweater dress and coat, hoping they would blend in with the quiet, everyday atmosphere of Richmond Hill, Jacqueline looked at the Venetian Antiquities glossies and asked herself.

"Why?"

If this man should be her Richard Kimberly, why had he never contacted her, nor even sent her a single sign of his existence?

The best answer, the happiest for her was her most selfish thought. He had been injured in the accident and lost his memory. But amnesia didn't last this long, did it? She remembered reading somewhere that amnesiacs recovered in hours, days, weeks. But then, there had been a case where a man left his wife one morning and never came back for ten or fifteen years. It wasn't another woman. It was amnesia.

There were other possibilities, the worst scenarios: First, he had been hiding out because of that IRS problem of his and he no longer trusted or wanted her. Second, perhaps worst of all, Richard actually was dead and this man was simply a look-alike. The Germans had a word for the weird phenomenon. *Doppelganger*. It always made her shudder. To see one's own *doppelganger* was to see one's own death.

Doppelganger or Richard himself, it might all be explained in an hour.

She left the suite twenty minutes after she had entered it and went to the elevator. As she stepped out into the lobby she remembered the unsavory or "furtive" little man who had been so interested in her.

The lobby was too busy now for her to make out a man more furtive than anyone else. She crossed the lobby toward the street entrance.

Belatedly, the answer came to her. Upon Nigel's orders, his dutiful slave, Esther Heffernan, had probably employed private agents for Jacqueline's protection, even in London. The little man the bellman and the assistant had seen might even be a spy, hired by Godart competitors. It was a nuisance and she would simply have to lose them if she didn't want Nigel or anyone else to know all her private business.

Although she was dying to get to Richmond, she stood outside, not far from the busy, uniformed doorman and pretended to be waiting for someone. While she gazed innocently around her, apparently oblivious to anything but her next appointment, she studied the men going into and out of the Savoy's lobby.

It was annoying to be the only one who never saw her pursuers. She made up her mind suddenly. She would walk the short distance to Charing Cross Station and take the Underground to Richmond. It seemed highly unlikely that anyone could follow her along the Strand as far as the station without her seeing them.

"O.K. Here goes. Let's get a good look at one of my dogged bloodhounds, anyway," Jacqueline said to herself.

Somewhat to the surprise of the doorman, she neither asked him to summon a cab, nor hailed anyone approaching the hotel. Her stride carried her half a block down the Strand before she found herself in the mid-afternoon pedestrian crush. Even so, she was fairly sure she would be able to make out the man following her. So far, no one looked suspicious.

Letting her handbag slip off her shoulder and down to her wrist, she stopped at a corner. While she fussed with the bag, she managed to get a good look at the sidewalk behind her. No one stopped or lingered or peered into a shop window, the way they did in all the old television detective shows. She waited long enough for everyone to pass her. They kept coming, several small men among them. They paid no attention to her.

So much for the hotel's observations.

No matter. Jacqueline decided to keep her eyes open, just in case the Little Man was not imaginary.

She was the last person to squeeze into the Richmond train before it rumbled off. The "tube" train car wasn't full at this hour and she gave each person a long, hard look. One elderly woman with a worn tweed coat and a highly respectable countenance stared back at her, clearly resenting her interest.

On the other hand, no one else seemed to be interested in her except a shrivelled little woman in the far corner. On her lap was a basket covered by a hand-embroidered napkin. Every once in a while as she gazed unblinkingly at Jacqueline, she reached into the basket, broke off something that appeared to be a pastry, and nibbled with great relish. She enjoyed it so much she aroused all Jacqueline's professional instincts.

She wished she knew what that pastry was. Godart's might be missing a bet.

When everyone poured out at the end of the line she walked close behind the tiny woman and as they came up the steps to the street she was able to see the greasy paper bag wadded up and tossed away. With the bag went the remnants of a currant bun, one of thousands sold every day by London bakeries.

Jacqueline laughed at her own industrial spying and went swiftly past the others onto the street. She walked the short distance through the town which still retained traces of its old rural charm. A few minutes later she reached Richmond Hill above the distant, winding Thames.

Flaky clouds had passed across the sun and the walk up the hill was cooler than she had expected when she dressed before lunch. She hugged her arms briskly while searching for the Tudor inn to which she had been directed by Prince von Ulsbach.

It was not difficult to find. A charming, even quaint old two-and-a-half-story building with Tudor timbering, it did not look like the kind of place Richard Kimberly would choose. It was so remote from the center of London. Still, the prince had ferreted it out.

Jacqueline wondered at the sudden fall in the temperature. She rubbed her palms together, wrung her hands to get warm, and then realized the problem was with her, not the notorious English weather. She was trembling with nerves.

In a few minutes she would know, once and for all. Had her husband survived that terrible night in the lagoon? Or would this turn out to be one more phantom, one last hope gone? She hardly knew how she would act when she saw him if, of course, he was her Richard. She wanted to throw her arms around him or better, have him embrace her. She wanted him to be glad to see her. If only she could meet him without witnesses! Maybe she could convince him that his identity was safe with her . . . if he was in some kind of trouble.

But above all, she wanted him to be her Richard.

The interior of the building, especially the reception hall and desk, were all dark and shadowy, but off to the left was a friendly-looking bar, like an English pub. It took the curse off the stuffy reception area. The reception clerk (or manager?) looked like a genial pirate. He raised his rough, dark head and gave her a toothy grin. He wore a kind of plaid vest over his shirt, and one sleeve was rolled up.

"And what'll it be for you, Madam? Looking to book a room, by some chance?" He reached for a pack of index cards, all very informal. "You're from the States. I can tell 'em every time."

She smiled. "How clever you are! I'm from the States, right enough. But my husband is already registered."

She had no idea what other name he was using; so she rattled on hurriedly. "Conor doesn't expect me until tonight, but I was lucky. Caught an early flight."

The pirate was so pleased she almost regretted having lied to him.

"Well, now. So you're Mrs. Devlin Conor. Good news it is. Mr. Conor – he's a solitary man. Kept my Missus on the fret about him. A man on his own, she says. It's not natural. Nosy old biddy. She'll be that pleased." He raised the counter and came out of his dark little cubicle. "Would you care to wait in the lounge, Mrs. Conor?"

She hesitated. This was an opportunity not to be missed. "I wonder if – I'm so tired. That tedious flight. Do you suppose I might wait in my husband's room? It might give me a chance to rest for a few minutes. He will be back shortly; won't he?"

He scratched his head. "Well – it's not the usual – not but what there's no harm in a lady like yourself. Still –"

She thought of something and reached into her bag, taking out one of the old Instant prints that had been taken by the Italian gentleman in Torcello. There they were, Mr. and Mrs. Kimberly, on their honeymoon. She showed it to him, sighing the same time and looking wistful.

"Our honeymoon. It seems like yesterday."

He examined the picture with interest, murmuring, "I don't see as how he'd mind . . ."

She hardly recognized herself in the little scene she enacted for him. "I know. It's just that I'm wearing these wretched high heels and if I could slip them off for a little, what a joy that would be!"

He looked furtively at her shoes, then her ankles and legs. He raised his head and she knew she had won. Her legs had tipped the scale.

"It's a harmless little bending of the rules. My lady wife is the same. Many's the time and often I've had a good long search for her shoes at the pictures. And then, Mr. Conor, he'll be coming back soon. Follow me, Madam."

He hadn't asked her to register yet or requested her passport, so she could worry about that later. She followed him to the floor above. The stairs were ancient and creaking but very solid. Devlin Conor had a room on the front of the house, over-looking the road and the Thames far below.

She thanked the manager-clerk and settled into a big, much-used wing chair. Then she sighed deeply, slipping her feet out of her pumps. The landlord gave them a glance and looked away quickly. She called after him,

"Maybe I can surprise him if he doesn't know I've come. How thrilled I'll be to see my dear Conor . . . Dev," she corrected. "It's been ages. I had to wind up my job, you know. I want to be a good wife to him." That part was true, anyhow.

The landlord considered her sentiments very proper.

In the doorway he pointed out a few necessary bits of information. "The facilities. You'll find them across the hall. The bathtub is in the room next door." He hesitated. "You'll understand, Madam, if Mr. Conor should chance to be gone the night, I must sign you to another room. It's the law, and all. I'll be stopping back shortly. To see how things be. I mean to say – You might like to get comfortable in the lounge. During the bar hours you may just fancy a drop of the hard stuff."

"Thank you."

She tried to look as small and harmless as possible, since it was clear he was having second thoughts about leaving her here alone. She must have succeeded. He closed the door after one more furtive glance at her long, trim legs, exposed to the thigh as she crossed them.

When he had gone she rushed to the door and waited until she heard his heavy footsteps descending the stairs. Then she turned around, still leaning against the door, and studied the room. It was singularly spartan, with very little in sight that suggested the personality of the owner.

Since the room had no closet she started with the big oaken armoire and found Devlin Conor's wardrobe hanging on one side. An English raincoat, a genuine Burberry, surprised her. It was well-worn but of excellent quality. A golden-beige corduroy mackinaw was likewise old, but if Devlin Conor was the man in the Venetian Antiquities picture the jacket should be flattering. The colors would look great on Richard Kimberly. It was also something he was likely to wear.

A dinner jacket chilled her for a moment. The rest of the suit was missing but even so, she could hardly imagine Richard, with his penchant for tight, faded jeans and sweaters flung over his shoulder, ever wearing a dinner jacket.

She moved to the drawers beside the wardrobe. The highest drawer revealed no clues. A brown turtleneck sweater appeared to be of cashmere. One shirt stud.

Pearl? Probably imitation if it belonged to Richard. A leather shaving kit with its gold initials almost worn away. She thought she could make out a "C". An elaborate, twisted "C" that might almost be a "K".

Please let it be a "K".

Although there had been no sound, quite suddenly she realized she was no longer alone. She stood very still. One hand remained inside the drawer, caught in the act.

A voice from across the room instructed her in frigidly civil tones, "Try the third drawer. You may find the contents more worthwhile. I keep my foreign currency there. Francs, lire, Deutschmarks, some pesetas. Or do you prefer Sterling? Here. Catch."

Shivering with anticipation and dread of disappointment, she swung around just in time to be struck by a leather wallet that hit her shoulder and fell to the floor.

Richard Kimberly stood in the doorway, watching her.

Twelve

She didn't know why he was so coldly angry. Her own reaction was an almost overwhelming desire to burst into tears of joy and relief. She found her mouth dry and she could barely speak his name.

"Richard?" Still confused, she asked brokenly, "Why?"

She saw that her hands were held out toward him now, pleading with him to say something. She dropped her hands. But she wanted to touch his flesh, the high planes of his face, the faint crinkle around his eyes that hadn't been there three years ago. Had he lost the wondrous, irresponsible charm of those days? Life must have done that to him.

He moved into the room, into the pale afternoon light from the cloudy sky. He was not so angry now, thank heaven! More puzzled. He looked older, with a kind of sophistication he had lacked before. In a strange way, though he was as attractive to her as ever, she found him frightening.

His voice was more authoritative than it had been in

those few glorious Venetian weeks but his manner of speaking still sounded like the Richard she had known and loved.

"Who the devil are you?"

She knew perfectly well that amnesia was possible, but she could hardly grasp its reality when she saw it. She felt behind her for something firm, the heavy door of the armoire. She remained there trying to study him. His features, seen on this dark afternoon, were unmistakeably those of the man in the glossy photos. His body, lean and slightly taller than she remembered, appeared to be Richard's body. He had slung his leather jacket over one shoulder in exactly the way Richard carried his, jauntily pinched between two fingers.

If he would only smile, she could be sure. Richard had grinned a lot. No smile though. He watched her with narrowed eyes, as if she might be crazy. She managed finally, in a strained voice,

"I'm Jacqueline."

He threw the jacket onto the ladderback chair beside the door and came into the room. His stride – graceful, she had always thought – was not as easy and carefree as it had been. Richard loped along sometimes with shoulders a little hunched. Had amnesia changed him? The grace remained but there was more determination now.

"Sorry. I don't know any Jacqueline." He stooped to pick up his wallet at her feet, holding it out to her, asking with light, careless sarcasm, "Sure you don't want this?"

She backed against the armoire which creaked and protested behind her. She tried not to be offended or to give way to her devastating disappointment.

"You knew me once." She forced a smile that was far too bright and artificial. "Maybe, if you got a good look at me . . ."

He stuck the wallet into his pocket without paying any attention to it. He was within a few feet of her and she became aware of the old sexual excitement his nearness had produced in her long ago. He frowned as he looked her over, but for the first time she thought she saw the spark of humor in his eyes. Vivid blue; as she remembered them.

Was this some kind of awful game he had decided to play with her?

"Yes. I certainly would have remembered you, Miss –"

"Kimberly." She waited a second or two, watching him with all the careful attention he gave her. She added, "Mrs. Richard Kimberly."

His eyes narrowed. She had at least aroused his interest. Had he felt some twinge of recognition? Surely, even an amnesiac must remember bits and pieces of the past.

Unless, of course, he really wasn't Richard.

He took her numb body by the shoulders and shifted her over toward the window. She went along obediently. In the afternoon light he studied her.

"Am I supposed to be your husband?"

"You know you are."

He went on smiling but with a more friendly edge. She began to hope until he let her go abruptly.

"I'm not, you know. Though I will say, you tempt me. I'm Dev Conor. Devlin Conor, from Los Angeles, California, among other stopping places. Is this some game you're playing? Bring back a stranger? One of those things you jet-setters play with the common herd to amuse yourselves?"

She was hurt but she leaped onto what she considered a clue. "How do you know I'm a jet-setter? They were phased out years ago."

"Well, whatever you Idle Rich call yourselves."

"What makes you think I am rich?"

"My dear girl." He sounded so exactly like Richard that her heart leaped and she forgave him for his denial of her. "In my profession you learn to observe details. Everything about you shrieks it. Your manner. Your outfit. Your shoes. That bag. Everything. What do you get for bringing me in? I hope it isn't much. I'm not worth it. I'm only an itinerant sketch artist."

"And photographer."

"When necessary. This is a game. Admit it. Who are you? Really?"

He was being deliberately cruel. Surely, her Richard would never tease her along, torment her in this way, even if he didn't remember her.

She started to speak, knew she was on the verge of crying and shrugged instead. She swore to herself that she wouldn't give him the satisfaction of knowing how he had hurt her. She started away from the window but couldn't resist looking back once, to see his face in the light.

Hauntingly like her memory of Richard. Except for the sarcasm and the unexpected strength. Probably strength of character as well. It wasn't something she needed right now. She had to get away from that potent effect he had on her, so she could make up her mind about his identity, and his total lack of recognition.

"Running away like Cinderella?" he taunted her. "Not even leaving a glass slipper?"

At the door she stopped.

"How could that possibly concern you? In my life Prince Charming died long ago."

She didn't wait to see how her bitterness affected him but walked out into the dark hall, letting the door close behind her. She went rapidly down the stairs, past the empty reception booth. The piratical-looking manager was busy in the bar, drawing beer for two local workmen.

She went out to the street, forcing herself not to look up at Devlin Conor's window. She never knew whether he was watching her or not.

It occurred to her on the way back to London that it would be far less painful for her to hire detectives to trace Devlin Conor and his past. But it would take considerable will power. She had thought of nothing but Richard during the entire trip.

Was he, or wasn't he masquerading as Devlin Conor? If he was the same man, could she learn to forget him? After those interminable years of dreaming, desperately wanting him, remembering every detail of their short lives together, could she erase the most important – the only important part of her life?

In London she went blindly out of the Charing Cross Station. Wilder than Old Broadway, the bright theatre signs, heavy on the reds, blinded and confused her. She felt herself flowing along with the crowd. She envied the chatter and laughter of the theatregoers.

An especially enthusiastic rush past her reminded her of the dangerous shove she had received on State Street in Chicago. She glanced around, instinctively looking for the faceless enemy. So many people passed her as she stood in their way that she told herself this was just the usual state of frenzy in the hour before the curtain went up.

Suddenly, a roaring wind whirled through the air. The noise unnerved her, made her think of an earthquake she had experienced on a business visit to a small Californian town.

Around her all movement seemed to stop for a few seconds. To her astonishment few people screamed. But they began to run, a panicked, heedless movement in all directions at once. There were sirens and clanging bells and trucks and men looking like Martians in strange uniforms. Clouds of black smoke soared above the rooftops across the street, coming from somewhere beyond the theatre district. Jacqueline began to run with everyone else. On all sides she heard the breathless words, the whispers:

"It's them."

"They've done it again."

Belatedly, she understood that the hideous "earthquake" had been a terrorist explosion. The horror at least distracted her thoughts from her own morbid self-pity. She rushed up the street, into the hotel, blindly making her way to the lifts. As soon as she reached her suite she called her mother at the country estate where she was a house guest.

She was enormously relieved when Matilde called Angela to the phone.

"Did you have a good flight, dear?"

"Mother! Thank God! I thought you might have stayed in the city to shop or something."

"Darling Girl, not at this hour. It's after dark. Cocktail time. In fact, I was on my way to cocktails with General Sears' widow. She owns the Featherstonaugh Estate, you know."

So that was how the prince knew Viola Sears, the woman who had struck out with Devlin Conor.

"Mother, excuse me. I feel kind of edgy. We've had a bombing in the city."

Angela was horrified.

"Jacqui, for heaven's sake, are you all right? Were people hurt? Where was it?"

The day's tensions, climaxing in the nearness of the bombing, had left Jacqueline badly shaken.

"I'll find out. But I wasn't anywhere near the actual bombing. God knows how many people were hurt. Or killed. It was awful. And it brought back those terrible days and nights after Richard's – accident. Made me kind of shaky."

"Jacqui, he is gone. You must learn to accept his death."

Had Richard actually died in the Venetian Lagoon that night? Then who was Devlin Conor? And that middle name. So much like Kimberly. Was this Richard's *doppelganger*? How did he differ from Richard? In small ways, ways that might be accounted for by amnesia or his accident. And then too, her hopes might have played tricks with her memory. She wanted so desperately to believe Richard was alive, but she didn't want him to be Devlin Conor as he was today. It was that simple.

"Yes." She pretended to agree with her mother. "I know he is dead."

"Take care, dear. No more naughty bombs, now. Mind." Before she rang off, Jacqueline could hear her calling to Matilde, "For heaven's sake, turn on the TV! There has been another of those ghastly bombings. I thought they had finished with that kind of thing. And cancel my luncheon with Lenore tomorrow. I'm not going back into the city until they get these things under some kind of control."

"Dear Mother," Jacqueline thought when she replaced the receiver. "I wish we could all live in that silk-lined cocoon of yours. The whole world was created expressly for your comfort."

During the evening she listened intermittently to the brief bulletins on the television. The bombing was suspected to be the work of an IRA splinter group. The device had been planted in an old car outside a theatre where a charity film performance was due to start within the hour. But aside from a hole in the street and some broken windows, no definite target seemed to be marked. There was a rumor that the explosive device might be similar to that used by Iranian terrorists, but this had not been confirmed. Two people were dead, a policeman and a passing Belgian tourist.

Between the bombing, Devlin Conor, and jet lag, Jacqueline was too tired to go down to dinner. She settled for an easy meal in her rooms: a dry martini, a mushroom omelet, and a green salad.

Feeling a good deal calmer afterward, she ran herself a bath in the enormous tub. She was just getting in when the phone buzzed. Wrapping her cream satin travel robe around her, she answered it reluctantly, sure it must be some invitation that she wasn't in the mood to accept in the next few days.

Nigel Chilton-Brown's voice had never been so welcome.

"Hello, Old Girl. Didn't catch you on the way out to something glamorous, did I? I've been prowling about among my old friends here. Found out very little. Am I interrupting you?"

She stifled a yawn as quietly as possible. "Heavens, Just finished dinner. What will you be doing next?"

"A little more investigative work. Ultimately, I'll have to work on connections in Bern and Zurich. If that doesn't pay out, it's probably Venice, where the Dragon Lady started."

"Sounds intriguing, all this spy work."

"It isn't. How's your new project going?"

"New project?" She felt suddenly chilled. Had he guessed that she was off chasing a dead man?

"Certainly. Those Banbury Cakes you are so fond of."

"Oh. Marvelous. I mean – I'm going to start sampling them tomorrow. I can hardly wait."

He chuckled. "Happy eating. I must say, it's a bit of luck that you are so lean and lank."

"Thank you. I think."

"Why don't you amble out to Banbury? See the birthplace of those precious cakes of yours. And be sure to look up the Banbury Cross. Not that you can miss it. Right in the center of things. Well, love, I'm off."

"Good hunting. We'll be looking forward to seeing you."

"What do you say to just a dash of affection in that farewell?"

"All right. Love you, Mr C."

"Sounds like Esther Heffernan. But I suppose it will have to do."

She laughed and he rang off.

She stepped into the bathtub, settled herself and wallowed in the fragrant bubbles connected by an exclusive Californian designer. The bath foam was a Christmas present from her father and too expensive for her tastes. She wondered what Richard would think of it. Her Richard might have accepted it as sexy and alluring but she suspected the man she had seen today would despise it. Nowadays, he didn't look as if unearned money would impress him. Yes, she admitted finally. Whatever had happened to him in the accident had marked and changed him from the careless, irresponsible man she knew.

She let the perfumed suds run through her fingers, dripping down upon the pale gold flesh of her upper thigh. What would Richard think of her flesh now? She had taken excellent care of it for him. However, it seemed that her husband's amnesia had led him to forget everything about her.

But of course, he might not be Richard Kimberly at all. If only there was something, perhaps one simple object, that would tie the man who called himself Devlin Conor in with her Richard. Then at least she would know the truth, and could blame his cutting sarcasm on the amnesia.

Meanwhile, here was Nigel Chilton-Brown accomplishing things right and left in his investigation of the contessa's past. At least, if he hadn't proved she was up to no good, he had eliminated some suspicions about her in England. Maybe she was innocent after all.

Jacqueline had just curled up in bed with an Agatha Christie paperback when the phone buzzed again. Marking her place with one finger, she reached for the phone, said "Hello?" and heard the light static of an open line. Gently, quietly, the party on the other end hung up.

"Damn!" The idiot hadn't even had the courtesy to say "Sorry."

She removed her finger from the page and began to read. Agatha Christie reminded her of Richard, who had brought a half-dozen well-thumbed mysteries on his honeymoon.

She slept surprisingly well. Although her dreams were a discordant jumble, she couldn't recall any of the details when she woke up.

The day was cloudy "with sunny intervals", as the radio had it. While she ate breakfast (she had requested a "Banbury Cake" but settled for scones) she decided on the spur of the moment to make a pilgrimage to the town of Banbury, as Nigel had suggested.

She had hired a car for her use in England. The right-hand drive always took getting used to, but luckily, British drivers seemed prepared for Americans who were apt to realize suddenly that they were racing along on the wrong side of a very narrow rural lane.

She found her spirits considerably brightened as she drove through the pleasant green countryside. Serene as the Cotswolds looked, their rolling hills dotted with sheep kept the view from monotony and around every corner there seemed to be yet another time – worn stone village. She seldom glimpsed the inhabitants but spent the drive – about an hour – wondering what their lives were like.

In this way she was able to keep her thoughts off Richard Kimberly, and his alter-ego, Devlin Conor, for most of the morning. She still hadn't decided what to do about his denial of her. Some day, if he persisted, she might have to settle the matter by having Richard pronounced legally dead, but the idea was like a knife in her heart. She would have to prepare herself for the legal step.

Occasionally, she had admitted to those who knew and cared about her that he was dead, but her mind hadn't accepted it and even today she couldn't quite bring herself to cut all legal ties.

Following the little map drawn for her by the Hall Porter at the Savoy, she had no difficulty pulling into Banbury about lunch time. At the northerly end of the Cotswolds, it was a market town, according to her British Automobile Association guidebook, and her arrival coincided with the noon traffic.

She made her way around the celebrated Banbury Cross which drew numerous buses and cars, all circling the area to get a good look at what appeared to be a medieval cross but whose real age was betrayed by the AA book as a mere hundred and eighty years, give or take a few.

Jacqueline looked around for a parking spot. She thought she had found it about half a block away. Then a London tour bus moved in on her, towering over her little Mini Metro and lumbering into her spot. She moved a few yards away and climbed out just as a score of tourists, loaded with parcels, cameras and cassette recorders poured from the bus. Trapped between three women, Jacqueline found herself edged back against another tourist, a male who caught her and added a friendly warning.

"Watch it. You're liable to be inundated. Have to be careful in this crowd."

"Thank you. Maybe it's something to do with this left-handed driving." She raised her eyes, and saw that her rescuer was Richard Kimberly. She was shocked not to have recognized his voice out of all the voices in the world.

Slowly, his pleasant expression faded.

"Good God! You again."

She couldn't remember a single man who had ever greeted her in such a casually insulting manner.

Thirteen

For a minute she felt stunned. Nudged and shoved by the rest of the passengers wandering away from the bus, she had to submit to the indignity of being pulled back and "rescued", not urgently, by the puzzled "Conor."

"Here. I'm sorry. Are you all right?"

She managed a big, stiff smile.

"Certainly. Don't I look it? Thanks for the hand up."

In a daze, motivated by pride, she pushed his hands aside and walked past him, around her tiny car, on up the street. Her knees felt weak with shock. She tried not to think about the meeting, his manner, the way he had softened somewhat after that first impatient outburst.

She caught a glimpse of a woman's face reflected in the window of a shop displaying decorative porcelain plates and animal miniatures. It was only on second glance that she realized those strained, pale features were her own. The huge eyes with their intensely dark depths fringed with sooty black lashes made her look like a wraith.

"This is ridiculous," she thought and had the satisfaction of seeing a little color appear in that haunted face.

At the same time she became aware that another passer by had stopped behind her. The shadowy silhouette blurred her own reflection.

She wondered for an instant if she really was being followed. So much had happened lately. Yesterday she had been sure that some tireless character had tagged her all the way to Richmond Hill. But after the sickening disappointment of That Man's conduct toward her, she had almost forgotten her earlier fear.

Even now, she didn't know whether she was relieved or unnerved when she recognized Richard Kimberly's reflection behind her.

"Am I blocking your view?" she demanded and stepped aside.

He appeared to be concerned. "Not at all. But you seemed ill. Anything I can do?"

For some reason his compassion angered her more than his indifference.

"No, thanks. Since you absolutely refuse to be my husband," she said flippantly.

This time he grinned and revived her most painfully vivid memories.

"I deny that. I never said I wouldn't play your husband. I simply state categorically that I am not Donald Kimberly."

"Richard."

"Whatever." He looked around the busy little street. "What brings you to this out-of-the-way spot? I don't suppose I can flatter myself that you are following me."

"You forget. I got here first."

"Now, how can you say that? We parked first." He took her arm in a proprietary way.

"Only because your stupid bus stole my parking place. Where are we going?"

"I've no idea. Ever been here before?"

"No. You?"

"All I know is a nursery rhyme about a ride to Banbury Cross. Mom was a war bride. She came from Oxfordshire. She used to recite the rhyme when she made the cakes. Kind of a pastry with sweet, dried fruit."

She was excited by this, a clear connection between Richard and this man who claimed to be someone else. But she ignored it for the time being; he obviously resented being mistaken for Richard Kimberly. She resorted to an argument.

"Excuse me, but they are filled with almond paste."

"Don't be ridiculous. You think my own mother lied to me about the Banbury Cakes? Next, you'll be saying she lied to me about the nursery rhyme."

"I couldn't care less about your mother and her nursery rhyme." She saw then that he was amusing himself by making her angry and she added on a less belligerent note, "Did you ever hear of Godart Bakeries? Godart frozen foods, breads and pastries, et cetera?"

To accommodate their argument they had reduced their pace to a saunter and crossed a street, just missing another tour bus. Devlin Conor dismissed Godart's with a quick chop of his free hand.

"If there's one thing I can't stand, it's a frozen pastry, and Godart's seems to have a patent on them."

"Thousands of people will disagree with you. Me, for one. My name, in case you ask, is Jacqueline Godart Kimberly."

He lowered his voice confidentially. "Don't worry. I won't tell if you don't."

She burst out laughing, startling two women who came from a corner shop.

She couldn't remember when she had laughed so spontaneously and she gave her companion full credit, whoever he was.

By this time she had become almost convinced that he really was Richard Kimberly. There were only two explanations for his denial. Either he had permanently lost his memory, which she knew was most uncommon, or he was hiding his identity because Richard Kimberly was still in trouble, wanted by someone. Gangsters? Mafia? IRS? This seemed likely. It would explain everything except his cutting indifference to her when they met yesterday.

"Ah!" He stopped suddenly in the middle of the block and then hurried her along. "A bake shop. Now, we'll get some real Banbury Cakes. No frozen Godart garbage here."

She tried not to be annoyed at his insulting opinion. As she ran along with him, wishing she had worn walking shoes, she reminded herself that all her impossible dreams had come true. She was with Richard. He was alive and well, as handsome and maddeningly exciting as ever.

How often did such dreams come true? When did the dead return to glorious life as her husband had?

She decided not to press him yet on his other identity. Let him think she had given up that point. She also kept up their bantering quarrel. He seemed to be his old, lighthearted self again when he was teasing her.

They argued about the pastries and especially their contents, generously loaded in between the flaky layers of pastry.

"What did I tell you?" he asked proudly. "Look at that filling."

"Yes, yes. Your precious Mom was right. But personally, I prefer my almond paste."

He took one of the cakes out of the sack and held it by the waxed paper wrapped around the other end.

"Here. Bite."

She did so and considered the savory, spicy result.

"Tolerable." It was exceedingly good.

"I resent that. It's delicious. I'll take a dozen."

The baker's wife was somewhat confused when Jacqueline also ordered a dozen.

"We're running a bit short, Madam. What with luncheon gone and tea coming up."

With a fine show of reluctance, Dev Conor promised Jacqueline, "All right. You may share mine. In exchange . . . Well, who knows? I'm bound to think of some way you may pay me back."

They started out to the street while he added, "You might begin by telling me all about this husband who deserted you."

"He didn't desert me. There was an accident. I thought he had died."

"I see." The clowning was over for the moment. He studied her with narrowed eyes.

Like that analyst they made me go to, she thought. He's another one who thinks I'm crazy.

She tried again, sneaking up on the heart of the mystery. She still wasn't sure of his reaction.

"Do you know Europe very well, Mr. Conor?"

He didn't seem to think her formality was unusual. Surely, Richard would have objected.

"As well as any tourist. Less than most, I imagine. Why?"

"What cities have you touched on?"

He offered her a Banbury Cake but she waved it away.

He looked at the cake. "Rejected." He put it back in the bag. "Well, there's the Louvre, of course. And the Riiksmuseum. And the Prado. I wanted to make the Hermitage but couldn't swing it all the way to Russia. I was just out of college in those days and scraping by."

"You've never been to Italy?"

"Of course. Rome and the Uffizi in Florence."

"But not Venice."

He shrugged this off. "No. I'm supposed to sketch some palaces in Venice but they haven't decided which ones I'm to do. They are still arguing about that. I do a pretty fair sketch. Period. I went broke in Paris and sold some stuff at a sidewalk exhibit on the Boulevard Raspail. Not to the French, I needn't add. German tourists bought two of my masterpieces. Blessings on the good burghers."

They saw her little Mini-Metro parked in the next block and, with mutual understanding, slowed their steps. She asked casually, "Were you always an artist? Most artists start out in some dull job, like book-keeping. Were you ever a book-keeper?"

They stopped in the middle of the street while he picked up the bag of cakes that had dropped unexpectedly. He looked into the bag. "I hope they aren't crushed. After all my bragging about them." He saw that she was watching him and dismissed the matter of the cakes. "They look O.K. to me. Now, where were we?"

"Book-keeping."

He shuddered. "Sounds murderously dull to me."

After a little pause in the conversation she remarked, "That's practically what my husband said."

"Excellent judgment. Did he really resemble me?"

"To be precise, you resemble him. Although you look considerably older."

"That puts me in my place."

They both realized at the same time that the tour bus was gone. Devlin Conor said ruefully.

"It appears that I'll be thumbing my way back to London."

She couldn't bear to lose him now. Who knew what he would take it into his head to do? She might never see him again. But instinctively, she knew it would be dangerous to crowd him. She was cool in her offer.

"If you can fold up into my Mini, I'll guarantee to get you back to London. I'll even spring for Richmond Hill, if you insist."

To her surprise and disappointment he refused.

"Thanks. That won't be necessary. I have a few places to check out. Family ties. Places where my mother lived."

Things I want to do alone.

She was sure that had been his real meaning. She could appreciate that. But the thought of losing him again, and perhaps forever, depressed her heavily.

She put on a fair imitation of indifference. It cost her something.

"Fine. If you're sure you can manage. I'll be on my way." She held out her hand. "It was nice, Mr. Conor. Maybe we can go shopping again some time. For my kind of Banbury Cakes."

"Sounds good to me."

He took her hand, held it briefly, then dropped it in order to open the car door for her. His easy, pleasant expression, almost but not quite a smile, reminded her of the man she had met in Richmond. She stared at him, noting something else, a familiar line or shadow, that brought back memories of that chance meeting long ago in a shop on the Merceria of Venice.

He had looked just this way, casually interested, when he picked up her spilled handbag; yet, from that tentative meeting had come the love of her life.

It had happened once. It could happen again.

She got into the car, flipped him a salute, then reminded him with false gaiety.

"I'm at the Savoy, in case you get a sudden craving for Banbury Cakes. Just ask for Jacqueline Kimberly. *Bon appetit.*"

She waited briefly. Would he give her a small hope?

He didn't, though. He nodded, smiled and left her.

She pulled out in a spurt of noise and speed, heading toward London as fast as the little car could make it.

She had psyched herself up to remain angry in the hope that the pain of his rejection would gradually fade. To be doubly sure she stopped at a bar off the lobby of the hotel and mulled over her husband's behavior while numbing her feelings with two Scotches. She was signalling for a third when she caught sight of Nigel Chilton-Brown in the doorway.

A friendly face, thank God! She waved to him. He nodded and crossed the highly modern and functional American Bar. She was gratified by his pleasure at the sight of her. He leaned across the table and kissed her forehead. The warmth of his presence was better comfort than a lineup of whisky.

"Just checked in, Old Girl, and they obligingly told me where to find you."

"Nigel, you are a pearl beyond price. Join me."

He pulled one of the chairs closer and raised an eyebrow at her drink. The second was being removed and the third set down while he watched.

"Drowning your sorrows? And if so, what are the troubles? Any way I can help?"

"Just being here." She reached over and hugged him. He accepted this with wry diffidence.

"Anything to oblige. Want me to rob a bank? Murder some luckless customer who returned our sacred Godart products? Just give me the signal."

She laughed. Even to herself she heard a note of wildness in that sound. "Any and all of the above."

He signalled to the waiter. "Give me whatever the lady is drinking." When they were alone again he glanced around at the room, almost deserted at this early afternoon hour. He returned to the subject at hand. "You've got a look in your eye, Jacqueline. Is it the Scotch or are you – as we British say – gunning for someone?"

Her eyes were too bright and she closed them for an instant, relieved that he thought she was angry.

"You're so right. I'm gunning for my husband."

He choked on a peanut. "Beg pardon?"

"Richard. I could swear he is alive and doing very well, thank you."

A brief fit of coughing took some of his attention from her, which gave her a chance to swipe a hand across her eyes. It was so quickly done she felt sure he hadn't noticed.

He sipped the drink set down before him and then gave businesslike attention to her claim.

"You really believe you saw Kimberly?"

"*Believe* nothing. I know I saw him. You think I don't know my own husband?"

"Well, frankly, my dear, I mean to say – Good Lord! The poor chap drowned over three years ago."

"They never found his body."

"Yes, but you are speaking about that profile in the contessa's picture, of course. And a few others equally uncertain. As I recall, you couldn't make out more than the head and shoulders."

"To the waist. Maybe the hips." He shook his head at her gullibility, so she added the clincher. "I spent half an hour with him yesterday and an hour today.

You must think I'm ready for the looney bin. Wouldn't I know my own husband after an hour and a half with him?"

He took another sip, chose his words carefully.

"I don't think you are a looney at all. I simply think you've let your hopes rule your head, so to speak. You want this man to be your husband. Superficially, he appears to answer the description. I can understand that. I remember talking to a friend about a flight we were both booked on, back in '72. It crashed. Two weeks later I saw this chap strolling along the street toward me. I would have known him in a thousand. We had talked about conducting some business on that flight. Needless to say, my real friend had gone down with the plane. The fellow on the street was a total stranger. But it took me several minutes to convince myself."

She said haughtily, "I claim an hour and a half is a longer time to judge than several minutes."

"I understand, Old Girl. Actually, I do understand. But this thing is unhealthy. You really must let the past go."

He reached for her hand but she drew it back, locking her fingers around her glass. She drank slowly, aware that he was watching her, as if he might have to rush her off to a padded cell any minute. She wished now that she hadn't invited him to sit down.

"Nigel, *Old Boy*, you aren't helping at all. Why don't you just run up to your room and attend to your little spying?"

He was annoying anxious to avoid a quarrel. She hated being humored.

"You haven't asked me about my activities in the spy department."

"All right. What have you found out?" Not that I care, she thought.

He settled back more expansively into his chair. "Interesting work, espionage. I rather fancy myself as a C.I.D. Inspector. However, I'm afraid the lady in question has covered her tracks very cleverly."

"Or she is innocent."

He snapped his fingers, dismissing this as absurd.

"I have an instinct about people. That woman is up to something. I can smell it. This nose is sensitive to frauds. Esther Heffernan says the woman has adopted an 'easy does it' attitude. I suspect she's discovered that we are investigating her." He didn't get much reaction, so he reverted to what was on her mind as well.

"Where did you meet this Kimberly? Where do I find him?"

"In Richmond. Oh, no you don't! I don't want you bothering him. He's annoyed enough with me, as it is."

"I see."

"You don't see at all. He has amnesia."

He nodded. "Which has lasted for three years. That explains the matter."

"Don't be sarcastic. I know you don't believe me. But you have no way of knowing all the little things that make Devlin Conor exactly like my Richard. Banbury Cakes, for instance." That didn't sound too convincing and she was trying to describe the other signs when she realized they meant nothing to the legal-eagle brain of Nigel Chilton-Brown.

"Banbury Cakes? Good Lord!"

That had really scotched her meagre hopes of getting him to believe her. She changed the subject but she knew she hadn't fooled him. When he left her at her suite half an hour later all his earlier concern about her seemed to have resurfaced. It was as maddening as ever.

"You look depressed, my dear. Can't blame an old admirer for worrying just a little about you. Incidentally, we're all dining at Capuchin's tonight."

"All?"

"Your mother, the noble prince, you and I."

She wondered if she could trust the switchboard to take all messages. Especially any from Richmond Hill.

The dinner at Capuchin's, a formal, feminine single room with Regency furnishings, was lively and pleasant for the most part, thanks to her mother and Prince von Ulsbach. Nigel spent his time watching Jacqueline and asking vaguely, "Beg pardon. You were saying . . ." when he was spoken to.

At one time it looked as though they would get onto the one subject Jacqueline hoped they would avoid: her "business trip" to interview the photographer, Devlin Conor.

The prince brought it up. "I hope you found the man is worth it, after all your efforts to find him, Jacqui."

"She prefers to be called Jacqueline," Angela put in. "Sigurd, will you signal the maitre d'? I definitely feel a draft on my shoulders."

Jacqueline said immediately, "Be careful. A lot of colds going around."

Her mother took the bait. "I assure you, Darling, I am no more susceptible than you. I'm not decrepit quite yet, you know."

By the time they got that worked out the subject had been nicely switched away from Devlin Conor. Jacqueline breathed again. She didn't want any of these well-meaning people harassing Richard. He would be sure to blame her.

When they all left her at her door that night, however, it was Angela who got Nigel worked up all over again, to Jacqueline's disgust.

"Jacqui, you simply must get some more sleep these nights. You are looking quite sallow."

"Mother dear, I always look sallow. It's the nature of the beast."

Nigel had to open his mouth and make matters worse.

"If you find yourself depressed, Old Dear, give me a ring. Any time. Johnny-on-the-spot, I was known as in my youth."

Jacqueline tried to play this awkward moment lightly.

"Insults, insults. Are you sure you don't want to add something to all these insults, Your Highness?"

"No, indeed," the prince answered her gallantly. "In my opinion, the young lady has never looked lovelier." He bowed but this graceful gesture was cut short when Angela, having received Jacqueline's quick kiss, started down the hall, barely tossing him the command, "Are you coming?" over her shoulder.

Just before Jacqueline closed her foyer door, Nigel made one last effort to be helpful.

"I'm sorry we seem to be hounding you, Jacqueline. It's just that we hate to see you so depressed."

She said, "Oh, shut up!" and slammed the door. But he meant well. She knew that; so she opened the door, called down the elegant, silent hall, "'Night, Old Thing. How about breakfast, nine-ish?"

He waved without looking around.

She was so relieved to be out from under their pressure that she felt more cheerful than she had all day. She bathed, took three of her maid, Milly Yee's health store capsules of valerian, guaranteed to help her sleep without drugs, and crawled beneath the covers. The health products had been Milly's idea to take the place of the prescription drugs Jacqueline had taken after Richard's death. The effect might have been all imaginary, but it had worked so far.

On this night it seemed to work all too well.

She was awakened by pounding and keys rattling, followed by Nigel Chilton-Brown calling her name and actually shaking her awake.

She was furious. The room seemed to be crowded with people, a bellman, the Hall Porter, Nigel, and a benign young man with a Fu Manchu mustache. Nigel cried louder than necessary,

"She's awake. All's well."

"Of course, I'm awake." She began to realize this was serious. "What is it? A bombing? An earthquake? A fire?"

"Never mind, Doctor. She will do nicely now," Nigel told young Fu Manchu. "These modern young women. They will insist on overdosing themselves with sleeping pills."

She sat straight up in bed indignantly. "I didn't take a sleeping pill. Get these people out of here, damn it!"

There was a slow, awkward exodus. Jacqueline could hear them all talking about her in the foyer. She had awakened with a headache and this confusion infuriated her. Then she looked at her little gold bedside clock.

Eleven-thirty.

Obviously a.m. A murky sun was trying to pierce the fog outside the windows.

She had slept twelve hours. Preposterous idea, unless she had taken sleeping pills. "Which I didn't," she reminded herself.

Nigel came back looking haggard.

"My dear girl, I told you, if you felt in any way –"

"I didn't feel in any way. I was fine. I took capsules Milly Yee got at the health stores. Harmless herbs and roots ground up. I do wish you would mind your own business."

He hesitated. He was still looking somewhat peaked. Feeling angry enough to be cruel, she laughed at him.

"You're the one who needs help. You look like the wrath of God."

"Sorry." At the door he reminded her stiffly, "Since you missed that nine o'clock breakfast with me, I would like to take you to lunch. Unfortunately, I have an appointment with Mediterranean Delight, Limited. About importing their Baklava."

"Have a lovely time."

She was sorry for his concern but awfully glad he couldn't make lunch. Before she got up, however, she sat there with her arms locked around her knees, trying to figure out what had happened to make her sleep so long.

She had been frantically hopeful ever since she had seen the contessa's eight-by-ten glossy. But long before that she had been torn by hopes, then fears, and above all by the intrusive common sense of everyone who "reasoned with her" about Richard's death. Small wonder that her body had finally given her the sleep she required.

That must be the explanation.

Two hours later, when she had showered and eaten and was dressing to visit the exciting modern piazza and mall of Covent Garden, the phone rang. Obviously Nigel again. Or her mother. She reached for the phone, said abruptly, harshly,

"Yes?"

"This is Devlin Conor. Remember me?"

It was Richard.

Fourteen

Her fingers squeezed hard around the phone. She forced herself to sound cool. Bantering.

"Well, hello there. Banbury time already?"

He chuckled. "Not this time. Do you by any chance happen to like Agatha Christie?"

Her heart almost missed a beat. Richard's beloved Agatha.

"Sure. Doesn't everyone?"

"I was just wondering if you'd like to take in her old play, 'The Mousetrap'. The one that's been running since God knows when. We could get something to eat afterward."

"Love it." She decided that he didn't have to know she had seen it half a dozen times with various acquaintances who had insisted it was part of her London education.

He didn't waste words, unlike the Richard of long ago. "Great. I'll call you from the lobby."

No fooling around in her rooms, having drinks, breaking the ice, making love . . .

He rang off.

O.K. I can live with that, Mr. Devlin Conor, alias Richard Kimberly.

She spent most of the day getting her hair done and shopping for something special to wear that night, buying two glitzy dinner outfits off the rack. It was an elegant rack and according to Viola Sears whom she met while modelling the silver mesh, she looked smashing.

"A special date?" Mrs. Sears guessed at once.

"Very special."

"Lucky girl. Siggy was saying only this morning that you had seemed depressed since your arrival." She shook a gaunt finger coyly. "We can't have that. Very naughty of you."

Siggy? Poor mother! Was she about to lose her gigolo?

Jacqueline gave her the fixed smile, accepted among her parents' international friends.

"On the contrary. I'm having a lovely time. Great fun."

Mrs. Sears caught a glimpse of her own gaunt, carefully starved figure in the exquisite old bevilled mirror and smoothed the long torso of her suit.

"Did you ever find that photographer you were so desperate to locate? Siggy –" She caught Jacqueline's expression in the mirror. "Prince Sigurd had me hunting through all my Venice Antiquities correspondence to find the man. Will he do?"

Jacqueline was uneasy. "Do what?"

"Weren't you looking for a man to handle the telly promotion about Eccles Cakes or Banbury Tarts, something of that sort, for your company?"

Jacqueline held a cream-colored *peau de soie* gown up before the mirror, cursing her own stupidity. She needn't worry about other people ruining her relationship with Dev Conor. She would betray herself if she wasn't careful. If Richard did have something to hide, he would never forgive her for letting the world in on his real identity.

"Oh, that. He may just do. His work isn't too bad. The fellow is a bit standoffish but nobody's perfect."

"Certainly not I, my dear. Well, have fun tonight. I must say, I envy you. Ah, to be young again!" She had started out into the spacious Empire Reception Hall but stopped, stuck her head around a pillar and asked, "Darling, do you think that is quite your color?"

It was hard to take offense at the truth. Jacqueline grimaced at her own reflection and gave the dress back to the sales-woman. "She is so right."

She decided to take a chance on the silver mesh and a one-shouldered coral matte jersey.

She added to this unfashionably quick decision by taking the boxes with her in the taxi. All the way back to the hotel she debated which outfit to wear but it wasn't until evening that she realized how wrong she had been in the entire day's efforts.

Where was the girl in the swinging skirt and the peasant blouse, the girl Richard Kimberly had married?

A little older, she admitted. A great deal more sophisticated. But the same figure. The same size. Same woman? Not the same. That was the problem.

Maybe she could go halfway. Forget the glamor and simply wear something that would remind him – just a little – of the girl he married over three years ago.

She tore off the silver mesh, stepped out of her silk evening slippers, and studied the elegant travel wardrobe hanging in the wardrobe.

When Dev Conor's call came from the lobby Jacqueline was still brushing lacquer and "styling" out of her hair. She finished with one long, full sweep that made her black hair crackle. But at least, she looked a lot more like the girl Richard Kimberly had married. A maroon velvet skirt and a scoop-necked silk blouse with a paisley pattern managed to look sophisticated on her in spite of her efforts. Her big, gypsy earrings reduced that problem.

She grabbed up her old vicuna coat, swung it around her shoulders and started out.

Naturally, she shared the "lift" with a party of four, heavily formal, even to pristine white silk scarves on the men and an extraordinary combination of mini-skirts and sable maxi-coats on the ageing blonde women. They looked Jacqueline up and down. She gave them the same treatment.

As the women elbowed their way out of the lift before her, one murmured in a broad American accent, "You sure see everything here."

Jacqueline swept between them offering, "Cross my palm with silver, I tell you fortune, Ladies."

One of the two men grinned but the women were speechless. Gypsies in the Savoy? What next?

Feeling almost drunkenly exhilarated, Jacqueline crossed the lobby, looking for Richard. Or Devlin. She must remember his pseudonym.

At first, she missed him. Theatregoers and diners crowded the big main lobby and it wasn't until half a dozen couples vanished into cabs outside that the lobby cleared enough for her to spot Dev Conor in a business suit and Burberry, talking to a solid-looking elderly woman in a brimmed rain hat and a cloth coat with a rolled fur collar.

It was impossible to make out her face. She left Conor almost immediately and headed for the lift. She clutched a folded umbrella and a large handbag held close to her body.

Jacqueline cut across the lobby, remembering to play the meeting flippantly.

"Hello. Who's the girlfriend?"

Conor grinned and shook the hand she offered. It wasn't as good as a Continental cheek-to-cheek greeting, but his hand was warm and firm.

"She wanted to know if I was waiting for her. She'd been hired by some Americans to baby-sit tonight. Are we ready?"

"Ready as we'll ever be."

He looked her over as he took her arm. They walked out to the taxi line. He took the long strides she remembered well. His voice was so casual she didn't expect anything but some prosaic remark when he said,

"You really are."

"Are what?"

"As beautiful as I remembered."

She knew how easily these compliments came to Richard who enjoyed seeing her (and no doubt his previous girlfriends) in a happy mood, but she was caught by surprise when she looked up and saw that he was not teasing. He seemed very matter-of-fact. Maturity became him, and this was certainly more flattering than an easy compliment. If only maturity could do as much for her!

An early evening mist had stopped now and Conor pointed out a couple of stars that appeared timidly on the horizon.

"It's an interesting town. All kinds of weather in one day."

After they got into the cab she asked, "Is there variety in your own town?"

"Not much. With smog and without smog."

She was careful not to show any excitement at this information. "You must come from Los Angeles." Long ago she had guessed he came from Southern California.

"We're not the only ones with smog. But yes. I live there. In tacky old Hollywood. Matter of fact. On Franklin Avenue. Near Vine. You can't get much more Hollywood than that."

"My father lives there. In Malibu, I mean." She hesitated, then went on. "I had a friend who lived there but he moved to Boise, Idaho. I guess he wanted variety in his weather."

She thought he would dismiss this or even lose patience, imagining she wanted to trap him, but instead, he said, "There's a coincidence for you. I had two aunts in Boise. Well, Garden City, actually. It's sort of surrounded by Boise. They're gone now. I was very fond of them. Nice people."

"I suppose you never sent them cards when you travelled."

She waited breathlessly. Had his mind completely blotted out all that talk about Boise, Idaho and how pointless it was to send cards from Europe, or news of his wedding?

He frowned. In the dark of the cab she felt him staring at her. "They've been dead for years. Aunt Belle in 1974 and Aunt Eunice in '77. They were lively, interesting women, both of them. But about the post cards – Is that what you meant?"

"More or less."

"Maybe I've sent them. I don't really remember. I never travelled much except that museum thing in Europe." He looked out as they whirled around the Nelson Monument in Trafalgar Square. "We're pretty near. Lucky about the weather . . . Are you a card sender?"

"Not as often as I should have been. I wasn't away from – from my husband long enough. And my parents travelled a lot. They were very social. I had my grandmother, of course. Berthe Godart. I loved her."

She hadn't realized the betrayal of emotion in her voice but he looked at her again and said something he had never said to her before.

"You must have been a lonely little girl."

"Not at all. I had more than most little girls have, believe me."

After a silence that puzzled her he said, "You think a lot about money. That's what you meant, isn't it? That you had money and all that goes with it."

She was hurt. "It's a hell of a lot better than being poor, let me tell you."

"Oh, I don't know. Anyway, you may have been lucky, having absentee parents. I had a father who was a conniving bastard."

"Good Lord!"

His laugh had an edge to it. "Runs in the family. You should have known my grandfather. He stole a claim from a drunk in Goldfield, Nevada, back in 1906. That's how he got his start. Runs in the family."

The taxi pulled up. Theatre crowds from several theatres were all around them and he took her arm, leading her past the box office and into the modest lobby. She could hardly wait to bring Agatha Christie into the conversation and judge his reaction to the author he had been so crazy about three years ago, but she had to be careful. He already showed signs of suspecting what she was up to.

Every link between him and his past seemed to annoy him. And he showed no sign of the old, teasing, flirtatious Richard Kimberly; yet all the circumstantial evidence proved he was the same man. That comment about his Boise Aunts, Agatha Christie, the Banbury Cross meeting. Too many coincidences.

She was relieved when he brought up the Christie subject just before the first act.

"I hope you like this. I've never seen "The Mouse-trap", but it's supposed to be vintage Christie."

She confessed in part. "I saw it some years ago. As you say, it's the good old vintage stuff. The last person you'd ever guess committed the murders . . . So you read English mysteries."

"Every few years I re-read a batch of them. I have one with me in Richmond Hill now." He gave her a sideglance. "But I imagine you saw that when you rifled my room."

"I didn't rifle it. I was looking for some sign that you were you."

"I am. I give you my word."

"No. I meant –"

"I know what you meant."

Luckily, the play opened, the light oldfashioned banter onstage was seasoned with scary outbreaks, hints of a killer somewhere near the snowbound lodge, and the plot was on. Jacqueline let her mind wander over the real mystery of the man beside her.

Late in the first act her neck began to prickle and she reached back, thinking the collar of her coat had rubbed her flesh. The collar was down. Her neck was bare. She decided finally that she had imagined the feeling.

She smiled at a thought dredged up from her childhood.

Somebody is watching me. That's why my neck prickles.

She looked around into the semi-darkness. Hundreds of eyes were all focussed on the stage and the finale of Act One.

It was too ridiculous, even if her childish explanation was the right one. People frequently stared at patrons sitting in front of them. No crime in that.

She remembered oversleeping this morning and didn't like the juxtaposition of the two ideas. Anybody can oversleep, just as anybody can be stared at.

Damn Nigel Chilton-Brown for planting the first seed in her mind!

Everyone began to stir. She came out of her unpleasant thoughts. It was intermission. Conor said,

"Well, knowing Agatha, I've figured out whodunnit."

"Don't be cocky. No one has ever guessed."

He told her.

She gasped and began to laugh. "No one figures it out. How did you do it?"

"I told you. I've studied her thought processes."

She shook her head, but of course he was right.

The rest of the play merely reinforced Conor's correct guess. He turned to Jacqueline at the unmasking of the murderer with an exaggerated air of pride.

"Told you so."

Her laughter was "shushed" by several neighbors. Then the players took their curtains calls and Jacqueline gathered her coat around her throat. Conor helped her. She liked the warm strength of his fingers. Perhaps he sensed that. His hand lingered over her throat and jawline while he looked deep into her eyes, as if caught by some message in them.

His touch brought back vivid, tingling memories of the first time they had made love, in that old hotel behind St. Mark's undeterred by the smell of canal sewage wafting its way up.

"How happy we were!"

He frowned. "What?"

"Nothing. I was thinking of the first time I saw 'The Mousetrap', my family and I, a long time ago."

Out in the unexpectedly warm autumn night they found themselves surrounded by the crowds from several theatres that were also letting out, all of the crowd hailing cabs. It looked like being a long wait.

Conor confessed, "I'm not much into theatre-going. I certainly didn't count on this."

She was feeling hopeful, thrilled by his proximity. The cab shortage seemed like a marvelous way to spend more time alone with him.

"It's turned out to be a lovely night. Why don't we walk back to the Savoy? We're not likely to get mugged with so many people pouring out along all those streets."

He looked up at the sky. There were half a dozen stars on view now. The night would be impressively beautiful, once they got beyond the garish theatre lights.

"Why not? Are you an outdoor girl?"

"No way. But here goes."

They started down in the general direction of the Strand.

"I love walking in Venice," she said when they had crossed the street against a mass of foot traffic.

"I didn't know anybody walked in Venice. I thought everything was done in gondolas."

Nervously, she tried to keep on the subject of Venetian waters without arousing his anger which would inevitably be aroused if he hadn't lost his memory and was just putting on an act by denying he was Richard Kimberly. On the other hand, he might betray something that would let her know one way or the other.

"Most visitors to Venice spend more time in motorboats. Even speedboats." She shivered. In spite of her firm efforts to banish it, the old nightmare returned . . . The black waters. Then the blinding light flashed on them by the Yugoslavian freighter. Her last sight of Richard's agony . . .

She clutched his hand. He put an arm around her, asking with concern, "All right, now? Did you stumble? These streets aren't as well-lit as they might be."

"I'm fine. I just remembered something. A nightmare. About drowning."

"It's a common nightmare. Even to good swimmers."

"Are you –" She moistened her lips. "Are you a good swimmer?"

The idea didn't seem to dredge up any painful memories.

"About like most landlubbers. I can swim across a pool. Maybe the length of it, if the painful necessity arises. But no. I'm not rich enough to afford a pool. Never really missed one, either." He boosted her over a curb. "Here. Watch it. Maybe we should have waited for the cab, after all."

But her problem had nothing to do with curbs and side-walks.

He was watching her with a growing tenderness. Maybe it was only compassion.

"Do you want to talk about him sometime?" When she raised her head, he added firmly, "Not tonight. Tonight we're going to have nothing but laughs. And come to think of it, food. Where would you rather eat than any place else? Sky's the limit." Then he added with quick humor so like the old days, "Let's make that – the roof's the limit."

She grinned and felt better. They found themselves caught up in a trail of teenagers, at least half of them skinheads, looking badly outdated by their more modern companions. As the group snaked along the sidewalk, trying to separate men and women they saw walking in pairs, Conor suddenly called out, "Watch it!" and pushed Jacqueline halfway across the sidewalk. She reeled up against a shop wall, unable to believe what had happened. The snaking line rushed onward, laughing, calling to each other. The last of them wore a peaked cap pulled far down over his eyes. Nobody looked back. It was as if they didn't know what had happened.

Jacqueline caught her breath and staggered out to Conor who stared after the group, holding one hand in the other palm.

She demanded, "Why did you do that? It's not funny."

"No," he agreed. "Not really. I supposed they meant it as a joke."

"Some joke."

He said, "Come along. We need either a Bobby or an all-night restaurant. I'm hungry."

"A Bobby?" Then she saw the back of his hand. Something sharp had slashed across his knuckles. It didn't seem to be a deep cut, but a trickle of blood trailed along it. She cried, "You're hurt. Why did they do that? The bastards!"

He began to show impatience. "It's stopped already. Don't fuss."

She ignored that. "Wait. Grandmother always made me carry a clean linen handkerchief. Here." She fished in her handbag and brought out the carefully folded white handkerchief. "Shall I do it, or do you want to? It must hurt awfully."

He was reasonably nonchalant. "Smarts a little. I doubt if I'll bleed to death. The question is, why did the fellow do it? I don't think the others knew anything about it. And he was no fun-loving teenager."

"Did you get a good look at him?"

He took the handkerchief, laid it over the cut, and walked on with her. "Not much. But I saw the switchblade and his hand. No kid, that one."

She pointed out a brightly lit little restaurant two shops away.

"We can call the police from there."

But he had changed his mind.

"It's O.K. now. Lucky I saw the damn thing in his hand. Can we take a chance eating in this place?"

"I think it's reasonably safe," she joked, trying to bring back the warm banter of their earlier moments together. "How's the hand?"

"Practically like new. Just a scratch. But you sure were right in the path of that knife. The creep was probably on something. Unless –"

She looked at him. "Unless what?"

"Nothing. He just didn't fit the pattern of the other kids. In fact, he was no kid, as I said. I wish I could have gotten a look at his face. Well, here we are."

In the nearly deserted restaurant the waitress was shocked by the stains on Jacqueline's handkerchief. She urged that somebody, the local Policeman, Scotland Yard, the Metropolitan Police, *somebody*, should be called, but Conor, examining the cut by the gaudy restaurant light, complained that it was much ado about nothing. The bleeding had stopped. Only a thread of a stain remained, and it seemed clear that the attack must have been merely a nasty joke.

"I'll report it to the first cop I see," Conor promised the woman, but though Jacqueline was relieved at his cheerfulness, she still felt a little of the horror she had experienced when she first saw the blood, and remembered how she had lost Richard once before.

"This isn't exactly the Savoy Grill," Conor remarked ruefully, when the waitress and Jacqueline had wrapped his knuckles with oldfashioned tape and gauze. "What sounds good to you? Miss, what is the specialty?"

The girl came back, fluffing up the heavily sprayed white-gold hair behind her starched linen head-ruff.

"This hour, Mate? Bean Sandwiches. About it."

He looked so horrified that Jacqueline laughed. "Think of it this way, it's nourishing."

"Bean Sandwiches. Now I've heard everything. I don't believe it. Who thought that one up?"

"I'll try it if you will. After all, I'm the one who was caught eating greasy Soft Shell Crabs."

"Oh well, at least, crabs are American."

"Not in Venice."

He had taken her first mention of the crabs without question and she waited breathlessly for him to connect the crabs with Venice. He hesitated, looked at her for a moment without speaking, then dismissed the whole idea.

"Anyway, this doesn't look like a seagoing restaurant to me. So I guess it'll be Bean Sandwiches. I owe you one. Dinner, I mean."

"I'll hold you to that."

It was pretty bad. Fortunately, they ordered tea with their meal, and while Conor said it was strong enough to melt the spoons, they both enjoyed it.

Afterward, they sauntered along the Strand which was still crowded and brightly lighted, until they reached the Savoy. Jacqueline noticed with satisfaction that Conor slowed his pace even more as they entered the lobby. Would she be able to manage it so he thought it was his idea that he should come up to her suite "for a nightcap?"

He made a good start, teasing her with, "I'm beginning to think your burglarizing my room was a great idea. You must do it again some day."

"Any time. I took a great fancy to your landlord. A nice, big, woolly bear."

He was amused but from the way he tightened the fingers of his good hand around her elbow and headed toward the lifts, he showed definite signs of jealousy. She was delighted.

Then the bubble burst. The balloon was punctured. They were accosted by Nigel Chilton-Brown and Prince Sigurd von Ulsbach. Nigel looked uncomfortable. Obviously, he wasn't enthused by the prince's company. The prince, however, was positively gushing with pleasure at this new encounter.

"But this is delightful, Jacqui." He recognized Conor at once and further aroused her fury by doing the two things she had been afraid of.

"And this, of course, is the man you had me chasing all over London to find. You are a man of secrets, Mr. Conor . . . My dear Nigel, this is our Jacqueline's young man, the one in the Contess Fabrini's picture. It was this picture that brought our Jacqui to London. But perhaps I speak out of turn. She did show you that picture; did she not?"

Almost in one breath he had managed to betray Conor's identity to Nigel and let Conor know he had been wildly pursued by a crackpot woman who thought he was her dead husband.

Conor's hand slowly left her arm. Otherwise, he was the essence of cool indifference. "I'm flattered. Actually, I've been trying to persuade Mrs. Kimberly to use my sketches rather than my photographs. That was what your company had in mind for me; wasn't it, Mr. – Mr. –"

The way he snapped his fingers in his effort to "recall" Nigel's name was insulting, but Jacqueline was too angry to care. She said brusquely, "Oh, that's Nigel. He doesn't own the company. Matter of fact, you are looking at one of the owners. And I think your sketch idea is terrific. Don't you, Nigel?"

Nigel held out his hand, determined to be dignified but pleasant. "Quite so. Chilton-Brown. I manage the Godart Eastern and European connections." His eyebrows rose as he indicated Jacqueline. "Subject, of course, to the views of the Godart Family."

After shaking hands – everyone avoided the prince – Conor said, "I'll be getting along now, Mrs. Kimberly. If you decide on those sketches, we might discuss them at some later time."

He turned and walked away.

She couldn't imagine what he really thought of her, or if he thought about her at all, after this disclosure.

She swallowed hard, squared her shoulders, and moved past the two men with the suggestion, "You gentlemen seem to have had a hard day. Why don't you just run along home, like good little boys."

Prince Sigurd was nothing if not accommodating. He bowed. "Of course, Jacqui. Just as you say. My Angela will be expecting you down in the country tomorrow for dinner." He glanced after the retreating Conor. "If you can make it."

She shrugged. She would think about that tomorrow. Without wasting more anger on Nigel who, from his point of view, hadn't been guilty of anything, she started for the lift. As she might have expected, he followed her.

"The resemblance is very close, considering the time that has passed. I can see why you were startled. Who is he, really?"

"He is –" She broke off. "He says he is an artist named Conor. Devlin Kimball Conor. He comes from Los Angeles." She smiled sweetly and lied. "Just like Richard."

He looked back thoughtfully, but Conor had gone. "I suppose they could have been related. But you must allow that your husband was hiding something. Remember, we never could track his family."

Don't spoil it for me, she prayed, hating him for puncturing the balloon of her dream. "If you start putting detectives on his trail, you and I are through, Nigel. Just a friendly warning."

The old, familiar, troubled look came into his gray eyes. As if she were crazy, or something. He had looked like that in those first awful months after Richard died. No. After he disappeared. And she hadn't been crazy then either. He tried to be patient. His patience was as bad as his doubts about her.

"Jacqueline, is it possible that a sensible, well-informed modern woman like you can deliberately blind herself to reality? I'm afraid the truth is, you want to believe he is Kimberly, even when you know better."

She reddened with anger. "Do you know better?" With an effort she managed a cutting laugh.

"Darling, if only you were as smart as you think you are. Run along now and leave Mr. Conor alone. He has one great asset. He's an artist. We are using him on our spring campaign."

She was glad when the lift separated her from his all-seeing eyes. He had tried to crush her dream, but she wouldn't let him succeed.

It seemed to her that the longer she knew Devlin Conor, the more of Richard Kimberly was unfolded to her. All he needed was to develop those qualities that he had probably stored in the back of his mind after the appalling accident. Heaven knew what suffering he had gone through after his close brush with death.

Some way, somehow, she would help to recreate Richard Kimberly out of the man who had been turned by fate into Devlin Conor. But they certainly must avoid any more near-misses like that switchblade weirdo's attack tonight. She wished he had reported it to the police.

Fifteen

Nigel was playing the busy little beaver again. He called her just before she left for Featherstonaugh Lodge next afternoon and she answered the phone, thinking it was her mother or even, if she was lucky, Dev Conor.

She greeted Nigel appropriately.

"Make this a quickie, Old Boy. I'm late now."

He sounded a bit rattled by her tones. "Just a reassuringly word. I – er – happened to – That is, I was discussing the new plant near Long Beach, California, and the plant manager, a chap I used to know from the Aurora affiliation, was familiar with the new artist, this Conor person."

"Really? How nice!" She was glacial.

"It seems our chap's wife is a collector. She has three sketches of Conor's. Thinks he's tops among the newer artists. Not much known about him until 1988, but he's come up fast lately."

Surely, this fitted Richard Kimberly. It had taken him years to find his real profession. He had been floundering when she first met him. The memory loss (it must be that) had washed away all the irresponsible side of his nature and actually turned him into another man.

"Glad to hear it. Then you approve of our using him if he agrees to the offer."

"Sounds like a popular approach. His sketches are comical, you know. By the way, this may make your day, Old Girl. Know how he signs his sketches? The initials DKC."

He didn't die. He exists. He is my Richard.

After recovering her breath she asked as casually as she could, "What's the K for? I've forgotten."

"Kimball."

"Yes. Of course. How nice to think I was right! All I have to do is convince him. He's had a memory loss, you know. He must have been badly injured in the accident."

"I see. You still feel there should be no further investigation?"

"Absolutely." Then she had another thought. "Except in Venice. If it can be done discreetly. We might try again to see if an injured man was rescued that spring night three years ago. A fresh reward. You know the routine."

"It didn't work before," he reminded her.

"Maybe we didn't try hard enough."

He wasn't enthusiastic over the chances but he agreed.

After that conversation her world seemed to brighten.

That evening Angela and her friend, Viola Sears, not to mention Prince Sigurd, congratulated Jacqueline on her scintillating manner, her sparkle, and even her wit. She accepted all compliments graciously, knowing quite well that her so-called sparkle was the result of one blazing fact: Nigel's information had convinced her that Richard Kimberly had come back from the dead.

She spent the night at Featherstonaugh and in the contrary way of dreams, found herself reliving the horror of her old nightmare. She awoke shortly after dawn at the usual moment, just as Richard went under for the last time. She heard herself cry out and sat up in bed, reminding herself,

"He didn't die."

She had always known that. Curiously enough, a part of her had never accepted what had seemed to be the plain truth.

She got up, showered and dressed, all the while trying to plan some sort of campaign that would open up the past, and their marriage, to his memory.

When she got back to London there were several messages, two invitations from the wives of company executives, one from Nigel, and two from Esther Heffernan who complained that her beloved Mr. Chilton-Brown never returned her business calls and asked what she should do about the contract with Bernstein and Kent.

At the moment Jacqueline wasn't keen to discuss advertising executives with the chattery Miss Heffernan. Nothing must interfere with her campaign to rouse Dev Conor's latent memories. It wasn't very businesslike, but the Godart Corporation had taken up most of her adult life and right now she wanted more than stock profits out of that life.

She cabled to Miss Heffernan: "Hold B & K spring campaign. New proposal pending."

She pushed the corporation invitations aside and let their messages join Nigel's in the "sometime" file. A cable from her father "and your loving Irina" was more urgent.

They were on their way to open the contessa's Venetian palazzo for the Autumn-to-Winter Season and would be delighted if Jacqueline joined them. "Many balls, *intime* parties, and exquisite Affairs for the Preservation of our Heritage," the contessa carefully explained, adding, never at a loss for words, even in a cable, "Do come and make our triumph complete."

Jacqueline wondered how "delighted" the contessa would be to see if she showed up with her husband. Always assuming that Devlin Conor still loved Jacqueline.

Nigel had been right about one thing. The contessa was already manipulating to take a place on the board of Godart's. Considering her ambition, she would find any marriage of Jacqueline's a serious threat to her plans. Suppose Jacqueline and her husband produced an heir. Much more likely than that Marcel and Irina should have children.

Jacqueline was almost, but not quite, amused enough to wish Nigel was here so she could enjoy the idea with him. All the same, when she heard the door buzzer, she went to the door grumbling, and threw it open, saying in a bored voice,

"Not you again."

Dev Conor looked surprised but assured her, "So far as I know."

Meanwhile, between amusement and embarrassment, she cried, "Oh, my Lord! Do come in. I'm so sorry. I was expecting Nigel Chilton-Brown. You met him."

"Then I'm glad I'm not that good a friend."

He came in with her, looked the living room over, and reminded her, "Better hurry. These business conferences sometimes take all day." He settled down in an armchair, stretched out his long legs before him and looked up at her innocently.

"Business –?"

"The minute your buddy, Chilton-Brown, called me this morning I said to myself, I'd rather deal with the owner. Might get better terms. For my sketching or whatever. Hurry up. These rental car agencies may charge by the hour. Or is it the kilo?"

"You are really impossible." She went into the bedroom happily, stopping in the doorway to ask, "Where are we going?"

"To Rye, of course. Quaint little hill town on the Sussex Coast. It's only about an hour from here. Smuggler's hide-out in the good old days. Great place for me to hold you up on terms."

She had just nodded as if this were the most natural arrangement in the world when he went on, "If we work it right, you might be able to avoid dear old Chilton-Brown for an entire day. I'll try and make stiff demands. Then we can quarrel a lot. That ought to kill some time."

She laughed. "Thanks for the warning. I'm a tough bargainer. Just give me a minute."

She had almost gotten used to his reserved and even sophisticated manner as Devlin Conor, but now he seemed to show more of the old carefree Richard Kimberly spirit. Hearing him joke like this brought back poignant memories of those few weeks they had spent together. Maybe they could recapture them in spite of the insistence of everyone else, including Conor himself, that he was not her Richard.

What on earth was he up to today?

No matter. She packed a new case made especially for her by Hermès in Paris. It was no bigger than a large handbag but opened a few inches, accordion-fashion and carried a tissue-thin nightgown, silk Teddies, a sexy dinner blouse, her makeup and money. She regarded this little case as her Home-Away From-Home. If she and Conor came back to London this afternoon, he would never know about the little case. She had often used the case on less sensuously promising overnight travel but never until now with the definite plan for a seduction.

"How goes the war wound?" she asked as they rode down in the lift a few minutes later.

He held up his hand, making a fist. "Good as new. Dull blade, maybe."

The scar was faint and already scabbed over except for one end of wound where the blade had dug deeper. There would soon be no sign of the unpleasant encounter.

"I still say you should have reported it."

"What? And be hounded the rest of my stay here by the sinister minions of MI5? Or do I mean MI6?"

"They're on our side, remember? Anyway, I doubt if MI5 spends much time pursuing street punks."

"Street punks." After a few seconds she noticed that he was frowning at her. His next question startled her. "You are pretty well-known. I just got to wondering if someone in your position might have enemies. You know. In business. Or someone who has it in for your family."

The idea made her uncomfortable. It brought out things she would rather not think about, like the push and shove on State Street in Chicago, the fact that someone had been following her, or the peculiar long sleep the other morning. She had thrown out the Valerian root, but the herbs had never bothered her before.

"I guess I should have kept it," she thought aloud. Also, she should have had it analyzed; yet the idea horrified her. She would almost rather not know. He was still puzzled and she explained in part. "Nigel thought I was taking too many sleeping pills." She tried to play it lightly. "I wasn't taking uppers or downers or pills of any other kind, except an occasional aspirin. What has this got to do with street punks?"

"Nothing, actually. Except that the fellow with the switchblade was no kid. He didn't fit the pattern of the others in that daisy chain. Then too, he seemed to be headed for you, though I could be wrong about that. It happened so fast . . . Here we are."

She was relieved to find his American hired car waiting and to change the subject as they drove out to the crowded street. Luckily for her peace of mind, they discussed nothing but the traffic and the difference between English-English and American-English until they were beyond the positively-final, absolute end of sprawling Greater London.

"You handle left-hand traffic very well," she said when he had skillfully eluded a cyclist and a lorry.

He disagreed. "I should have ordered a British car, like that Mini of yours. American cars just weren't designed for country lanes."

"Have you been in the U.K. before?" Hadn't Richard mentioned something about his travels in England before he came to Venice? But so had Conor.

"That one time. The Great Museum Caper. I was big on art. I don't know that it made me a better artist." He caught himself. "But maybe I shouldn't remind you of that. I'm bargaining for a job on one of your commercials."

"I'll forget I heard it. Then you don't consider commercials beneath you?"

"Nothing is beneath me, except starvation."

"There should be a law – no starving for artists."

He reached for her hand. They made no effort to dislodge their hands, nor did they say anything. It was almost as if they had resumed the loving closeness they shared three years ago.

They drove through lanes of trees with their leaves turning brown, picking up traffic headed for Hastings and other popular coastal towns. The Sussex Marshes with their roaming sheep and their peculiar out-croppings of little hillocks here and there began to take over the scene. Jacqueline felt as if she had retreated far into the past, to another time which she shared with this man.

It was scary because she kept asking herself if it would last. It had vanished once, this close companionship with another human being, the only companionship of that kind she had ever really known.

Grandmother Berthe Godart had been a vastly superior person, like a goddess, never an equal. You did not feel equal to a goddess whom you adored. Only with her husband had Jacqueline known that delicious closeness, almost as if they were one.

When she had confessed this to the psychiatrist he had asked whether she regarded this as a normal state of affairs for anyone else.

"How do I know?" she had asked, hurt and already fed up with him. "I never was anyone else."

Sharing the excitement of Conor's close companionship now she was convinced that she had been right to wait for his return from the dead. To wait and to believe. Gradually, ever so carefully, she would make him over into the man he used to be, but without losing this new responsibility that she liked in him.

He caught her looking at him and asked quietly, "What was he like? Tell me about him." She hesitated, not knowing where to begin. He encouraged her. "Not his looks. I mean, how did he behave?"

It was easier that way, just describing the funny little restaurant where she had bought the soft shell crabs, and the events which followed on that first day, including her lost money and the way Richard Kimberly had come to the rescue.

Conor shook her hand in his, trying to make his accusation sound casual. "Are you sure this paragon didn't steal your money himself?"

"Would you?"

He sighed. "Hoist with my own petard."

"What is that supposed to mean?"

"Damned if I know. But it sounds impressive . . . So our hero rescued you. And then?"

She went on. It was painful reliving all those precious moments but she kept hoping a picture – a memory – would come back to him as she talked. Perhaps his slightly cynical attitude was put on, and he was either confused or jealous of what he thought of as the other man in her life.

She wondered about his probing.. Did he hope to remember the love they had shared for such a pitifully short time? There were moments when she felt that he was trying to contrast the Richard of her memories with his new identity as Dev Conor. Perhaps he simply wanted to make her see something special in him that she hadn't enjoyed with Richard in Venice. If this was so, then he couldn't possibly be that other man, and that would be the greatest hurt of all.

He kept referring to Richard as "he" or "him". Nothing she told him appeared to ring a bell. She had to be satisfied with the sympathy he offered her in his look, his touch, his warm concern. Until she came to the abbreviated details of the honeymoon on Torcello.

She tried to make it light. She didn't want her real emotions to take over.

"A heavenly place. I mean, if the accident hadn't happened. It was the boatman's fault, you know. He was drunk. And Richard wasn't a very good swimmer." She cleared her throat but it was no use. She couldn't get any more words out for a minute.

Luckily, Conor pretended not to notice. He kept strictly to business. "I get it. That's why you asked about my own swimming. O.K. It's not the greatest. On the other hand, what else do you know about our hero's background?"

She had to accept the dubious fact. She had known nothing about Richard when she married him, and she had suspected his past, even then. However, she said quickly, "I know his family live- or lived – in Idaho."

"Idaho. What a coincidence. I can see why you got me tangled up with – with your husband. Not that I mind." He slowed down to make a turn into a smaller road leading to "Royal Rye." Then he leaned over and kissed her lips.

He took her by surprise but her lips parted under his pressure and she was aware of her body's deep, hot response. She had dreamed of this for so long. It was better than her dream. There were force and power in his touch, in his firm, insistent mouth, and his tenderness; his genuine care for her feelings had already been demonstrated. He lingered, prolonging the ecstatic sensation as if it were an invasion of her body, as in a sense, it was. Still, there was the gentleness she sensed in him that was only now coming to the fore.

He must have had a lot of practice lately.

She backed away, staring at him.

"Not the same?" he asked, though he didn't seem sorry about it. Was he testing her again, hoping she would love this new personality more than the old one?

"The jury is still out."

He seemed to find all this highly amusing but his tension told her that he too had been aroused.

Then he dismissed the mood, as if he shrugged it off.

"The verdict will have to wait. We park in the garage at the foot of the hill."

She had been to the hill town of Royal Rye with a British nanny many years before, and remembered the steep climb up Mermaid Street to the historic inn, as well as the dinner she had enjoyed in the Mermaid Tavern. She had been thunderstruck to find a graveyard crowning the hill, a graveyard that appeared to be the Village Green. The townspeople crossed it all day, and probably half the night. At first sight it had seemed frightening but later, thanks to her wise, history-loving companion, she had learned to read the big tombstones and connect them with families and descendants. The people resting in those graves were old friends by the time she and the nanny left.

As she and Conor started up the hill she told him about the graveyard. He was already pointing out the bow windows and shop fronts that he wanted to sketch. He described how he personalized such places. She thought he must make them almost human enough to speak.

"Maybe I'll do the same with your gravestones." He carried an old, beaten-up airline bag and pulled out a camera. She was fascinated by his rapid collection of shots "for future use," and a tiny seed of doubt made her wonder how Richard could have acquired all these talents and interests in so short a time. Then she remembered how many snapshots Richard had taken on Torcello and how often he had photographed the little Italian children.

"Do you ever sketch children?" she asked.

"Sometimes. If they have character. I'm not a mad lover of children in the aggregate, but sometimes, I have memories of . . . of the past, and my childhood."

It was almost exactly what he had said on Torcello.

She tried to make a deal with him. "If you will tell me where you were three years ago, in the spring, I promise not to ask you any more questions."

He stopped on the steep, cobbled street and looked at her. He said evenly, "Can I count on that? As a matter of fact, I was doing just what I'm doing now. Taking pictures and planning sketches."

"Where?"

"That's two questions. But I don't mind telling you. It was in Death Valley. Later, I hiked on above Bishop toward June Lake. I packed in. Mighty cold in the early spring."

He would be unlikely to carry any traces of this picturesque adventure. Was there some significance in that?

He gave her the gratuitous information, "Late in spring I tried to get north into the Mt. St. Helens region for photographs of the changes since the big blowup. I had to give it up." He softened his final question with a smile. "Satisfied?"

"I'm sorry. I didn't mean to pry."

He said briskly, "Enough of the past. Let's give the future a chance. We'll start here at Rye's answer to the Hilton chain." He stopped at the ancient door of the Mermaid Tavern. "Good God! Talk about living in the past. This is right out of Treasure Island. Shall we take a chance?"

"Don't be silly. I adore it."

Inside the old timbered walls a pleasant young woman took their reservations for dinner in the celebrated restaurant and asked if they would be staying at the inn. Conor and Jacqueline looked at each other. He reminded her, "We haven't talked business yet."

"Very true." She added gravely, "That's quite essential. It may take hours. But make it a room full of history. And a bath, if possible."

The young woman studied her register. "The Dr. Syn room will be occupied tonight. It was just reserved a minute or two before you arrived. It has twin beds and a secret passage."

"A secret passage. I certainly hate to miss that. But what about the Elizabethan Room?" Jacqueline gave Conor an angelic smile. "That's better than the Dr. Syn Room. It's haunted."

Conor raised his eyebrows but agreed, "We certainly have to have that one."

"The Elizabethan Room is our finest. If you like atmosphere. Except the bathroom. That is highly modern."

Conor sighed. "Well, we can't have everything."

He was about to sign for them both but hesitated. Jacqueline had been hoping against hope that he would sign "Mr. and Mrs. Richard Kimberly" but he wrote "Devlin Conor" and presented the young woman with his problem. "My wife is rigidly feminist; so she always uses her – dare I say it? – her maiden name."

"Very funny." She signed "Jacqueline Godart Kimberly."

The young woman was puzzled but amused. She rang for the small, elderly bellman who had a mischievous twinkle and seemed to think they were newlyweds.

As they went up the stairs Conor put his arm around Jacqueline, whether to impress the bellman or simply out of a desire to have her close, she couldn't tell. He let her go when they reached the room at the end of the hall.

The little bellman had opened the bathroom door, pointing out just how modern it was, and pressed his knuckles down on the mattress of the huge double bed. Then he assured them "A body was sealed inside the wall. Just there in that corner behind you Madam." Jacqueline jumped, but the bellman was quick to add, "Happened hundreds of years ago. Must've been removed by now. Stands to reason; wouldn't you say, Sir?"

"Let's hope so."

Conor gave him his tip and he left, pocketing the pound notes and looking wise.

Conor strolled around, fingering the excellent reproduction furniture. "This is it, all right. But I'm never going to look right in this place without a dirk and a – whatever the old smugglers used to deck themselves out with."

He stood there with his hands on his hips, his hair dishevelled by the salt wind off the marshes, and he looked as young as he had the day she met him in the Merceria of Venice.

Mentally, she sought out the small network of lines barely visible at the corners of his eyes, and the way his straight nose had a scar over the bridge that she didn't remember from the old days. Very probably he got it the night of the accident. He combed his hair differently now, in a casual pompadour, not as he used to, like a cock's comb. She had always remembered it as a shade lighter, but his hair didn't look as if it had been dyed.

Memory plays tricks on the mind, she thought.

Never mind that. Right now, he looked young enough to be whatever age she wanted him to be.

Anxious to hold onto these precious moments, she pointed out the heavy canopy over the bed.

"Did you ever read that old story about the Terribly Strange Bed? The wooden cover-thing up there, it came down in the night . . . slowly . . . slowly . . ."

He laughed, caught her expressive hands and held her there, assuring her, "I'll be afraid to sleep tonight."

"Poor dear. And I thought you were so brave. What would you have done with Dr. Syn's Secret Passage?"

Beginning playfully, then aroused at her touch, he drew her to him by her wrists, pulling her up against his chest. Abruptly, he shifted his hands to her shoulder blades, holding her firmly in place.

"Suppose we christen this place in style. Kiss me. That ought to do it."

"What? Are you sure it will?"

"Positive. I wanted this little trip to wake you up to my fatal charms. No ghost out of the past. Just me. Devlin Conor."

She wriggled her arms out from between their bodies and locked them around his neck. When she kissed him she brought to it every ounce of feeling, leaving herself breathless, but though Conor responded, it seemed to her that he was still suspicious of her sincerity. The sensuous power his mouth had formerly exerted over her was there, and she succumbed to it passionately.

It was only afterwards, when she saw the intense look in his eyes, the way he studied her face with a painful, questioning expression, that she wondered if she had betrayed her Richard after all. She realized how he had really changed inside. The Richard of Venice would never believe he lacked sexual power over her. He was too sure of himself in that department.

She couldn't hurt him like this.

"Let's do it again. I guess you think I'm bonkers, but I found myself playing the shy maiden. That was only a rehearsal. Here comes Opening Night."

He laughed at that. He returned her exuberant kiss playfully and followed it with a boyish hug. He believed her. He said, "Good. That's settled. You make me hungry. Let's go down to lunch."

She thanked heaven silently that the little scene was over and he had been placated. They went down to lunch lightly teasing each other and acting as if nothing had happened. Only once, when she called him "Richard", his eyes seemed to darken slightly.

They joked about the food. He thought he had received two kinds of mashed potatoes, white and creamy-beige. She explained.

"Those tannish ones are parsnips. Or turnips. Something gruesome that they do a delicious job on here."

He examined the vegetable and agreed. "Mother used to make turnips, diced, with a kind of white sauce. Good, too."

She remembered their discussion at Banbury.

"You loved your mother very much; didn't you?"

"She was actually my – I guess you'd call her my confidante. She believed in me. As an artist, I mean. Turns out, she thought I was better than I am."

She loved the tenderness in his voice. It was something acquired since the old days, something to do with his amnesia, perhaps. It had been painful before to hear him talk of his family as "bastards" in that hard, bitter voice.

She wanted this to be a light, happy time; so she didn't bring up the comparison that leaped to her mind. It must be wonderful to have a parent one could love, respect and trust. She smiled at the dismal prospect of confiding her deep, personal hopes to either Angela or Marcel.

Still, she was luckier than her parents. She had Richard. Meanwhile, from time to time that afternoon she wondered if "Dev" had gotten over his curious doubt of her love. She was haunted by his expression when he had asked her to kiss him. He had seemed to be looking for some feeling, some reaction he didn't find in her eyes.

She was deeply touched by the thought and tried to make up for any earlier omission by her warm, loving trust as they wandered past quaint shops while she debated whether or not to pay five pounds for a three-inch goose made of glossy white china.

"They're made locally and they are darling. Nigel's secretary collects little china animals. But five pounds?"

He laughed at her quibbling over less than ten dollars. Everything about her spelled money.

They crossed the old graveyard at the top of the hill.

She said, "Thank you for coming here with me. It was heavenly, under this blue sky, and all these quaint –"

"Tombstones?"

"O.K. That and the place itself. It's good to get away from all that pressure in London and Chicago."

He began to reach the names on the tombstones, pointing out one luckless fellow who had died in 1820 while his loving wife survived until 1865. Another age. A wildly different period.

It might have been like that for her and Richard if she hadn't found him again.

To his surprise she put her arm around his waist and hugged him. After a few seconds, remembering the double tombstones, he understood.

Several shoppers hurried past them, completely ignoring the placid, or unplacid, sleepers below those lichen-covered tombstones.

Conor and Jacqueline took the hint and strolled on until they had covered the entire hill and each of its precipitous streets before they returned to the Mermaid Tavern.

The receptionist greeted them in her quiet, pleasant way. "Did you enjoy your stroll?"

They assured her they had and were starting up to their haunted room when the woman called after them, "Shall I ask them to book a table for four in the restaurant?"

They were puzzled. Conor said, "Not that I know of. Who are the other two?"

The woman apologized. "I'm afraid I misunderstood. But as she was such a friend of yours, I assumed you would wish – My mistake, obviously."

Jacqueline felt chilled. To her surprise, however, Conor was angry. He seemed to be suspicious of these unknown friends as well. "What friends are these?"

The woman consulted her register. "A Mrs. McAllister. She and her husband are in Dr. Syn's room. The gentleman is in religious orders. Methodist, I believe."

Jacqueline, however, was delighted. "What a good omen! Darling, don't you see? It's a lucky coincidence." She explained to the receptionist. "Dr. McAllister married us in Venice three years ago. Where are they now? Can we see them?"

Conor was less enthusiastic.

"I thought we were going to enjoy this place alone."

"We will. We will, Darling. But we owe it to them to be civil, at least. They put themselves out for us in a hundred ways. We can surely buy them a drink."

He never did agree, but Jacqueline was swept away by the idea of this omen. Nothing would bring more vividly to Richard's mind the memories of their absurd but romantic marriage in a flower-scented salon of the Gritti Palace.

Sixteen

He continued to object and brought up, for the first time in hours, the fact that this minister and his wife would get the wrong impression of Jacqueline if they found her sharing the best room in the house with a man.

Jacqueline joked at his views on sexual behaviour. "Even if you persist in not being my husband, this is not the Middle Ages. We weren't married when you met them in Venice. Wait." As he opened his mouth. "You're going to tell me you don't remember the wedding. Do me a favor. If they recognize you, leave it at that."

"And if they don't?" He unlocked the door but stopped in the hall to look at her. "What then? How will you feel?"

"I'll just tell them they are way off base. I will remind them that I ought to know my own husband."

He laughed, threw up his hands and then bowed her into the Elizabethan Room. "Enter my haunted lair and tell me all I ought to know about our famous wedding."

"Make that infamous. Poor Dr. McAllister! His wife

had smothered the hotel room with flowers and he was allergic. He punctuated the entire service with sneezes. Remember how we laughed as soon as we got out of there? No. I can see you don't. But think about it, Darling. We went off to Torcello right away. I left most of my stuff at the Danieli, but we didn't need much, after all."

"After all, we had each other."

She stared at him with anxious hope. "You remembered."

He touched her lips, his forefinger following their soft outline. It was a tender touch. "Maybe, Sweetheart. Or maybe I was just remembering how it ought to have been." To brighten her lowered spirits he said briskly, "Now, where do you suppose that ghost is? Probably the corner where he was buried."

He strolled across the room to the corner which was plastered up as if it really did hide a body. He felt around the wall.

"No secret passages. No hollow sounds. I wonder if the McCandlesses are having any better luck with their secret passage."

"The name is McAllister. Don't be cute. And the secret passage was sealed up a long time ago. Shall I call Myrtle and ask them to cocktails?"

"Myrtle, I take it, refers to our esteemed minister's wife. Oh well, let's get it over with." Just as she reached for the phone on the night stand he added, "I hope we didn't have this much trouble finding time alone on our honeymoon."

She made a face at him and then asked for the Syn Room.

The gush of words started the minute Jacqueline introduced herself. Mrs. McAllister had thought it the most extraordinary coincidence that here "in the boondocks of England," as she said, "We run into you, dear. And with a new husband. How perfectly romantic! Honeymooning again, of course."

"No. Same husband. Second honeymoon."

Across the room she could feel Conor looking at her; so she tried to explain hurriedly but Myrtle beat her to the punch.

"Jacqueline! I thought the poor man was drowned while you were – Well, where did I get that idea? George, didn't Angela Godart tell us that when we met her at Marbella? George, for heaven's sake, I'm talking to you!" Into the phone she complained, "Honestly, George would forget his own name if I wasn't around to remind him."

Jacqueline jumped in. "That's a coincidence. Because it's just what happened to my Richard. He lost his memory. Yes. Isn't it weird? He hit his head at the time of the accident and just . . . went home when he recovered. We only found each other recently."

Myrtle gasped. "I've never heard anything so romantic. I hope it wasn't like Enoch Arden in the poem, marrying somebody else and all that."

"It was Enoch Arden's wife who got married, and I can promise you, I didn't. It was always Richard for me."

"Well, if that isn't the – George, let me tell you the most fantastic –"

"How about cocktails in our haunted room?"

"Love it, dear. Wouldn't you, George? He's delighted. You are delighted, George? Yes. He just nodded. What time? Sixish?"

"Fine. You know where to find us?"

"Heavens, yes. We stayed there last year. George adored it. Sat up half the night hoping to catch a glimpse of the ghost. Well, you were certainly up and down all night, George. All right, Jacqui. Expect us at six. We can't wait to see that Man Returned From the Dead. 'Bye, dear. And say goodbye to that handsome Enoch Arden of yours."

"Great," Conor said when Jacqueline had replaced the phone.

Jacqueline was beginning to regret the call.

"You know, I'd forgotten how boring that woman is. Still, she means well, and she was terribly good to us. Besides, she may help you remember things."

He remained stubborn in his refusal to allow for a possible breakthrough of his memory. "But just on the offchance that I'm not your Richard, can you give me a few more pointers on the famous wedding? Did anything else happen that day?"

She tried to be casual. "Yes. You paid your fond respects to your old girlfriend."

That startled and amused him. "How typical of me! What was her name? Is she worth looking up?"

"Don't be funny. Her name was Babette Cuneo. Your landlady's daughter."

"You mean I didn't live with you?"

"Certainly not. You aren't a gigolo."

"Thanks. It's nice to have your word for it. Though, of course, you could easily afford me. My rates are modest."

If he meant to provoke her, he failed. This was her old, teasing Richard. "I know. We went halves on everything."

He shifted his gaze to the ceiling.

"I see that marrying you was the smartest thing I ever did. Out goes my easel. Out goes my sketch pad. The hell with my oils, and my watercolors. Although I never was very good with oils, now I come to think of it. But my wife is rich. Come here."

However, even love would only get her so far. "You come here. That corner is where the body was buried four hundred years ago, or whenever. I'm not going near it."

He reached for her. She made a pretense of resisting. The excitement of the surrender was all the sweeter. When they acted out their charade of a tussle all the hours of their honeymoon came back to her.

She found herself locked tightly against his body. One of his hands cupped the back of her head and forced her to stare up into his eyes. He looked subtly different, more intense than he had been in Venice. Now, instead of kissing her as she ardently expected, he demanded harshly,

"Do you love me? Say it. You love *me*."

What a question! "Of course, I love you. There isn't a single hour, not a minute, when I don't love you, darling. Now, you say it."

Her neck ached where he held her head captive and he bent his head only a little to take possession of her mouth, this time fiercely smothering her with his kiss while his fingers worked their magic through the cloud of her dark hair.

When he released her she staggered. He caught her with one hand, grinning at her condition.

"Does that answer your question."

"I didn't say choke me to death," but she laughed and recovered her breath. "Who've you been practicing with? Or are you the type that doesn't kiss and tell?"

"That's me. Don Juan Conor. Shall we order up some liquor and stuff? I suppose this place has the usual weird pub hours."

It was all wonderfully domestic, the way she had pictured her future life with Richard when she married him.

"Great. And don't forget. When you order Scotch just ask for whisky. They have only a nodding acquaintance with Bourbon and Rye. Dr. McAllister may drink a little wine. Try a wine spritzer. Also tonic water, just to be safe. Champagne for Myrtle." She thought about it. She was in a champagne mood. "Me, too. And you're going to make us all sick with that sweet Campari."

"Not me. Those were my salad days, when I thought all painters stuck to French and Italian stuff. I was discouraged early when I tried to order Absinthe at my first Paris bar. No. I'll make mine Scotch. Sorry. I mean whisky."

He was about to pick up the phone and order when he put in a postscript. "If we keep ordering champagne, I'm going to have to take you up on that gigolo business. Split the bill down the middle." As she started to speak, he cut her off. "Only kidding. Don't get cute."

He took up the phone, eventually got the bar and put in his order. He added, "Better send up the usual stuff that goes with cocktails."

She watched him behave like a husband again, giving her the delicious feeling that she was no longer absolutely alone in her private world. She thanked God that she hadn't given up on Richard and let his brief but all-important place in her life be filled by someone else.

When the McAllisters arrived Jacqueline was prepared for difficulties from the officious and all-seeing Myrtle who would be sure to think Jacqueline's husband had changed a lot in these months. Then Dev might have to make up some plausible story. The McAllisters would hardly believe the truth. Whatever that was.

One consolation. Although it was now possible that Richard Kimberly had been a false name, the secret problem he had formerly carried around with him seemed to have been solved. Today, he wasn't afraid of pursuit, or of strangers in the lobby of her hotel. Some day he would tell her. But she was afraid to rock the boat now. His acceptance of her was too recent. Even today she was afraid to call him by the name she had known so briefly and loved so long.

A few pounds heavier, and tinting her hair a lighter shade, Myrtle McAllister plunged into the Elizabethan Room like a windjammer with all sails set.

Dr. McAllister was a bit more careworn, but then, he spent much of his time repairing any damage left in the wake of Myrtle's determined voyage through life.

Today, however, it was the good minister who made waves.

Myrtle leaped into Jacqueline's arms with the glad tidings. "My dear, you've never looked better. You absolutely radiate happiness. So different from the

World Hunger Drive last winter in Chicago when, frankly, you looked like death warmed over."

"Thank you, Myrtle. You are as subtle as ever."

In spite of her husband's throat-clearings, Myrtle shook a finger at her hostess. "Now, don't deny it. You were miserably unhappy. And all the time –" She jabbed Conor in the ribs. "– you sly dog, you were alive and well and pretending to have amnesia."

No one paid much attention to Dr. McAllister's plaintive "Really, my dear."

Mrs. McAllister's large, prominent eyes opened wider as she looked over the resurrected Conor.

"Alive and well indeed. Our Enoch Arden looks handsomer than ever. Maturity does that. Or maybe amnesia agrees with him; doesn't it, George? George?"

Dr. McAllister had been shaking hands with Jacqueline.

"Very true, dear." He turned his full attention to Conor, offering his hand and then studying him with an interest that made Jacqueline nervous, though Conor seemed amused by all this attention. "So this is our famous Enoch Arden. Your face looks familiar. I mean, since Venice. Haven't we run across each other somewhere?"

"George, good heavens! You married them."

"No. I mean in the States. No matter. Well, sir, you and our Jacqueline have had quite a sad aventure. But Divine Providence has intervened to give you a happy ending."

Conor agreed. A certain grim note in his voice troubled Jacqueline. "In many ways, I consider myself a lucky man. I didn't think so three years ago, I can tell you."

What on earth did he mean by that, Jacqueline wondered. If he had really had amnesia after the accident, why would he have been so unlucky or unhappy? He wouldn't have known what he had lost, surely.

"Oh, yes, do tell," Myrtle begged as she pulled a chair nearer the collapsible table with its miniature sandwiches, its patés, crackers, salmon paste, an ice bucket and an assortment of bottles. She began to make a daisy pattern on her plate with samples of all the hors d'oeuvres.

Busily taking orders for the drinks, Conor ignored her remark. Dr. McAllister stuck to Quinine Water. The two women voted for champagne, in between Myrtle's insistence that Conor tell the story of his amnesia.

The subject abruptly changed when the champagne cork shot out to the casement window and only Conor's quick action with the towel kept the rest of the champagne from showering Myrtle.

Jacqueline was sure he had caused the confusion deliberately. If so, he had succeeded in his purpose and the subject was changed.

Dr. McAllister gallantly proposed a toast to "the long, happy marriage of Jacqueline and – and –"

"Devlin," he put in casually, ignoring Jacqueline's stare.

Myrtle said at once, "Of course, George. Jacqueline and Devlin. You remember."

"Sorry." Dr. McAllister sipped his tonic water. "I seem to recall another name. Strange. I wonder where I got that idea. Well, no matter. Enjoying England?"

"Very much," Conor said. "My mother was born here. Near a town called Banbury."

"Banbury." Myrtle turned to her husband, sprinkling champagne over the remaining hors d'oeuvres in the tray. "We've been there. They invented Hot Cross Buns."

Her husband said patiently, "I don't think so, dear. Tell me, you two, what are your plans now? Not a second honeymoon in Venice, I hope."

"Why not?" Conor asked, to Jacqueline's surprise. "To finish what we began."

The startled minister said, "I beg your pardon?"

"To pick up the pieces we lost at the time of the accident. And we hope to wipe out the years we lost."

Jacqueline reached out and touched his knuckles where the thread of a scar was faintly visible from their adventure on the street a few nights before. He smiled and kissed her fingers, to Myrtle McAllister's delight.

"Did you see that, George? How often have you kissed my hand?"

"My dear, I promise faithfully to do so, next time we have been apart for three years."

Everyone laughed, including his wife, after a slight delay to analyze the remark.

Dr. McAllister apologized belatedly for his behavior at the wedding. "Allergies are one of Job's Torments. My sneezes were appalling. But I will say, my wife did a bangup job of decorating the salon; don't you think?"

"Lovely." Jacqueline glanced at Conor. "We thought the flowers were exceedingly romantic, and I love the hotel. My father and my grandmother always stayed there, but Mother had different ideas. Didn't we love the decorations, darling?"

Conor poured more champagne into the glass Mrs. McAllister extended. "Absolutely. There's nothing like the Danieli for the real feeling, tradition and all. The look of Renaissance Venice. The others have their points, but you're right. The Danieli is probably tops."

Myrtle frowned and Jacqueline started to speak hurriedly but it was Dr. McAllister who explained the problem to Conor.

"Afraid you've got it a little mixed up, my boy. You were married at the Gritti Palace, Ernest Hemingway's favorite. And I am sure my good wife is about to remind you that the Gritti is as good as the Danieli, any day." He chuckled. "But we forgive you. After all, you do have an excuse. The memory lapse."

Conor looked at Jacqueline. His eyebrows went up but he didn't seem too sorry for his embarrassing mistake. He had failed to praise the right hotel, where the McAllisters had worked so hard to give them a romantic wedding.

Unfortunately, he also gave Myrtle a chance to satisfy her insatiable curiosity.

"Naturally, you don't remember where you were married. Stands to reason. Your amnesia. Does it still bother you? How does it feel? Like great blanks in your mind, I guess. Imagine living three years and not knowing who you are or where you live, or anything."

"It wasn't quite that bad," Conor said, somewhat to Jacqueline's disappointment.

But things got worse.

"You see, I had amnesia when I met Jacqueline. Came about after a fall I had. I was trying to scale Mt. Whitney. Stupid business. I didn't really know the terrain. I had some idea of sketching a group of climbers. Anyway, I don't remember anything until I woke up months later in a hospital in –" He shook the whisky in his glass and swallowed the dregs. "Let's see. It was that town with the walls. Historical. Yugoslavia."

Myrtle cried, "Horrors!"

Dr. McAllister said, "Dubrovnic, probably. And then?"

"I'd been picked up by the crew of the tanker that rammed us. They said nothing to the Venetian authorities. I imagine they didn't want to wait around for investigations. Anyway, I'd completely blocked out memories between Mt. Whitney and Yugoslavia. Couldn't imagine how I got there. So I did the logical thing. I took the first flight home. To Los Angeles."

Mrs. McAllister's romantic dreams were shattered. "It isn't the way I pictured it, at all. I must say, you seemed perfectly normal when we met you in Venice."

Jacqueline felt desolated by his absurd story. It shut her out completely. Suppose, in some ghastly way, it was true. But she managed to add her cheerful explanation.

"You see? He never remembered anything between his two accidents. How he got to Venice, or what he was doing there, or anything. Isn't that ridiculous?"

"But typical of me, you've got to admit." He smiled at Jacqueline. She couldn't bring herself to reply.

Dr. McAllister, however, took the story at face value. "And three years later you found Jacqueline and your memory came back. I've heard of such cases."

"Oh, no. I didn't know her from Adam. Make that Eve. It was Jacqui who recognized me. I'm still trying to piece the whole story together."

Mrs. McAllister sighed deeply. "I must say, I hope George never forgets me like that."

The minister's voice was dry. "Highly unlikely, my dear. And now, I do think we must be on our way. Dr. and Mrs. Pervis will be waiting for us at the Sussex Inn. Charming pair. He is a Presbyterian, but eminently respectable and quite an authority on these old English relics."

Myrtle bustled around, looking for her purse and her fox-jacket. "Good night! I'd completely forgotten. My dear children, no matter what went before, you did get together at last. And that's romantic. Say what you will. Hold it a minute, George. Kevin, or do I mean Devin, may I have a teensy bit more of that bubbly? One for the road, as they say?"

Dr. McAllister cleared his throat, but the message did not reach his wife. She watched carefully as Conor poured three-quarters of a glassful of champagne. She drank it down with impressive ease before joining her husband on his way to the door.

Conor hurried to open the door for them while Jacqueline embraced Myrtle.

Dr. McAllister was the last to shake hands with Conor. He turned to go, stopped, cocked his head on one side and said,

"I know I've seen your picture somewhere. Out west, it was. We flew out to visit our daughter in, of all places, Las Vegas. Strange place. However, that is neither here nor there. But about your picture, I couldn't have seen it in a newspaper there; could I?"

"I hardly think so."

"He's probably being modest," Myrtle put in. "Come along, George. If you don't stop these silly questions, Jacqueline is liable to think you're tiddly. He means well, my dear, but he is so curious about everyone. Next, he'll be saying Kevin's picture is in the local post office. Bye-bye, dears. Have a nice second honeymoon."

A minute later Conor bolted the door behind the McAllisters. "Thank God for the Presbyterian. I don't envy him."

Jacqueline scarcely heard him. She was thinking bitterly that, judging by Conor's story, he didn't even know for sure he'd had a first honeymoon.

Seventeen

Conor rubbed his hands together. He seemed in excellent spirits. "So that's over, thank God! What a pest that fellow is!"

She shook off her depression and tried to play up to to his mood. "Dr. McAllister? I would have thought Myrtle annoyed you."

"Oh, she's all right. You forget. We penniless artists get in the habit of catering to women like her. They aren't too bright but they mean well. They are a little like clay. They mould well. His kind are rigid, like stone. I was never a stonemason. Do you want any of this stuff? Shall we have it taken away?"

She eyed what remained of the sandwiches and crackers that Myrtle hadn't eaten. She smiled.

"She has quite an appetite. I'm surprised she hasn't gained more weight." She hesitated, fingered a cracker and asked in most casual voice she could muster, "Did she look much changed to you?"

He offered her a salmon paste finger-sandwich which she refused. Then he said, "Not much. A little older.

But aren't we all? Shall we eat in the restaurant, or is there another good place? And don't say The Sussex Inn, for God's sake!"

She made an attempt to smile. It was only half-hearted.

How do I begin? she asked herself. How can I explain my real feelings, that his story may or may not be true, but it was the telling of it that hurt me so much. The way he referred so coolly to our lost days of happiness? Did he have no tender memories of them at all?

Worst of all, she couldn't forget his emphatic, hurtful remark that he didn't think he was lucky in their Venice days. He didn't remember the loss of their relationship or indeed, their relationship at all. So this bad luck he hinted at must be his fall on the slopes of Mt. Whitney. She could understand that, but surely, the events that occurred in Venice had brought him some happiness in retrospect, when he was reminded of their brief but passionate relationship.

It was almost as if he dreaded his life as Richard Kimberly, a life he claimed not to remember.

She said, "I'm not awfully hungry. Too much champagne maybe." She was still fingering her first glass which was half full.

He had been gathering the bottles together. He kept on with his job, placing everything on the littered tray, but his attention had been caught by her manner more than her words. In spite of her doubts and fears she felt the warmth in his eyes, his genuine concern.

She cheered up a little and tried to be flippant. "You do that very well. You may have a whole new career before you."

"My professional touch. I've been a waiter, among other things."

"Really?" She didn't know why it surprised her, except that in the old days he never talked about his past.

"My dear Miss Godart Industries, how do you think artists survive? They aren't all Van Goghs. Besides, I've got only two ears and I hope to keep them both. For a while, anyway."

He dropped the empty tonic bottle and moved toward her, frowning. "Are you all right, Sweetheart?"

"Right as a trivet. Whatever that means?"

With the tip of his forefinger he tilted her chin up, looked into her eyes. "Then, where's the sparkle you have when we talk about the old days? Were they so much better than today?"

She wondered if he could possibly be jealous of those Venice days that he couldn't remember. It seemed reasonable, and it explained so much. She wanted to believe this was the answer.

"No, darling. It just hurts to relive all that horror with people like the McAllisters."

"Do you want me to drive you back to London tonight? Sweetheart, I only seduce willing beauties. No caveman tactics. Can't help it. Just the plain old Take-It-Or-Leave-It type, I guess. What do you say?"

She loved his quirky little smile that seemed half-sad, a kind of questioning beyond words. He had succeeded in changing her mood.

"Seduce me, darling. I came all prepared. Look into my case there on the bed."

"Your purse?"

"Yes. Only it's more than a purse."

He took up the case, found the lock and pressed it. He laughed when he saw what was inside.

"Preparedness, Verily thy name is woman." Then another thought occurred to him and he dropped the case as if it had scorched him. "Do you use this often?"

"Of course." She saw that he was taking this a little too seriously and added, "But only when I am alone. By the way, I really am getting hungry. Do seducers include supper in their itineraries?"

He took a deep breath, laughed and agreed. "Best in town. Within limits. At least, I've got the training if we have to wash dishes afterward."

"Fair enough. You can wash. I'll dry."

Ten minutes later, arm in arm, they left the Elizabethan Chamber and went downstairs only to find that there would be an hour's wait for a table in the popular restaurant.

They looked at each other. Both started to speak. He said, "I think they are trying to tell us something."

She said, "Do you know, that tray of hors d'oeuvres is getting more appetizing every minute."

"A shame to waste it."

"And the extra bottles of champagne. And the Scotch."

"You mean whisky," he reminded her.

"Quick. Before they clear it all away."

With the head waiter staring after them, superior but puzzled, they hurried through the ancient hall, back to the staircase, and on up to their room, taking the last few steps two at a time.

Inside the Elizabethan Chamber, with the door bolted behind them, they both leaned against the door, still laughing. Conor got out the words.

"My God, I love your laugh! But you are a witch. No getting around it."

"Me? Witch? Why, for heaven's sake?"

He turned his head to look at he· as if she had bewitched him again. The bright light in his eyes gave her an exciting sense of power over him. Or even, she thought, it just might warn her of his power over her.

"Because I meant to despise you and I couldn't help myself. I fell for you the very first time I caught you there, impudent as the devil. Proud, too."

"I remember. In that funny little shop in the Merceria."

He stared at her while she might have counted to ten. Then he blinked and she guessed that the peculiar fire – a kind of love-hate – had burned out. The tenderness was back, and the humor, the joy of life.

"Let's say, the first time I remember seeing you. That day when I caught you trying to rob me. On Richmond Hill."

She played along with his mood. Half a loaf was a lot better than none.

"O.K. I don't care when it started. Just don't let it stop."

They left the door and started across the room. They were thinking about the great Elizabethan bed, but after more than three years she was a little shy of him. She didn't want to behave like a virginal child, but still –

She reached for her deserted champagne glass, took a big swallow. "What is more exciting than flat, warm champagne?" she asked brightly.

He had taken off his jacket and hung it over a chair. He was amused at her comment but he didn't seem the least disappointed. Maybe he didn't want her to be a sexy sophisticate in bed. Now that she thought of it, he never had wanted her to demonstrate any wild sex fantasies, even a few small liberties with his body.

No danger of that. In the time since Venice her sexual experience had been limited to dreams.

Whatever his private thoughts, he understood her present dilemma and took a new bottle out of the ice bucket. The champagne was still nicely chilled, though the ice had seen better times. He surprised her by pouring himself a glass after giving her a new one generously filled.

He touched the rim of her glass with his. "Here's to us, sweetheart. May this honeymoon last a lifetime."

"I'll buy that." She felt the tickle of the bubbles and drank again in a sudden glow of happiness that was only partially due to the wine.

He was apparently affected the same way. With her glass between them, he leaned over it and kissed her lips. "That tastes good. I think I prefer my champagne this way."

Her glass was empty in a surprisingly short time. He took it from her fingers. "More?"

"Later."

He set his glass down saying, "Let's do this right. Imagine we're in an old movie." He pretended to be worried. "You do like romantic old movies?"

"The more romantic the better."

"Well, you asked for it."

She didn't quite know what to expect but was ready for anything. With what she considered wonderful agility, not to mention strength, he cupped one arm under her knees and the other around her shoulders, sweeping her deftly into his arms. She was so close to his cheek she brushed it with her lips.

"Just like the old movies," she murmured huskily.

His eyes looked into hers the way she had dreamed it would be for so many nights. On their first honeymoon they had barely gotten started on this easy, titillating game of love. Now, they could look forward to the glorious future they had missed before.

She expected to be dropped on the bed with its many layers of mattress but he laid her down gently, hovering over her and then running his hands over her throat. He slid her blouse off her shoulders and pressed his lips warmly, sensuously, on the bared flesh.

She turned, touched his rough, lean fingers with her own lips and raised her hands to caress him. When she had tried to initiate sexual advances with him years ago he hadn't reacted as she hoped. His masculine pride seemed to be affronted. Now, maturity, and perhaps his amnesiac status had made him appreciate her own feelings.

She sensed his quick reaction as she began to free him from the constriction of his belt and shirt. Her attentions aroused him as he excited her. She whispered, "Who needs champagne?"

"Depends." His mouth covered hers. She clung to him. When the flesh of their bodies joined hotly, she told herself in her happiness that the last doubts were gone. Now he must remember the other time. How could he help it? His driving force within her might be gentler, more deliberate and careful, even more skilled, than on their first honeymoon, but the act itself would bring him vivid memories of Torcello.

The first tremors of excitement faded into a light euphoria. He lay back beside her with only the flesh of their arms and hips touching; yet, the throb of remembered passion kept them joined.

Eventually, the evening wore on. They hadn't turned on the lamps. A maid knocked at the door, wanting to turn down the bed, and was asked to return. In the meanwhile, Jacqueline and Conor rustled around, buttoning up, zipping up, and laughing. It was Jacqueline who brought the obvious reminder,

"After all, it isn't as if we're doing something criminal. We are legal, you know."

She was still laughing over their panic when the maid came back.

While the maid worked, the reunited lovers wandered around the big room in an awkward, nervous way, still under the pulsating influence of lovemaking. They had separated the minute the maid knocked and now Conor appeared so sombre Jacqueline wondered if he was reliving snatches of their Torcello nights for the first time since his amnesia.

He went to the casement window, opened it to look out at the starry night, then shut it when the maid shivered. Mid-autumn was here and the night air had a freezing edge. Jacqueline watched him with slowly rising anxiety.

What was he thinking about if not the past? He didn't look as happy as she felt . . . Had felt.

With the maid gone he relaxed. His pacing had brought him to the temporary bar, or what remained of it. He poured some more champagne and held it out to her. When she took it he picked up the tray. This looked as if a small army had run through it. He bowed to her considerable grace and inquired,

"Will Madame try these exquisite tidbits?"

Delighted to find him in a teasing humor again, she curtzied, spilling a few drops of wine.

"A pleasure, I'm sure, Monsieur. Ah! Fish paste. Just what I've dreamed of so often. And Scotch Egg. What a beauty!" She took up the strange loaf-slice of ground meat and hard-boiled egg and tried to eat it daintily. It was good to taste but impossible to eat dantily.

He laughed at her efforts and his odd, restless mood faded away. he poured himself champagne and fished among the debris to find a fresh, crisp cracker, finally located one and put it between her lips.

She bit down on it. The crumbs dropped over his shirt and she brushed them off, murmuring, "Sorry, Monsieur. I'll do better next time." She looked into his eyes and saw, for one terrible second, an expression that made her doubt. She saw an intensity that seemed to mirror painful thoughts.

She put on her light mood. "There will be a next time; won't there?"

"I hope so." She caught her breath and he added with sudden force, "Yes, of course, there will." He grinned and chucked her under the chin. "Don't mind me,

Sweetheart. I'm still knocked out. I don't make love to a goddess every day."

"You'd better not." She became lively, hoping her good spirits would rub off on him. She fussed around the debris on the tray. "I'm hungry, thirsty, too. Fill 'er up."

He filled her glass and when she had drunk the champagne she felt better. She was relieved to see him refilling his own glass.

Eventually, the champagne was gone and the hors d'oeuvres tray was nothing but crumbs.

Setting their glasses back in unison they looked at each other with the makeshift table between them. She was determined to restore their earlier gaiety, the wonderful camaraderie they had enjoyed during their long walk around town, in and out of shops, through the graveyard, and then home. It had been genuine; hadn't it?

"Much as I admire that Terribly Strange Bed," she began, "I think I need a little fresh air. What do you say we go up to the little shop with the china figures? Maybe it's still open."

"I doubt it." he glanced at his wristwatch, then looked at her, his expression softening. "Well, what if it isn't. Let's go."

"O.K. Give me ten minutes. I'll put on a new face."

He walked around the table, kissed her lips, and gave her the obvious line, "The old one is good enough for me."

She wrinkled her nose at him playfully, then swung her overnight case onto her arm and went off to the bathroom in great spirits. The truth was, she didn't want tonight to end. She still had the creepy feeling that when they returned to London it would all collapse somehow. He would go back to his life, whatever that was. She would resume hers, and the beauty of this interlude might become a memory for her, like Torcello.

In spite of the heavy, ancient timbering, she could hear voices very faintly. Not voices. A voice, now and then. With a mascara wand in hand she stopped, listened, wondering idly who was next door. When she was this close to the bathroom mirror the sound became a bit more audible and the mirror was near the door.

She glanced around the little room. The door into the Elizabethan Chamber was still ajar. The voice she heard occasionally was her husband's.

Puzzled, she moved to the door. He had the phone in his hand. He did a lot of listening. Then she heard his voice raised for the first time in the conversation. Impatient. Or angry.

"No. Not so far . . . Well, that's your – All right! But you've got to do better than you've been doing . . . I said 'All right.' And no more calls."

Shaking with nerves, she pressed her cheek against the mirror. Her confidence revived a little at the chilly contact.

This is ridiculous. It's something perfectly normal.

She pulled herself together, stood tall, as Grand-mama Berthe used to say, and rattled the doorknob as she walked out of the bathroom.

"Hi, darling. Do I look reasonably human?"

He had set down the phone. "Not human. Let's say: inhumanly beautiful."

She scoffed, "Idle flattery. But I love it. Were you on the phone?"

He said easily, "It was the restaurant. They've sent us our final warning. They are giving away our table. I told them to go fly a kite. Are you hungry?"

"After all Myrtle's leftovers? No, thanks. We've had our feast."

"Good. We're on our way." He tucked her arm in his and they started out. He pulled her close. "It's been pretty good; hasn't it?"

She hoped he was being funny. She played it in the same mood. "Yes. On the whole, pretty good."

"Better than before?"

She shuddered. It took several seconds to recover. Of course, it was better than before, because they were now more used to each other. But did he want to wipe out the most beautiful memory of her life? To make her exactly like him, with the dearest part of her life erased? He acted as if he was jealous of those days.

"I wouldn't go –" She coughed and started again. "I wouldn't go that far. Darling, would you, really?" His cruelty in bringing up such a comparison hurt as much as the words.

"I'd go a lot further to relive today. And tonight."

Was he actually disappointed in the vividness of her memory? Didn't he have any sensitivity? He knew what that early time meant to her. And then the miracle had happened. Like all her dreams and prayers. He had come back from the dead. It should have cancelled out the darkness of those first months after the accident.

Maybe she was pressing too hard and too soon.

"Slowly does it."

He was puzzled by her remark which she found herself murmuring aloud, but he only said, "Very profound. I think."

The hilly street with its picturesque but uncomfortable cobblestones was fairly deserted, though at this hour in London most of the fashionable supper clubs were just beginning to hum. Conor frowned.

"I thought there would be more lights. It is the main street, after all."

"Who cares? I doubt if we'll see muggers and serpentines of kids in this town. I love the brisk, cold air, right off the marshes and the Channel."

"We'll go to see your precious china ducks and whatnot, and then come back. Unless, of course, you'd rather saunter across the village green and wake the dead."

"Thanks a whole heap but I visit cemeteries only in daylight."

There were still lights on in the shop that sold locally made figurines, although the oldfashioned brass latch was fastened. They could see an elderly man and two young women inside the shop. One of the women was balanced somewhat precariously on a high wooden stool. She seemed to be calling down items from the top shelf.

"Inventory," Jacqueline whispered. "They're going to hate us for lousing up their count. I hope they hurry. I can feel that graveyard right behind us."

Conor rattled the latch. One of the girls grinned at them but the man looked around, shook his head and mouthed the word "closed."

When Conor persisted the man shrugged, nodded, and the younger woman unlocked the door.

"Most awf'lly sorry, Sir. But we are closed for the night. P'raps tomorrow?"

"We are leaving early. I wonder if my wife could buy one of the white geese over there. That is what you want, darling?"

At the endearment the two girls exchanged glances and looked wistfully at the man who was undoubtedly the owner. He dropped his lengthy sheet of figures on the counter and, stroking his mustache, came over to wait on them.

All the geese were delicately done, made by a local pottery, and Jacqueline chose the "domestic" about three inches tall, who looked as if he might take off any minute, clumsy body and all.

When they left the shop after many thanks all around, they were face to face with the cemetery which acted as the Village Green. Although Conor studied it curiously, Jacqueline avoided it after one glance. The moon was up, almost a full moon. It managed to cast the entire square in vivid contrasts of light and darkness. The lean, standing slabs of the tombstones marched across the green, making shadows like jail bars.

The square was not deserted. Two townspeople strolled on the diagonal path across the cemetery, and half a dozen others still had business on the street that bordered the square.

Jacqueline found that the graveyard, which captivated her in daylight with its historic associations, affected her differently by night. She wondered if she would always get these moods of depression, quick flashes of Richard – no – Dev – struggling in murky black waters.

"Let's go back to the inn," she suggested. "I'm ready now."

"Had enough fresh air?" He was looking around interestedly, into the shadowy corners of the little town. He acted as if he expected to see some sinister character following them.

"What on earth are you looking for?" she asked nervously.

"Getting on toward winter. I can feel it in the air."

They strolled back down the hill.

Ahead of them a small, elderly woman who had been walking her Yorkie picked up the dog, put him in a straw basket and threw what appeared to be a napkin over the suddenly quiet contents. With this on her arm she dissolved into the darkness of a path down to the street running parallel to Mermaid Street.

Jacqueline laughed and guessed, "Her landlady forbids pets."

Conor said nothing. He too had been looking down that crooked little path. Now he stopped, turned and gazed around. Nothing in sight. Curtains and shutters sealed in the comfortable warmth of household lights.

"They must really pull in the sidewalks here at eight o'clock," he said finally.

"I don't mind. I loved the walk; didn't you?"

"You know I did." He smiled at her but his thoughts were elsewhere. "It's just a question of your safety. What with your experiences recently . . . Ah, here we are. Home again."

She was surprised but touched by his attention to her safety. At least, he didn't believe she was going around taking over-doses of sleeping pills and what-not.

A party of four on their way out met them in the doorway. Everybody begged pardon and the group went out into the quiet street which soon rang with voices. Conor looked after them. Was he still concerned for her safety?

Jacqueline said nothing until they were in the Elizabethan Chamber with the door bolted. Then she faced what she considered a far more important matter than her own presumed danger.

He gave her an opening when he picked up her overnight case that had fallen under the edge of the bed hours ago when they made love. She opened it, looked in at the jumbled contents, and played it lightly.

"Wonder where we'll be and what we'll be doing this time tomorrow night."

She was conscious of his steady, serious look.

"What do you want to be doing? Be honest." He tried to match her light, easy tone. "I can take it, even if my memory isn't all you'd like it to be."

She thought this was an effort and she loved him for it.

"Darling, what a goon you are! Do you think I'd let you go out of my life again? Besides, we need your sketches for the spring campaign."

"That's another thing. Any job with Godart's is definitely out."

"What?"

"I straightened out your buddy, Chilton-Brown, when he called me this morning."

"Why did he call you? To offer you a job?"

"Probably to find out as much as he could about me. Not that there's much to tell. Anyway, I made it clear, I get my own jobs. No hassle. I do have a small following. Of sorts."

"Of course, you do. He had no right to question you."

"I don't mind that. He was just looking out for your interests. The thing is, they aren't mine. Your financial interests, I mean."

"But when, what are your plans?"

He kissed her. His fingers pressed hard into her shoulders. He silenced her effectively. Having done so, he laid out a plan that removed a good deal of her dread.

"It's going to be endlessly complicated if we announce that I've come back to life and my mind was a blank during our marriage. My idea is that we simply continue our relationship and say we intend to marry when we get around to it. Pretend I'm going to be your second husband. We'll know better. And what do we care about the others?"

"I don't like it. In fact, I hate it."

"Sweetheart," he reminded her, "We haven't got a hell of a lot of choices. Amnesia may work on TV and in old movies, but in real life you won't get anyone to believe it except the Myrtles of this world. Not over three years of amnesia."

What did he mean by that? It was the truth, after all.

She stood there opening and shutting the case, knowing he was right, yet crushed by the implication everyone would get, that Richard Kimberly had actually died many months ago, and there had been no miracle.

"But all the time I'd be the only one who knew my real husband was alive."

"Frankly, thank God I am alive. I certainly know it."

"Are we going to live together, like a normal husband and wife?"

He hesitated, then picked up that cheerful, upbeat spirit he had shown so far. "I wouldn't have it any other way. But that's for you to say. We may find it a bit awkward about household expenses, considering the difference in our lifestyles. But I can work it out. I hope."

"If we were merely lovers," she pointed out, "We'd be paying our own way. It's done all the time. If I want to go to dear old Grand Vefour in Paris, I invite you. If you want to go to –"

"Barney's Beanery?"

She grinned. "Barney's it is. But it's on you. Darling, we'll work it out."

"The thing is, will you be happy? Think about it." He was so earnest she hugged him. The arrangement was a whole lot better than going their separate ways, which had haunted her for the last few hours.

"Do we ever get married again, or just say we are?" she asked, trying to make it sound casual.

"Of course, we get married." He was in good spirits once more. "It would be highly unseemly if we didn't. At least, that's what our very proper Mr. Chilton-Brown would say. But that's up to you. If you still want me, even without the memories."

"I'll want you forever. No matter what the memories are."

Nevertheless, a lot of important decisions had been made today, and much had happened. They were both secretly sure when they got into the old Renaissance bed that they wouldn't make love again so soon. The tensions of the evening remained in spite of their assurances to each other of their happiness.

But propinquity is persuasive and, when they touched each other in the bed while saying their "good nights," the sensuous brushing of flesh on flesh was too much. With one accord they turned to each other, pulses beating heavily, and they made love.

It was even better than before. This was what marriage was all about. They became playfully active, teasing and exciting each other in all the erogenous areas that Jacqueline had only thought about in the long nights since Venice.

They slept almost at the same time.

Jacqueline slept soundly until about three a.m. For years she had not been used to sharing her bed, and she awoke to find she had curled into a fetal position on her side of the huge bed.

It was cold in the night but not entirely dark. Somewhere outside the back window a light from the street that climbed the flank of the hill cast a little streak of light through the room.

"Our haunted room," she thought, only half awake. "Ours. Richard's and mine. But I must call him Devlin. I'll get used to it. . . . Imagine living in this cold, huge room all the time, like our ancestors did. Surrounded by all this heavy, shadowy furniture . . . I wonder what the poor ghost did in order to get walled up over there in the corner . . ."

She looked across the far end of the room where the body had once been sealed up. (Had he been sealed up alive?)

The darkness seemed to take shape as she stared. She told herself, "Imagination is an awful thing sometimes." Out of the dark, against the contrast of the lighter wall, Richard's slim, slightly raffish figure seemed to form. He turned then, to face her.

Her imagination saw him as he must have looked during those last few seconds, dripping with the slime of that oily water, his face pale as death, his eyes so desperate. He held out his arms to her.

A dream . . . More real than the others . . . so achingly real.

She screamed.

Conor crossed the room in quick strides.

"Sweetheart, it's me. I didn't mean to startle you. I just couldn't sleep. I got to thinking. Never start thinking in the middle of the night. My poor darling, I'm sorry."

He took her in his arms, holding her against him, trying to comfort her with his warmth and his strength, and above all, his reality. No drowning phantom here.

Why had she thought he was dead?

But though she clung to him as though he were that Yugoslavian life-preserver long ago, it took her a while to stop shaking.

"You're alive. You didn't die. Promise me."

"I'm alive, Sweetheart." With his chin resting on the crown of her head he stared at the corner where the luckless Elizabethan had been walled up. He broke the spell deliberately with his teasing reminder, "Don't I feel alive? I love you, Sweetheart. Did I ever tell you that?"

"I could hear it forever." She stirred around until she could brush his bare throat with a feathery kiss. "I adore you. I'll adore you as long as I live. Do you want to know why?"

"Why?"

"Because I can touch you and squeeze you, and especially, I can feel you."

He wrinkled his nose at this dubious compliment.

"Well, you can feel me, all right. I'm right here. Now, you're going to go to sleep again and nothing can hurt you. I've got you safe."

Eighteen

In spite of their interrupted sleep they got up early and after drinking the hot, strong tea left on a tray at their door, they prepared for the trip back to London. During those first few minutes of the morning there was a camaraderie, a certain amount of joking, teasing, teacups raised to each other in a toast, and Jacqueline's slow survey of the room with its many spots which reminded her of their happiness yesterday. All but that one awful moment in the night. And that was nothing but another crazy nightmare. She would soon be done with them. Richard was here beside her. Why should he haunt her dreams as if he returned from the dead to accuse her of betraying him? *He was here*.

Conor was happy watching her, smiling when she mentioned something that had happened in this or that spot, especially the laughable memories of Myrtle and Dr. McAllister. Then he began to talk about new assignments ahead, work he was anxious to start on.

"That general's widow, Viola Sears, suggested to the Venetian Committee that I do the sketches of the palazzos in their book on past glories. Going to be big stuff, I'll have you know. Too expensive for people like me to buy. All for sweet charity. I wonder how you'd feel, returning to Venice, just long enough for me to complete the job."

Her immediate reaction was shock. For three years she had avoided Venice, sometimes walked away when people mentioned it. She was torn by conflicting emotions over the possibility of returning with her husband. If the sight of those places, both beautiful and agonizing, brought back Dev's memory of the "Richard" days it would be blessedly worth it.

But what if some fate was drawing him back to a repetition of the other horror, a horror he was not meant to escape? She couldn't remember when she had first heard the old fable about "Samarkand" but it leaped to her mind now.

"Darling," she began, "Did you ever read a little fable from the Arabian Nights or somewhere, about Samarkand and predestination?"

He zipped up his old flight bag thoughtfully. Then he brightened. "You mean 'Appointment in Samarra'?"

"That's it. Samarra. A traveller sees Death on a road and Death gives him a threatening look. So the traveller runs the other way, toward Samarra."

He nodded. "I remember. Another man asks Death why he made the threatening gesture and Death denies it. Death says –"

"'It wasn't a threat. I was only surprised to see him on that road. Because I have an appointment with him in Samarra.'" She shuddered. "Dear God! I've always been haunted by that."

He set the bag down and came over to her, looking into her eyes with that half-humorous, half-reassuring gaze she was learning to love all over again.

"Jacqueline, this is real life, not the Arabian Nights. And I swear to you on a stack of Bibles that I will positively, absolutely, never go to Samarra. Frankly, I don't even know where it is."

She tried to laugh. "It was dumb of me. I seem to be scared of my own shadow these days. You see, I just got you back and I don't want to lose you."

"If it comes to that, I don't want to lose you, sweetheart. But I learned something a long time ago. When I was a kid and fell off a horse, I made up my mind to get right up there in the saddle. Otherwise, I might never have had the nerve to ride again. If there's a curse on that beautiful Venice, we have to take off the curse. Thumb our noses at it. Don't you agree?"

"Sure." She felt that his brusque common sense was like an infusion of courage. She would make herself face Venice. Even Torcello. But no speedboats. And especially, no drunken pilots on the canals or the lagoon.

They looked around once more from the doorway, arm in arm. He was the first to speak.

"It was a nice honeymoon of sorts; wasn't it?"

"Lovely. Perfect."

"As nice as the first one?"

She was startled but said hurriedly, "Darling, you know the answer to that. Couldn't you tell?"

He shifted their bags to his other hand while he took the key out of the door, and he had already changed the subject when they started along the hall.

"They keep the place up remarkably well without destroying the – whatever it is."

"The ambiance?"

"A two-bit word. I was going to say – the atmosphere."

How stupid of me, she reminded herself. Richard had been just as proud three years ago. She would have to be careful when she hinted about the small details that would make him the same man she had loved in Venice.

On the way back to London she was surprised to find out how much importance he attached to the Venice job. He discussed it from different perspectives, and seemed convinced that Venice was the answer to "everything," whatever that meant.

They had a brief argument about where they would both spend the night. From his occasional mention of familiar hotels she knew he was no stranger to luxury establishments; so his objection to joining her at the Savoy was based on the appearance it would present to the world, especially Jacqueline's family and the Godart officers.

"But that's silly. Dad and his precious contessa are headed for Venice. She is opening her palazzo for that Venice Preservation Antiquities thing. The one they want you for. We can't very well live in too small a place, once they recognize you."

"Suppose they don't recognize me. I thought we had all that worked out."

"To other people, yes. Outsiders. But naturally, sooner or later the folks will realize the truth, in spite of all your changes in the last few years."

"Am I so changed?" Her hesitation and the way she looked at him with a baffled expression made him ask, "How? Tell me. I'm curious."

"Not inside." She pinched his wrist playfully. "Inside, you're just the way I always remembered you."

"But?"

"On the outside, it's just that I used to imagine you smaller. I knew you were tall and slim –"

"Lean."

She laughed. "No. Not lean. It sounds like a pork chop. Anyway, you look older, but so do I. And I didn't remember that scar on your nose. How did it happen?"

With his free hand he rubbed the bridge of his nose. "That? Just a little dispute with a palamino. He wanted to go west and I wanted to go south. So he went west and I ended up against an oak tree. Old Kim was mighty sorry. He came back and almost tongued me to death."

"I'm glad he came back. You spent a lot of time out of doors; didn't you? It doesn't sound at all like the Los Angeles my father knows. Was this in Boise?"

He glanced at the rear-view mirror, then answered her with some amusement.

"Surprisingly enough, nobody I knew ever rode into Boise on horseback. The state has riding country, but Boise is a city. No. I'm talking about desert country. Fertile valleys, dry washes, and just plain desert. Except at sunset. Nothing plain about a desert sunset."

Was he being evasive, as he had been in Venice? Where was this riding country? Why hide it?

Nevertheless, she was enthusiastic. "It's nice to have you so normal about your life. You don't mind talking about your past, things you like and don't like." Within limits, she thought.

"Why shouldn't I?"

"I don't know. But when we were first married you were awfully vague. Hard to pin down. I thought you might be in trouble with the – Well, in trouble."

"I'm not surprised." He was grim. After a little pause, guessing her surprise, he made good sense. "I didn't know my past. Seems reasonable. Considering."

Without taking his eyes off the rearview mirror, he reached for her, pulled her closer. She responded warmly and they drove on, into the late morning traffic between the suburbs and London.

At the Savoy Hotel he surrendered his rented car and started up to Jacqueline's suite with her.

"I'll get you settled and then hike out to Richmond on their precious Underground."

"Richmond. Oh, no!"

"Work, Sweetheart. I'll be with you tonight. I just want to work on the calendar I'm doing for a cat commercial. It's to be a giveaway with coupons. May not be art with a capital 'A' but it pays my rent."

She said loyally, "I think it's awfully clever of you. Making money out of your own paintbrush."

When they turned a corner in the hall they found Nigel lounging in front of her door, arms folded, and looking as bored as he must feel. Jacqueline was a good deal surprised and beginning to be annoyed, especially since he acted as if his long wait was their fault.

He said, "I rather thought I'd spare you another ten minutes before I gave up."

"Sorry, Nigel." She presented her cheek for his kiss while she gave him the big news. "We're getting married. Eventually, Now, please don't give me all the sensible reasons why we shouldn't."

"Quite. matter of fact, if I said 'Isn't it about time you made a new life?', I'm sure you would take offense."

"I certainly would." She might have gone on but Conor put a hand on her shoulder and she calmed down. "All right. So long as you don't put a spoke in the works."

He gave Conor a quick glance, then said, "You have nothing to worry about from me. Your parents may be upset, but at your age you hardly have to answer to them." He reached around to shake hands with Conor. "I guess you know you have a great deal to live up to, Conor. Mrs. Kimberly has enshrined her late husband, and everyone will consider you an interloper."

"That doesn't come under the heading of news, believe me." She had expected he would laugh at Nigel's warning in the circumstances, and it always hurt a little when he spoke so coldly about his Venice days.

Nigel said, "You have changed somewhat. But you must have been told that."

"Have I! If you'll excuse me, both of you, I'll be on my way. I have some work waiting for me at Richmond."

Before Jacqueline could say anything Nigel cut in sharply, "You are staying with Jacqueline? I mean, isn't that your plan?"

Jacqueline could hardly believe her ears. This from staid and proper Nigel Chilton-Brown. Then she remembered that Nigel obviously knew all about Dev's true identity, the only person who did.

"Certainly I'll be back." Conor embraced Jacqueline. She started to ask him if he simply must go at once, but he strode over to the elevator, leaving Nigel to inform Jacqueline, "Not a bad chap. I've checked him out. Seems to be genuinely in love with you."

"Why not? He always was. We've got a lot of lost time to make up for." She unlocked the door and Nigel followed her in. She would rather he hadn't. She wanted to relive in her mind all the tender and yet exciting moments she and Richard/Devlin had known, both in Venice and during the last few days.

"Then you agree that Devin is my husband?"

"More or less."

"You do know about his amnesia and why he didn't remember me?"

"Certainly. Certainly. Went into it all on the phone yesterday." He added, "You're looking happy, Jacqueline. That chap is good for you." And then he spoiled it. "No more pills and over-sleeping?"

"Oversleeping, my clavicle! I don't know what happened, but I give you my word, if it ever happens to me again, I'm going to have my capsules analyzed."

He looked surprised but then agreed. "Excellent. I know just the man to do it. He's a chemist. Old acquaintance."

"Thank you. But frankly, I'd almost rather think it was too many pills. Or something."

He seemed to understand that she didn't want to think someone had given her the capsules deliberately. At least, he was beginning to admit that she hadn't consciously taken an overdose. She wondered if he would investigate the matter. If not, then she must.

On the other hand, it was quite possible she had only overslept, after all.

"And now comes my good news." He raised his eyebrows and rolled his eyes like a man who doesn't expect to be believed.

"I'm almost afraid to ask," she joked.

"London is getting some new visitors. Esther Heffernan cabled me that she has been brought along to London to take dictation from the contessa. Dictation about Godart products."

"What? I thought they were on their way to Venice for the Season."

"All in good time. But you miss the good part. Our Irina is worming her way – if you will pardon the expression – worming her way rapidly into the presidency of Godart's. I have someone who will throw a wrench into the monkeyworks, or whatever, but I thought it might be entertaining to see her work her way into a morass she can't dig herself out of. I happen to have a Swiss employee in my pocket who dealt with her formerly. Shall we persuade Marcel to see her for what she is? Not that I think there's much hope of a sudden, blinding revelation. Given his age and her beauty."

"Why not give her enough rope and see what happens? You say you have a witness. Get all the evidence together; so she can't possibly crawl out of it. Then, maybe Father will see through her. I wish there was some way we could avoid hurting him."

"Afraid that goes with the territory."

She went into the bedroom to wash and change, leaving the door open. "When does Father arrive?"

"Today."

She groaned. There went the precious time alone with Dev. However, it seemed a suitable occasion to introduce Dev into the family as her fiancé.

He guessed her problem. "It might be easier if we all accepted Conor as a different man. By his true name"

"Did you talk this over with Rich – with Dev?"

He looked guilty when she peered around the door and looked at him. That annoyed her. "It was mentioned in passing." He went on rapidly, persuasively. "Don't forget. This is the true man. The one you knew was amnesiac."

"He should have remembered me."

"But he didn't," Nigel reminded her. "And I think you will agree that one of those Return-From-the-Grave things would bring endless publicity."

"Bad for business. We mustn't have that."

"But very true, all the same." He got up. "See here, Old Girl, I'll get back to the subject of Godart, and wait for their call. If you contact them first, will you call me?"

"Righto, Old Thing."

He grimaced. "Don't overdo it."

She walked with him to the door. "I'll see you out."

In the doorway she patted his arm, suddenly remembering their long, close friendship. They cheek-to-cheeked in the old way. Jacqueline was grateful that he had taken the news about Dev Conor-Richard Kimberly so well. It made her future relationship with her husband that much easier.

The jangle of the phone jarred them both.

"Please wait," she urged him. "It's probably Father. Worse. It may be the Dragon Lady."

He stepped back into the room.

It was Matilde, her mother's maid.

"Mrs. Kimberly? Madame Godart here. Please hold the line."

How many times that woman had pulled the same trick, getting Jacqueline all lined up and waiting while she went to find Angela. More waiting. Jacqueline drummed on the telephone stand, giving Nigel the comprehensive story, "Mother."

He came over to the phone and waited.

Angela's first gush of words was typical of her: "Jacqui, is it true? The dreadful, awful contessa is using the Heffernan Woman on Godart business?"

"Sounds like it. I suppose Esther notified you as well. How have you been, Mother?"

"Terrible. That is, since we heard this. Sigurd tells me it's the worst possible sign. The creature has made too many friendships among the Board. She is moving in to take over the company."

"Don't worry. Nigel Chilton is on top of it."

"How dare she! It means she is bound and determined to marry Marcel. Sigurd says she's just trying to marry that poor, silly man so she can get control of his stock and the company itself."

Sigurd certainly ought to know, Jacqueline thought.

Her mother said finally, "Maybe it would be reassuring if I had a little talk with you. We might drop by. We've got theatre tickets for tonight but we could have an early dinner with you."

Heaven forbid.

"Not tonight, Mother. I have an engagement. I'm sorry."

Her mother spoke sharply to someone nearby, probably Sigurd. "She says she can't make it. Well, I can't force her; can I? . . . All right, Jacqui. I'll call Chilton-Brown. He's always such a tower of strength."

She rang off and Jacqueline told Nigel, "You're such a tower of strength. She's going to call you."

"Good Lord! And Esther Heffernan is sure to be sending the bloodhounds after me. I'd better be on my way. I'll try and keep them all from you as much as possible."

"Thank you, dear Nigel. What would I do without you?"

"Probably just what you want to do. You do that anyway. Although that man of yours may change your mind about a few things. He's no weakling. I wonder if . . . I'd like to have a little talk with him." He walked down the hall, still deep in thought. What did Dev have to do with it, she wondered.

An hour later Jacqueline went down to the Grill Room for a late lunch. Fried Plaice was on the menu, a dish she had enjoyed dozens of times in small cafes on the Continent, but the commonplace fish was elegantly prepared here and as usual, the meal was highly satisfactory, even when eaten alone.

She had just crossed the lobby, hoping she and Dev could avoid the family tonight, when she was paged by a young bellman.

"That's bound to be the contessa," she decided. "Calling in Father's place. His Little Helper."

It was Nigel Chilton-Brown.

"Jacqui, I'm out at Richmond."

That was unexpected. "You did go to see Devlin?"

"Right." His voice lacked that epic calm of the Imperial Englishman. He was clipped and even a bit nervous. "We've had a bit of a – what you might call – an accident."

"What would you call it?" Her fingers tightened on the phone. Nigel and not Dev had called her. It sounded bad.

"I don't quite know. Perhaps a joke in bad taste. Youngsters involved. Combined with a street accident. Runaway lorry."

"My God! Tell me."

"It seems a lorry – I mean a truck, got loose. Brake problem. Who knows? The driver swears the truck was parked, motor dead, etcetera. Rolled down the hill. Not much of a hill. But at that very minute some idiot, probably a boy, threw a golf ball at one of us, Conor or me. Probably me. Thought me too tailored by half, it seems. Children enjoy taking me down a peg."

"Get on!"

"At all events, it hit Conor between the shoulder-blades. Absurd business, really. Just as we were about to cross the street. If he hadn't exerted enormous muscular control, he'd have fallen directly in front of the lorry. Nimblest thing I ever saw. He scuttled out into the street. The lorry missed him by a hair. And he landed on his feet."

She felt dizzy with relief. "He's all right?"

"Practically. Here he is. We're in a chemist's shop. He refused a physician."

And then Conor's voice, warm and dear and cheerful.

"I told you, Sweetheart. I've taken tumbles before. From Kim, my Palamino. No Kim to lick my face this time. And Old Chilton-Brown here won't oblige."

In the background she heard Nigel chuckling. Her hands on the telephone were moist with sweat.

"And you weren't hurt. Honestly?"

"To tell the truth, I managed to acquire a problem shoulder. No harm done but the druggist – I mean the chemist – says I've got to apply ice and then heat. Not at the same time. Anyway, further inventory, sore elbow. Oh, yes. Skinned arm and a broken finger, I think. My little finger. The one I stick out when I drink tea. I landed standing up; but I did something to my arm. Don't ask me how it all happened."

She was so unnerved by his near-miss that she began to cry. She knew it would bother him; so she sniffed mightily and got hold of herself.

"How did it happen? Haven't they arrested the truck-driver? And who threw the golf ball?"

"Some little fellow coming out of a tobacconist's said he saw the boy throw the golf ball. The truck matter is one of those things. No one can prove the driver didn't put on the brakes. He seems to be a reliable guy. He was in my hotel, delivering courgettes. That's a vegetable, they tell me. The golf ball just hit me by chance. Nobody owns up to anything except the little man who was a kind of timid witness, and he's gone by now."

"Darling, darling, make Nigel bring you here right away. This minute. No. I'll go there."

"Wait. Chilton-Brown agrees with me on this. We're going to settle our own affairs first. He thinks we ought to be out of town. Don't tell me that golf ball was a deliberate – Chilton-Brown, you've got some imagination . . . Anyway, you and I are off to Venice. Not you, Chilton-Brown. You, Sweetheart."

"But we can't. My folks will be here any minute."

"Venice first. One mess straightened out at a time. Besides, they will all be celebrating that Venice Palazzo Antiquities Affair at the contessa's palazzo. That should make it handy for us. Meanwhile, we'll have a couple of days to go over the places you remember from three years ago."

She wished he would say "places *we* remember." Just once.

"But I can't pick up and walk out overnight."

It was more than that. His accident only brought back the old fear. It had been a warning. Don't return to Venice.

"Not overnight, Sweetheart. Now. Chilton has connections. He's going to get us on our way this afternoon. In – How long, Old Buddy? . . . He says an hour and forty-five minutes."

She panicked. "Impossible."

"On your way, Sweetheart. I want to find out what really happened. I'm sick of guessing. Start packing, I love you."

"I love you. Please, let's talk this over."

The connection was cut.

While she threw things together, she was still baffled by the entire Richmond episode. Why were Nigel and Dev buddies all of a sudden?

Furthermore, she wasn't sure that the new "accident" had been an accident. She lived in horror of losing Dev a second time. The only obvious motive for all these accidents, both to her and Dev, was her position in Godart's.

The revival of her marriage was a threat to the two outsiders. Irina and Sigurd were young enough to outlive their respective Godart connections. They would not welcome a possible direct heir, a child of Jacqueline's. Dev himself might be absorbed into the business, for all they knew. Another piece of the pie stolen from them.

Any way you look at it, she thought, the resumption of our marriage threatens them all financially, even Nigel.

In the circumstances, it was generous of Nigel to accept Dev so wholeheartedly, but that was like Nigel.

Maybe it was better to get away before the folks met Dev. Venice might even be a refuge from all these "accidents" and "overdoses" in London.

Nineteen

To awaken with the Grand Canal glistening in hazy morning light outside their long, Nineteenth Century window was a far cry from yesterday's awakening in the Elizabethan Chamber of the Mermaid Inn.

They had the view of the Canal in front of them and a long, ramshackle, rooftop balcony along the east side of their large, double room. The hotel was not the most elegant in Venice. It was the best Esther Heffernan could reserve for them by phone in those last, hectic minutes before they left for the airport, and Jacqueline was delighted with it. Even more so when she found out how pleased her husband had been by the two views, one over tiled rooftops in the moonlight, and the other over the mysterious, twinkling lights of the Canal's late traffic.

It had all happened too fast. Jacqueline lay in bed watching Dev as he stood by the window, having stopped shaving long enough to study the celebrated view before him. He still held his left arm a little stiffly, the elbow sticking out and his lower arm wrapped in gauze to the wrist. As he had guessed, his little finger was in a splint, the metacarpal bone neatly cracked, according to the doctor called by the concierge of the Grand Hotel Splendide upon their arrival last evening.

Dev had been surprised at this quick service and remarked, "Money certainly talks."

"Dr. Benedetti knows Mother awfully well," Jacqueline explained. "I've always suspected he is a little in love with her."

She watched him now, marvelling that he was actually here, alive and reasonably well, in the Venice where she thought his life had ended three years ago.

In slacks and still naked above the waist, he looked lean, tanned and very fit, but less flippant and boyish than in the old days. Such an experience does something to a man. Or a woman if it comes to that. She wished he would fill her in about those days. Sometimes she felt as if they lived in a vacuum with no past that they could share.

Aware at last that she was watching him, he turned from the window, wiped a towel over his face and remarked, "This view is one way to acquire an inferiority complex. My brush isn't good enough, my pen isn't up to it, and my pencil is too crude. What does a poor artist do before a scene like that? It's all been done."

"Photograph it, imaginatively."

He softened his jeer with a smile. "There speaks the amateur." He glanced once more at the morning traffic, the crowded ferryboat, the motorboats making their racket, now and then a black gondola riding the rumpled waters, and across the canal the heavy, baroque dome of Santa Maria della Salute.

He said, "The thing that fascinates me is how little it changes."

"It hasn't changed since we were here."

"I was thinking more in the line of centuries. It probably looked very much this way to Tintoretto and Titian. Not to mention Henry James and Browning. Give or take a vaporetto and a motor-boat."

"You surprise me, Darling. I didn't think you cared about history."

He came to the bed, leaned over and kissed her. "There is a lot you don't know about me, Sweetheart."

She wondered. It was more than a wife's natural curiosity about his past. Didn't he know that? It was her desire to share his memories, to picture in her mind all the little events of his childhood.

Dressed and ready for the day, he suggested they eat breakfast down on the terrace overlooking the canal. From the bathroom where hot water was thundering into the tub, making her wish she had brought some of Millie Yee's scented oils, Jacqueline called out,

"Fine with me. You really like Venice better this time; don't you?"

He stuck his head around the bathroom door.

"It doesn't just pretend to be the past. It really is." He whistled then at sight of her as she stepped into the bathtub. "Did anyone ever tell you, Sweetheart, you make a glorious nude?"

She surprised herself by flushing a little. She hadn't thought, after all these years, that she could be modest about her naked body. All she knew was that she had been overwhelmingly pleased at his praise. She sank into the water and flipped a few soapy, gleaming bubbles at him.

While she bathed she wondered at the wild changes in her life since she discovered the contessa's photograph of the Venetian Antiquities Ball. She was convinced now that someone was out to remove her and Dev from the Godart interests. She couldn't figure out why anyone else was trying to kill him, or at least, scare them both away from – what?

He might have private enemies that she knew nothing about, but it seemed far more likely that this was all connected with the odd things that had happened to her and the man she loved.

The plot required an intimate knowledge of her comings and goings. The contessa hadn't been in London when the recent events occurred. But Prince Sigurd had been on the spot all the time, and he knew his way around. Jacqueline suspected he also had an acquaintance with useful connections on the fringe of the business underworld. His past had a few suspicious blanks, and when he emerged he was always in a better position.

But Nigel knew all this. He had more power than the prince or the contessa, unless Irina had enormous, unsuspected forces behind her.

The minute Nigel's adoring secretary had landed the day before, and called him with complaints about Irina Fabrini's officiousness, Nigel had set her to work acquiring air tickets, including transfers on the Continent, plus reservations at the Splendide in Venice, all in under two hours. If he had asked for six hired assassins, she would probably have tried to contact them as well.

With that thought it occurred to Jacqueline that Nigel knew quite as much about the criminal class as the business world ever knows, and rather more than most men in his position. She had never pursued the matter when she wondered how he got a great deal of his inside information on the backgrounds and secret meetings of rival corporations.

During the minutes before Dev and Jacqueline left for Venice, Nigel had given orders that both the prince and the contessa should be shadowed. Miss Heffernan cared little about the prince, assuming as Jacqueline did, that eventually Angela would tire of him. Angela was a hedonist, but not a fool. However, Miss Heffernan was delighted to oblige when it came to "punishing that impudent female who calls herself a countess. Countess, my foot!"

"Mark me, she's no better than she should be," she had warned Jacqueline. "I wouldn't be surprised if she tried to seduce Mr. C. Not that he would fall for her wiles, of course. He's not that kind of person, as we all know."

"You're so right," Jacqueline had agreed hurriedly. She was trying to find the little white china goose she had bought for Esther and packed somewhere in her tote bag.

So here they were, Richard and Jacqueline, alone for a precious few days, in which Jacqueline, at least, hoped to get back the lost years.

At breakfast on the sunny terrace, with the rhythmic lapping of the Canal waters against the Splendide's cement foundations and pilings only a few yards away, Jacqueline discovered an oddity in one of their fellow diners.

"Don't look now," she murmured to Dev, "But that elderly woman in the far corner seems awfully familiar."

Dev raised his head, set his cup down and tried to look discreetly over his left shoulder. This wasn't easy because his neck and shoulder muscles were still sore but he managed to get a look at the elderly woman in the gray tailored suit with the white blouse and the female version of a derby hat. He frowned.

"Somebody you know?"

"Not an acquaintance. No. But I have a kind of nebulous idea."

He looked at the woman again. She seemed unconscious of having aroused any interest, He returned to his coffee, but he was watching Jacqueline over the rim of the cup. He looked concerned, or perhaps thoughtful. She couldn't be sure. He surprised and touched her by asking apropos of nothing, "Still happy, Sweetheart?"

"Of course, I am. I've never been so happy in my whole life."

"I wish I could believe that."

He reached across the table for her hand and took it in his. She felt the roughness of the wrappings around the little splint on his finger and caressed it gently.

"You can, Darling."

Suddenly, in her mind's eye, she saw the lobby of London's Savoy Hotel and Dev standing there across the room, talking to an elderly woman. What was it he had said? She had been hired to babysit with some children and had thought Dev might be her employer.

Jacqueline tried to play her suspicion mockingly. A joke on herself. Only it hurt that he should lie to her so easily. And lie again today.

"Are we the children she is babysitting with?"

"Who. Oh, her. Why?" Perhaps he thought this was her own joke. "Do we need babysitting?"

"Nigel thinks so. Don't tell me she could ever protect both of us."

"Kind of a Ma Barker type, I guess."

It wasn't funny. He was evading.

"What a busy little beaver Nigel has been. He hired her; didn't he?" When Dev shrugged she muttered, "If he is going to protect us from golf balls and runaway trucks, he ought to at least hire a man with a little muscle."

"I'm ashamed of you, Sweetheart. A woman who runs a business worth millions, and you want to cheat a little old lady out of her job. You're an anti-female chauvinist."

She didn't think it was funny, but she let it go. She would settle with Nigel later.

"Where shall we go first?" he asked, seeing that she had thrown aside her napkin and was obviously done with her half-eaten breakfast. To Jacqueline it seemed to be a second thought when he added with a delightful grin, like the teasing Richard of the old days, "I'll let you pilot me around to all the places you remember from those days with – Well, You can tell me what happened. Every single place."

"And wake up that stupid memory of yours," she added, somewhat mollified. "Let's lead that old woman a merry chase. Make her earn her salary."

"Ruthless creature." But he got up at once, pulled her chair out and behaved in exemplary fashion.

By the time they got to the lobby and Jacqueline looked back through the glass doors she was able to say with perverse satisfaction, "We fooled her. She hasn't budged."

"Maybe she isn't one of Chilton-Brown's little hirelings."

"One thing I do know. She's the same one who talked to you in the lobby. I know that face. It seems sweet, but she's got a hard jaw and it doesn't fit the Sweet Little Old Lady portrait. I'll bet her eyes are steel blue."

Dev touched her temple, close to her dark right eyebrow. "Be generous. They can't all have eyes as deep and ravishing as yours."

"Don't be silly." Just the same, she was pleased.

"Where do we start?" He knew her object was to retrace the places and things that were a part of the other experience. He didn't appear to mind. She passionately hoped he was anxious to recover those memories.

They began to walk through a sunny little courtyard between the Splendide and another canal-front hotel. An old fountain, dry and full of cigarette butts and other debris, served as the back-up for a moist hole in the pavement where a half-dozen of Venice's ubiquitous cat population hung out.

"Rat-catchers?" Dev asked.

"Don't forget. This is a city on water. The rats come with the territory. And those cats can be mighty useful."

He was interested in these malevolent felines, most of whom were the worse for wear, like aging fighters still too tough to die. Cauliflower ears, missing teeth and extremities had no effect on them. It was clear that they were fed somehow, though they looked lanky and proved to be almost boneless, the way they wriggled their way in and out of impossibly small corners.

Dev was about to turn right toward the canal, but Jacqueline headed determinedly into the labyrinth of little alleys and bridges that led to St. Mark's Square. Though she had conquered her haunting fear of Venice as much as possible, she still felt a chill of horror when she caught a glimpse of the watery expanse where the Grand Canal emptied into the lagoon.

They reached the Square, coming out of tunnelled obscurity into the breathtaking full sweep of the Piazza San Marco and somewhat to Jacqueline's surprise, Dev found it as magnificent as it must have been the first time he saw it. She could hardly believe he had forgotten its immensity and the Byzantine splendor of that sight.

It was strange that when she first knew him his artistic feelings and abilities were not only dormant but dead. He hadn't even known what he wanted to do with his life. But then, of course, he had been suffering from real amnesia, a blackout that only the speedboat accident cleared up.

They strolled past Quadri's, the cafe opposite Florian's, and headed for the Merceria under the clock tower. She tried not to give him surreptitious little glances, to see if he remembered anything, but he caught her at it, and she looked away, embarrassed. She knew this close surveillance must be annoying to him. If he did recall any sight along the way, he would tell her so.

After crossing the little hump-backed bridge where he had once boosted her along in a sexy, joking way, they passed the shop where she had bought an apricot-colored blouse only minutes before meeting "Richard Kimberly."

She thought she felt her heartbeat increasing. Excitement engulfed her. Surely, he must feel something. They were coming to the place where she and Richard had met, the open-front cafe that was part delicatessen. Almost in spite of herself, she slowed her steps.

He looked at her and then around at the tight little shops jammed against each other.

"Did something happen around here?"

"Pretty soon. Do you feel any thing?"

"Matter of fact, I do," he confessed. "A kind of déjà vu, as they call it. I've been here before. You know the feeling."

"Ah!"

"But a long time ago. Hundreds of years, Not in our time. Funny how you get these ideas."

With a sinking feeling she confessed, "Often. Especially in France where my grandparents were born. But this is different." She clutched his hand. "Try, Darling. To please me, if nothing else."

In a playful way he swung her fingers, laced with his, but there was nothing playful about his own plea.

"I wish to God you would accept me for what I am, and not the Ghost of Weddings Past."

"I know."

She hung her head, feeling like a scolded child, knowing she was wrong and that she was hurting him. But she wasn't strong enough to throw off the old dream.

They walked on and she found herself carried away by the thrill of seeing again the place where they met. Around the next corner. Beyond this big red palazzo that had become a hotel on a tiny canal.

"It's on the left side. Just beyond the next building."

She closed her eyes to make ready for the great moment.

He was puzzled. "The luggage shop?"

"No, no. The café. There's an open front." Her voice trailed off.

The café was gone. The open front was now a wall with a display window through which a set of imitation Gucci luggage could be seen.

She stopped dead still, feeling the hot bite of tears which she blinked back angrily, insisting, "I am positively not going to cry; so don't worry. It's so stupid. After all, every year there are bound to be changes."

He said nothing. He was staring at the window, or maybe the luggage. He left her and walked over to the wall, touching it with his fingertips. He examined his fingers. A young woman and a stout, short man stopped, watched him and then, shaking their heads, went on.

Jacqueline joined him. "Nothing? No vibrations? No memories?"

"I'm sorry."

She walked on with him, remembering how she had walked along with her soft-shelled crabs. The route hadn't changed much. If she closed her eyes she could almost revert to that day and relive those moments.

With dazzling suddenness they found themselves out on the busy, sunlit Grand Canal. She cried in delight, "It's still here."

"What? The Canal? It certainly twists around like a sidewinder."

"No, Silly. The sidewalk cafe where we really got acquainted. Could we sit here a few minutes? have a drink?"

"Why not?"

There were two vacant tables next to the canal rail, but Dev pulled out a chair for her, the very chair and the same table where she had sat that other time. He took a chair close to her, facing the canal.

"What will it be?"

She tried to remember what she had drunk that day. Probably Cinzano. He ordered two, luckily pronouncing it in the Italian way. The waiter was different, but you couldn't have everything, she thought. Automatically, she began to relive that other day long ago. She reached into her handbag.

He asked, "Lost something?"

She stared at him.

He went on lightly, "Don't tell me your pocket's been picked. There's a lot of that in those narrow alleys we've just passed through."

"Why did you say that?"

"What? About pickpockets? Don't worry. I can cover the check. If it isn't too inflated."

It was almost exactly as it had been before. He saw that she was looking serious and he added, still playing it with a grin, "Tell you what. You can pay me back in ten easy instalments."

Whatever he was pretending, and for whatever reason, he had re-enacted the business between them.

She was delighted. Maybe he didn't remember, but subconsciously he repeated those magic moments of their first meeting.

They both drank the Cinzano, enjoying their companionship, the lack of pressure on this relationship. They made small talk and when they got up he made no objection to her idea that they walk back to the Royal Danieli before heading toward their own hotel. For her they would be reliving everything they had done on that first meeting.

They had just gotten up, planning to retrace their steps toward the Merceria, when Jacqueline saw the old woman they had noticed at their hotel. She was calmly sipping Campari at a table strategically hidden from hers and Dev's by a group of tall, chattering American girls at an intermediate table.

Jacqueline muttered, "That woman really annoys me. She looks like a Nazi storm trooper in that suit."

He was looking at the woman over the heads of the girls. "Maybe. But from what I remember, she has the accent of a pure Brit. If she is the nanny who spoke to me at the Savoy, she said her name was Dimblby." He took her arm. "What do you say we lose her?"

"I'd love to. She isn't likely to guess where we are going this time."

Sauntering along, they reached the Merceria, started through a serpentine byway and increased their speed, turning to the left at the first little offshoot of an alley.

"Did she see us go?" Jacqueline asked as they stopped to get their breath on another shopping street which branched off the alley.

"She signalled to the waiter. I don't think there is any doubt we're her big interest."

Jacqueline felt guilty but pleased. "If she is sent by Nigel to protect us, this is a dumb thing to do. And if she's sent by someone else – I wish I hadn't thought of that."

She waited for him to laugh. Unfortunately, he didn't. The idea that some unseen enemy might have employed the woman was enough to give Jacqueline a case of the chills. She forgot her fatigue and found herself easily keeping up with his long stride.

They walked out of the labyrinth, across St. Mark's Square, and found themselves on the Fondamenta just beyond the Hotel Danieli. Jacqueline watched Dev without seeming to. He showed no recognition of the hotel and was solely interested in its historic qualities. Here they were much closer to the lagoon and in spite of herself she glanced out over the waters toward the Lido.

Somewhere under those waters she had lost Dev when he had thought he was "Richard." It still appeared to her as a miracle that he should have survived. She tried not to think of it, but already the fog of a late autumn day was creeping over the islands, Murano, Burano and Torcello, and over the waters which began to turn a dull blue-green, then murky gray.

"I hate it!"

Dev was startled. "What? The Danieli?"

"No. No. The fog. Shall we go in?"

"Why not?"

True. But that other time he had definitely been afraid he would meet people. What people? Who were his enemies, and how had he rid himself of that past which seemed slightly sinister in those days?

Somewhat to her amusement, he examined everything historic that he could find in the lobby, along the staircase and even in the lobby ceiling. The artist in him might have been retarded before but it was in full flower now.

They didn't get home to the Hotel Splendide until after three, having enjoyed Czechoslovakian Beer and an Italian form of the toasted cheese sandwich "Croque Monsieur" at Florian's. Their gray-haired, gray-eyed nemesis, Mrs. Dimblby, was nowhere to be seen. Jacqueline felt that they had been very clever in eluding her.

They found several phone messages waiting for Jacqueline. Nigel's was brief and to the point:

"Trust you made it. Good luck. See you soon."

Jacqueline's mother was more verbose:

"Please call me. Imperative. Heartbroken. Can say no more. Have spoken to Marcel. So sympathetic, dear boy. He demands that I appear at the Venetian Gala. Will see you there, but call soonest."

Jacqueline showed this to Dev who whistled. "Sounds serious."

"It is. Mother has probably just broken with Prince Sigurd over some peccadillo of his."

"Yes, but the woman seems to be suffering."

"There is one thing you must learn about Mother. Her heart is frequently cracked, but so far, it has never quite broken. This sounds as if she were after Father again. Any port in a storm."

He smiled, not without sympathy. "Am I permitted to make a bet on your mother against the redoubtable contessa?"

She sparkled at the thought. "Both Father and Mother are very jealous of each other's outside interests. Wouldn't it be marvelous if they got back together? I used to dream about that years ago."

The last message they found was sealed. She turned over the envelope. It had the embossed name of the Grand Hotel Splendide. The message had apparently been written at one of the lobby desks, on hotel stationery.

Whom did she knew in Venice after all this time? The contessa, of course, but she would hardly use hotel stationery.

She remarked, "Probably some local executive of the company who wants to be sociable. But why seal it?"

Dev said, "Look on the front. It says 'private.' It would seem they want to exclude me. O.K. I'll be a sport and let you read it by yourself. But just tell your boyfriends they should be more discreet."

She laughed and ripped the envelope open.

When she saw the signature she thought she understood what it was all about.

"Darling, here's the other side of the coin that Mother has just flipped. It must be Prince von Ulsbach's version of the great breakup."

"I'll bet he wants you to put in a good word for him." He came back to read it over her shoulder.

"Jacqueline, my good friend,

"You will have heard the news by this time. You, who know me so well, are probably the only person who would understand. The relationship with Viola Sears hardly qualifies as a 'relationhip' but a simple encounter and, if you will forgive my immodesty, a once-only attempt on my part to satisfy a woman who has pursued me since we first arrived in England."

Dev wasn't overwhelmed by the prince's frankness. "Nice, modest little fellow."

But Jacqueline could accept Sigurd for what he was, an attractive purchase made by her mother. No doubt, any gifts he had received from Viola Sears were in the form of a tip, so to speak. His main paymistress had certainly been Angela Godart and it looked as though he could kiss that income goodbye.

Jacqueline murmured, "It doesn't look good for His Highness and Mama."

But the prince had other irons in the fire and was pursuing them:

"I have not been idle, however. Since we first learned of the difficulties pending at Godart, I employed the services of various friends, insiders, and my own nose for the scent of chicanery. You will find my information is of great, even supreme value to you. The warning of this danger should be my entry to you.

"Because, my lovely Jacqueline, you are in danger. I can tell you what you have not guessed about the man whom you know as Devlin Kimball Conor, and about others as close to you.

"I must see you at once. I confess I am personally afraid for my life; so I will meet you on the canal terrace of your hotel at seventeen hours, five o'clock your time. I will remain for half an hour. I will occupy a table surrounded by others. I do not think it is wise to isolate myself. I will wear a blue Italian beret, and a blue corduroy jacket. If you do not receive this before that hour, I will return again, having called you before arriving.

"I beg of you, come to the lobby and terrace alone. If I see your companion with you, I will know you have foolishly betrayed me. My life may depend on it.

"Your friend always,

"Sigurd Erich Reitler von Ulsbach."

Jacqueline was left speechless. It was Dev who said lightly, "I like his nerve. What does he think he has on me? That I'm really Devlin Conor? I told you that." An idea occurred to him. "Maybe he's going to tell you I'm actually Richard Kimberly. That would be a laugh."

"One thing is certain," she said finally after glancing at her wristwatch. "It's a quarter to five now. I'd better be on my way down to the lobby."

"Not alone, you won't."

She turned and looked at him.

"What he says about you is poppycock. We know that. But for a long time now I've been having accidents. You had one yesterday. Someone connected with Godart's is trying to get rid of me. And probably you. Sigurd has found out something, for which he will expect to be paid, and he's asked me to meet him in the most public place possible, in my own hotel. I don't even have to go out in one of those spooky alleys. I'm going down to meet him."

He shrugged. "Very well. I'll be discreet. I'll just go down early. Now, as a matter of fact. I'll remain in that alcove off the inside dining room where I can watch the terrace through the glass without being seen."

"I don't like it. He's bound to suspect something."

Dev had been thinking it over. "Not if I take the elevator the room waiters use. It will bring me into a corner where he can't possibly see me."

She wanted to argue, but she knew he was right.

"All right. I'll come down at five exactly."

"I'm off. Be careful, Sweetheart."

It was with some tension that she watched him go.

When she was alone she re-read the letter. She knew, and she suspected Dev knew, that for all her quick dismissal of the reference to "the man who calls himself Devlin Kimball Conor," she was more obsessed by this subject than whatever else the prince might have dug up. Maybe there was a plot against her, and maybe also, it was all a series of accidents which she had blown up out of all proportion. But this mention of her husband was the signal that sent her hurrying down to meet the prince.

If he knew something in Dev/Richard's past and meant to blackmail her, she would have to pay, but first, she must know what it was.

Twenty

At five o'clock exactly she hurried out to the elevator and down to the lobby. She found herself trembling, which was no way to meet a blackmailing gigolo. By the time she stepped out into the lobby she had achieved control of herself.

The sunset light sparkling on the canal had briefly pierced the usual haze that spread over the island city like a cancer with its core in the mainland manufacturing centers. So strong was the vermillion light across the waters beyond the terrace that Jacqueline was momentarily blinded. She stopped, blinked, and looked out at the terrace and canal through the wall of glass that separated the formal dining room, now empty, from the tables where she had been directed to find Sigurd von Ulsbach.

The terrace would soon be crowded with the cocktail crowd. Already, the tables were filling up. One little table in the center had a Reserved sign on it. Obviously, the prince must have tipped someone. Jacqueline wondered if she should go out and take one of the two chairs at the table, but she thought better of it. She would probably look conspicuous, waiting for him, and the prince seemed to be afraid of attracting attention.

Knowing the prince would arrive any minute, she was particularly casual when she looked toward the alcove by the far windows where Dev would be standing.

No one was there.

She glanced around, touching her hair, pretending she was impatiently waiting for her cocktail date. Dev had certainly concealed himself well. He was nowhere in sight.

Meanwhile, it was five-ten and Prince Sigurd hadn't arrived yet.

She studied her watch with her mind on other matters . . . "Someone close to her who also knew Dev." Sigurd's letter had given her the distinct impression that there was a conspiracy against her and stemming from those two, Dev and that other person "close to her." Or was that a separate problem he wanted to discuss? What had he discovered about someone close to her? Someone trusted.

She had to know. A long time ago she had said she didn't care what Richard Kimberly had done, she would go on loving him. Well and good. But what if there was a conspiracy against her and what if Richard (or Dev) was part of it?

"No. I don't believe it."

She almost said it out loud but luckily controlled her nerves, fed by these sudden suspicions.

It was five-twenty and still no Sigurd von Ulsbach, nor anyone who looked like him. There was one man in an oldfashioned country beret and a corduroy jacket, but she couldn't imagine Sigurd in a worker's beret, even if he did want to remain incognito.

She strolled the length of the glass wall, keeping her attention on the terrace, but when she approached the alcove where Dev had promised to wait, he was still missing.

"Now, I've got both of them to worry about," she thought impatiently. By this time the impatience was tinged with apprehension, and the beginning of something else.

She was afraid. Not of Sigurd. And it couldn't be that she was afraid of Dev. Impossible. She feared what she didn't know, the information she was supposed to buy from Sigurd.

Suppose she never learned it . . .

These were idiotic thoughts. Good thing she had no psychiatrist to prod her about them now, she thought, trying to make a joke of it.

Five-twenty-five.

He had said, "If I don't see you, I'll call and make another appointment . . ."

But that was because he was afraid she might not arrive back at the hotel in time. There was no question that he himself wouldn't keep the appointment.

She walked around the partition. A goodlooking fortyish man in a black suit with the hotel's logo on the pocket opened the door onto the terrace. These late autumn days turned chilly when you weren't in the direct sunlight.

The maitre d' wove his way between the tables and came to meet her. He was all smiles.

She explained that she was to meet the gentleman

at the vacant center table and only just caught herself before giving Sigurd's name and title. The waiter looked at the table, then at her again.

"The gentleman does not seem to arrive. It was to be half an hour ago. Perhaps – if the Signora wishes to take the table, it should be permitted. A pleasure."

He pulled out a chair for her and she sat down in a gingerly way, still searching for Sigurd von Ulsbach among the new arrivals on the terrace. It was past five-thirty now and the sun had gone below the western wing of the hotel, bringing evening to the busy, noisy terrace.

By five-forty-five she had given up. Lingering over her Campari Vermouth, she was relieved to see Dev coming across the terrace toward her.

"No show?" he asked with amused sympathy.

"You said it. Darling, do sit down and keep me from looking so conspicuous."

He leaned over to kiss her before sitting down, then frowned at the bright, wine-red drink in her glass. "What's that gruesome thing you are drinking?"

She stared at the Campari, remembering a similar glass sitting near Richard's hand on more than one occasion. She was shaken by this contradiction on top of Sigurd's letter and his failure to appear.

Dev ordered a "whisky" and remarked after a glance around, "Looks like he changed his mind."

"Looks like it." She waited a few seconds, then asked, "Where on earth were you?"

"Some flunky laying on the silver in the dining room reported me and they shooed me out. Very nice, but very definite."

She stared at the Campari, held it up. "Why don't you like this? It's a beautiful color."

"I don't know whether I like it or not. I've never drunk any."

"I'd forgotten. Of course not . . . Where did you go?"

"When?"

"Before five, when you were supposed to be watching for Sigurd without his knowing it?"

"Oh. That." He received his drink, left money on the saucer and drank a little. "I played it rather neatly, I thought. I took that passage to the kitchens and went a few steps beyond, where I could watch eveyone entering the hotel from the land side."

"Then he saw you. That's why he didn't come in."

"That is impossible," he said patiently. "I was behind the door. He simply didn't arrive. It's my opinion he was bought off."

She shivered. "The minute the sun goes down, we freeze to death."

He reached out, closed his fingers over her hand, and squeezed it in a warm gesture. "Drink up. There's a good girl. We'll eat inside, where it's warm."

She withdrew her fingers slowly from his grip.

"Don't you care why he didn't show up?"

Impatience began to show for the first time.

"Yes, I care. That is to say, I am curious. I've known a lot of worthless flotsam like him. He loses out as a gigolo; so he takes up blackmail." His voice remained even but something had been added to it, a terrifying little note of implacable coldness. "To be honest, I wouldn't care whether he lived or died, except that he had possibly taken money from an enemy of yours instead of telling you where the danger came from."

"I don't believe it. If he knows who is back of these attacks on me, he intended to tell me. Only something got in his way."

"I don't doubt that for a minute."

"If you mean, he blackmailed the person back of this –"

"Probably."

"But he could get himself killed."

He made no reply. He was finishing his drink. She thought over that letter Sigurd had written and knew Dev was wrong.

"It can't be true, and I know why."

"Really? Why?"

"Because that letter was written by a terrified man. Look at all these precautions. Almost ridiculous. The disguise. A center table, so his enemy couldn't get to him without a lot of hassle. The timing. The last person in the world he wants to meet is the person he is afraid of. Richard! Could it be that woman this morning, the one who followed us? Maybe she's a hired – Who knows what?"

He didn't reply at once but looked around at everyone on the terrace. His lighthearted, cynical mood had vanished. He said finally, "Well, the woman isn't here now, at any rate."

"Neither is Sigurd."

They finished their drinks in silence. They were both occupied with their thoughts. But were they the same thoughts? Were they even on the same track?

One of the first fogs of the winter season was drifting

in when they finished their drinks and Dev looked out at the canal with an artist's eye.

"I'd like to get some pictures of the way the fog softens all the gaudy brightness. Makes it look like some unearthly place that exists only in dreams."

"Nightmares."

He stared at her surprised, then remembered. "Was it like this that night?"

She nodded.

"I'm sorry." He put his arm around her and they walked into the hotel's big lobby.

She realized that the artist in him genuinely wanted to see the great square all bathed in ghostly gray mist and she suggested, "That doesn't stop us from seeing St. Mark's."

"No."

She stared. "Why not? It was out in the lagoon where it happened before. The night lights in St. Mark's might be very picturesque. I'm game if you are. But please, not until we've had a hot dinner and I've changed into something warmer than this outfit."

He looked around, hesitated, then seemed satisfied. "It's a deal."

After leaving a message with both the telephone service and the desk, they ate in the dining room, earlier than the crowd. It served no purpose. There were no calls.

Jacqueline shook her head when she heard this and asked them to be sure and give her all messages when she returned from their walk.

As they left the hotel, she said, "Looks like he's forsaken us." She laughed and gave him a sideways glance that was meant to be humorous. "Whatever he has against you, he apparently thinks I'm safe with you, or he would have tried again tonight."

He was frowning at the dusty little cul de sac outside the land entrance of the hotel. The homeless cats had slunk away to their makeshift holes and the place was deserted. It was clear, however, that his thoughts weren't on the surroundings. He drew her close to him.

"I wonder how many people connected with Godart's know he is here in Venice. And more important, who knows you are here?"

"Nobody but Nigel."

"Then how did this prince know where to find you?"

She was chilled by the question but then she remembered. The answer was obvious. They had registered as Jacqueline Kimberly and Devlin Conor. Their passports made it obligatory according to the various continental laws, Europe had only the most casual interest in who was sleeping with whom, but everyone cared a great deal if the signature on the registration didn't match the name on the passport.

When they stepped out of the dark arcade into one end of the great Square with the cathedral in the far distance, Dev had to work on the gadgets of his camera for those light-and-darkness shots. He found a dozen compositions of the square, the arcades, the cathedral, and the scattered pairs of lovers or lone drinkers in the cafés.

He seemed to enjoy looking into dark corners, apparently finding some perverse fascination in places he couldn't possibly photograph.

For her part Jacqueline couldn't get Sigurd von Ulsbach out of her mind. She was still trying to discover what he had intended to tell her. She was pretty sure he had misinterpreted anything he discovered about Dev "and someone close to her", but she would like to know who that someone was.

She was still torn between her undoubted love for this man who called himself Devlin Conor, and her memories of Dev the way he used to be, careless, reckless, irresponsible, with no career and no ambition. Common sense told her that she herself had changed with time and business pressures. An irresponsible ne'er do well, with a dubious past of some kind, would not suit the present Jacqueline Godart. But what, precisely, had become of Richard that he could change so much in only three years!

Unless of course, there was no Richard Kimberly, and the last agonizing moments of his life had been spent in the waters of the lagoon?

Don't think of that!

She closed her eyes tightly, forced other pictures into her mind, and heard her name called from across the sparsely populated square.

"Jacqui, ma petite . . ."

To her surprise, when she turned, Dev was in her way. She cried, "It's father. He and the contessa, over in front of Quadri's."

He studied the pair, the man wearing a Fedora and the blonde woman bundled in furs. Then he let Jacqueline go. She ran across the square to her father. Dev followed her. He was given the once-over by the contessa before she greeted him as a vaguely remembered acquaintance.

It was always amusing to outsiders when little Marcel called his tall daughter "My little one." Jacqueline saw Dev smile as she and her father hugged each other hard, followed by an exchange of enthusiastic kisses.

"And have you no greeting for your future – for Irina?" Marcel reminded her when she stepped back to introduce Dev.

There were embraces all around, cheek-to-cheek, including the contessa's gracious acceptance of Dev as Jacqueline's future husband. It was so easy, so gracious, and so unsurprised that Jacqueline wondered if she had known about Dev's presence all along. Marcel, on the contrary, had to be convinced.

"Yes, young man. Do I understand you wish to marry my little girl?"

"Exactly, Sir."

Jacqueline put in quickly, "In a sense, Father. I've always loved – I mean I love him. Dev. I love Dev."

"You see, dear Marcel?" the contessa remind him. "Romance is easily come by. We need not spend all our thoughts upon my poor friend Angela. She too will find another love very easily."

Jacqueline resented the "very easily" and wondered if it was her own prejudice or the myriad lights of the square that made the contessa's smile look so fixed, almost glued upon her lovely face. Jacqueline started to ask about her mother but Marcel interupted. He was bubbling with enthusiasm.

"My poor, sweet Angela, when her heart was broken by that gigolo, what haven did she run to? In a word, myself. Her old Marcel."

Jacqueline could see difficulties ahead. She wondered if Marcel sensed them.

"You mean Mother came to see you in London?"

"Dear child," the contessa announced in her pleasant, social voice, "Much more. Angela came to us here at the Palazzo. I was delighted to receive my old friend."

Jacqueline had never recalled anything of this old friendship and suspected that many reasons went into the invitation, of which friendship was the least.

While Marcel was explaining to Dev that his ex-wife had "suffered a deep loss of trust in the wretched fellow," the contessa confirmed Jacqueline's suspicion of her motives by confiding,

"You will not believe how ravaged the poor woman is over this affair. One cannot help pitying her. Angela was always so careful not to look her age." She sighed. "I'm afraid that is all over now. Gigolos age one so."

"Really?" Jacqueline asked. "I didn't know. My experience of them has been somewhat limited."

The contessa hastily agreed. "And mine also. Indeed. We are fortunate not to know more of them."

"Has His Highness tried to contact Mother?"

"Not that I know of. *Per dio*! Is he in Venice?"

Jacqueline was evasive. "I just wondered."

Marcel locked arms with his daughter and his prospective son-in-law. "Come. Shall we all go into Florian's and have a *kir*? We will drink to the future happiness of these two. If only my poor Angela had come along tonight, we would be a family again." He murmured dreamily, "How beautiful she looked! It is always so, Jacqui. My Angela never changes."

"Yes," the contessa agreed. "Do let us have an aperitif at Florian's. Then home to bed. It is so damp tonight. I feel this fog in my bones. Now, Jacqui, you and our young artist must come to stay at the Palazzo. In three days, our first ball opens the Season. I am honored that the Palazzo Fabrini has been chosen for our great charity."

On their way into the picturesque and warmly inviting little rooms of Florian's the contessa attached herself to Dev.

"We may count upon your sketches, and perhaps photographs for our book? It will sell at seventy-five American dollars. That is our object, at any rate. You are so very clever with that pencil of yours, Devlin. I may call you Devlin?"

Jacqueline was amused when he wrinkled his nose at Devlin but he accepted the commission without hestitation.

By the time they were getting ready to leave the café, Marcel, who had been seated by the window, remarked suddenly,

"She is very odd, that female."

Everyone looked out. Several couples were passing and it was difficult to see the person he pointed out.

"A woman of a certain age, you understand. Not young. She was in the next room when we came in. She has passed Florian's twice."

Jacqueline looked up quickly. "Like an English nanny? In a gray suit?"

"It may be. But this one wears a rain cape and a felt hat with a brim floppy."

The contessa did not see the woman, nor did Jacqueline, but she suspected it was their earlier shadow, the lady in the gray suit, the woman Dev thought was called Mrs. Dimblby. Did he know her better than he claimed? She might look harmless but she made Jacqueline nervous.

When they had seen her father and the contessa into the motorboat that waited for them beyond the Piazzetta, Jacqueline told Dev her suspicions about the woman.

He shrugged. "Probably the same. But she may serve some good purpose. She looks strong enough. I wouldn't be surprised if she was hired by Chilton-Brown's people to keep a general lookout." He laughed shortly. "Not the most flattering idea in the world, to find a nanny looking out for you when you do have a husband of sorts."

"That's all right. I'll rely on you, thanks."

She squeezed his arm and he tightened his hold around her waist. They walked together through the night-shrouded little passageways, over humped bridges, past closed shops and forbidding, darkened churches to the cul de sac of the homeless cats. In the dim lantern light outside the land entrance to their hotel they made out savage, frightened little eyes staring up at them from holes they hadn't known existed. The nocturnal cats were on the watch.

There was a telephone message for Jacqueline at the desk.

"Thank heaven! It must be the prince. Now, we'll find out what it's all about."

But the message was from Nigel Chilton.

"Have been invited to Palazzo Fabrini for the Antiquities Ball. Have news about our beautiful friend. See you there. Love to you both, from N C-B"

Jacqueline showed it to Dev. "Looks like he's going to uncover whatever there is to be found out about the contessa."

"I wonder if she has anything to do with your prince."

"What!"

"I mean, is there any reason they might be working together? I shouldn't think either of them would want you and me to marry, for obvious reasons."

She doubted this theory. "Sigurd didn't trust anyone except me. That includes the contessa."

The phone was ringing when they finally reached their rooms. She rushed to answer it while Dev locked the door behind them.

It was Angela.

She had never heard her mother in such a state. Angela was gasping and breathless, trying to get the words out, with difficulty.

"Thank God, Marcel told me where you are. Oh, Jacqui, they found him on some slimy steps. Just above the water."

"Who, Mother, please?"

"Sigurd. They r-robbed him. His wallet was gone. But he had my name in his shoe. His shoe! Marcel, your handkerchief, there's a dear . . . Anyway, Jacqui, it was one of those places where you can signal to gondolas."

"Dead?"

"Oh, horribly. Hit on the back of the head."

Jacqueline stared at Dev. For some reason, she wanted to cry. The prince hadn't been worth much but still, he had helped her find Dev, and in an odd sort of way, he had been a friend.

Dev, too, was shaken. "The prince?"

Jacqueline covered the mouthpiece of the phone with her palm. "Now, will you believe he was afraid of somebody?" She turned her attention to her mother. "Where did it happen?"

"I told you. On the lowest step above the water. That little canal that runs into the Grand Canal near your hotel."

Jacqueline's mouth felt dry as cotton.

"What time?"

"They found him right away. He was barely dead. It was between four-thirty and five or so. Jacqui, isn't that pitiful? He had a card with my name in his shoe."

Jacqueline's hands were shaking and she sat down abruptly in the little desk chair Dev pushed forward. She looked up at him.

"Before five. He was on his way to meet me on the terrace when he was murdered."

Twenty-One

Jacqueline set the phone back. "At least, she isn't in hysterics. Poor Sigurd. Even Mother doesn't shed a tear over him. She wants us at the Palazzo with the rest of the family. Right away."

Dev pulled a chair up to face her and straddled it. He took both her cold hands in his.

"Sweetheart, you aren't going to that woman's house now or any other time. I don't like the whole setup."

She understood and loved him for his care of her, but she reminded him, "You have a job at the Palazzo. Sketches. Photographs. And my folks are there, both my father and my mother."

He shook their entwined hands, trying to express something – anger, anguish. Something inexpressible.

"That damned job didn't bring me to Venice. You did."

"You mean our safety? Running away? That was Nigel's idea, and we've run right into whatever it is."

"I mean you. Your love. That's why we came to Venice. Didn't you know that?"

Across their clasped hands she kissed his cheek tenderly. "You have that. But if you insist, we'll go tomorrow. Besides, Nigel will be there and he knows the danger. In fact, he expects to find us there."

He let her hands go with an impatient gesture.

"I don't know. I don't like it."

She didn't want to argue. She was too depressed.

"O.K. We'll see how we feel tomorrow."

When she was bathing that night, trying to wash away depression and her memory of some amusing, light adventures with Prince Sigurd, it came to her slowly that the shock of the prince's death wasn't what haunted her.

She remembered almost every word of his note to her and one phrase blazed in her memory:

"– what you have not guessed about the man whom you know as Devlin Kimball Conor, and about others close to you."

Dev hadn't liked her meeting with Sigurd. Not a bit. Talked of her danger; yet it was Sigurd who was murdered before he could tell her what he knew about Dev and "someone close." She had no doubt whatever that it was a murder to silence him and not simply a mugging.

The murderer might have hoped Sigurd's identity would be confused for a while. The steps where Sigurd had been found were usually in the deep shadow of a Renaissance church, but the murderer had still taken a chance. He (or she) would not take the time to search Sigurd's shoes.

But what had Sigurd known about Dev?

Luckily, nobody could connect Dev with the dead man if she failed to show the police the note Sigurd had left for her. Besides, Dev had been with her until five o'clock today.

No. More like a quarter to five. She hadn't seen him down in that dining room alcove afterward. In fact, she hadn't seen him at all until five-thirty.

And Sigurd's body was found on the steps of that little canal only two or three blocks from the hotel.

"Please, God, no!"

She sat straight up in the tub with foamy water draining off her flesh, as the dirty canal water must have drained from the prince's silly disguise, his blue beret and corduroy jacket.

Seconds later, she was towelling herself vigorously and closing her thoughts to that ghastly suspicion.

They slept close that night, seeking solace for their dreams and fears in each other's arms. In the middle of the night Jacqueline woke up thinking of the haunting night in Torcello, her last night with Richard the way he used to be.

He had been upset that night, dreaming or afraid of something, just as she was sure Dev felt haunted by some secret now.

Haunted by what mystery that threatened to ruin their lives together? Was it the same problem that had troubled him when he was "Richard?"

In the morning the world looked better. The fog seemed to be burning off, thanks to the efforts of sun and wind. They hadn't yet discussed their plans about the contessa's palazzo. They were both afraid to argue the subject, and the love between them still seemed to be secure.

During their continental breakfast which Dev thought

was inadequate to what he called "a growing boy" she reached across the table as usual to touch his hand. He raised her fingers and kissed the tips.

She laughed. "This reminds me of your taste in eggs. Hardboiled at breakfast? Ye Gods!"

He slowly let her hand go.

She couldn't help thinking his answering smile was forced. She knew he was jealous of those old days which he still couldn't seem to remember, and she changed the subject quickly.

They were just finishing breakfast in their room when they had a visitor who settled the matter of the cozy invitation to join the family in the Palazzo Fabrini.

Thinking the room waiter had come back, Dev called, "Come in," but the knocking resumed. He got up, shrugged at Jacqueline's question, and went to the door.

Nigel Chilton-Brown offered his hand to Dev.

"Good to see you looking so fit. According to Marcel, you must be good for our Jacqueline. He says she is her old, sparkling self again."

"I assure you, I am," Jacqueline called out. Wrapping her travel robe more closely around her, she came to join them. "And why not? I always told you Richard was the light of my life." She caught Nigel's frown as he looked Dev over. Then she and Nigel were exchanging hugs.

"It's really good to see you, dear Nigel. We were so worried after poor Sigurd was found. But now that you are here, maybe you can figure out what happened."

"A mugging?" he suggested as Dev led the way into the living room where the remains of breakfast were still spread out.

"No way. Excuse me, Gentlemen. I'll go and get dressed."

While she dressed she heard the murmur of their voices and wondered what they could find in common to talk about. Nigel had poured himself a cup of coffee and the two men seemed to have their heads together discussing something very serious when she came out, but, contrary to her expectations, it wasn't the death of Sigurd von Ulsbach.

Nigel had concluded, "I think it wise to wait before denouncing the lady. I don't want it on my conscience that the Antiquities Charity failed because of her part in quite a different scam. She evidently counts on hundreds showing up. She has hired half the young girls in Venice as maids, secretaries and what-nots."

"But can she be counted on to handle the profits honestly?" Jacqueline put in.

"Oh, yes. I've made certain of that. The general's widow, Mrs. Sears, is handling the money, and she is a discreet woman."

"Not when it comes to men. She stole Prince Sigurd from Mother."

Dev was somewhat amused but Nigel assured her, "The Sears Woman is passionately involved with raising as much money as possible. For her own reputation, if you ask me. She is not a woman to put sex above her own personal glory. And that goes for stealing money, as well."

Jacqueline, resenting the woman on Angela's behalf, suggested flippantly, "Maybe she killed poor Sigurd."

As the two men looked at her, she added, "Well, somebody did. And don't give me all that stuff about muggings."

"Why is a mugging so impossible?" Nigel wanted to know.

"Because of what he was coming to tell me. It's perfectly –" She broke off, remembering with horror what that note had contained.

Nigel set his cup down in its saucer. The crackling sound made her more nervous.

"What on earth do you mean? Ulsbach was coming to see you? Why?"

She glanced surreptitiously at Dev whose expression hadn't changed. He was a good actor. She thought as she fumbled for an answer. "Because he – he said he was."

"Let Chilton-Brown see the note the fellow left," Dev suggested. "Maybe he can make something out of it."

He spoke so innocently she couldn't look at him, for fear of giving away her secret terrors.

"That's impossible." She saw that Nigel was surprised by her sharp denial and added, "I was so disgusted with him, for what he did to Mother, that I threw the note into the waste basket beside the desk there."

Both men looked into the basket, finding nothing. They could hardly have found the note, since it was folded up and stuck behind her credit card case in her handbag.

"So he told you he wanted to see you," Nigel went on. "Did he say why?"

Dev opened his mouth to speak. She cut him off.

"No. Just that he had been looking into those funny accidents of mine. He said he had set some shady friends of his to work and they found something about people close to me in the company."

Nigel nodded wisely. "Clever chap. He must have found out about the contessa's connection with Willems-Binet of Bern, Switzerland. She was employed by one of their former officers, Willy Stadtmeister, in a hostile takeover about four years ago. A Danish firm. Had to do with designs of some kind."

"And we have to go to this woman's masquerade, for heaven's sake? What is she coming as? A female bandit?"

Nigel rubbed his jaw with his thumb but his amusement was plain.

"No. I believe our gentle contessa will come as Elizabeth Barrett Browning. She wanted Marcel to appear as Robert Browning but Marcel says he lacks the height for it; so he will be Doge Dandolo. You children are to be given your choice. I'm sending Esther over this afternoon with several outfits."

"Not me," Dev said.

But Nigel had other ideas. "I'd like it all to go as smoothly as possible. There will be international coverage and God knows, the cause is worth it. Conor, why don't you come as Henry James? Then you can swear reasonably modern trousers."

"What are you to be, Prince Charming?" Dev wanted to know.

Nigel did not take offense. "Quite the contrary. I think you will agree, my costume is well chosen, considering that my little discourse to Marcel and you at the end of the evening will very likely destroy the contessa's dreams of becoming Mrs. Godard. I come as the executioner of Venice, the chap who used to whack off the heads there in the Piazzetta. Esther Heffernan is to be my assistant."

Picturing stout little Miss Heffernan as an executioner's assistant was a bit much and Jacqueline ventured, "I almost hate to ask what Mother is coming as."

"She wasn't going to make an appearance. Out of respect to the prince. She had to identify him, of course. Marcel went with her. But Marcel talked her into attending the ball, as Juliet. He said she owed it to these ancient walls, or something of that nature."

Dev looked dubious and Jacqueline rolled her eyes heavenward but Nigel wasn't in the least disturbed by the idea.

"Actually, Angela is still lovely enough to look well in the costume. I'm told that a dashing new Italian movie hero, Ricardo Famagusta, is coming as Romeo. That was the contessa's idea."

"She wants to keep Mother away from Father."

"Probably."

Jacqueline shook her head. "Doesn't anyone else care that the prince was murdered only yesterday?"

"I'm afraid muggings are a commonplace these days. Even in Venice."

"That may be," Dev said. "But I still don't think it's a good idea for Jacqueline to be staying in that creaky palace."

"I'm inclined to agree. Let's just leave it this way until the night of the ball. If you feel tired enough to stay over, Jacqui, then we can figure out how best to protect you."

"There is an elderly woman in gray who hangs around us a lot. Looks like a nanny. She seems to take a great interest in us. And once or twice in London I saw a weaselly little man. I thought he was following me when I went to Richmond."

"That was a weaselly little chap who acted as our witness the day Conor took that tumble in front of the lorry," Nigel suggested. "Have you seen him here?" Dev shook his head. Nigel added, "You may dismiss your fears about the woman in gray. Highly capable. A Mrs. Dimblby. We know about her. Well now, I'll send Miss Heffernan over with costumes. Take your choice. You will probably see your parents some time today, or this evening. But –" He laughed. "At least, we need not worry about them."

When they walked with him to the door Dev asked, "Are we to believe she is safe here? I don't have much faith in this mugging theory about Ulsbach."

Nigel waved it aside. "Jacqueline is being watched, and we count on you as well, my dear fellow."

Jacqueline was gratified by his confidence in Dev and kissed Nigel goodbye.

Angela came along that afternoon with Miss Heffernan, accompanied by a Fabrini servant, and some pretty outlandish costumes. Jacqueline was glad to see her mother but she was depressed by the full details of how Angela had been forced to identify the unfortunate prince.

Angela got no sympathy from Miss Heffernan who whispered to Jacqueline, "Frankly, the man probably got what he deserved. Mr. C thought he was nothing but a gigolo."

"He was a human being."

"Humph. Mr. C believes the man –"

Jacqueline said abruptly. "The hell with Mr. C's opinions! When people are murdered, somebody ought to be a little sorry. It looks like I'm the only one. And there were times when I despised him. But he didn't deserve to be murdered. You can tell Nigel I said so."

Esther twittered nervously. "I'm sure I didn't mean – That is, of course, in Christian charity we all regret that wretched man's death. I was only quoting what I happen to know was dear Mr. Chilton's opinion."

"The devil with Mr. Chilton!"

"Now, now, Children," Angela calmed troubled waters. "We all shed tears for poor Sigurd. I certainly did last night. Anybody will tell you that. Ask dear Marcel. He was there . . . You know, Jacqueline, it was the strangest thing. Sigurd was wearing an old beat-up jacket and they found a beret beside him. Imagine Sigurd von Ulsbach in a beret! I can't think why."

Jacqueline and Dev looked at each other. Dev put his arm across her shoulders.

"People say things they don't always mean."

"Oh, that's ever so true," Esther Heffernan gushed. "I'm sure I didn't mean anything. It's only that Mr. C – Has Mrs. Godard told you what she is wearing to the Gala? She looks divine."

Angela looked as pleased as if she had never heard the compliment before.

"Thank you, dear. What are you children going to wear?"

"I thought I'd –" Jacqueline began, only to be interrupted oddly by Dev.

"Haven't made up our minds yet. We want to choose a matching pair. Can you leave them all here?"

It was arranged that they would send back the unused costumes before the Antiquities Ball and Angela left with Esther Heffernan, both women chattering about the "romantic notions" of youth.

Jacqueline was puzzled by his excuse to keep the costumes but she had no objection.

"What shall we be? Twin pirates? Or mandarins? Or – Well, we can't very well be twin ballerinas."

He laughed. He was tossing the costumes into their boxes. "Don't worry, sweetheart. We aren't wearing anything they expect."

She had no trouble guessing why he didn't want anyone to know what they were wearing.

"Dev, let's face it. You know as well as I do that Sigurd was murdered because he was about to tell me about some danger in the company."

He stopped sealing the top box. "Actually, all this is childish. You shouldn't be in Venice at all. Or do you, by any chance, think the danger is from me?"

"Don't say things like that." She reached for him. "You're all I have in the world. I mean it."

He avoided her hands, saying firmly, "The costume switch was Chilton's idea. But the real answer seems to be that someone your size should wear the costume while you are safe out of Venice."

She was overwhelmed by the old panic of her nightmares. "No! If I leave you, I might never see you again."

He didn't deny it. That hurt most of all.

"All right," he agreed finally. "But we are going to get costumes nobody knows about. Not even your parents."

"Don't tell me you suspect my parents."

"No, but they aren't the brightest pair in the world. And I doubt very much if they could keep their mouths shut."

She sat down on the bed beside the boxes he stacked up and closed her eyes. He was right but the fact didn't make her feel any more secure.

In the days before the Antiquities Gala she and Dev spent very little time in the area around St. Mark's Square where they might expect to be found by Jacqueline's large acquaintance. Dev was always thinking up walks across endless bridges to the Rialto or the Railroad Station or, of course, the churches and museums where the paintings interested him. She even thought him selfish at first, with his insistence on following up these interests, but she caught him looking around so often she realized he too was thinking about Prince Sigurd's death and the murderer who was still at large.

The night of the ball at the Palazzo Fabrini crept up on them before Jacqueline was ready for it. To her surprise, Dev had suggested that they not come in twin costumes after all. As a result, they had located ready-made outfits in a little shop not far from the ancient Arsenal, and had them adapted to their own taller, thinner figures, and then sneaked out of the hotel by the cul de sac of cats, rather than the main canal entrance below the terrace, where anyone watching them would expect them to hire a boat.

Ever since Jacqueline's arrival in Venice it had taken all her nerve to get into a boat. A rocking, swaying gondola was bad enough but motorboats were worse, with the memories they invoked. Tonight everyone would be arriving in trim, funereal black gondolas with the ever-present silver teeth at the prow that caught the lantern light as they pulled up to the striped mooring poles. There was no way to escape travelling on the choppy Grand Canal in Venice.

Jacqueline braced herself for the "voyage" and kept telling herself it was the height of romance to ride along in her husband's company, heeling over to one side all too often as a motorboat or big, clumsy *vaporetto* passed them. It seemed to her that the whole of the Grand Canal was lighted up in honor of the Antiquities Gala. The glow of many colors flashed over the murky green canal waters from a score of Sixteenth and Seventeenth Century facades, including the lacy front of the Palazzo Fabrini.

Jacqueline came as Harlequin, all black and white diamond designs in her tunic, over slim black trousers and a saucy black and white cap over a wig of lustrous red hair. Beside her, Dev was a priest in a biretta, a black cassock gracefully sashed, to conceal the tiny camera he had pocketed. With his pale, umblemished complexion, his slender height and poise, he looked extraordinarly handsome to Jacqueline.

They both wore masks. Dev's was a mere black eye mask, but Jacqueline had also painted her face half black, half white. Though her mask covered little more than her deep, expressive eyes and her nose, it was difficult to recognize her well-known features.

The Contessa Irina Fabrini waited with little Marcel Godart in the Central Hall at the head of the marble staircase above the canal floor. She was looking the height of glamor in a hooped green skirt and 1840s jacket and blouse. The contessa did not seem to know Jacqueline or Dev. Luckily, Marcel's attention was called away at that minute by a word from Nigel Chilton-Brown, looking more stately than terrifying in what he conceived to be the robe of an executioner. In his belt was a toy ax, the symbol of his profession.

The Englishman had been watching the new arrivals intently and Jacqueline did not doubt he recognized her and Dev.

Some of the guests appeared to have arrived intoxicated. It was hard to believe they could be so thoroughly drunk so soon. The canal floor, with its veined marble columns and exquisite diamond-patterned marble floor, heavily waterstained from Adriatic high tides, was crowded with a chain of masqueraders, some of them parading out toward the lantern-lit garden in the rear.

A learned Italian wearing the frightening red robes of a Venetian Inquisitor in the days of the Serene Republic, was lecturing to half a dozen foreign masqueraders that: "The canal floor is the *andron*. Then comes the *portego*, and at times after the mezzanine, the *piano nobile*. Not to mention the veined steps."

Jacqueline was surprised to find Nigel paying no attention to her, but he had also maneuvered matters so that her parents didn't get a good look at her either. Dev left her to snap some pictures of other guests, especially an attractive brunette in the costume of a Fifteenth Century male courtier, which featured tights with one leg striped yellow and black, the other pure black. Jacqueline recognized her own jealousy at this desertion. Curiously enough, the girl looked a bit like Jacqueline, around the head and general figure.

Jacqueline took champagne from the tray offered to her by a sexy, curvacious young woman who did not seem as well trained as she might be. One of the local girls hired for the night, probably. Jacqueline watched her with sympathy. It wasn't easy for an untrained person, balancing the silver tray without letting drops of champagne spill out of the glasses.

Two flirtatious young men in lumbering face card tabards pulled at Jacqueline, begging her in Italian to "join the daisy chain in the garden." While she gave them a laughing refusal, a tall figure passed between Jacqueline and the colored glass *torcheres*. His shadow distracted her attention and she recognized the Executioner with his obsequious follower, Esther Heffernan, trotting to keep up with his long strides. He slowed his pace beyond Jacqueline so rapidly that his stout little "assistant" bumped into him. This must be Nigel's way of keeping Jacqueline under observation.

From somewhere on the canal floor or "andron," below the long, open mezzanine came orchestral music, pleasantly if anachronistically playing *CATARI, CATARI*.

When Dev joined her she remarked coolly that the brunette in the male costume had quite good legs.

"That's what Chilton-Brown had in mind. Most of the crowd thinks she's you."

"Is it deliberate?"

He smiled. "What do you think? I'll admit, in order to look like you she would have to be pretty special."

He stood back, snapped two shots of her. “Look that way, toward the staircase. I want to get your profile.”

She did as he ordered, guessing he wanted to make it appear that he had stopped her only to take some pictures. Within her view was an oblong tabaret near a veined marble pillar.

The blonde girl with the champagne tray, whom she had noticed before, was setting the now half-empty tray on the tabaret. Thinking no one saw her, she raised one foot and massaged the instep. Her face looked petulant and unhappy, which was not surprising.

To Jacqueline the surprising aspect of her expression was its familiarity. She knew she had seen the girl before, and not in the capacity of a servant. She nudged Dev.

“Do you remember that girl at all?”

He studied her, shook his head. “Not that I know of. Is this something that Chilton-Brown or the police should know?”

They really had her safety on the brain. But she knew she should be grateful.

“No. Nothing like that. She reminds me of someone I saw once several years ago. She’s a little older now. But aren’t we all?”

Could it be someone who had waited on her in a cafe? No. This was outdoors. On a bridge? A bridge was in it somewhere. A little square where an outdoor cafe had been set up. Jacqueline had seen it first from a bridge.

Richard was in the picture. Sitting at a table reading, and across from him was a pretty, petulant girl with pouting, heavy lips, the daughter of his landlady at the Pensione Cuneo. She was Italian but she had a French name.

With her pulses beating rapidly, Jacqueline watched Dev as she repeated the name aloud.

"Babette something. Babette Cuneo."

Dev's mask was so small it was easy to tell whether the name produced a reaction. It didn't. He was examining his camera and looked up, perplexed.

"Oh? Do I know her?"

"I thought you did."

"Not that I'm aware of. Does she say she knows me? Look this way, Sweetheart. There. Should I hold out and demand they put you on the cover of their precious Palazzo book?"

She laughed off his flattery but her thoughts remained fixed on Babette Cuneo.

Meanwhile, he added, "By the way, your parents wanted to know what you were wearing. I told them you were playing a game. You wanted to fool them until the unmasking. Here comes our gray-haired nanny, Mrs. Dimblby. I'll let you go for the moment, Sweetheart. She'll look out for you. If I'm seen with you too long, your cover is going to be blown, to put it melodramatically."

Sure enough, an elderly woman in a nun's coif and robes swept along, headed for the champagne tray. Jacqueline got a good look at her face when the woman removed her mask, letting it dangle from two fingers while, with the other hand, she took a champagne glass from the tray. The girl who looked like Babette Cuneo hurriedly straightened up.

Sipping champagne, Mrs. Dimblby, the gray-suited detective, or bodyguard – whatever she was – kept an eye on Jacqueline. The woman had a hard, strong, alert face. She had probably never been pretty and certainly wasn't now, but in front of Jacqueline's eyes she had the ability to change from a forceful, strong woman of fifty to a sweet, reserved little creature who might be seventy. She turned this look on a masked ballerina and a Pierrot who came up the stairs breathless, probably after having been a part of the hurlyburly in the garden.

Jacqueline took this opportunity to escape Mrs. Dimblby's eagle eye and look for a friend in the crowd now milling around the long buffets of food and the footmen with other trays of drinks.

A footman, looking into various masked faces, stopped in front of Jacqueline, saying in Italian, "A gentleman wishes to speak with you in private, Signora Kimberly. Signor Chilton-Brown. There on the balcony."

Jacqueline looked in that direction, wondering why Nigel would ask her to join him in the tiny space high over the Grand Canal, with its lacy white fretwork and a railing scarcely two feet high. It seemed highly improbable. She started in that direction, intending to get a look at "the gentleman named Cheelton-Brown," and no more. In doing so she crossed the path of Esther Heffernan balancing two champagne glasses and trotting toward the mezzanine. She had abandoned her mask entirely and her round face was sweating with her exertions.

Seeing Jacqueline about to speak to her, the harried Esther excused herself. "Sorry. Dear Mr. C has been talking to a Swiss gentleman. He is quite hoarse. A lubricant ought to put everything to rights."

Jacqueline glanced in the direction of the canal and the little decorative "balcony."

"Wait. Please. Where is Nigel?"

Esther stopped reluctantly, trying to point with her head. "As I say. Over there. At the far end of the mezzanine."

"Esther, send him to me."

"But he is busy talk –"

"At once. Fast. I can't leave here. Tell him it's life or death."

Surely, that would get him. It got Esther. With eyes wide she scampered off, showering champagne as she went.

What was the supposed guard's name? No matter. Jacqueline didn't want to scare away whoever was out there. Without taking her eyes off the balcony, Jacqueline called, "Babette?" Her voice didn't quite cut through the pandemonium. Turning a few inches, she raised her voice. "Babette Cuneo."

This time the gray-suit female guard, or whatever she was, heard her. With fluttering black robes she stalked over toward Jacqueline, followed by the puzzled Babette Cuneo.

"At least, I was right about the girl's name," Jacqueline told herself. By calling her, she had also gotten the more important female guard.

Meanwhile, nothing moved on the half-curtained balcony.

With any luck, she thought, they could find the answer to all those attempts on her life.

She refused to think about the implications of her husband's failure to recognize his old girlfriend. It might be an effort to spare Jacqueline any jealousy. It might be a part of his amnesia during the "Richard Kimberly" days.

Or was there another, more terrible reason, something she could not face?

Twenty-Two

It took Esther some minutes to locate Nigel in the midst of the noise, the music, the laughter, and what seemed to be the echo of all the activities that had gone on in this building for the past four hundred years.

Meanwhile, the woman who introduced herself as "Mrs. Dimblby," asked Jacqueline quietly, "What happened? Some kind of threat?" She dismissed the wildly curious Babette with an authoritative, "Don't hang about. Go into another room."

Jacqueline added, "Not too far, please. I'd like to talk to you later, Miss Cuneo, if you don't mind."

The girl stared at each of them, then shrugged, returned to her tray and went out into the mezzanine, looking back several times.

Still, there was no significant movement from the balcony. A couple of times the heavy green velvet drapes swayed as if the wind off the canal had rustled them.

Jacqueline explained, "I was asked to meet Mr. Chilton-Brown out there. His assistant had gone to get him. In the mezzanine."

"Ah!" Mrs. Dimblby said. "Interesting. Shall I rout this person out?"

"Do you have a weapon?"

Like Dev's costume, the woman's habit concealed several pockets. She showed Jacqueline something dark and metallic that Jacqueline supposed was a handgun. The idea was unnerving but she had no doubt Mrs. Dimblby knew how to use it.

"This will do nicely. We probably won't need it."

"I devoutly hope not." Jacqueline looked around at the curious figures, masked and costumed, all focussing their interest on her and Mrs. Dimblby. She had a sensation of being in some unearthly place where only inhuman creatures looked back at her out of weird, multi-colored faces. She supposed her own black and white painted face was also eery.

There was a disturbance among the milling crowds in the adjoining salon as Dev made his way through, not too careful how he cleared a passage for himself. He slowed down to a long stride when he saw that Jacqueline was with Mrs. Dimblby and unhurt.

"My God, Sweetheart! You had me going. I heard the Heffernan Woman. What about this life or death business?"

Mrs. Dimblby nudged him. Two pirates walking by turned to stare at Dev. Jacqueline explained in a voice that was scarcely audible. He took her arm.

"The hell with Chilton and his schemes. I'm taking you out of this squirrel cage."

Jacqueline was about to point out that this might be their best chance to learn about The Enemy when Nigel arrived on the scene with Mrs. Heffernan still trying to explain the matter to him.

Mrs. Dimblby was succint. "Someone is claiming to be yourself, Sir. Asked Mrs. Kimberly to meet him out on that little balcony. With your permission . . ."

The Contessa Fabrini had been summoned by the hullabaloo and said with freezing politeness, "Certainly, you may. Is someone playing hide-and-seek on my little balcony? I assure you, there is no room."

Nigel said, "I don't understand. You wouldn't have been so foolish as to go out there, Jacqueline?"

"Of course not. Especially since the footman claimed Nigel Chilton-Brown was out there and I discovered from Esther that you were in the mezzanine."

The contessa kept her wits. She signalled a girl passing through the long salon with an empty champagne tray.

"Send every footman to me. At once. As for the man out on the balcony, is anyone armed?"

Mrs. Dimblby patted the heavy weight in the pocket of her habit and started across the room toward the balcony as she produced the small but dangerous Biretta. The audience which had flocked around to watch the excitement, now scattered toward the mezzanine in one direction and the second salon in the other, leaving only a handful of onlookers including those immediately concerned.

Dev stepped in front of Jacqueline and Nigel moved forward somewhat cautiously on Mrs. Dimblby's trail. She had reached the green portieres. Her left hand pushed them aside suddenly. Everyone could see that nothing was on the balcony and only the lights across the Grand Canal were visible.

Jacqueline insisted, "I've been watching every minute since the message. No one went near that balcony or came out."

Just as three footmen in black livery with yellow stockings hurried into the salon from the staircase and another approached from the mezzanine, Angela Godart as a golden "Juliet" appeared upon the scene, unmasked, accompanied by stocky Marcel and a dashing Romeo, also unmasked, who provoked "Ah!" and little screams from girls as he strode by.

Poor Father! Jacqueline thought, trying to get her mind off the sinister invitation she had not accepted. It was clear that Marcel would be outclassed by movie star Ricardo Famagusta who had twined the fingers of one hand with Angela's. Seeing Jacqueline remove her mask exhaustedly, Marcel started across the room to her but Esther Heffernan said imperiously,

"Hush! Mr. Chilton-Brown is speaking."

"I think we must agree that someone was having a little fun with Mrs. Kimberly. May I speak to your footmen, my dear Contessa?"

"By all means, my dear Mr. Chilton-Brown. Augusto will translate if your Italian is not up to it."

None of these three had delivered the message but Jacqueline recognized the fourth who came up late from the *andron* or canal floor. He was a short, pleasant-spoken young man, flustered now by this unwanted attention. His Italian was clear to Jacqueline and Nigel, though Dev frowned, trying to follow it.

"The gentleman was English or American, Signor. I cannot say. He wore a mask with the lower cloth that covered the mouth loosely. He was in clown costume.

Of height? Taller than myself but not tall. The message? To ask the Signora Kimberly –"

"How did you know me?" Jacqueline asked.

"But Signora, he pointed you out."

Nigel said, "Where was he when all this happened?"

"In the alcove beyond the portieres. Was it a bad thing to bring the message, Signore?"

"Would you know him again?"

The young footman scratched his head, apologized, then admitted, "I can not say, Signore. The voice was like a cold. Hoarse."

"Disguised," the contessa suggested, and looked around at what remained of the witnesses, fortunately too far away to hear all the details.

"I will walk through the rooms with you and see if you can point him out. Do not make it obvious. You understand?"

The contessa said, "I will go with you. To translate."

"That will not be necessary."

The contessa smiled. "I understand perfectly. Augusto, go with them."

Watching them leave, Marcel demanded of the contessa, "What has happened? Is there danger to my daughter?"

Jacqueline removed his mask and kissed his cheek "Certainly not, Father. It was a joke. That is all."

She and Dev were beseiged by her mother afterward. Angela, being assured that Jacqueline was safe, wanted to present the Signor Famagusta whose slanting eyes opened wider, doubtless in shock, when introduced to Jacqueline who still wore the red wig, the soft cap and the ghastly black and white makeup.

Under the interested eyes of the contessa, who clutched Marcel's arm, Jacqueline interrupted Famagusta's practiced flattery to remind Angela,

"You haven't said hello to my Richard."

Dev corrected her politely, "Dev Conor," as he took Angela's hand in his. Angela was not averse to the charm of any good-looking man and let her small hand lie in his while she expressed her delight with her "son-in-law" and said after cocking her head on one side prettily,

"I could never forget you, my dear Mr. Conor. May I call you Dev? The London Antiquities party. You were snapping pictures and sketching."

While Angela flirted with Dev Jacqueline studied her father's expression, the way he never took his eyes off his ex-wife. She glittered like the gold coins on the little net cap she wore over the crown of her head. She was certainly as much "Juliet" as any forty-year old Shakespearean actress.

But to Jacqueline's disappointment her poor father's feelings didn't seem to be reciprocated.

The crowds had shuffled into smaller groups presided over by members of the Antiquities Committee, and many of the rowdier guests were streaming out to their gondolas to kill the rest of the night in St. Mark's Square or on the Lido.

Jacqueline saw Babette Cuneo once while she and Dev waited for Chilton-Brown but Jacqueline said nothing. She didn't want to pursue the truth at this minute. Not if it might threaten her happiness with Dev.

When she went to wipe off the weird black and white paint from her face with theatrical cream, Dev waited on guard outside one of the bathrooms. While she was making herself look halfway presentable, Angela came in. She was at her best, delighted with the evening.

"When Irina asked me to stay here – at Marcel's suggestion, I'm sure – it seemed like the best *entrée* to the Venice Season, and of course, I was broken-hearted over Sigurd's awful death – poor dear Sigurd! And besides, I felt that Marcel needed a little looking after. Don't tell Irina but I think he is looking peaked. She seems to have lost her grip on him. But little did I expect that a young man Ricardo's age would take such a fancy to me. Quite absurd, that boy."

"Father loves you very much. He always has."

Angela examined the gold powder on her eyelids thoughtfully. "Do I see a wrinkle there? God, what will I do when I grow old?"

"Mother, you will never grow old. Some maddened lover will shoot you out of sheer desperation."

Angela smiled and chucked Jacqueline under the chin. "You are a dear."

When they left the elegant little marble room, obviously a recent addition enlarged from an ancient powdering closet, Dev drew Jacqueline aside.

"Miss Heffernan got the word from Chilton-Brown. The footman couldn't identify anybody. I figured that. But he intends to expose the contessa. I'm afraid we are stuck to meet in the library. It's across the mezzanine."

Jacqueline winced at the thought. "I wish it was over. I don't want to see anybody humiliated. And in front of witnesses."

"He needs the heavy stockholders, your father and Mother, and you. It's going to be rough on your father."

Jacqueline considered the idea. "Somehow, I don't think it will hurt Father as much as this Famagusta character . . . What do you think happened to the man who wanted to get me out on the balcony?"

"Probably hustled out with some of those drunks."

They walked in silence around the balustrade high above the canal floor which they could see more than a dozen feet below. Before they opened the heavy, panelled door of the library, Dev suddenly remarked, "I don't know why but the whole business about the balcony and the mysterious invitation sounds phoney to me."

She tried to laugh. "You don't think I made it up!"

"It happened, all right. I just don't believe whoever is back of this expected to meet you there. It was a – I guess you'd call it a red herring. Somebody sent the message but never went near the balcony. Why it was done, I've no idea." He shrugged and grinned. "Anyway, that's my theory."

"We'd better tell Nigel."

With his hand on the door latch he looked at her.

"Let's just keep this to ourselves for a while."

She was puzzled but said briskly, "Righto." As they went into the room lined to the high ceiling with leather-bound books, she whispered, "I hate this. I'd rather be anywhere else."

His expression told her he agreed. He avoided looking at Angela who sparkled so much Jacqueline suspected she knew what this was all about. Obviously, her pleasure did not reflect a guest's normal discomfort at her hostess's bad luck.

To Jacqueline's surprise her father and a stout, gray-haired man came in with Nigel, the latter looking severe and formidable. Marcel seemed to have shrivelled into himself. He didn't look shocked, only lost. Jacqueline longed to hug and encourage him. Nigel must have told him the truth about the contessa's machinations.

The contessa herself entered alone, radiant but stately in her Elizabeth Barrett costume. She made a graceful gesture of welcome to the others, with her arms extended.

"I do not know what it is about, but you are all welcome. Is it the profits for the Gala? Viola Sears said there would be word shortly. Gentlemen – Ladies, you will find decanters on the desk behind you, Nigel." Her gaze shifted from Nigel to the stout, gray-haired man. Her eyes dilated. She took one step back, felt the aged brass door latch behind her, and mentally pulled herself together so rapidly Jacqueline had to admire her.

"I suppose I may thank you for locating Herr Stadtmeister."

"Quite," the Swiss gentleman agreed. "I have had long chats with Herr Chilton-Brown. My sincere regrets if there is embarrassment in any quarter."

Nigel took over in his most dry and bookish manner.

"I have here statements authorized and sworn to by officers at Willems-Binet that Irina Salvio Fabrini is a member of the board of a corporation directly subordinate to Willems-Binet which has been buying up substantial blocks of stock in Godart's during the last few months."

Everyone looked at Marcel Godart who reddened and stared at the terrazzo floor partially covered by a Persian carpet. He cleared his throat.

"I wanted to please my – fiancée. I have given her stock certificates as gifts now and then." He added in a low voice, "Quite heavily."

Nigel covered Marcel's humiliation. "Herr Stadtmeister was an officer in the Helvetian Stadtmeister Corporation which absorbs the Godart assets. He has now – retired."

Perhaps by request of the parent company, Jacqueline thought cynically. The Swiss were less likely than anyone else to forgive an officer who revealed inside deals.

The contessa's first uneasy reaction had firmed up into a matter-of-fact approach. "I am sure we can come to an agreement. As you may imagine, I will make any accommodation that seems reasonable to you. Although –" She gave Marcel a soft smile, "I did not forcibly extract the shares from Monsieur Godart." She looked at the others then, especially Nigel and Herr Stadtmeister. "I do know when the game is up and I am naturally anxious that this affair should not go beyond this room."

Jacqueline understood very well that the contessa had hoped to continue to do business with her Swiss allies, moving on to another company in the States whose assets were desired by outside interests. The fact that she had been found out was a body blow to her future hopes and plans, not only at Godart, but at the next of her company interests.

The contessa crossed the room, gently elbowed her way between Dev and Marcel, and poured herself two fingers of Scotch. She drank while everyone except Marcel stared at her. Over the edge of the glass she smiled at Nigel.

"I am quite willing to sell my Godart shares. If the matter goes no further than this room, you may find my terms generous."

Herr Stadtmeister said, "The Contessa is all of that."

Jacqueline had been growing more and more uncomfortable.

"Please, can't we handle it as the contessa suggests? Surely, nothing will be accomplished by bringing in outsiders."

The contessa smiled over her whisky. "I could not agree with you more. Gentlemen?"

"I think it's disgusting," Angela said. She walked to the door, opened it and flounced out onto the mezzanine where they could see the handsome Italian movie star lounged against the wrought-iron railing above the canal floor, unmasked and clearly waiting for her.

Marcel hurried after her, calling, "It was stupid. I am aware now. Angela? Let me explain."

The contessa shook her head. "Poor little man. It's perhaps just as well. I'm afraid I would have quite worn him out."

Nobody laughed and Jacqueline girded herself for the battle to get back the stock.

She was exhausted by the tensions of the evening before she and Dev left the library, the Godart stock safely in Godart hands and Nigel efficiently handling the long-distance transfer. At the parting in front of their gondola, she kissed her father who was followed by a Fabrini servant carrying three large suitcases. He explained, "Nigel is arranging rooms for me at his hotel."

"Yes, Papa. Things will look better in the morning."

"Angela went off with that movie actor."

Jacqueline hugged him again. "She'll be back."

He didn't answer and stood there forlornly, waiting for Nigel.

Nigel lowered his voice so that Marcel wouldn't hear him. "I think we may say tonight's business puts an end to those *accidents* you were having, Jacqueline."

"How do you figure that?" Dev wanted to know.

"Because it all seemed to be tied up with the months since the contessa came into Marcel's life. I doubt if they were actually attempts. Just unsettling efforts that would turn you against the business, upset you, Jacqueline. She had heard about your problem several years ago, and this seemed a good way to wean you away from the company. If you really wanted to get away from the whole scare, you might have sold your shares."

Jacqueline wanted to believe that. It was possible, but Dev didn't seem to accept it. He looked around for their gondolier who had been in the lower regions of the palazzo, and then studied him before helping Jacqueline into the gondola.

"Does he look safe?" she asked half-humorously.

"He's the one we had coming here, at any rate."

Their voices had attracted a young woman bundled up in a heavy cloth coat and waiting beyond the palazzo for a motorboat. She looked around just as Jacqueline's face was illuminated by the lights at the water entrance of the Palazzo Fabrini. The girl stopped, then came back to them, her kinky blonde hair blowing about her petulant face. She was Babette Cuneo.

"It is you," she called. She showed a fine set of teeth and her eyes flashed. "I thought I remembered your voice."

Jacqueline was surprised that the girl's jealousy had lasted so long. Obviously, she still held a grudge because Richard had fallen in love with Jacqueline. There had never been anything between her and Richard. At least, Richard said so.

"Turn around, Darling," she told Dev. "There's an old friend of yours."

Puzzled by this curious encounter, Dev looked back. He didn't seem to recognize the girl yet. He was still puzzled when he remembered. "The girl with the champagne tray."

The astonishing reaction was Babette's.

"Well?" Then, addressing Jacqueline again, "You took your sweet time coming back. My Richard's death was not even worth a tribute from you."

Jacqueline grasped Dev's hand and stepped out of the rocking gondola. She raised his hand with hers.

"Because Richard was rescued. He is here. You see?"

Dev frowned. "Obviously, she doesn't know me."

Babette came close to him staring into his face. Then she waved a hand in front of him, as if he were a fly who annoyed her.

"You think he is like my Richard? He is nothing like him." She spat at the worn paving with its green water-stains. "I spit upon him. My Richard was not so tall, and he had a freckle on his neck, beneath the ear. I loved that freckle. But this one, no."

She signalled to the motorboat that approached at the end of the narrow paving stones, and got in.

Dev watched her and then turned to help Jacqueline into the gondola again. They sat down together. The gondolier, yawning, leaned on his oar and they moved away from the Palazzo Fabrini.

Jacqueline and Dev sat in silence until the gondola was in midstream. Then Jacqueline asked in a voice she hardly recognized,

"Who are you? Really?"

Twenty-Three

The gondolier had begun to hum to himself. There was no effort to entertain his tourist passengers in the usual tourist fashion. His main object, apparently, was to keep himself awake until he got back to the water landing of the Grand Hotel Splendide.

The more he hummed, the better, so far as Jacqueline was concerned. The occasional night sounds, an infrequent boatman calling signals across the Grand Canal, along with the gondolier leaning forward and back on his great oar, helped to cover Dev's reply. She knew what he was bound to say, but she prayed that he would surprise her.

He did not.

"I told you that day in Richmond when we met what my name was," he said evenly. "It has never been anything else. Unlike Richard – What did he call himself? Kimberly? I was born – I was even christened Devlin Kimball Conor, in Minersfield, Nevada, on the twenty-sixth of May, 1959. My birth certificate is somewhere in the archives of Nevada. Try that with your beloved Richard Kimberly."

She felt a keen stab of anguish. "You let me think you were Richard. You know you did. Maybe not at first, but afterwards. I remember when you changed. Really changed and seemed to love me as you used to. I mean – he did. It was after we met at Banbury." She turned and stared at him, seeing his face only in fleeting light and shadow from the varied unknown lights of the Grand Canal. It was the same face she had loved all these days and nights. "Why did you tell me that cruel lie about your mother being from Banbury, and how you loved Eccles cakes, or whatever they call them?"

He examined his hands, especially his nails, as if all his thoughts were focussed on them.

"They happen to have been a favorite in my family. My mother baked them for us. She actually was from Banbury."

"What a coincidence!"

"Not at all." He looked up at the gondolier and made no further effort to explain.

She sat there without saying another word until the Grand Canal began to flow together with the Venetian Lagoon and the gondolier pulled up between the mooring poles of their hotel.

"Have I been nothing but the mistress of a stranger all this time?" Jacqueline asked herself. "How could I have been so blind, so faithless to Richard?"

Had Richard really drowned out there in that ghastly black water, the constant scene of her nightmares?

They went silently to their pleasant rooms that overlooked the terrace and the canal in one direction, the balcony and red tiled rooftops in the other. Jacqueline caught a glimpse of herself in the mirror with Dev behind her, reaching around her in that tender, sensuous way of his to unfasten and remove her black velvet cape. She had loved his touch, his gentleness and warm caring. He was Richard as she dreamed of him.

Now she asked herself: "Why did he go though with this pretense? Granted, I insisted, like a crazy woman, but surely, he could have made me see the truth some way. Showed me his past, his real life."

She looked at his face in the mirror and then at her reflection. It showed her a tall, pallid, thin woman in a garish Harlequin costume that was far from flattering. Behind her Dev was looking directly into her eyes in the mirror. She avoided his gaze, doubtful, hurt, puzzled. It troubled her too much. She tried to concentrate on his luggage stacked in a far corner, his suitcase and the old-fashioned canvas roll that reminded her of the blue canvas roll Richard had carried on his shoulders when they left Torcello. Even in this Dev had copied Richard Kimberly.

Looking back on her relationship with Dev Conor, she added up so many things, clues, signs that pointed to a direct attempt at imitating Richard Kimberly. The Agatha Christie play. The Boise reference of all things. The . . .

A hundred things.

A hundred things.

Because her life had been lived in the center of power, which meant money in most instances, and suspicion had been instilled in her from infancy, she knew at once why Dev Conor had gone to this trouble to win her love. Money.

Jacqueline and Dev.

Marcel and the contessa.

Like father, like daughter.

She said finally, "There must be an explanation."

His hands slipped away from her throat and shoulders. She was astonished by what she assumed was a lightness in his voice.

"I take it that just plain loving you isn't enough."

"No. That's the kind of answer Sigurd would have ready."

She realized the minute she said it that it was a disastrous comparison. But the insiduous comparison had leaped to her mind. She was used to men like Sigurd von Ulsbach. They had all been like that. Except Richard, of course. Richard had been honest.

Without saying a word in his defense he stared at her, his eyes wide, as if he had taken a blow and was numb before the pain set in. The silence made her regret more and more that she had blurted out that secret thought, but she could do nothing to reassure him. He would read her insincerity if she told him, "I believe you."

She fumbled behind her for a chair. Her hands were shaking. "Tell me how it happened. How did you find out all about Richard Kimberly, the little things, his tastes, about his mother and the Boise aunts."

"Tell you? And hope you will believe me?" He cleared his throat, tried to laugh. It was not a success and he shrugged. "Well, why not? I'll give it a try. But I think it was all useless from the beginning. You'll never get over him. It's a gift he has. Had."

She frowned, trying to follow him. "You knew Richard Kimberly?"

He seemed to think her question was funny.

"Did I know – Oh, yes. I knew him. At least, I knew Rick Kimball Conor. From the day he was born."

"You were Richard Kimberly's – what? His brother? Cousin? What?"

"There is no Richard Kimberly. There never was one, legally, although he must have gotten someone to forge whatever he needed. He and Dad had a lot of funny friends. Associates."

How simple! The perfect explanation for the resemblance. The knowledge of Richard's past. Their mother born near Banbury in England. The aunts in Boise. Everything. And now, he was going to try and destroy her faith in Richard.

"You hated your brother. One of those sibling rivalries psychiatrists are always babbling about." She had had her own bitter dealings with psychiatrists. "They told me I was all mixed up because I *had* no siblings. No sisters. Brothers. Did you hate him because he was a younger child, maybe more popular, more charming?"

He threw his hands up in the air and brought them down hard, slapping his thighs.

"Don't give me that crap. We loved each other. He was only a year younger. We looked a lot alike. We were always having wild adventures together. We got lost several times. The Nevada Desert is no picnic. Once, we had half the county out after us. We made it back ourselves, though, thanks to Rick's sense of direction."

To her relief he relaxed a little, although he started to walk up and down, thinking back. Reliving old, warm days of youth.

She was haunted by the knowledge that the worst was coming. Obviously, something had happened between them. Something unforgivable. And Dev would make it appear to be entirely Richard's fault. Maybe it had been, but it was all too much to absorb now. The emotions that had absorbed her entire life for over three-years would have to be overturned. She ventured hopefully,

"People don't always get along. You can't expect miracles. Were your parents partial to one of you?"

He didn't get angry again as she expected. His thoughts still seemed to linger over the good days.

"Mother wasn't. She treated us as equals. Father took to Rick, but it's understandable. He had a lot of easy charm. Everybody liked him right away. But after Mother died – I was fifteen. Rick was almost fourteen, things were different."

He looked at her. "I told you once that the men in our family were pretty crooked. Grandfather stole a mine from his partner by getting him drunk and and then riding hell-for-leather into Carson City and staking his claim. He aced another fellow out of a little gambling hole in Minersfield and eventually got my father wrapped up in it. 'Conor's Ace' it is – was called. After Mother died Rick fell into it quite naturally. At his age, he couldn't do much publicly. For a while he studied bookkeeping, but that wasn't his bag, as he said repeatedly."

"He said it to me," she murmured, thinking back.

"Anyway, gambling may have been in the blood. I don't know."

"I find that odd, considering that we never went near a casino, and he certainly didn't suggest gambling."

His smile was more than a little sardonic.

"I'm not surprised."

It came back to her then, Richard's fear of someone or something. She had teased him about the Mafia. Whatever it was, Richard's fear had been there. No one knew anything about his past. He had never confided in her. If only he had, she might have been able to help him.

"Did he lose a lot of money?"

He shook his head. "No. But something just as stupid. I never went in for the gambling bit; so I left for L.A. when I was almost eighteen. Didn't make any money, I can tell you. Thought I was an artist. I got a job, sort of a gofer for a photographer on the *Times*. Father had put Mother's name on record as co-owner of 'Conor's Ace'. When she died he transferred her interest to Rick and me."

"At least, your father tried to help his family."

"I don't know if he meant it or not. I'll never know, but after what happened, I have my suspicions. I didn't want any part of it. You've got examiners and commissioners breathing down your neck, and ultimately, the IRS."

Richard had mentioned the IRS. "He said he 'might be running from them, not the Mafia.'"

"Anyway," he went on, "Father took me at my word and we were both happy. I had nothing to do with 'Conor's Ace' and he wouldn't be needling me about any sissy art stuff as he called it. Father died of angina four years ago while I was photographing and sketching in the High Sierra. So I came back to Nevada for the funeral and to help Rick clean things up. It was then I discovered Father had willed his share of Conor's Ace to me."

"What?"

"Generous to a fault. I was the proprietor of more than three-quarters of Conor's Ace. Rick was sort of an also-ran. For about two weeks I felt lousy. I got in the legal boys to make the whole things more equitable and put Rick in charge, with the advantage of the profits that would bring him. Rick nobly refused."

"But – I can't believe it."

"There were reasons. Reasons my grandfather would have understood very well. My father certainly did. He and Rick had been skimming for more than a year."

"Skimming?"

"Taking profits off the top before reporting. That's a severe no-no as far as the IRS is concerned. You usually land in the slammer. I give Father this much credit. He probably thought I'd get out of it. My record was O.K., whereas, if he had left it in Rick's name, he might have gone to jail. Of course, Rick said he would stand by me and blame it all on Father."

"My God!"

He waved off her concern. "I was just about stony broke. I couldn't possibly dig up what we owed the IRS, but Rick thought, with my so-called clean reputation, I'd get off easy. Two days before our appointment with the IRS Rick disappeared. I haven't seen him since. I guess you know more than I do from here on."

The story was sickening. She wondered if it was even true. There must be something, some allowance made, but why should it be made? She murmured inanely,

"I know he thought about the good times you had as boys. I remember, on our honeymoon in Torcello, the way he watched the children playing. Thoughtful and tender. I asked if he loved children and he said almost what you said one day. 'Not particularly.' You see, he was thinking of his youth. With his brother. The good days."

Dev pressed the tips of his fingers against the two parallel lines that marred his otherwise unlined forehead. The two wrinkles between his eyes seemed more prominent and she had no doubt he was suffering as much as she suffered from all this.

"I don't doubt he was sorry about the whole thing. Rick was always sorry. But during his halcyon honeymoon days with you I was starting through two long trials, paying legal fees which looked like Mt. Whitney for two years, and aren't completely cleared yet. I finally got a judgement in my favor. That noble edifice, Conor's Ace, went to pay the IRS. I can't complain. I'm just relieved that I didn't go to prison. As it was, I had enough of a taste of jail to last me awhile." He laughed. "I'm clear now, though, except for monthly payments I make to half a dozen Legal Eagles."

Her own thoughts were chaotic. She knew he was looking at her, wondering what her reaction would be, and she had none to give him. The greatest pain might still lie between them. She got up and went to the windows overlooking the now darkened terrace and the canal beyond. She rested her hot cheek against the cool window pane. After an unhappy silence between them, she asked tiredly,

'Why did you play up to my insane fantasies and let me go on pretending you were Richard? Why didn't you tell me the whole truth when we first met? You must have know even then that I confused you with your brother. If you had mentioned your relationship I would have believed you."

He stopped pacing to look at her. "Would you? You don't believe me now. I've lost you because I told you the truth. Chilton-Brown warned me it would be like this. He wanted me to wait a little longer." He added more gently, "Has it never occurred to you in all your life that someone might simply fall in love with you besides my brother, and not want to lose you?"

Nigel's disgusting influence prejudiced her as much as Dev's playacting. "You despised me before you knew about Godart Bakeries and all."

"I don't give a damn for your crummy frozen waffles or whatever. Matter of fact, I can't stand frozen breakfasts. I resented your going through my things. I thought you must be on some kind of scavenger hunt and I was *it*. Then I bumped into you at Banbury."

His strong features had softened when he mentioned their second meeting.

She was relieved. The world didn't look quite so bleak. She too softened at the memory. "We had fun that day. And then, you vanished. I kept hoping you would call. No way. What made you change your mind? Tell me the truth. Honestly."

It had been heavenly, that unexpected call that had reopened for her the doors of love and need that she had kept locked for so long.

"I wanted to, God knows. But there was that damned Bakery Heiress business in the way. It was only Chilton-Brown who made it all possible. He walked in on me at Richmond Hill. Told me what a bad time you'd been having. I figured it was the fault of us Conors. I didn't doubt that Rick had run off and left you in the lurch. But the truth is, I wanted to see more of –"

"Stop it!"

The cold of the window pane had seeped into her bones, but nothing else was as bad as this confession. "I suppose Nigel told you I had passed out from a suicidal overdose. That was a lie. But he would also have added something about the psychiatrists and the fact that he though I was going nuts dwelling on my lost love. So you were to help me live out my fantasy. Like the good fellow you are, you came trotting into London to keep me occupied, just so I wouldn't kill myself."

"That's not the way it was at all. Matter of fact, I was half in love with you before we left the theatre that night." She rolled her eyes skyward in disbelief and disillusionment. He was trying hard to reason with her, she knew that. But she was crushed by the knowledge that the only reason he kept hanging around her was because he believed Nigel and thought she was whacko.

He tried once more. "The night we went to 'The Mouse-trap', we were attacked on the street by a nondescript little man with a knife. He was aiming for you. I knew then that you weren't suicidal. Somebody had been trying to make it look that way, and when the old gaslighting business failed, they came out and tried it another way. But the point is, by that time, the only thing that mattered was our relationship. I was in love with you."

"Thank you for that."

"Maybe you think it didn't cost me something to realize every time you looked at me that you were thinking of Rick. I only hoped you would eventually see the real me and find you'd – outgrown Rick. I took you to Rye to be with you, and also to keep you out of harm's way. Chilton-Brown agreed. We went. And I knew then that I would do anything to keep you, even let you go on mixing me up in your mind with Good Old Dashing Rick."

She stared at him across the dimly lightly room. "It was Nigel who told you to take me to Rye. I'm surprised he didn't come to Venice with us." Obviously, the man he talked to on the phone from the Elizabethan Chamber in Rye was Nigel.

He stood there a couple of long minutes, studying the painting of the last Doge of Venice across the room. She said nothing and with a sudden spurt of energy he went across the room to his suitcase and the blue canvas roll.

He's going to be childish, she thought. He's going to be childish and walk out.

She would not beg him to stay, even though the empty feeling of loss inside her made her think of the future as a cave with no way out.

Her cape lay in a heap on the floor. For some reason Dev stopped packing and picked up the cape. He brushed it with his hand and threw it over the back of a chair. She wanted to thank him but the words stuck in her throat. She was afraid she would cry in front of him and she wanted none of his pity. She stared out at the canal. From one position she could see the dark, oily lagoon beyond. The old nightmare had come to life. Richard had never been saved. And Dev's love for her had been maneuvered by Nigel.

Sensing movements behind her, she looked around. He had removed his priest's cassock and was wearing brown slacks, a worn brown turtleneck sweater and his English raincoat thrown over his shoulders. She remembered the clothes. They had belonged to Dev Conor, the cool, unfriendly man who had surprised her in his Richmond Hill room the day they met. Near the door were his suitcase and the canvas roll.

He picked up the suitcase. In another few seconds he would be gone.

She couldn't bear to lose Richard . . . No, Dev, again.

Her voice hoarse with emotion, she asked, "Don't you think I'm entitled to at least some resentment?" She made a ghastly attempt at lightness. "Who knows? I'm a sucker for a good love story."

He didn't look the way she felt, sad, depressed, sickened. He looked furious, more angry that she had ever seen him.

"Believe me, my story is nothing to Richard Kimberly's story. I was idiot enough to fall in love with you. I'll bet Richard's little buddy, Babette, whoever she is, could straighten you out about your Dream Man."

He was gone and she hadn't stopped him. With her cheek pressed against the window she stood there a long time, wondering, missing him.

Was it his imitation of Richard she missed or was it Dev himself? She had driven him to that masquerade, trying to turn him into Richard.

They looked so much alike. And yet, Babette Cuneo had known the difference at once. And Nigel refused to believe they were the same man; yet Nigel had accepted him later in some odd way. They had become almost confidantes.

Eventually, she went over to a chair and sat there reliving all he had told her, trying to excuse Richard. Trying to excuse Dev. There seemed little to compare in their lives. If only she had been sure that Dev loved her, without that shadowy feeling that Nigel Chilton-Brown had put him up to it! The longer she remembered those days with Dev, the more she blamed herself. Nigel must have ignored her warning not to check on Dev, and finding he was trustworthy, had told him of her troubles, her background.

But later, it was more than pity. It had to be. Every moment of their time together told her that.

When she awoke in the foggy, hazy morning, she showered, restored some life to her tired muscles, and dressed. Surely Nigel would be up by now. She called his hotel. She wanted to tell him how she resented his interference but she also wanted him to find out where Dev had gone.

Nigel didn't answer. Wondering what to do next, she asked for her father's room.

Marcel was up and dressed and surprisingly cheerful.

"What do you think, *Chérie*? My Angela will share my breakfast. She seems pleased. She has quite forgotten that prince-fellow."

"Oh, Father, how wonderful!"

She could almost see his eloquent shrug. "But she lunches with this Famagusta. One cannot win always. Your mother is like the honey-bee. Flitting from flower to flower."

Jacqueline laughed. "You are by far the nicest flower, Papa."

"When she hung up she was momentarily happy for him, but this didn't solve her own problem. She called back and got Esther Heffernan. If Dev had contacted Nigel, Esther would probably know about it.

Luckily, the ever-faithful assistant was very much present and anxious to hear from Jacqueline.

"Mr. C wanted you to know your father is feeling ever so much better. He and Mr. C talked about it. They were worried about you though. You *are* all right?"

Jacqueline's voice was crisp. "Certainly. Why wouldn't I be." When Esther used that tone it always sounded to Jacqueline as if they expected to find her laid out in a morgue.

"Oh, thank heaven. He didn't want to wake you, but he was awfully anxious, especially after talking to your – to Mr. Conor. I was supposed to call you within an hour, just to be sure."

"Well, you can be sure." But the adrenalin seemed to be pumping back into her heart or veins, or wherever it normally went. "Then Nigel saw Mr. Conor this morning?"

"Of course. They had something to do together. Something about Torcello, that little island where you spent your honeymoon. Unfortunately, I wasn't dressed yet; so I couldn't leave when they did. I'm to take notes."

"Notes? on what?"

Were they looking into the details of Jacqueline's honeymoon with Richard? Or possibly even wondering about the details of his death?

"I don't quite know, but of course, Mr. C needs me; so I'm on my way. But no motorboat for me. Not after your horrid experience. I'll take the tour boat."

I must go there, Jacqueline thought. It will end, once and for all, this terrible mooning about the past. "Bless you, Esther."

"Really? Why. Mrs. Kimberly, how very nice! Will we have the pleasure of seeing you out there by any chance?"

"Don't tell the men. Please."

"Not if you say so."

They both rang off together.

Jacqueline made up her mind to chance a meeting with Dev and Nigel. At the same time it was even possible that she could blur the old memories entirely. It hurt to confess it, but apparently, Richard had been dishonest and evasive, and to his own brother.

Every time she tried to remember Richard's face now, she saw, instead, Dev Conor's face and his tenderness, his gentle care of her, his reserve that she had denied, thought of as cold, unlike his warm brother. And their love had somehow been more of a partnership between man and woman, less like Richard's quick, exuberant love-making that suggested only his own urge for satisfaction.

She knew her entire future happiness, if any, depended on that trip to Torcello, and putting to rest the old, dear, ever-youthful Richard who seemed to have died as he lived, still the same irresponsible "boy."

Twenty-Four

She knew perfectly well that if she was ever going to free herself from the clutches of the past, she must take a motor-boat, or speedboat, to Torcello, over those same waters that had destroyed Richard and haunted her dreams. She must force herself to relive those last minutes. Then, if she failed to banish the spectre of that lost love, there was no hope for her and Dev.

Dev's story and the implication that he had only come to her out of pity, one of Nigel's tiresome efforts on her behalf, occupied most of her thoughts before morning. But in the daylight, foggy and misty though it might look from her windows, she added up all the clues she remembered from her all-too-short love affair with Richard.

On Torcello he had been terribly troubled. Obviously, his conscience bothered him over his flight from responsibility. She had known even then that he had committed some wrong. They had left Torcello early at his request. He had said he must go back and "straighten things out." If only Dev could believe that, maybe the old bitterness against his brother would be softened a little.

Unfortunately, there was no way to convince Dev that she hadn't made up the story. Dev would certainly suspect her motives.

Jacqueline walked over toward the Piazzetta, passing the steps below the little bridge where Sigurd had been murdered. The attack on him and the attempts on her life hadn't been solved yet. She wondered if Nigel really believed his easy dismissal of those "attempts to scare her."

What had Sigurd been about to tell her when he was silenced? The bit about Dev was easy. He had probably found out that Nigel had persuaded Dev to befriend and protect her. In other words, that the two men were closer than they pretended to be. But the other – about someone who knew everything? The contessa? Nigel was obvious, but she didn't believe it was possible. She had known him too long, too well.

She stopped for a minute or two, looked down from the bridge, remembering the prince's shallow charm and his open avowal of his vocation in life, to decorate rich women. She had liked him even while she despised him and now she paid a moment's tribute to the murdered prince.

The fog gathered along the narrow canals like eery, formless creatures, gray and opaque. She remembered that foggy night when she and Richard left Torcello. Those creeping, gray fingers . . .

She blinked and went on, more rapidly.

St. Mark's Square looked forlorn and deserted on this day so close to winter. The tourists had gone and the Venetians who went about their business paid little attention to their fabulous surroundings. Like the others, Jacqueline had her own important concerns. She walked the length of the great square at a rapid pace, avoiding the arcades where the fog seemed to grapple with everyone hurrying along.

In front of the cathedral she turned and headed through the Piazzetta to the canal with its idle gondolas rocking on the choppy water, and a scattered few passengers for Torcello huddled in their coats with collars pulled up around their faces.

She didn't recognize anyone. At the same time she realized that she was still suspicious. The person who murdered Sigurd von Ulsbach had not been captured. She was convinced, in spite of Nigel's reassurance, that the person responsible for the State Street accident, the overdose of sleeping powders in London, and the weird summons to a tiny balcony last night, was still out there, waiting to make good on the next attempt.

The island tour boat had pulled in and was taking on passengers. Jacqueline yielded to temptation. Instead of hiring a motorboat she followed the others on board, recognizing her own cowardice. She wanted company out there on the mist-shrouded lagoon.

Most of the passengers proved to be young, off-season back-packers, a group she was more than happy to see. There was a good deal of joking as the old ferry started off and they got a blast of winter air from the Adriatic. They began to point out the several "leaning towers" that Jacqueline and Richard had noticed on their run to Torcello. They argued about the Lido, but presently were confusing Murano with Burano.

It was shortly after that Jacqueline forced herself to look down into the dark waters of the lagoon. She shuddered but reminded herself that poor Rick Kimball Conor, as she must think of him now, was beyond feeling any of the pain and horror that had haunted her for so long.

She closed her eyes, forcing herself to turn away. One of the girls with an old-fashioned, well-worn back-pack asked sympathetically in English,

"A touch of the old *mal de mer*, maybe?"

Jacqueline smiled. "Not exactly. It looks a long way down; doesn't it?"

"Yeah." The girl's lengthy red hair lashed her face as she leaned out over the rail. "But they say it's the easiest way to go." She added with a wry chuckle, "If you gotta go."

"I suppose it is. I never thought of it like that."

The girl's green eyes sparkled. "Now, me, I see myself flying out into space, maybe from a hang-glider, or falling off the Matterhorn or some place. You're bound to be dead before you reach the bottom. All those fierce cross-winds and all."

Jacqueline found her spirits oddly lifted by this morbid conversation. "Well, whatever turns you on. Good luck, anyway."

The bell tower of Torcello formed itself out of the mist and everyone got ready to pour out onto the landing with its wild, grassy look, and a little, rambling canal that must once have been a creek. The green-eyed girl muttered something to her athletic-looking boyfriend. He looked around over his shoulder, then shrugged.

The girl nudged Jacqueline. "You got an admirer over there. Sure couldn't take his eyes off you."

Jacqueline swung around, instantly on watch.

"Where? What does he look like?"

"He left in that bunch that crowded off first. Not too big. Kind of a middle-aged nothing."

Jacqueline had heard that description before, in Chicago, and last night at the Palazzo Fabrini.

"Thanks. He's no friend of mine. If you don't mind, I'll just fade into your group when we're getting off."

"Sure. Help yourself."

With a vivid recollection of Prince Sigurd's murder, Jacqueline took care to stay within the little group of laughing, chattering back-packers.

When they started along the path beside the little canal Jacqueline was still trying to catch a glimpse of the nondescript little man who had become the bane of her life. The green-eyed girl, too, had been on the watch. She said after another couple of minutes.

"You needn't worry about your friend. He didn't take the path. He went around through the field toward the church, or whatever it is."

Jacqueline thanked her but remained guarded.

Walking toward the inn on the path she and Richard had taken three years ago, Jacqueline fell into a dream-like state, in which she experienced the scene at a distance, with no personal involvement. Two lovers had walked here hand in hand in a foggy mist like this, but she was no longer the girl in the scene. Too much had happened since.

Now, she thought of deep companionship and love, a communion of experiences together, a man of strength, not that troubled, reckless, irresponsible young man she had clung to in memory for so long.

But would Dev ever believe her?

She must try to explain now on her pilgrimage to Torcello. She had wanted to exorcize that old stubborn dream and she believed she had done so.

By the time she reached the inn she found the rest of the passengers had drifted off toward the church and the occasional stone house surrounded by unkempt grass and a tiny, dry fountain. They recognized her at the desk and the clerk mentioned her long absence. She knew they must be aware of her husband's death three years ago but since she didn't mention it they politely ignored it.

She asked, "Have Mr. Conor and Mr. Chilton-Brown arrived yet?"

He wasn't surprised at her question. "Not yet, no, Signora. But there has been another inquiry. Would you care to join the other lady?"

Little Miss Heffernan sat looking a bit forlorn at a table on the edge of the flower garden. Hearing Jacqueline call her name, she jumped up eagerly.

"Thank goodness! It's so embarrassing, sitting here all by my lonesome. They look funny at me. The men, I mean. Do you suppose they think I'm a pickup?"

"Well, we'll straighten that out in a hurry." Jacqueline pulled out a chair opposite her before the waiter could do so. "The men haven't arrived yet, I take it." She looked around, noted only two sets of diners on the terrace, another pair – apparently young honeymooners

– strolling through the garden, and a tall, light-haired gardener in a blue smock, kneeling at the rose trellis. Although the sun began to peer weakly through the fog now and then, it was still clammy under the shelter of the terrace roof.

"They should have been here long before this," Esther protested, glancing hopefully at the inner foyer that opened out upon the terrace. "They left almost an hour before I did."

"Why were they coming to Torcello?"

"Search me." Esther finished her little glass of Cinzano and signalled to the waiter. She grimaced as she studied the empty glass. "This sweet stuff makes you sick, honestly. Would you like to order lunch before they get here? I think I'll settle for a big, steaming mug of coffee right now."

"Coffee for me too."

"I can't say I'm surprised to see you, Mrs. Kimberly. This being so close to your past, and all. But I just can't imagine what delayed Mr. C. You don't think something has happened to him?"

Jacqueline dismissed that unpleasant idea.

"Not if Dev is with him. I doubt if they could both have been waylaid." She felt sure their trip to Torcello would be connected in some way with Richard and the past. Maybe they were still wandering over the island.

A severe-looking woman in a straight-skirted suit of unfashionable cut and length, and wearing laced arch-support shoes, was seated at a table behind Esther. Her iron-gray hair, wound around her head tightly, made her look even more forbidding. She took her time ordering while the waiter showed an exemplary patience. Jacqueline smiled at the sight and Esther was puzzled at what interested her, trying in vain to look over her own shoulder.

"Do you see them? Are they coming?"

"No. It was nothing. Just someone who looks like my old Math teacher. Bless her heart. She tried hard. I wish I had been more receptive."

The large cups of coffee were set down before Esther and Jacqueline, along with toast, butter, croissants and bright little pots of confiture, cherry and blueberry. But they were of little use to Esther who had seen two men crossing the far end of the garden. She tried to stand up, crying.

"Mr. C? Over here. Oh, I do hope he sees us." She sat back down abruptly, embarrassed. "I guess it wasn't. Oh, Lord! I've walked out of my shoe."

Jacqueline laughed and got up. She signalled to the waiter who did not catch her eye. She dropped back into her seat, only to find she was stepping on Esther's oxford. She bent to pick it up and finally got hold of it.

"Please don't let anyone see," Esther begged.

"Sorry." Jacqueline passed the shoe to her under the table.

Flustered and muttering her thanks, Esther slipped her foot into the shoe and raised her coffee cup to her lips. She said coyly, "Here's to us, anyway. We've been stood up by the gentlemen."

Jacqueline laughed, raised her her own cup and clinked their cups together. As she brought the coffee cup to her lips an extraordinary thing happened.

The "math" teacher with the iron-gray hair was staring hard at Jacqueline. Jacqueline realized two things: first, that the woman was actually Mrs. Dimblby, and second, that she shook her head and started to rise. It was no accidental gesture.

It was a warning.

Jacqueline had been about to drink the steaming coffee. Over her own cup Esther smiled at her.

"Good on a cold day, isn't it?" She drank and waited for Jacqueline to follow suit. It was the intensity of her look in conjunction with Mrs. Dimblby's odd behavior that made the whole ghastly truth fit. Had Esther put something in that cup while Jacqueline scrambled on the floor for her shoe? Jacqueline brought her cup to her lips again and pretended to drink. But her thoughts were in hideous disarray.

"Drink up, Mrs. Kimberly," Esther urged her with a new tone of anxiety. Her stare was glassy and fixed, like her smile.

Not Esther. Not loyal, faithful little Miss Heffernan who adored her beloved Mr. C. What could be her motive? Jacqueline had never consciously wronged her.

But the evidence mounted.

Nigel had always been the most obvious suspect because he knew Jacqueline's moves and advised her on most of them. Only one other person knew as much about Jacqueline and was constantly hiring people, either to "protect her" or to follow her.

Nothing else mattered in Esther's life than to enrich her "Mr. C." In a sense, Esther was already married to Nigel. He was her obsession.

One question remained. Was Nigel in on these attempts against Jacqueline? Had Nigel ordered Sigurd's death because he got too close to the truth? Jacqueline couldn't believe it. The whole complex plot would have been handled more simply if Nigel were back of it. This was the scheme of someone unbalanced.

Obviously, in trying to find out what he could about Godart's stock or Nigel himself, Sigurd had stumbled onto the fact that Esther was Jacqueline's active enemy. As for his hints about Dev, that Dev and Nigel were now allies, it would shock Jacqueline, as it certainly had.

If Jacqueline married Nigel, all her inheritance, especially her stock, would go to Nigel who had been her adviser and friend. She had only to marry him and die. Maybe, in her warped mind and hopes, Esther had hoped to marry Nigel when she had made him the head of Godart's. She had certainly made herself close to indispensible in his business life.

But what a calamity if Jacqueline married Dev Conor! Obviously, Esther had to work fast.

Jacqueline pretended to drink but it was not easy. She let her glance run vaguely to Mrs. Dimblby who seemed ready to interfere. She patted the pocket of her coat significantly. But this would prove nothing except that Mrs. Dimblby had evidently seen Esther dose the coffee. A small offense. Esther would claim it was for Jacqueline's own good. It must be a sleeping powder of some kind, like that used on Jacqueline in London. She could hardly murder Jacqueline with poison while they sat drinking together.

What did she intend?

Even if the little man who followed Jacqueline on the boat was lurking around, Mrs. Dimblby had a weapon.

Jacqueline made up her mind. The main thing was to get rid of the coffee, yet appear to be drinking it. After that, with Mrs. Dimblby's help, Jacqueline could see what Esther was up to.

To distract Esther as she herself had been distracted, Jacqueline jumped and squinted up at the beamed ceiling over the terrace.

"It's raining."

"Just a little mist," Esther objected. "The sun is trying to shine. Drink up. You'll feel better."

If she had any doubt of Esther's guilt, this persistence would have settled the matter.

"But my sleeve is damp."

Jacqueline got up, carrying her cup and pretended to take another sip. She avoided Mrs. Dimblby's table and headed for the inn's interior where most of the little tables were still vacant.

After protesting, Esther followed her, but she had to feel around for her handbag. During those few seconds that Jacqueline was alone in the little dining room, she threw the contents of her cup into the corner beyond the floor mat. Unfortunately, there was no planter handy, but at least, the liquid was not readily visible. In spite of all this rapid activity, Jacqueline's thoughts whirled with her incredible suspicions.

Not good old reliable Esther Heffernan.

Yet who was more likely? Who knew more about Jacqueline's every movement? With Jacqueline out of the way, Esther would have no rival for Nigel Chilton-Brown's trust. She would be closer to her idol than ever.

Mrs. Dimblby seemed to understand at once that Jacqueline wanted to make Esther reveal her hand.

"I hope I don't have to die to settle the matter," Jacqueline thought wryly and managed to give Esther a wan smile above the rim of the coffee cup. She was wondering what reaction was expected of her.

Esther settled the matter. "Mrs. Kimberly, you look quite peaked. You must be tired after all that hullabaloo at the countess's last night."

"Yes. I suppose I am." Sleepy? She pretended to yawn. This seemed to be the expected reaction.

Esther was watching her solicitously. Jacqueline drained the cup.

"This ought to wake me up."

"Yes, indeed. But you really look tired. Maybe we should leave the gentlemen a message and I'll take you back to your hotel."

I must be doing something right, Jacqueline told herself. She sat down in a gingerly way, aware that Esther's birdlike little eyes were watching her intently. Jacqueline gave the pantomime another minute or so, yawned again, begged pardon, and murmured, "I believe you're right. I feel a little woozy. Better – back to hotel."

Evidently, the woman wasn't surprised that whatever she had put in Jacqueline's coffee had acted so fast. Or maybe she just didn't know. She knew what she expected and Jacqueline was behaving correctly.

"Do let me help you, Mrs. Kimberly."

Jacqueline tried to rise, wavered a little and accepted her hand.

"Thanks. I'll be on my – way. Is it – too early for tour boat?"

"Don't you worry about a thing. Just lean on me. Here we go. Oh, I'll take care of the check. Don't worry." Esther dismissed the waiter who started toward them solicitously. "Quite all right. Mrs. Kimberly had a bad reaction to some medicine she took. Tell Mr. Chilton-Brown we couldn't wait."

The medicine she took.

So that was how this witch intended to pave the way for Jacqueline's fate, whatever it was! To get her to sleep and then have her die, accidentally, no doubt. Drowning seemed the likeliest way.

Jacqueline found herself shaking so badly it wasn't necessary to act. Even Esther's hand and arm giving her support seemed revolting. Had anyone ever guessed what depths lay beneath Esther Heffernan's adoration and ambition for her beloved Mr. C?

Yes. Sigurd had guessed, or found out. Probably through some unsavory friend who had heard about Esther's search for a confederate. Remembering all the "accidents," the "odd little man following her," and the death of Sigurd himself, Jacqueline knew Esther must have her hired assassin somewhere. As Nigel had remarked one day: "Esther will know how to find someone to watch over you . . . Esther can find anything."

Leaning heavily on Esther's shoulder, Jacqueline glanced behind the shorter woman's head. In a moment of panic she saw that Mrs. Dimblby was gone, but the woman must have concealed herself from Esther who looked back, saw nothing suspicious and suggested, "Shall we go?"

Jacqueline obeyed. It was only then that she saw Mrs. Dimblby who had moved behind the rose arbor and was partially concealed by the kneeling gardener.

Relieved that she could count on the woman, Jacqueline stumbled out with Esther onto the path beside the canal. They were headed for the boat landing. Jacqueline had a very good idea that the nondescript little man who had followed her on the tour boat was somewhere around here, lurking behind the old farmhouse near the landing, or hidden by a gnarled and twisted tree. There were bushes growing high and unpruned as well. But at least, if Esther and her murderous buddy had gone to this much trouble to provide a convincing "accident" Jacqueline was better prepared than for an outright murder attack.

She thought it might be time to protest.

"Where – what happened? Feel odd. Why didn't Dev – Nigel come?"

Esther was her consoling, gentle self. "That wasn't quite true, Dear. You misunderstood me."

"But – bodyguard. The woman . . ."

Esther's sweet smile was insufferable. "Heavens, no! I sent her off to the Lido. Come along now. You're just going to lie down and take a long sleep . . . To dream about meeting your Richard. Isn't that lovely?"

Jacqueline felt a thrill of horror. No doubt of the woman's intentions now. Jacqueline looked around vaguely. The tour boat was certainly not going to be their transportation. A motor-boat had been pulled up to the landing and she had no difficulty identifying the nondescript little man who extended his hands to help her into the boat.

She pulled back as if confused. "Saw him before. Followed me in London. Cut my Richard's hand on street . . ."

"You've had a good run of luck, dear. What with that drunken boatman who nearly managed to get himself drowned, for all I know, and then the –"

"*You knew that boatman*?"

"My dear Mrs. Kimberly, he wasn't any of my doing. Stupidity and drunkenness I will not tolerate in those who work for me. A pure accident, that wreck of yours, unfortunately."

The woman's pride was overwhelming. Clearly she had no notion of right and wrong. Had she always been unbalanced? Or was it only her passion for Nigel that had driven her into this black abyss of insanity?

Esther became businesslike:

"Well, dear, it won't matter much longer. Your Richard is waiting. Get in."

Jacqueline was beginning to wish she hadn't gone through with this dangerous charade. But if she had let the whole plot unravel at the inn, Mrs. Dimblby would have witnessed nothing worse than Esther dropping something in Jacqueline's coffee. Obviously, a sleeping powder. So she went on acting.

"Going to see Richard?"

She tried to make a glance over Esther's shoulder as vague as possible. She could have sworn she saw something move near the canal-side wall of the farmhouse.

The Dimblby Woman. And other figures. Thank heaven for that.

The little man had both hands out; so there could be no weapon there. If Esther had a weapon it was not in her hands. Everything in their plan apparently depended upon it looking like an accident. The little man gave Jacqueline's arms a sharp tug, hoping to tumble her into the boat beside him. She pulled back with all her strength. Her unexpected resistance caught them both unawares.

Esther gave her a stinging slap across the cheek. Her little eyes were bright with anger.

"Oh, no, you don't. You're not going back to marry some idiot and take away everything my Mr. C's worked a lifetime for. He's too decent to give you what you deserve for sponging off him all these years. But I'm not. It's for my Mr. C, you understand?"

Jacqueline jerked her hands away from the little man and tried to push Esther aside. Esther's furious order warned her.

"No knife, Simpson. No knife, I tell you! When she's found it's got to look like suicide."

Jacqueline scrambled to her feet, trying to pass Esther. She had no idea what was going on behind her but seconds later she heard the pistol shot, a sound surprisingly low out here in the muffled fog, and the little man tumbled backward, his head cracking against the side of the boat.

Jacqueline and Esther stared back at the path beside the canal. To Jacqueline's intense relief Mrs. Dimblby emerged from the fog. During the seconds in which Esther had been stunned by this interruption, the bodyguard was joined by the tall, goodlooking young gardener of the inn who lowered a dark, compact, dangerous handgun in an embarrassed way and murmured,

"No resistance, I think."

Jacqueline realized that the gardener was a policeman. Thank God for that, although Mrs. Dimblby looked determined enough to handle the matter all by herself. Behind Mrs. Dimblby two men raced along the canal path. One of them, Dev Conor, reached out to Jacqueline, lifting her to her feet. It was the sight of Nigel Chilton-Brown that shook Esther Heffernan.

He moved onto the boat landing. There was something stunned but coldly inexorable about his strained features, an expression the adoring Esther must never have seen before.

She stammered, "For you, Sir. Some – somebody had to. You wouldn't help yourself. It was for you, Sir. I'd do it again to help you. You know that. Please, don't look at me like that. I can't b-bear it."

Nigel avoided her desperate eyes. He turned to the Italian police official. "The woman was my secretary. From what she says, I take it she thought she was helping me."

"Please, Mr. C . . . don't shut me out. . . ." the luckless woman pleaded.

Nigel bit his lip and turned toward Dev and Jacqueline. Jacqueline could hear Esther's sobs as the policeman reached for her chubby wrist and his free hand helped up the cringing man in the boat who was nursing his arm and screamed at the Italian's touch.

Dev had said nothing, although Jacqueline had the comfort of his arm around her as she pulled herself together. It was Nigel who explained,

"Thank God for Mrs. Dimblby. She just called as we were leaving the hotel. We were headed out to find your elusive friend, Babette. Thought she could explain a little about Dev's dead brother."

"Cuneo," Jacqueline said flatly. "Babette Cuneo. But that was a long time ago. We can't go on living in the past. Like –" She did not say "like Esther," but the thought was clear. It was painful to love a man who could be that cold about your passion.

She hadn't yet seen any demonstration of Dev's forgiveness.

Twenty-Five

It was the most excitement little Torcello had seen in years. An American lady had been doped and kidnapped by another American lady who was crazy, and by her hired hand, a man named Simpson, who was singing his head off now, blaming the crazy American for the murder of a certain Prince von Ulsbach.

"She may have watched and I don't doubt she gave this Simpson the order to kill Ulsbach," Nigel told Dev who stood beside Jacqueline's chair in the comfortable old lounge of the inn. "But nobody can convince me that Esther hit that tall fellow with a piece of stone, as Simpson keeps insisting."

Jacqueline shuddered. "Won't it be over soon? We've been here since before noon. We know she isn't responsible. Poor devil!"

This must have appealed to Dev. For the first time in hours he showed some personal feeling for her, taking her hand and holding it briefly. He asked Nigel,

"Does she admit to all the attempts on Jacqueline's life, the thing she tried to do today, for instance? And that absurd balcony summons at the ball last night?"

"Simpson claims she set that up to draw suspicion away from herself. She wanted to be seen around Jacqueline when the message was delivered."

"You see, Dev, you were right," Jacqueline reminded him. "You believed it was some sort of trick."

He made no reply and Nigel went on. "Anyway, there seems no doubt about it. Her idea was to drop Jacqueline off around that area where your brother drowned, Conor. Since Jacqueline would be asleep by that time, or otherwise incapacitated, she would . . . go down. You could never have found her in this weather." He shook his head. "No. I'm afraid sympathy is out of place here. It was too cold-blooded. They have a pretty valuable witness in Simpson. He'll be anxious to cover his own tracks."

They all looked around anxiously when Mrs. Dimblby crossed the lobby toward them.

"You are free to go now, Mrs. Kimberly. You've been extremely helpful. The Commander says he will want to check some items in your story tomorrow. I told him you would be available."

"Yes. Certainly." Jacqueline held out her hand which was still a bit shaky. "I want to thank you and the young man, the Commander? If you hadn't given me that signal at the table, I'd have drunk that coffee."

"We all owe you a vote of thanks," Nigel agreed, offering the woman his own hand. "Thank God you had sense enough not to trust my assistant. Technically, she was your employer, I realize."

"I make it a point never to trust anyone, employer or otherwise," Mrs. Dimblby said calmly.

"Excellent plan," Nigel agreed, determined not to take offense at the hint in the woman's voice. "At any rate, the matter has been handled very – expeditiously."

"Shall I take you back to the hotel now?" Dev asked Jacqueline who looked up hopefully, but he was busy throwing her coat around her shoulders.

Nigel and Mrs. Dimblby discussed what was to be done about the wretched Esther Heffernan.

"I can't let her rot in jail," he pointed out. "She needs psychiatric help."

"She needs a good lawyer," Mrs. Dimblby snapped. "The woman is a menace and a murderess."

"Yes. But unbalanced."

They were still arguing when Jacqueline and Dev left the island. Since a tour boat was loading, they got on, although Jacqueline insisted that she was willing to face a ride in a motor-boat.

"No need for that," Dev assured her, but his cool, polite manner warned her that their differences were by no means at an end.

As they stood at the rail by themselves, avoiding the chatter among the other tourists about "attempted kidnapping" and "an old crazy woman" involved, Jacqueline asked plaintively.

"Aren't we ever going to be friends again?"

He almost smiled at that but said "That depends on you. Chilton-Brown and I spent the morning looking for Rick's girlfriend. It was Chilton-Brown's idea. I think he hoped to wean you away from Rick's memory."

"Rick is dead," she said flatly. "He died long ago. It was Esther Heffernan's idea that I join him out there. I assure you, it wasn't mine."

He looked at her and then turned his attention to the gray, choppy waters that a distant sunset glow was trying to brighten.

"Then you wouldn't mind visiting this Babette?"

"Certainly not. I'm better off than you and Nigel. I have a pretty good idea where to find her. The Cuneo Pension or the Pensione Cuneo was just off the Calle San Giovanni, at a little cafe in a square. The Piazza San Giovanni."

He was genuinely surprised. "You are willing to go with me? Suppose she turns out to have been his mistress?"

"So?"

He began to relax. She sensed it in his body, so close beside hers. He gazed out at the lagoon, adding thoughtfully, "I came to Europe to find Rick, to tell him just what he had done to my life, but I couldn't trace him. Then I met you in England. It was the first time I knew he was dead."

"You were sorry about that, surely."

"I was. We had a good childhood together. But you seemed to have been divinely happy with him. I figured he had lived one hell of a life until that last minute. He had no regrets, no guilt . . ."

"I think he did. He had terrible dreams. He intended to return with me and make things right. He said so." She looked into his face pleadingly but he merely shook his head.

"He had plenty of time to return. It's too easy to say what he might have done. Besides, there is his other girlfriend, this Babette. If it hadn't been you, or Babette, it would have been someone else."

But by the time they were piling out of the boat near St. Mark's with the others, they had tacitly agreed to pursue Babette Cuneo. It was the only way Jacqueline could prove to Dev that she was no longer obsessed by her love for "Richard Kimberly," even if this Italian girl had been his mistress.

The horror of her possible fate at Esther Heffernan's hands had shown her that she loved the living and not the dead. It wasn't quite so easy to convince Dev.

They hired a motorboat near the hotel and were taken across the Grand Canal just as the late afternoon sun burst out again from behind the sullen, foggy mist. It was blinding but at least it was warm; Jacqueline hoped it would be a good omen.

Dev's arm was around her shoulders and when they were let out in the little Piazza San Giovanni he waved to the retreating boatman for both of them. This seemed encouraging.

At her suggestion Dev inquired about the Pensione Cuneo from a waiter at the cafe in the piazza where Jacqueline had seen Rick and Babette long go.

The waiter grinned. "But of course, Signor. Babette is here each evening. The house is hers but the pensione is gone. Her mother died over a year ago. Babette? You will find her on the top floor of the third building beyond the bridge."

Richard Kimberly's old room.

Dev turned to Jacqueline. "Still willing?"

"Lead on, *Mon Générale*."

He smiled for the first time and offered her his arm with mock gallantry.

As they walked over the little bridge she remembered

that she had seen Richard and Babette from this bridge. How jealous she had been then, but she did not mention this out loud.

Babette Cuneo's name was scrawled upon the bottom half of an old café menu on the wall beside the door. They started up the rickety stairs. Jacqueline felt calm, confident, rather pleased to have the matter of Babette and Rick beyond them, but to her surprise, Dev became stiff and silent, unsure about the meeting.

The stairs felt more than usually long to Jacqueline after her unusual exertions with Esther Heffernan and her accomplice. By the time Dev and Jacqueline reached the top floor she was breathing hard.

"Want to turn back?" Dev asked, eying her carefully.

"No way. I haven't done all this mountain-climbing for nothing."

"O.K. Here goes." He knocked with unexpected force, surprising himself, and Jacqueline laughed at his expression.

"You don't know your own strength. Try again."

A few minutes later it seemed very evident that they had missed Babette Cuneo. They both felt let down after their discussion about whether Jacqueline was willing to face the woman or not.

They were wondering what to do next when Babette's voice challenged them in reasonably good English from the staircase behind them.

"I have callers, have I? My Rick's faithless wife."

"Tell us about it," Dev encouraged her.

Babette glanced down at the key in her hand. "Why not? It may be worth something to you. I'm in the market, as you say."

She turned the key noisily in the lock, pushed the door open and gestured for them to follow her in. They did so before she could change her mind.

Jacqueline found the room smaller than she remembered, but the view remained. The red tiled rooftops looked as if they were on fire at this hour. The room was crowded with knick-knacks, souvenirs dolls, dozens of cushions everywhere, a huge day-bed, and a single hot plate. There was hardly room for one guest, much less two. Babette's taste reminded Jacqueline very much of her father's crowded, over-heated apartments.

"Poor Papa!" she murmured, to Dev's surprise.

Babette made a graceful if exaggerated curtsy.

"Come. Sit. It will cost you. Be of good comfort. Since last night I have thought about this thing I have for you to buy."

Not at all sure what was coming next, or what Babette had to sell. Possibly love letters from Richard. It would not have surprised Jacqueline now. Or things that had belonged to him. Jacqueline dropped onto the big couch. Dev took over.

"We wondered if you could tell us something about your relationship with my brother."

Babette rubbed thumb and middle finger together.

"What do you say to five . . . No. Ten thousand lire?"

Jacqueline reached into her handbag. Dev's hand stopped her.

"Wait. If we're buying, let's not buy a pig in a poke."

Babette was confused. "Who sells pigs? You ask what is Rick to me? For ten thousand lire I tell you. We are friends. My Mama would not permit more." Her big eyes narrowed. "But I tell you this for free. He thinks of Mama and me as his friends. His only friends. He leaves his last letter for Mama to post."

There was a letter. Richard had told Jacqueline it would go out on the last day of their honeymoon. She asked Babette anxiously, "Did you send it? It was very important."

Babette shrugged. "But he does not pay to send it. It cost much to send to America. So we wait and wait, but he never comes back. He dies. He does not pay."

Dev had noticed Jacqueline's tension. "And the letter?"

"Mama was to post it after three days. He said he wished his honeymoon first. But he does not pay; so it is ours. No?"

Dev and Jacqueline exchanged glances. Jacqueline had no doubt that Babette, at least, had held onto the letter because Richard was marrying her rival. It was her only chance for revenge.

"Who was it addressed to?" Dev demanded.

Babette's moist lips parted in a smile. "Your letter will cost you much."

"*My letter*?"

"But yes. You are the brother Devlin, no? Of Minersfield in the State of Nevada?"

Jacqueline saw that Dev was badly shaken. She reached for his hand. He clutched hers, scarcely aware of the movement.

"May I see that letter?"

Babette looked scornfully at Jacqueline. "You let him die. Why should I help your new lover? I would not help him, not for a million lire."

The matter was too critical to Dev for them to haggle at this moment. It was worth a couple of thousand dollars for him to know that his brother's last words were for him. Jacqueline opened her handbag again, got out her cheekbook and pen. She began to write.

Dev turned from one woman to the other.

"No. It isn't worth paying for. He probably wants to apologize. It won't change anything."

"We must have it," Jacqueline said. She showed the check to Babette who laughed, then read it again. This time her fingers were unsteady. She looked up.

"You will make it no good. Cancel. I never saw a check of so much. Never."

Jacqueline took the check out of her fingers. Babette stared hungrily after it. Neither of them paid any attention to Dev who paced up and down in the few yards of the room left to him and said, "No blackmail. Absolutely none."

Jacqueline reached into her handbag again, took out the entire roll of thousand and ten thousand lire notes and said, "This is less. But it is real. It can't be cancelled. What do you say?"

Even Dev was silenced, waiting for Babette's reaction. She was hypnotized by the sight of all those bills. Finally, she reached for them.

"The letter," Jacqueline said crisply, holding the money back.

While they watched, Babette went down on her knees and crawled halfway under the couch. She brought out a chamber-pot filled with little souvenirs, pins, brooches, something that looked like lines of poetry, and a letter. It was stamped. Babette had lied about that. Or perhaps her mother had stamped it and left it to Babette to mail. But it hadn't been through the Italian Post Office. Jacqueline and Dev both read the inscription.

It was written in Richard Kimberly's hand and addressed to his brother in Minersfield, Nevada.

Dev caught his breath. Babette looked at Jaqueline with eyebrows raised. Jacqueline nodded and the transaction was completed. Babette slipped the letter into Dev's hand while her other hand stuck the roll of bills into the chamber-pot.

Jacqueline said, "Why didn't you mail the letter after Richard died, Miss Cuneo? Just as a matter of curiosity."

Babette wrinkled her nose. "Mama sent me to mail it. But it was the least I could do, hold onto this, when he'd run off with you. And then he got himself killed for you. Neither of you deserved anything from me."

Jacqueline glanced at Dev but he was too interested in the envelope and hadn't noticed this exchange. He shook the envelope. "Something small and flat in it. Cardboard?" The envelope had been opened and resealed, obviously by Babette. He slipped the envelope into the pocket of his jacket. Jacqueline got up and joined him.

Babette's eyes still gleamed at the memory of those thousand lire bills. As Dev opened the door, she roused herself to offer,

"Will you take an aperitif? We drink to the memory of my Rick?"

"Another time, thank you," Dev told her politely, and they went down the stairs, Dev holding Jacqueline's arm and hand in the old, dear way she had come to love before their quarrel.

Babette watched over the bannisters until they reached the street far below, then she ran back into her room and locked the door. Dev watched her disappear. There was unexpected compassion in his look. When he walked out into the little street with Jacqueline she said,

"You were sorry for her; weren't you?"

"I know what it's like to be poor."

She was ashamed for having failed to share his feeling. "I'm sorry. I have a lot to learn from you."

To her delight he kissed the top of her head. It was so unexpected she hugged him and burst out passionately, "This is the happiest moment of my whole life."

He looked into her eyes, as if to verify this extravagant claim. He seemed to be satisfied. Arm in arm, they hurried over the little bridge and down toward the outdoor cafe in the square.

"Shall we read the letter there?" he suggested, and then, more hesitantly, "Whatever it says, will it matter to us?"

"Not any more. The past is gone. From now on, all we both care about is the future."

He agreed firmly. "Amen to that."

The tables were filling up fast but they made a run for the last one, feeling like teenagers, and slid into the two chairs. He orderd cognac and she ordered a *kir*, delightfully relieved that she no longer expected him to behave like a carbon copy of his dead brother.

"You're dying to open that letter," she teased him, seeing the way he touched the pocket of his mackinaw.

He tried to grin but it was an effort. "I just can't imagine what his apology will sound like. He was always good at it."

"I'm afraid so. Poor Rick."

He nodded. "I can pity the poor devil now. Jealousy and bitterness are like a cancer. They ate at me for so long. And I fell in love with my brother's girl. And every time she looked at me she kept seeing Rick."

She reached across the table to touch his hand. "I've grown up now. I'm with the only man I will ever love."

He raised his glass. This time his grin was genuine. "I'll drink to that." He took another long sip, winced at the burning warmth of the brandy and reached into his pocket.

"Shall we?"

"Why not?"

He rattled the envelope. "I'll bet it's a key." He ripped open the thin Continental Airmail envelope and a piece of cardboard fell out. A flat key was taped to it. He and Jacqueline looked at it together.

"Safe deposit key," she said, taking up the cardboard and key while he unfolded the sheet of fragile airmail paper. He read the letter aloud:

"Dear Old Buddy Number One:

"It's taken me a long time to grow up. I figured from the first that with your spotless, driven-snow reputation, all you had to do was point to the fact that I'd ducked out and they'd see why. The IRS and the rest couldn't stick you with the bill. Everybody knew I shared ownership of Miner's Ace with the Old Man.

"I was pretty cocky. Nothing new about that. So I've been bumming around Europe for a month, telling myself you're free and clear by now. They were bound to have opened the safe deposit box I shared with the Old Man. Some of the books are there. Pa's figures. His bank books. He had quite a nest-egg in Vegas. He thought I might need it. To buy my way out, I guess.

"Like me, he figured they'd see through his idea of putting the Ace in your name, but it would give me a chance to beat it.

"Well, I've been living on all these pie-in-the-sky notions, and it's got a bit heavy. I met a nice girl here in Venice. We're in love. I mean love. She's got plenty of dough but so what? I'd want her if she was stony.

"We're getting married tonight. I'm turning over a new leaf. All shiny clean. If, by chance, you or the others haven't found the key to the Old Man's safe deposit box yet, I want you to take this key to the First Cal-Vada Bank in Vegas. All the stuff that's in there should clear you. We'll be along, my wife and me, within the week, and I'll face the music. Told you I'm a new man.

"I've asked that my landlady hold this letter up three days, just long enough for us to have our three-day honeymoon before the mess hits the fan.

"I don't ask your forgiveness. I don't deserve it. But I'm coming home anyway, Old Buddy.

"Sure hope you like my Jacky.

"Your Old Buddy Number Two."

All around them the cafe was growing noisier. Dev folded the letter. "You can shed a tear or two if you like. It won't hurt my feelings, Sweetheart."

"All that time," she said thoughtfully, "You had to struggle and suffer and get a bad name . . . All that, and this letter might have saved you."

He smoothed the letter with the palm of his hand.

"What's more important is, I spent most of the last few years hating him for not coming back, for not stepping in to testify. God! If I had only known!"

There were tears in her eyes but she laughed through them. "Sweetheart, we know now. Nobody's perfect. Not even us."

He replaced the letter in his pocket and his hand joined hers across the table.